Praise

"It's fast-paced, swoon ....
The next time anyone asks for a fantasy romance book, I'm
going to recommend this one!"
Madison Mary

"This is the adult, spicy, Fae, witchy, polyamorous, romance,
action flick, rom com book we've all been waiting for. We see
some of the tropes this genre is known for, and yet done
in a really healthy way."
Jessica Williamson

"I haven't been this sucked into a book in a while. Whether you
read a lot of Fae books, or this is your first dip into the Seelie
and Unseelie courts, this was one of the best and clearest
descriptions of how the Fae world works."
Chelsea Palmer

"It's sex positive, and the respect comes across on the page
clearly. I loved the intimacy within the relationships. I was
engaged from the first page to the last."
Amy McDougal

"Some characters you will love some you will love to hate, but
they will all wriggle down into your heart one way or another.
Don't sleep on this contemporary fantasy."
Ali Worsham

"An Irish love interest, polyamory, stunning communication,
and boundaries throughout, magic, mystery, diversity, and
exceptional worldbuilding. This is very much character driven
with fast-paced writing, and a plot that had me staring
wistfully out the window awaiting book two."
Aofie

"I finished it in one sitting because I couldn't put it down."
Ashe Grey

A PROPHECY IN ASH

Kate—
Fulfill your destiny!

JULIE ZANTOPOULOS

atmosphere press

*For my parents, who taught me home isn't a place,
it's people. I love you.*

GLOSSARY OF TERMS

Alate: An earth sprite. They can be bark, flower, or plantlike in appearance. Typically, very protective of their gardens and glens. Peaceful unless disturbed or molting. Useful for keeping garden pests away.

Dark/Unseelie Fae: Historically, the more "volatile" court. They want change in their favor, even at the cost of lives.

Fae Glamour: A disguise created through Fae magic to hide their true appearance. Can also be used to put humans under their spell and play on their emotions (negative or positive).

Familiar: Animal companion to Fae with the ability to assist and communicate with them.

Firinne: A council of elder witches that oversees bonds between witches and their Ravdi, as well as with humans.

Light/Seelie Fae: Typically, the more mild-mannered court. They want change through collaborative and mutually beneficial means.

Neapan: The most common type of water sprite. They lure people to the water's edge, strip their flesh and bleach their bones to wear as prizes.

Ravdi: Human magical conduit to witches capable of harnessing magic and channeling it to witches, through the bond, for the witch to wield. Ravdi are incapable of magic themselves but necessary for magic users.

Sifting: A bending of space and time allowing fast travel through Faerie by Fae, only.

Spark: A fire sprite seen as smoke or flame. They are typically destructive and temperamental.

Unaligned Fae: Fae who have chosen, or are forced, into exile. They live outside the Seelie or Unseelie Courts and therefore have no governing power to protect or rule them.

Veil: The divide between the human and the Fae realms. It is visible to all with Fae blood and some witches, but not to humans. Passing between the two worlds is possible for all Fae during the new moon, stronger Fae at all times, and all humans, witches, and Fae at border checkpoints.

Wisp: An air elemental capable of controlling winds. They can be invisible or take the form of small glowing lights. They're typically peaceful but can be moved to anger.

Seelie Court

King Kyteler: King of the Seelie for the past 483 years.

Queen Branwyn: Queen of the Seelie, wife to King Kyteler, and mother to Corinna.

Princess Corinna: Princess of the Seelie and heir to the Seelie throne.

Nevan, Regent of the Seelie Court: Servant to the King and Queen and father of Aisling. Role includes patrolling the borderlands of Faerie

Aisling Quinn: Daughter of Nevan and slated to unite the two courts and realms.

Unseelie Court

King Tynan: (Assassinated) Father to Rainer, Levinas, and Ceiren. Ruled for 754 years.

Queen Moura: Sitting ruler of the Unseelie Court.

Bloody Hand, Gabriel: Executioner and advisor to Queen Moura. Father to Brynach and Breena.

King Rainer: King, in name only, of the Unseelie

Court. Father to Beatrix. Widower- Brittany
(human).

☾ **Princess Beatrix:** First halfling Princess.
Daughter of King Rainer and (deceased) Queen
Brittany. Eventual heir to the Unseelie throne.

☾ **Prince Levinas:** Second son of the Unseelie Court.
Duties include overseeing disputes of Unseelie Fae.

☾ **Prince Ceiren:** Third son to Tynan and Moura.
Duties include being a liaison to Unaligned.

☾ **Prince Brynach:** Twin to Breena and betrothed to
Aisling Quinn. No "official" role in the royal
hierarchy.

☾ **Princess Breena:** Twin to Brynach. No "official" role
in the royal hierarchy.

CHAPTER 1

Aisling

Quietly, Aisling grabbed socks and sneakers and crept to the empty living room to lace up. The condo was quiet despite having three other people in it. What she didn't need was anyone waking up and noticing her. She desperately needed alone time. She stretched a little and then opened the front door.

"And where are you're going?"

She barely stifled the scream that crawled up her throat.

"What the fuck, Breena?" Aisling cried, a hand to her heart.

"Where do you think you're going, Ash?" Breena repeated her question.

The Fae Princess was dressed for battle. A leather halter top crossed over her breasts, leaving her flat stomach bare even though it was bitterly cold out. The snow hadn't started yet, but the air smelled like it was an inevitability.

Aisling knew Breena had at least three knives strapped to her body. What she didn't know was why the Fae was at her door. Aisling crossed her arms. "Am I being held prisoner, then?"

"Guard duty. Brother dearest said he wanted time with you."

Aisling nearly facepalmed. He'd mentioned something

about wanting to talk to her and she'd promised to carve out time. But then Lettie had shown up, her blue eyes red from crying, and Aisling had completely forgotten.

"I see that didn't happen, huh?" Breena rolled her eyes.

"Something came up," Aisling answered.

"Doesn't it always?" She straightened and stared Aisling down. "You've grown on me, Aisling, but not enough to tolerate you stringing him along."

"Anything else you'd like to scold me about?" Aisling checked her watch. "At seven in the morning?"

"You don't listen anyway." Her fiancé's twin shrugged. "You will listen when I tell you you're not going anywhere, though. I'm not in the mood to run and you're not going out alone. Get back inside."

Arguing with the stubborn Fae was useless. Aisling turned and closed the door behind her. Let her freeze out there.

"And lock it!" Breena called from the other side.

Aisling stuck her tongue out but did as instructed before walking to the sofa and sitting down. She put her head in her hands and tried to breathe through the frustration. She'd had shit sleep. Her fiancé was sprawled snoring in her bed, Riordan was in her shower, and her best friend had finally fallen asleep in the guest room after a rough night. Aisling desperately needed time for herself.

She was balancing so many spinning plates and was terrified she'd drop one. And Aisling loved all her plates. She had to do better. How long would it be before everyone tired of putting up with her half-assed attempts at maintaining healthy relationships with them? Too late, she remembered to put up the barrier on her bond with Riordan. She could only hope he was too distracted in the shower to recognize her emotions.

Aisling leaned her head back on the wall and closed her eyes, wallowing in self-pity.

"The bond went quiet. Are you okay?" her Ravdi asked,

sitting next to her and pulling her close.

"Yup." She put on a smile. "Just annoyed at She-Hulk. I wanted to go for a run."

Riordan quirked his head. "You wanted to go for a run? This early in the morning after no sleep when it's freezing out?"

Her face was disgruntled as she turned to him in a mock huff. "Are you insinuating that I don't take fitness seriously?"

Her boyfriend chuckled, "Yes, I am. Besides, she's not so bad."

"You're only saying that because she can hear you, and you're afraid of her," Aisling joked.

"It could be worse. We could have one of his other siblings," Riordan reminded her.

Ceiren or Rainer would be fine, but nowhere near as effective as Breena. But Aisling knew he was talking about Levinas. She didn't want him anywhere near her house.

Aisling shivered. "Having a hellhound is better than that slime ball. Is Bry still asleep?"

Her Ravdi nodded. "I showered and got dressed and he didn't even stir."

"He needs the rest," Aisling said. Her fiancé had been running between Faerie and her condo nearly every day. To say he was spread thin was an understatement.

Aisling needed the rest too, but not as much as she needed to help Lettie. The "Hive", which is what they were calling the collective that had woken from the curse, now shared sensory experiences. They could smell, hear, feel, see through one another at random times. It had been a few months since Lettie realized that she'd woken changed. The cursed may have broken but they woke different, connected. Aisling's best friend never knew when her reality would be replaced by that of someone else. When Lettie showed up exhausted and scared, Aisling welcomed her into her warded home so she could sleep soundly. She'd renewed the charms and protection spells around her friend. She'd do whatever she could to help her.

Riordan didn't let her change the subject. "You didn't feel okay to me. Want to talk about it?"

She shook her head. "It's nothing new and nothing anyone can fix, even me, which is infuriating."

He took her chin in his hand and angled her face to his. "You don't have to solve everyone's problems, Aisling. That's not your job."

Looking into his warm brown eyes, she wanted to believe him, but she didn't. "I'm responsible for the people I love, Riordan. You probably think it's silly, but it's how I feel."

"You're not silly. It's an admirable, if not completely impractical, trait." He kissed her. "You're going to run yourself into the ground. And then you'll be no good to anyone. Ash, we're all doing our best to take care of ourselves. You have to do the same."

"Riordan," Aisling warned.

"No. I'm serious. Your mother is planning our bonding ceremony. We are about to solidify our union as a team. You promised me at the beginning of our relationship that we would communicate openly. I'm telling you, honestly, that I don't think you're okay. And I don't know how to help you."

It was too much. She pushed to her feet. "That's not fair."

"Me loving you isn't fair?" he asked, and she could see the hurt in his eyes.

"No, it's not fair to make me feel bad for wanting to help people," her voice raised before she remembered Lettie and Brynach were still asleep. Then heavy footsteps sounded in the hall, and she knew she'd woken her fiancé.

"That's not what Riordan is saying," Brynach said. "But he's right. If we are your responsibility that means you are ours as well." He moved into her space, crowding her. Those predatory eyes scanning her as he stalked closer.

Aisling stayed still, heart pounding. She didn't want to do

anything that kicked his hunter instincts into hyperdrive. Even still, when he reached her and wrapped her in his arms he sniffed her hair and a low purr in his throat vibrated through her.

"You need a vacation. We all do." He nodded to Riordan.

Aisling laughed, "We don't have time for a vacation. There's too much going on."

Brynach dismissed her argument. "It will still be going on when we get back. It's been difficult since Riordan's loss and Lettie's change. We're all under a lot of stress and we need to turn off our brains and breathe a little."

"I like the sound of that," Riordan admitted.

If Aisling was being honest, she did, too. But how could she justify leaving Lettie? Or the police department, where shit hit the fan after she broke her "partnership" with Dexter? She had responsibilities.

Brynach ran a hand up her back to the base of her skull and tugged her hair gently until she gazed up at him. "You're thinking too hard. Do you want to go away with myself and Riordan? It's that simple."

"Of course, I do."

Riordan came up behind her and took her hand. "We need this. And with me moving out it will feel nice to know we're all still in this together."

She saw the sadness in his eyes. He'd decided to move in with Liam above Dawn's shop while he was here. Aisling understood the need to have his brother close. He had left an entire country to escape the pain of his parent's loss and here he was forced to live in a town where his aunt died, the least he could do was be close to his brother. But that didn't stop her missing him, and he hadn't even moved out yet.

And Brynach was away from Faerie just to be close to her and keep her safe. Their time together had been stress filled and about other people, and their wedding day was swiftly approaching. The guys deserved time with her that wasn't about court politics or justice for Aunt Maggie and Lettie. Hell, she deserved it, too.

"Okay." She smiled at them. Aisling was moving to hug them when a strangled cry rang from the guest room. Aisling turned and ran, her men at her back.

She entered the room and found Lettie sitting up, her eyes blank. Even after months she wasn't used to the way her best friend's eyes rolled back or went sightless. There was nothing to do but wait for her to come back around. The learning curve had been intense, and even though she'd done all she could to ease Lettie into a world of magic, she couldn't help feeling like she'd failed. She sat next to Lettie but gave her space. Riordan sat at Aisling's side and took her hand, offering what comfort he could through his touch and through the bond. She leaned her head against his shoulder.

Riordan commented, "I hope she's okay."

"She will be," Aisling attempted to reassure herself. She wasn't so sure anymore, though. The visions hadn't gotten any easier for Lettie to handle. Not even the protections and wards Aisling placed on her kept the majority of them away. Her friend's bright blue eyes were ringed with dark circles and the spirit she once possessed had dimmed. The weight of the trauma weighed heavily on Lettie.

"Hey," Riordan soothed. "It's going to be okay. You're doing all you can."

"Am I?" Aisling was spared further discussion when Lettie shook her head, coming out of the sensory high jacking. As Lettie started to stir Brynach showed up with a bottle of water. Aisling smiled at him in thanks then turned her attention back to her friend.

"The gang's all here," Lettie joked as she came back into herself.

Aisling knew her friend well enough to know she was using humor to hide her fear. These lapses in time upset her, losing your life to someone else's isn't something you get used to quickly. "Are you okay?"

Lettie nodded. "Honky dory. But you're not going to like what I have to share." She turned to Riordan and Brynach. "It's about Dexter."

Both men moved closer to her, whether subconsciously or not. Since Aisling had told the chief she wouldn't work with Dexter, he'd been nothing but a pain in their asses. Drunken phone calls, mild threats, and angry outbursts when she saw him were now commonplace. Both Riordan and Brynach were running out of what very little patience they'd ever had for the man. So, they'd focused the past two months on pinning him for Maggie's death. "What about him?" asked Brynach.

Lettie stared up at Aisling's looming Dark Fae Prince fiancé. "Well, I saw and heard him," she began, explaining which senses she'd been able to share. It normally wasn't all five. "He was in an alley, I think. Somewhere with overhead lighting but outside and secluded. I can't be sure. I didn't recognize it."

"And he was talking to someone from the Hive?" Riordan tried to gain clarification.

"No." Lettie shook her head. "Whoever I was tied to stayed hidden. I couldn't see who Dexter was talking to, but I could make out Dexter's face and voice."

Aisling put her hand on her friend's leg, removing it when Lettie jumped. "What happened?"

Lettie frowned and shrugged an unnecessary apology to Aisling. "He was threatening the other man. Or warning him, rather. He said that it wasn't a fucking game and that the other person had to be more careful. That things were already falling apart, and everyone needed to keep their shit together. The other guy said he was doing his fucking best and to back off. Dexter punched him and then walked away from whoever I was seeing through."

Aisling tilted her head at them. "Still think we should plan a getaway?"

CHAPTER 2

Riordan

R iordan was putting the last of his things into his bag, determined not to make his leaving into a "thing". Not that he wanted to leave Aisling, and she knew that. But Liam was only stateside for so long and he wanted more time with his brother.

"I don't like this. I understand, but I don't like it," Aisling said, coming up behind him and sliding her arms around him. They snaked around his hips, flat hands pushing up to his chest and holding him to her. He loved the feel of her, the sweet jasmine smell of her. He'd miss these small moments, but it's not like they wouldn't happen, just less frequently.

"Ash, we never planned for me to move in to begin with. But things happened and that's how it ended up. This isn't me leaving because I feel like I don't belong here." Riordan turned to hold her and saw Brynach standing in the doorway. "I know you both want me here. Liam's already been here longer than I anticipated, and I want to spend more time with him before he's called back home."

Aisling pulled back and tilted her head to him. Riordan gave her the silently requested kiss. "I'm leaving something to sleep in and a toothbrush. You'll still see me enough to be sick of me, believe me."

"I'll never be sick of you," Aisling promised, and the love shining in the bond was proof of her words.

Brynach dropped his arms from across his chest. "I'll text you later with a few rental options for the weekend."

Riordan nodded to Aisling. "Can I borrow your car? I'll bring it back later tonight. I can't get these bags over on the bike."

"Sure." Aisling ran out of the room.

"You don't have to leave to give us space, Riordan," Brynach said approaching him. "She'll feel better with you here and we find time for ourselves."

"It's not about her, or you. This is about me," Riordan confessed.

The Fae would have a freaking immortal lifetime with Aisling. Riordan kept reminding himself he'd have plenty of time with her too, but limited amounts with Liam state side.

Aisling handed the keys to him before moving to Brynach's side. Before, seeing his girlfriend move to the large Fae as he got ready to move out would have driven him mad with jealousy. He was also acutely aware that, more often than not, Lettie was in the guest room which meant Brynach was likely to share her bed. He searched for the anger but found none.

"I'm working with Liam this afternoon. I'll bring any new information about the investigation back with me tonight."

"Dinner at seven." Aisling tried to keep the smile on her face, but Riordan could feel her sadness through the bond.

He moved over and kissed her forehead. "Perfect."

Aisling followed him down the hallway with a sad smile. As soon as the door was closed behind him the desire to pinch the bond, let himself take a deep breath, and relax was strong. He didn't do it. Shutting down their bond right as he left would probably throw Aisling into a spiral.

Instead, he kept his mind as blank as possible as he got his bags into her car and made his way toward town. Riordan wasn't sure moving onto Main Street and passing the empty space that Sweet Escapes used to occupy would go. Liam had been living in the apartment for a week or so, after it had been professionally cleaned. But, he hadn't known Maggie's place. It wouldn't bother him the way it did Riordan.

He turned onto a wooded road between Aisling's condo and Main Street, ever alert to the sprites that tended to frequent the trees. They didn't bother him when he was in cars, preferring the access of his motorcycle. Then again, they hadn't shown themselves often since the explosion. Further proof in his mind that they were somehow involved. He just didn't know how. Liam was working on it, but new information was harder to come by than they hoped.

His brother was talented, but he was still one person. It wasn't fair to expect that much out of him, and yet, everyone was pinning their hopes for leads on him. Riordan needed something to occupy his spiraling thoughts, so he'd agreed to help Liam. He could work a search engine as well as anyone else.

Riordan parked in the extra alley spot next to Dawn's sedan. She'd given him a key to the backdoor since using the shop door would disrupt business. Riordan took extra care to stay on the stone path through the witch's garden.

The alate who called it home, a beautiful brightly colored floral variety, wouldn't take kindly to him veering into her territory. In fact, Dawn had already warned him to use caution around the temperamental alate. She'd advised an offering to keep it happy. Riordan reached into his pocket and pulled out the decorative tray he'd purchased. Then he poured the simple syrup from the stoppered bottle into the dish.

"Well met, sprite." He bowed as low as he could with bags on his shoulders. "Thank you for protecting my new home and allowing me safe passage."

The alate was already sitting on the edge of the tray, long tongue lapping at the syrup. "I'll tolerate you, conduit."

Riordan nodded and moved to the door, making sure to

lock it behind him. Aisling had already reinforced all the wards here, linking them to warnings at her own condo. If something broke them, she'd know right away. He appreciated the extra step but hated that she bore the responsibility of everyone's safety.

He made his way upstairs and acknowledged how excited he was to get settled in. Granted, he hadn't expected his older brother to be his new roommate when he'd made the agreement to rent from Dawn.

"Anyone home?" He called out as he unlocked the second door at the top of the stairs.

"It's not a castle, Rory. I'm right here." His brother's voice came from the wall of computer monitors on the dining room table. The room was large, the kitchen against the back wall and a bathroom to his right. The one walled off bedroom was Liam's. Riordan had agreed his brother could have it since he'd be spending a lot of nights at Aisling's. He would take the sleeper sofa.

"One second," Riordan called unloading his bags into the hall closet he'd agreed he'd use. Now wasn't the time to fully unpack. He hung up his black leather jacket and moved his folded jeans and t-shirts onto the shelf on top of the hanging rack his jacket occupied. Then he made his way to the table, flopping down in a wooden chair next to Liam.

"That was fast," Liam said without looking up from his keyboard.

"Don't really have much to move." Riordan shrugged and then winced as a wave of his witch's emotions slammed into him. "Aisling is sad."

"The bond is intense regardless of emotional romantic connections, and I assume sex?" His brother raised an eyebrow at the end of his sentence turned question.

"We are not having that discussion. But yes, it's been very intense. I'm not trying to hurt her, but maybe if I'm not around all the time, she won't feel so obligated to keep me smiling.

She looks at me like she expects me to break, even months later." If he could admit that to anyone, it was his brother.

"Ahhh. The pity face." He glanced up. "You know, you can freak the fuck out if you need to, right?"

"Don't do that, Liam." Riordan's voice rose, "You think I haven't freaked out already? I don't need her seeing it. And not because of some toxic masculinity bullshit, but because she's got enough on her plate."

"You're not a burden, Rory."

"I know that, you asshat. She's marrying Brynach way sooner than she thought she would. She has a best friend who can't sleep and is a part of a freaking sensory Hive. She was attacked and the threats against her aren't gone. Aisling doesn't have the emotional or mental capacity to save me, but she won't stop trying." He didn't know how to help her when she did so much to help others.

"You do realize how crazy that is, right?" Liam sat back in his chair. "Your girlfriend, and bonded witch, is marrying someone else."

"Are you really going to try and talk me out of being with her, Liam? Because that's not a fight I want to have with you," Riordan warned.

"You always wanted a quiet life, Rory. I can't believe this is where you've found yourself."

"Clearly, I've made mistakes. Aisling isn't one of them, though. I can't wait for our official ceremony." Riordan watched Liam's fingers fly across the keyboard. "Liam, you don't have to stay for me, you know that, right? I know you must be mad at me. You've been keeping a lid on it because of everything happening, but I can take it. I'd feel better if you yell at me."

"Yell at you? Rory, I'm not mad at you for leaving. I understand."

Riordan's frustration grew. Was he being deliberately obtuse? "That's not what I'm talking about, and you know it."

Liam held up a hand, his face red with thinly controlled anger. Riordan recognized that look. He'd seen it often as a kid.

"I'm not letting you do this, Rory. You want to own being a moody brat when you stormed off stage, fine. If you want to apologize for ignoring my calls and texts, that'd be grand. But I will not sit here and let you take the blame for Aunt Maggie's passing. I refuse to sit witness to your self-flagellation." His voice rose with every word. By the time he was done, his neck was straining and his voice was echoing off the brick walls.

Liam took a breath and continued, "I'm not going anywhere for a while. Not just because I like the idea of us being together, but because the Firinne have decided I'm needed here more than at home. But we're going to have serious problems if you don't knock that shit off, Rory."

Riordan shook his head. He wasn't going to cry. He sniffed once and then squared his shoulders. "Maybe tomorrow we can go to the pub and get a drink? I don't play there anymore, but it's still good craic."

Liam smiled. "I'd like that. Now, let's crack on. We have work to do."

CHAPTER 3

Brynach

Visiting Faerie so soon after Riordan left for his new place hadn't been easy. Sean picked Lettie up and Brynach had gone shortly after that once Aisling promised she'd be okay. Brynach would be more concerned if he didn't know Breena was guarding her. It didn't help that his tasks for the day had included seeing his mother.

"Stop being moody," the gruff voice in his head scolded him.

Kongur might have been Brynach's most constant companion, but he had no tolerance for his bullshit. He also held a serious grudge about Brynach abandoning him for the other side of the Veil. Unlike Aisling's familiar Kongur couldn't blend in. Not to mention, the horse refused to leave Faerie.

"You try being yelled at for the better part of an hour as an adult. I'm too old for this shit." Something about the honesty he shared with his familiar made Brynach whine more than normal. Still, that had been a rough encounter at court.

His mother's voice still rang in his head, "While you play with your human, things here are falling apart. We need to re-establish control and your proclivity for halflings make us look weak. You're bending to her will, to her court, when you should be firm for your own."

Now, he was seeking out Rainer, eager to talk to his eldest brother.

Through the halls he forced his shoulders back and his head high. Brynach couldn't show weakness within these walls. Not as a Prince of the Unseelie Court and not as Gabriel's son. He'd been hoping to see Rainer at court, but he'd been absent on the dais that held the thrones. His mother had been alone but for Brynach's father at her shoulder. You could count on the Bloody Hand to be close to the Queen, his opinions worming their way into her ear. Something had to be done about that.

"Ahh the court disgrace."

Brynach's fists clenched at his side.

"Calm down. Don't let him see how he gets to you," his familiar reminded him.

He was right, but that was easier said than done when faced with his oldest annoyance. It was the right of older siblings to harass the younger, but Levinas took a perverse pleasure in his torture of Brynach and Breena.

Brynach held his tongue. "What can I do for you?"

Levinas stood in front of him, forcing him to stop walking. He didn't want to waste any more time on unpleasant conversations. He certainly didn't have the patience for whatever this was.

"I have to get to the throne room and hear complaints. Our mother tires of the drivel and I do like to keep your father's blade wet," his voice was disgustingly soft for such cruel words.

"Don't let me delay you." Brynach stepped to the side hoping he'd walk past.

"How is your blushing bride to be?" Levinas asked.

Brynach's blood ran cold. He didn't want Levinas thinking about Aisling. He certainly didn't want him intrigued enough to ask after her. The Fae had always taken pleasure in breaking anything Brynach cared about. From his favorite toys to his first sword, Levinas found a way to ruin them.

"Protected," came Brynach's simple response.

"Touchy, touchy," Levinas laughed. He left without another word.

Brynach took a moment to calm down before walking directly to Rainer's suites.

"Can I be of service?" A Fae he didn't recognize stopped him as he neared the doors.

"I'm here to see my brother." Brynach didn't slow his stride as he reached for the handle.

"The King is busy," the guard answered.

"Not too busy for me." Brynach pushed the guard aside and moved into the suite. He stalked through the plush rooms, carpeted and decorated with muted gray and slate blue. A smile lit his face, remembering the palace scrambling to accommodate his late sister-in-law when she redecorated the once scarlet and black rooms.

The multiple sitting rooms, office, and private dining in this wing were all laden with memories of Brit. They were good ones, of laughter and joy that Beatrix and her mother had brought to the castle. It was one of the few places in the palace that Brynach felt free to be himself and not a scripted version of a Dark Prince.

"I said no visitors," Rainer barked when Brynach knocked on the doors to his personal rooms.

Brynach wasn't deterred. He entered with arms spread wide and a smile on his face. "Even for me, brother?"

Rainer groaned dramatically, "Especially for you." He embraced Brynach. "What brings you home?"

"I was summoned by the she demon."

"Mother have a sprite up her ass?" Rainer smirked.

"Something like that. Ranting about my needing to control Aisling and be a stronger presence in the Unseelie Court. As if anyone ever wanted me here."

"I'm afraid that may be partially my fault. My weakness in marrying Brit didn't make it any easier for the rest of you to find love where you chose. But if she thinks you can control Aisling, she's dumber than I thought," Rainer laughed.

Brynach shook his head. "You took your happiness and I'll never fault you for it. Mother has had so little of it she takes it in the unhealthiest of forms. That's her burden, but it doesn't need to be ours."

"What is your burden, brother?" Rainer asked, sitting back down.

"Too many to name, but that's not why I'm here. Do you have time to discuss a few things?" Brynach sat.

"Within reason."

He wasn't sure exactly how to begin this conversation, so he dove in. "For the sake of brevity, I will not mince words."

His brother waved him on.

"Mother can't be on the throne when I marry Aisling."

Rainer's face would have made Brynach laugh if he hadn't been serious.

"I don't believe that anyone wants our mother on the throne, Brynach. However, that's easier said than done." Rainer leaned back in his chair. "You seem to believe I enjoy being second fiddle to her and Gabriel. I don't. But staging a takeover is difficult when our mother's advisor is a ruthless murderer."

"It's dangerous to leave her in power. Your daughter resides here, Rainer. This is no home for her, not when danger lurks everywhere." It was a low blow.

Rainer leaned forward, voice quiet but stern, "Are you questioning my ability to parent my daughter? I don't want trouble with you brother."

Brynach shook his head. "No. Of course not. Only that her future is less secure with our mother on the throne, and you know this."

"Of course, I do, but I can't simply dethrone her."

Brynach disagreed, "Actually, it's within your rights to do exactly that. The role of King should be an active one. She married onto the throne, but you were born into it. You have a stronger claim to it than she ever will."

Brynach held up a hand when Rainer started to protest. "I understand why you didn't claim it before, but you've mourned, Rainer. It's time."

"Easy for you to say when the responsibility of being King won't weigh on your head. She won't go easily," he lowered his voice. Even within the personal confines of his suite, the walls could listen. "If I try to overthrow her, even if it's within my rights to do so, it will be messy. I don't have a Bloody Hand, Brynach. Unless this is you volunteering for the role?"

Brynach tried not to let his anger get the best of him. "You know I'm not. But we could still make it work."

"We? You're coming home?" Rainer's voice dripped with sarcasm. He knew Brynach would be doing no such thing. "Why the sudden itch to boot Mother?"

Brynach sat back in the chair and crossed his leg, resting his ankle on the opposite's knee. His relaxed posture might counteract how nervous he was that his brother was about to mock him.

"I have a theory that when we have our bonding ceremony, the Veil will fall."

"Excuse me?" Rainer's eyebrows shot into his hairline. Considering his not too tiny forehead, it was an impressive feat.

"Remember the story we were told as children about Larken and Kailyn?"

"You can't actually believe that, Brynach!" The shock in his voice made it clear he thought his brother had lost his mind.

"I'm not sure what I believe, Rainer, but the seers believe it, so I won't discount it. You have to admit, it fits. I'm an eternal one. Aisling is born of both Light and Dark and of both sides of the Veil. If we wed, if we fulfill the destiny that Kailyn and Larken were supposed to have, it stands to reason the Veil may fall."

"That is a considerable number of 'ifs', brother. It's a fairytale. A children's story. Nothing more." The look in Rainer's eyes was sad. Brynach felt suddenly silly under his scrutiny. His eldest brother's opinion of him still mattered.

"Are you willing to risk the safety and future of both our worlds? If the Veil drops and Mother is on the throne there will be war between the courts and the humans. She'll unleash Gabriel in a bid for power and control. Do you deny it?" Brynach could practically hear the wheels turning in his brother's mind.

Rainer was silent for a moment. "That's in keeping with her behavior."

"If we truly unite the realms and restore the balance back to what it was meant to be, if the Veil comes down and the sides become one, she'll destroy whatever peace we could hope for. Soon the talks between the Fae, humans, and witches will begin. Do you want mother speaking on the court's behalf? You'd make a better face for the Dark Court when discussing how the world will work once the Veil is no more."

"Talks?" Rainer asked, ignoring the questions.

"It's something I've discussed with Aisling. We can't risk the chaos that would ensue if the Veil falls and the other side isn't prepared. Or our side for that matter. We need meetings with those in power to prepare for the merger."

"Brynach, you're talking nonsense. The Veil has existed for as long as anyone can remember. It will not fall." Rainer threw up his hands in frustration.

"We can't know that. Not for certain, Rainer." Brynach was adamant that his brother understand his position. "Talk to the seers and the elders. If there's even a fraction of a chance that the Veil falls, ask yourself who should be in charge of the Unseelie Court when that happens? It's not her, Rainer. It's you."

His brother thrust his hands into his hair, then brought them down to cover his face. "This is crazy, Brynach. I love you, but I'm not planning a coup to appease your belief in a fairytale."

"Will you at least take it to the elders?" Brynach needed to make sure Rainer didn't dismiss this.

"Will it make you feel better, even if their answer is the same I've given you?"

"Yes," Brynach assured him. He didn't care if it made him seem sentimental or foolish. If it protected Aisling, if it meant their union was safe, he'd do it. "I'll let you get back to work."

Rainer accompanied him to the doors. "I'm not making any promises, Brynach. I won't risk the Unseelie Court or my future reign, not even for you."

"I'm not asking you to." Brynach clasped his brother's forearm and pulled him into a hug. "Thank you for making time for me."

"Enjoy your vacation," Rainer called from behind him. Brynach heard the faint muttering of, "running off with your lovers while you leave me with this crap."

He left feeling better than he had when he entered. At least the seed had been planted for change.

"So, how did it go?" Kongur never could mind his own business.

"Not as well as I'd have liked, but about as good as I expected," Brynach answered.

"You're asking the man to believe a children's story, Brynach. Give him time to process. If he believed blindly, he'd hardly be a King worth following," his familiar reminded him.

"I'm asking him to prepare for something, so he's not caught off guard. Besides, even if it doesn't come to pass, it's time for a change in the court." Reasoning with Kongur was wasting time, really. He was too logical for leaps of faith like Brynach was asking for. *"I have to leave now. I'm sorry."*

"Save your sorry. I'm used to it now," his voice was gruff, angry.

Brynach should stay, but he'd already been gone too long. He had to get back to Aisling. Besides, he'd talk himself blue in the face and still make no headway with Kongur. At least, not if he still had to leave Faerie. He sifted to the Veil, quickly parted it, and stepped through the tree line behind Aisling's condo.

Brynach's phone pinged with a text message as soon as he crossed. He loved technology but the immediate reminder of responsibilities when all he wanted was to get to Aisling was awful. He hurried up the steps, eager to make sure everything was okay. Since Riordan had moved out, the thought of her home alone with only Breena bothered him. Jashana had regained her guard status but was busy, more often than not, in Faerie. He took the steps two at a time until he reached the door, his keys already in his hand.

"You're home," Aisling called when he entered.

Seeing her set his heart racing. Hearing her call her condo his home had pride surging through him unlike any other he'd experienced in his long life. The condo was great, but Aisling was his true home. She centered him in a way nothing else could. And seeing her in flannel pajama pants and an oversized college sweatshirt, hair in a ponytail, made him eternally thankful he got to call her his.

He loved this woman to a degree she couldn't fathom. Hell, he could barely understand it. The urge to kiss her was overwhelming, but that hadn't happened again since the soul prison. As much as he cared for her, as much as she allowed him close to her, he didn't know what she wanted. When they were away, he intended to find out.

Brynach smiled and nodded. "It took me longer than expected, sorry."

"It's fine." She waved him off. "While you were in Faerie playing prince, I was over here trying to make sure Peggy stays the fuck in jail. But you know, it's whatever."

Brynach ignored the pang of hurt at her words. He hadn't been playing at anything but that didn't matter. If the witch was loose, then Aisling was in danger. That wasn't acceptable.

"Peggy got out?"

"No. She's still locked up. Some weird super fan tried to post bail. We had to talk to the judge to confirm she was a flight risk. And Dexter started shit because he wanted to discuss a case with me, and I told him I'd address it with the captain when I checked in," Aisling explained. "It's getting harder to pretend to not want to kick Dex's teeth through his skull."

"So violent," Brynach laughed. "Let me know if you want me to take care of him? I can do that for you, a stoirin."

"No. I don't need him dead. I need justice. Riordan needs it."

He understood that. "I'm sorry I was gone so long. I had a run in with my mother that made a detour to Rainer necessary."

Aisling looked up from her computer. "It's okay, Bry. I was busy, anyway." Her phone rang and she answered, walking in the other room her voice already lighter as she spoke to Riordan.

Brynach waited for the sound of her door closing before running his hands into his hair and sighing. Then he pulled out his own phone and the piece of paper in his pocket and dialed the number.

"Yes, I'd like to book your cabin." He paused for the woman to speak. "Is tomorrow too soon?" The faster they got away from here, the better. It was one thing to have life interfere with relationships, but the longer they waited to repair these cracks the harder it would be.

He waited for the woman to check availability and breathed deeper when she returned. "Yes, still here. I understand. No, don't move anyone around, we can wait a few days. Four days is perfect and yes, we can be out before your weekend renters. Thank you."

CHAPTER 4

Aisling

Aisling was a little nervous about this getaway. Brynach and Riordan were getting along better lately but being alone with the two of them without life as a distraction filled her with anxious energy. Could she split her time and make the vacation a good one for both men? Brynach had been vague about where they were going. What would the sleeping arrangements look like?

The truck was packed with all their bags and groceries. The music was loud, Riordan sitting up front with Brynach battling over channels. Aisling smiled up at them, wondering how she'd ended in the backseat with her two guys joking in the front.

Riordan put his hand back between the seats, running it up her leg. No doubt he'd felt her anxiety in the bond. Since he'd moved out a little over a week ago, he'd slept over only once. Aisling was looking forward to waking in his arms again. Not that sharing a bed with Brynach was bad, but the sexual tension was really becoming harder to ignore.

When they finally arrived at the cabin, Brynach's large shoulders blocked most of her view. From the front seat Riordan made an appreciative sound.

"Damn it, move your bulky self so I can see." Aisling scooted to the middle of the backseat to see between the two men.

They laughed and then the house came into view. It was pretty, nothing extravagant, but the ambiance was top notch. "Oh, guys, it's perfect."

They wouldn't let her bring any bags in, so Aisling wandered the path lined with lights to the porch. The forest of large trees dwarfed the two-story cabin. She ventured inside after Brynach called out the numeric code to the door. Inside, the décor was mountain chic. A lot of natural wood and forest green. A deep sofa, a large television, and a fireplace with wood stacked next to it. The kitchen was small but functional and the stairs to the second floor were raw edge wood.

The guys came in and Aisling trailed her hand along the railing and explored upstairs. Panic settled in her gut when she saw two rooms. One with a king size bed and one with a queen. There was a hall bathroom and one in the master.

"You're anxious," Riordan commented, his arms circling her hips. She leaned back into him.

"I don't want to hurt anyone. I won't decide. You and Brynach figure it out." She refused to be put in the middle.

"We already did," Brynach answered from the doorway where he held all three of their bags. "We'll all be sharing this room." He put them on the bed.

"We will?" She looked between the two men.

"It's not like we haven't done it before," Riordan commented and kissed her cheek before moving to his bag and unzipping it.

Brynach smiled at her Ravdi, and the two men unpacked their things, moving around one another to place items in dressers or on the bathroom counter. If they could be natural about this, so could she. Frankly, the thought of spending a weekend sandwiched between the two of them did things to her body. They might be okay with this, but how was she supposed to resist the temptation of both Riordan and Brynach for three nights?

Lucky for her, by the time night fell they were all too tired to make it awkward. After the excitement of the past month or so, they all fell into exhaustion once they let themselves relax. She'd been yawning by eight thirty and they'd all gone up to bed. She still didn't know what they had planned for the trip. Selfishly, she hoped it was very little. The peace the cabin brought was intoxicating.

Aisling woke to Riordan snoring softly next to her. At some point in the night, he'd released his hold on her and now she slid out of bed. She used the hall bathroom, so she didn't wake him and then tiptoed downstairs in her pajamas.

"Morning," Aisling called to Brynach quietly as she dove headfirst into the refrigerator. It was pretty empty, but they'd brought milk and cereal. She made herself a bowl and settled on the sofa next to the large Fae.

Aisling couldn't help but be distracted by his body. This morning he was wearing low slung black sweatpants and had opted to remain shirtless. She was in a flannel pajama set and sweatshirt. She was freezing, but he was half dressed and comfortable. She wanted to lean into the soap-clean scent of him and borrow the warmth of his chest. Immediately, she felt unfaithful. Feeling things like that as Riordan's girlfriend wasn't right.

Then again, she was Brynach's fiancé.

Honestly, she didn't know how she was supposed to feel or act in this situation. Riordan trusted her, but more and more she was starting to mistrust herself.

"A stoirin?" Brynach turned to her. "Are you okay?"

She shook herself out of her thoughts. "Yes."

Brynach quirked a brow. "You were quiet on the ride up. You seem distracted. Is it work? Dexter?"

"Is it okay if I don't think about any of that while I'm here?"

"If that's what you want," he answered and then commenced watching her eat.

Aisling lifted the spoon to her mouth and took a bite, milk

dripping on her chin. She flicked her tongue out to catch the rogue drop. Brynach's eyes followed her movements. If he was going to watch she'd at least make it fun. Aisling bit her lip and moaned. "It's so good," she drew out.

Brynach's eyes flashed. "Aisling. You're playing with fire. Keep it up and you may not go into our wedding night a maiden." His voice was light, but Aisling couldn't stop the way her pulse sped at the thought of a wedding night with Brynach.

She blushed and took her empty bowl to the kitchen before returning to the fire Brynach had built and warming her cold hands. He was still fiddling with the logs. Aisling was sure she'd made enough noise to alert him, but when he rose, he was so close she lost her balance trying to make room for him.

"Easy. You okay?" he asked, his arms wrapped around her to steady her.

"Fine. Just clumsy this morning."

"I don't mind."

Brynach's hair tickled her cheeks as he gazed down at her. Aisling didn't think, she acted. Her hands flattened on his chest, and she raised up on her toes the same moment he leaned down, and his large hand cupped her neck.

Briefly, she wondered if she was making a mistake. Then it was gone, and their lips met. Aisling fell into the sensation of being kissed by Brynach. Her mouth opened to him on a sigh then both his hands were on her, lifting her. She wrapped her legs around his waist, and his hands cupped her ass. Aisling let her fingers sink into his hair, holding him close as he claimed her mouth. And when she felt him hard against her core, she couldn't help the way her hips rocked against him. Brynach tugged at her lip with his teeth, and she pulled on his hair. When they parted, they were both panting.

"We can't keep doing this," Brynach whispered against her mouth.

Aisling's stomach dropped. "I'm sorry. I wasn't thinking." She loosened her legs, but he didn't put her down.

"That's not what I meant." Brynach's lips met her again. "I want to keep kissing you, but I don't want to keep doing this without talking about it." He set her down and Aisling tried not to fidget. "I'm not a rash decision you're making. I'm not a mistake. I'm here, Aisling. I want this. But I don't like the push and pull."

Aisling's heart hurt. She hadn't been very fair to him. "I'm sorry."

Brynach lifted a hand and smoothed the hair back from her face before kissing her once more softly. When he pulled away, he took her hand and led her to the sofa. "You and Riordan have discussed the dynamics of your relationship. We need to do the same."

With the memory of Brynach hard against her she knew what she wanted right now, but would it be fair to him? To Riordan? Could she keep them both happy without driving herself crazy with guilt?

Eventually this was something all three of them needed to discuss, but before they could agree on an arrangement for the group, they needed to straighten out individual needs. As far as she was concerned it was her job to make sure that both Riordan and Brynach were happy in their relationships with her.

She sat facing him, legs folded under her. Brynach frowned and unfolded them, placing them across his lap. His strong hands massaging her calf. "I want to build a life with you. One filled love where we both feel secure and safe."

"Oh, Bry. We'll have that. We already have that." And she meant it. "I haven't said it in so many words, and I can't honestly say I'm in love with you, yet. But I love you very much."

His black hair swung as he shook his head. "I want romantic love. I want passion and I want joy. We've both earned that. But I also want you to be fulfilled. And I need to know that whatever happens between us is because you want it and not because you think it's something that makes me happy. I need to know my touch and my kisses are welcome."

"They are," Aisling assured him.

"You're adorable when you blush." He brushed his fingers over her hot cheeks. "I'm glad to hear that. I enjoy sharing your bed. I look forward to sharing it for something other than sleep. But the prophecy isn't specific enough for me to feel safe doing that until we're married," he admitted.

"What a gentleman." She winked at him.

Brynach laughed, "Not at all. I'd happily ravage you here and now if you wanted it. But I have no desire to rush our physical relationship. The lead up can be just as fun."

Aisling felt heat settle in her stomach. "I look forward to that. I like the way you man handle me." She licked her lips.

"I welcome Riordan, too. I care for him." Brynach continued, "But I need to feel like an important and valued part of your life. I know we'll argue, but I need to feel like the one thing you aren't fighting is your feelings for me."

Her heart sank and she moved to him. "I'm past the point of trying to deny my feelings or attraction for you. But I'm in over my head." She let her hands wander along his jaw, feeling it clench and relax under her touch. She cupped his cheek and he turned into it, closing his eyes. "I have no idea how to keep one man, let alone two, happy. I'm so afraid I'm going to mess this up. And I don't know if I could handle that because I want this to work so badly."

"Then we'll make it work." He kissed her forehead. "But you haven't told me what you want from me."

"I need you to remind me that this isn't going away, and that you want me, not because of court politics, but because I matter to you." She paused. "I'm not going to be easy all the time, but you're used to that. But I want a partner, Brynach. I want someone who challenges me and who lets me breathe. A home and heart to come back to after my day. I want to be a team."

She watched his face for a reaction. Brynach took a deep breath, then spoke. "That's all I've ever wanted, Aisling. It would be my pleasure to give it to you. Where do we go from here?"

"Nowhere. Not until I talk to Riordan."

Brynach nodded. "That feels right. But, Aisling, I don't want to hide how I feel about you. That changes now. Today."

"I want that, too. I need you to understand that if it hurts Riordan or he can't handle it, then we have to revisit this." Aisling leaned forward and kissed him. Her lips against his, she murmured, "I'm a little sad you can't rail me right now." When his eyes went wide with shock, she grinned. "But if you want to wait, I'm okay with that, too."

"Damn you," he growled and lunged at her. Aisling squealed and jumped up, running away. A sleepy Riordan walked into the room.

"I thought I heard you," he said, rubbing his eyes and then taking in the scene. Aisling behind a table and Brynach crouched and ready to pounce on her. "Um, did I interrupt something?"

"Nope." Aisling winked at Brynach.

"Right. I'm going to make coffee." He turned to the kitchen. "Weirdos."

"It's already made. The pot should still be hot," Brynach called and snagged Aisling by the pocket of her hoodie. "You're in trouble."

Aisling put a hand to his chest and smiled up at him. Then she skipped to the kitchen to her boyfriend.

"Sleep well?" She asked, hugging his back as he made his coffee.

"Mhmm. Though it got cold once I was alone in bed." He stared out the window. "How about that, it's snowing."

Aisling followed his gaze out the window and sure enough, a light snowfall kissed the ground. "I know you guys want to hike but no part of me wants to go out there."

Brynach spoke from behind them, "There's a hot tub."

Aisling turned on him. "What? Where?"

Brynach laughed, "Out back. You can exit through the basement. I double checked this morning."

Riordan turned around. "You didn't tell us. I don't have a suit."

"Me either." Aisling sulked.

Her fiancé shrugged. "Didn't think we needed them."

Her Ravdi stiffened. "You knew about the hot tub and assumed we'd all climb in naked? You're handsome, Brynach, but that's not happening. You haven't wooed me enough." He was making light of it, but Aisling could sense the nerves through the bond.

Brynach waggled his eyebrows. "I haven't wooed you at all. I didn't know I was allowed to. Believe me, I'm happy to begin."

Riordan shook his head. "You're incorrigible."

It was time to break the ice. "Alright boys, I'm grabbing towels. Be ready to strip down to underwear. We're getting in that hot tub." Aisling ignored the way their jaws dropped and left the room smiling. She stripped off her clothes, immediately missing their warmth and wrapped a towel around herself. By the time she returned Brynach had gathered their boots.

She gazed from one to the other, both still dressed. "You're going to leave your clothes in the snow?"

The men shrugged and Aisling slid her feet into her boots. "Catch up." She made her way to the basement steps and soon they followed. She unlocked the sliding glass door and stepped out. Her breath a warm cloud in the cold air. Goosebumps rose all over her body and she started shivering. "Fuck!"

Brynach hurried outside, his boxer briefs black and revealing. Damn it, he was sexy. Riordan was nothing to laugh at in his grey boxers. He shivered and cursed as the cold hit him. "You took the damn towels."

Her fiancé laughed, unaffected by the cold. He lifted the cover, the steam off the water a welcome sight. After pushing a few buttons, the jets started bubbling. Riordan kicked off his boots and made the run. Aisling put the men's towels on the hooks she'd found by the door. Reluctantly she took her own off and hung it, before running to the tub.

"Fuck. Shit. Fuck. It's cold!" She yelped and hopped, kicking off her boots. She had no choice but to step, barefoot, on the snow-covered steps to the water. Riordan and Brynach had already settled into the steaming water. They both eyed her hard nipples through her pink bra. "Perverts," she joked.

"Opportunistic voyeurs," Brynach clarified.

Aisling sunk into the middle of the hot tub, only her head out of the water. They weren't covered by a deck. Snow was falling on them, but she felt incredibly warm. The men were sitting on opposite sides of the tub, leaving Aisling to decide who she sat next to.

"If we can share a bed, we can sit next to one another in a hot tub, for fuck's sake." Aisling moved to sit down, keeping as much of herself under the water as possible. "I want one of you on each side of me, pronto."

With a laugh, both men moved to her side. "Will we always do what she asks?" Riordan mused.

"I'm afraid so," Brynach answered.

Aisling let herself enjoy the view of the trees covered in snow, her hair collecting rogue flakes. Her hand on Riordan's leg and her foot wrapped around Brynach's calf. She closed her eyes and let her head fall to Riordan's shoulder.

"I overheard you," he said softly. "I saw you, too."

Aisling stiffened and then turned to Riordan. "I'm sorry! I'm so sorry. You asked me not to be with him until we talked, and we hadn't discussed it yet." Tears collected and spilled.

"Stop, they'll freeze on your face." He wiped the tear away. Brynach rubbed her back. "It's okay. I mean, it would have been nicer if we'd talked about it before you kissed him, but it's still okay. I'm not an idiot. That kiss at the soul prison would never be your last. You're marrying the man."

Brynach spoke, "I'm sorry, Riordan. I should have controlled myself."

Riordan ogled her now see-through bra and underwear under the bubbling water. "My friend, I commend you for controlling yourself as much as you have. Like I said, I understand."

"You don't mind that I kiss Brynach? It's okay if he touches me?" Aisling asked hesitantly.

Her Ravdi nodded. "It is. I can confidently speak for both of us when I say we'd still like alone time and not just group activities. But I love seeing you happy and cared for. Brynach loves you. I love you. I'm not going to ever ask that someone withhold that from you or make you feel bad about accepting it."

She let out a breath she'd been holding while waiting for his answer and actively tried to ignore the way her pulse raced at the mention of group activities. The images her mind conjured were probably not what he meant, but she was enjoying them none the less.

Riordan addressed her fiancé over her shoulder. "Do you have expectations of me?"

"Love her. Treat her well," Brynach answered simply.

But Riordan shook his head. "No. I meant in terms of our relationship."

Aisling turned enough to see the surprise on Brynach's face. Snowflakes collecting on his dark lashes as he blinked. "Well, I suppose I want to work with you to make sure Aisling is happy. But also, to communicate with one another so that jealousy, resentment, and anger don't build."

Riordan hummed his agreement, "That I can do."

"And I wouldn't mind kissing you, too," Brynach added cheekily.

With snow falling on their shoulders and laughter in the air, Aisling felt warmer than ever before.

CHAPTER 5

Riordan

W aking up without Aisling in his arms was the worst part of living with his brother. After their snowy getaway he missed the warmth of her at night. The sofa bed was garbage compared to her bed. Hell, he'd even take a snuggle with Brynach over the springs in his ass. And it's not like they hadn't both tried convincing him to come back. Especially when he had groaned falling into her bed one night, exalting the mattress as heavenly. But he'd been living with his brother only a month. He wasn't about to put his tail between his legs and move back into Aisling's that fast.

A part of him guiltily enjoyed waking without the weight of her emotions and expectations pressing in on him. He understood Aisling wanted him to be happy, to feel at home, but he couldn't do that all the damn time. He was still hurt, still healing. And even if looking at his brother reminded him that he'd robbed Liam of their last remaining blood relative because of his carelessness, it was still easier than feeling like he wasn't strong enough for Aisling.

Communication wasn't a problem for Riordan but there were things he didn't want to open up to her about. Not because he didn't trust her with it but because it would add to her heartache. So, after talking to Liam he took the leap and called Aisling's mother. He hadn't been sure if she'd see him, conflict of interest and all that, but she'd said that wouldn't be a problem and scheduled his first appointment.

It would be his first time seeking out therapy willingly instead of at the request of loved ones. Although, the reason wasn't all that different. The death of his parents had been a blow and even back then he could see the value in seeing a therapist. After Maggie's death and the responsibility he was shouldering for it, it felt right to start back up. Not only did he need to lift that burden, but he couldn't be a good partner to Aisling or brother to Liam while so deep in despair.

"Knock knock," called a bright and distinctly feminine voice.

Riordan looked to Liam. "Expecting company?"

"Actually, yes." Liam unlocked the door, letting in the dark-haired beauty with purple bags under her bright blue eyes.

"Lettie, this is a surprise," Riordan said when he saw who it was.

"It is?" She turned to Liam. "You didn't tell him I was coming?"

"It hadn't come up." Liam shrugged. "Lettie is helping with the investigation. Well, her and Sean. Where is he?"

Lettie set down her bag and moved toward the workspace. "He's right behind me. He's grabbing coffee."

"How are you?" He asked Lettie.

"I'd rather not, Riordan. I kinda need this space to just... not," she answered, her bright eyes looked tired.

He nodded. "So, what's on the agenda for today?"

Liam answered, voice excited, "We're going to use Lettie's insider knowledge to bring these dirtbags down."

She blushed. "Turns out the upside to this connection is that it has also connected us to the fuckers who did this. Whatever mental pathways we are following goes back to the source. Of course, none of us can control when or how the sensory sharing happens."

Liam jumped in, nearly bouncing with excitement. His brother lived for this kind of thing. "But they've exchanged numbers, or at least those who want to help have."

"Some are still living in denial. Like that's an option." Lettie rolled her eyes. "Um, he's not coming alone."

Liam's voice was high when he asked Lettie, "What do you mean? We can't have just anyone walking in here. This is sensitive information and not entirely, you know, legal."

"It's fine. She's been vetted. Ask your brother." She winked at Riordan.

What the hell did that mean? There were footsteps on the stairs, Sean opened the door, and Riordan's eyes went wide.

"Amber?"

The dark complected, half-shaved head of blue hair, and full time badass smirked at him. "You say that like you've forgotten my name. I'm hurt."

Riordan rolled his eyes. "As if I could forget you. What are you doing here?"

Sean answered after handing a coffee to Lettie, "She's got underground connections and tech experience. We could use the extra help."

Riordan turned to assess how much Liam was freaking out right now, but he wasn't. Instead, he was staring with almost literal heart eyes at Amber. He got it, she was impressive. But man, brother, play it cool.

"Um, Amber, this is my brother, Liam. Liam, this is Amber," Riordan made the introductions.

Amber winked at his brother before clapping her hands. "What are we doing?"

Lettie sipped her coffee. "Well, I've been talking to the other members. Turns out sometimes we're in the same place at the same time. I might have smells but someone else gets vision. Together we can piece together the whole scene. Through overheard conversations we believe we've seen into

Peggy's children a few times. And if we can use whatever the fuck this is to catch them, we're going to."

Surely, they'd already considered it, but Riordan had to ask, "Do they know you know? Can they sensory spy on the group?"

Lettie gestured in the air with her coffee. "We have no clue. We have to assume they can. But if we can't control it, maybe they can't either."

Sean rubbed circles on Lettie's back. "And you're going to bring them down. Nobody can hide, not with technology the way it is. We'll find them."

"Sean has...connections that are coming in handy." Liam winked.

Riordan remembered all too well what Sean's connections were. Dark web and drug deals. He hadn't wanted to know any more about it then and he didn't now. Let Sean handle the seedy internet underbelly, especially if it helped find Maggie's killer. He wondered how Amber would fit in.

"And I have connections to the area's, let's just say, less honorable community," Amber added.

"Sounds like you have plenty to work with," Riordan said, checking his watch. He had to get going if he was going to make his appointment. "I have to run, but I'll be back later."

The drive to Aisling's childhood home was fast, but even still he was almost late. Turns out that only having a motorcycle really sucks in the winter. He was frozen by the time he rang the doorbell and plastered on a smile.

"Hello, Riordan. I'm happy to see you," Mrs. Quinn welcomed him. He took a seat and she continued, "I have to admit, I was surprised you called me, but I'm very happy you did. It eases my mind to know that I'm planning a ceremony for my daughter and a man committed to taking care of himself. That's admirable. That said, I hope you're okay if things inside this office are a little different from when we're outside it."

"This isn't my first experience with therapy, Dr. Quinn. I

understand how this works," he clarified.

"Good, then you know you'll get out of this what you put in. This is a safe space and I hope you'll use both our time to engage in open and honest conversation. I know it might be strange talking to the mother of your partner but please know that anything you say here doesn't influence my feelings about you."

"Yes, it does. I wouldn't expect you to be able to separate your love for Aisling from your job. Besides, this isn't about her."

"Not entirely, but I doubt your struggles are that divided from your involvement with my daughter and the magical community," her voice was friendly, but she hadn't denied he was right.

"No, but the one at fault is me."

"And how does that feel?"

So it begins, he thought to himself and let his grief pour from his lips.

T herapy ended and Riordan dreaded getting back on the motorcycle in the frigid conditions. As much as he loved it, he could admit it was time to dip into his parent's money and get a car, too. It's amazing how much time you lose negotiating what ends up still being a pretty crap deal. By the time he was done at the car dealership it was too late to go back to the apartment and change so he drove to Aisling's. Brynach had already dropped his motorcycle into an empty spot. He'd come without complaint to bring Riordan's bike back so Riordan could sign the paperwork on his new SUV. The Fae's truck wasn't there, though.

He knocked on the condo's door despite having a key. Now that he wasn't officially living there it felt odd just walking in. Aisling's face when she opened the door said it all.

"I didn't know if I should come in." He toyed with the rings on the chain around his neck. As soon as he realized he was doing it, he stopped.

"Don't make it weird. Of course, you can come in." She turned back to her spot on the sofa and lifted her laptop. "You're early."

"I finished with errands but not with enough time to go to the apartment." He settled in next to her. "Whatcha working on?"

"Adult shit. Deciding to stop classes really sent my advisor into a tailspin. And I've asked Captain to send any requests for work through email and not text. I need a little distance from constant accessibility with all that's going on. So, I am checking in more often." She shrugged.

"I bought a car," he deadpanned.

Aisling nodded. "Adult shit, am I right? Do you love it?"

"You know, I think I do. At the very least it was nice not freezing my ass off. Safer, too," he admitted.

Aisling's fingers played on her neck and the scar. Riordan wondered if she realized how often she did that? He leaned over and kissed her cheek. "Don't go too deep into that pretty head of yours, Ash. I didn't mean to trigger anything."

"You didn't," she lied. "A few minutes and I'll be ready to go."

He sat while she finished what she was doing, taking her in. She was wearing leggings and a sweater so large it dwarfed her. He'd have no idea the shape of her body if he hadn't traced it with his fingertips and tongue. The sun pouring in through the glass doors to the balcony set her hair aflame. The reds and oranges swirling in a mesmerizing symphony of color. They were the only flames Riordan ever wanted to see for the rest of his life.

"You're staring. It's very distracting," she commented, eyes still on her screen and fingers tapping away.

He let his hand wander to her leg, traveling north and she smirked before lifting the laptop so he could rest his hand on her inner thigh, fingers brushing her core. "Where's Bry?"

"Grocery shopping," Aisling answered and set the laptop aside. "We have time if you wanna." She wiggled her brows and Riordan laughed.

"Oh, do we?" he asked, picking her up and settled her on his lap, his hands sliding under her large sweater and finding her breasts. Her mouth came down on his and he barely contained a groan as all things Aisling flooded his senses.

"I missed you," she whispered.

"Liam's a shit cuddle in the morning." Riordan tried for humor, but Aisling frowned at him. Which was impressive, considering he was currently fondling her hardened nipples. "You could stay at my place tonight? We won't be alone, but nobody will have superhero level hearing."

Aisling sat back, and he let his hands slide out of her shirt and settle on her hips. "That bothers you, doesn't it?" Aisling asked.

"It's awkward. I like Bry but I don't need him knowing every move we make," he confessed. "I love the lug, too. Fuck, even I've considered making out with him. But I don't need him hearing me moan your name."

"You have?"

He laughed, "Not really. Well, not much. That's not the point. You know I'm okay with the two of you being intimate, but it doesn't always have to be a group thing. Even when he's not in the room, if he's in the condo he might as well be in bed with us."

She settled back into his lap and brought her mouth down on his. The kiss was passionate. They wouldn't make it to the date after all. He lifted her and made his way down the hall to her bedroom. Aisling's laugh was music to his ears as he tossed her onto the bed.

"Get over here," she insisted with arms open, as if he'd rather be anywhere else.

"Grocery shopping, Aisling. We don't have time. Not for what I want to do to your body," he warned as he climbed slowly onto the bed until he could taste her lips again.

"Shut up and make the most of the time we do have, then." Aisling's hand was reaching for the button fly on his jeans when Riordan's phone rang. He scrambled to pull it from his pocket and silence it.

"Who was it?" Aisling asked, still undoing his buttons.

"Liam. He can wait."

"Hell yes, he can," she agreed, and dove for his mouth.

He pulled her sweater up over her head. His hands were hungry for her flesh. Aisling had finally worked the buttons on his fly and was eagerly pushing down his jeans, working them over his hips and reaching for him. And damn if he wasn't ready for her.

"Aisling!" Brynach's voice boomed from the front door.

She sat up, head almost smashing into Riordan's as she tugged her shirt back over her head. Riordan tucked himself away and was buttoning his fly in time for the large Fae to burst into the room.

At least he had the good grace to blush and turn his back before speaking. "Sorry! We were trying to reach you but neither of you were answering. I see why now."

"What's the emergency?" Aisling asked climbing off the bed.

Riordan reached for his phone. The text preview said, *"CALL ME."*

"We got a lead on Peggy. We want to move before anyone in the Hive can alert them."

Son of a bitch. He'd known he wouldn't have enough time to enjoy Aisling's body, but he'd anticipated a little more. He looked at her and sighed. If one thing could turn his attention it was justice for Aunt Maggie.

CHAPTER 6

Brynach

Aisling had concerns over Lettie and her exposure to magic and the Hive experience, but in this moment, he was glad for it. Without the connection they'd never have learned about the abandoned house that Peggy's sons were fleeing from. Instead, Sean was working on the web tracking down the names they'd gleaned from the vision. Sydney, Victor, and Callan.

Riordan looked a little pale, even more than usual. Finding information that could lead to putting away the people responsible for his aunt's murder and the curse that still plagued Lettie was important. But for Brynach, seeing some of the worry leave the creases in Riordan's forehead was a priority. He didn't deserve what he'd been through. The now disgraced elder Firinne was still in jail, but nobody believed her children were innocent. Bringing them to justice for the death of Peggy's partner and more than likely, her involvement in the fire, was the focus for a large part of the police force, not just the people in this room.

One was dead, good riddance. But who knew how many offspring were ready to continue their mother's agenda? Aisling's hand landed on his shoulder, and he turned toward her.

"You okay?" she asked.

"Yeah," he answered. Without asking he nodded nearly imperceptibly back at Riordan. Aisling bit her lip and shook her head. None of this could be easy on her Ravdi and Brynach hated that he was hurting, but also that it was adding to Aisling's own pain and guilt.

The window was down and Phlyren was overhead, observing the land they were about ready to drive onto. The property spanned acres and her familiar made it easier for him to feel safe allowing Aisling out of the truck. They'd pulled up Google earth and looked over the pictures, but a lot could change between snapshots. The driveway had weeds growing through the gravel but that didn't mean it was empty. They were waiting for Phlyren to report back.

"What's the game plan when we go in?" Aisling asked.

Brynach loved that she was a planner. No surprises for his girl. "I go in first."

"Obviously," Riordan quipped and Brynach frowned at him. "What happens after that?"

"Breena will take you and Aisling through the first floor. I will take Liam through the second," Brynach decided. Aisling would be safer with Riordan to aide her magic and Breena would protect them if something unexpected came up. Aisling's familiar swooped back overhead, landed on her shoulder, and nuzzled her cheek.

"We're good to go," she said, and they got back in the cars and drove up to the house. "Did you check the woods, or should we look through them better?" she asked her familiar. He bit her finger and Aisling grumbled, "I've insulted him."

The house was in complete disrepair. If this was where they'd been camping out, it hadn't been comfortable. The door was hanging open, the frame splintered. The stench of mildew hit them as soon as they entered the house. Even with Brynach's Fae hearing there was nothing but the rustle of little critters.

"It's empty," he confirmed, and immediately felt better about sending Aisling off without him. Still, this was the house of a powerful witch. Curses could have been left behind.

"I can still feel magic," Riordan observed.

Aisling closed her eyes, opened them again. "Her signature isn't here. At least, not that I can sense. We're safe. Look for anything that can give us clues about Peggy or her children."

"Be careful. Yell if you need me," Brynach instructed Aisling.

"We're fine," Breena said briskly. "Go."

Brynach and Liam walked toward the stairs. "How long has she owned the house?"

Liam answered as they searched the first room. It was a child's bedroom with a small bed and toys scattered across the floor. "The house was purchased by a Gavin Houndsworth in 1983."

Brynach's chest tightened. "You said Houndsworth?"

"Yup. Not sure the connection to Peggy, but that's what is on the deed," Liam said, opening dresser drawers. He turned on Brynach. "Are you going to help?"

"Yes. Of course." He moved to the closet, the doors broken and hanging by rusted hinges. Brynach searched the wall and ceiling for hidden pockets or panels. "Nothing in here."

"Here either," Liam said, leaving the dresser before lifting the mattress and finding nothing but bugs. "Gross."

Brynach checked the rest of the rooms on the second floor in a fog. Which is not to say he wasn't thorough, but his head was elsewhere. It had to be a coincidence, but Brynach didn't believe in coincidences. Houndsworth was the name his father used, and Gavin was close enough to Gabriel to be an alias. He didn't want to jump to conclusions, but he had digging of his own to do when they got home. Right now, he had to focus.

"Brynach!"

At the sound of Aisling's raised voice, he took off at a sprint. His feet barely touched the stairs as he cursed his inability to sift this side of the Veil.

"Aisling! Where are you?" he bellowed.

"In here."

Brynach followed the sound of her voice, but as soon as he entered the room, he could see she was okay. Breena was next to her, and Riordan was looking at him like he'd lost his mind.

"Are you okay?" the Ravdi asked.

"I thought something was wrong," Brynach admitted. "You screamed."

"We found something. Well, Riordan did," Aisling said, grinning at her bonded.

It was sweet seeing her pride in her Ravdi and Riordan's excitement at being helpful. He let himself observe their moment and acknowledged the jealousy that came and went.

"I was searching for concentrations of magic. Sometimes I can get a reading off of them, see how diluted it may be. Anyway, I found a whole lot in this area and when I tried to harness it, it wouldn't come to me. Which is weird, right? I told Aisling and she was brilliant. She blasted through the ward, and we found this stuff." Riordan's enthusiasm was endearing.

Brynach fought the urge to go to him and tell the man he'd done well. It was becoming second nature to feel affectionate toward Riordan.

"What is it?" he asked moving closer to the group.

Breena practically growled at him, "I wouldn't have let her get hurt."

"I know. I'm sorry. Instinct." He shrugged as Aisling began to spread paper on a table.

"It's letters. We found them in a heavily warded safe behind that picture." She pointed behind her. "They're old and brittle, so I'm trying to be careful. You don't think I'm fucking up fingerprints or anything, do you?"

"No, a stoirin, you're okay. They're too old for that," he said looking at the aged paper. "What do they say?"

He read over her shoulder and what he saw froze the blood in his veins.

"Love letters. I think they're from Peggy to a man she was clearly involved with. Maybe the father of her kids? This might be the clue we need." Aisling's excitement was genuine and so was Brynach's revulsion.

"Breena, can I speak to you outside?" Brynach led his sister from the room. Aisling and Riordan barely acknowledged their leaving, too wrapped up in the letters to notice.

Once outside and out of earshot from even Aisling, Breena turned on him. "What's with the look on your face?"

Brynach dragged a hand through his hair. "The house belongs to a Gavin Houndsworth. If those are love letters to Peggy's lover, it stands to reason that dear old dad may have sired those assholes."

"This isn't good!" Breena growled.

"Get her home and keep an eye on her. I have to get back to the court. I need to talk to..."

"Who? Who do we trust enough to go to with this? Ceiren will listen but Rainer can't do anything. And we can't trust this information with anyone outside our immediate circle until we know for sure." He recognized fear on his twin's face. He'd seen it often.

"I can talk to Alex," Brynach said nodding.

"To what end? What's he going to be able to do?"

Brynach thought for a moment. "I don't know, Breena, but I know we have to do something. I'll gather Ceiren and we'll visit. At the very least I can share this information and tell Ceiren to keep his eyes and ears open."

"Are you sure it's him?" Breena was chewing her lip.

"When we arrested Peggy's son, he called me brother. He's dead and Peggy isn't talking. Let's get what we can use and get the hell out of here." Brynach wanted to get back inside and be near Aisling.

Breena's hand slid to her leg, her fingers finding a blade

and slipping it from its hiding spot. Brynach wasn't sure she was doing it consciously, but she spun the blade on her finger before flinging it at a tree. It embedded itself inches deep. She stormed over, pulling it from the oak with little effort. So strong. So silent. So angry. That's how the Unseelie Court bred them.

Brynach scanned the woods, seeing a slip of Faerie running through them. Eyes looked back at him. A small red fox crouched in the brush. Then Breena cursed and he turned his attention back to his sister.

He hurt for her, his twin, who floundered without love or hope to ground her. Brynach wondered if Aisling would ever realize how caring for her had saved him? He wanted the same thing for his twin. She needed someone to tame the darkness inside her. When Breena returned, they joined the others. The need for Faerie crawled across Brynach's skin like a thousand wisps caressing him. Every hair on his arms stood up.

"I'm not going back with you. Breena will see you home safely. I'll be back later," he told Aisling.

"Bry, where are you going?" She moved toward him.

"You saw something. What was it?" Riordan asked, hand on Aisling's back while hers rested on Brynach's arm.

"I'll talk about it when I get home tonight. Riordan, stay with Aisling."

"Of course." The Ravdi pulled Aisling closer, then pushed her ever so gently toward Brynach.

Brynach's brow shot up and Aisling looked at Riordan. The Ravdi's brown eyes shone as he nodded, and Aisling stepped up to Brynach. Her hands braced on his shoulders, and she lifted herself until she could place a kiss on his lips. It was a salve on his anxiety, and he hugged her close. He breathed in her jasmine scent before letting go.

"I'll see you later tonight." Brynach waited for their cars to drive out of sight before turning toward the woods and parting the Veil to Faerie.

S ifting to Alex's house was instinctual. He'd done it countless times in his lifetime. What didn't come as naturally was confiding in him that he thought his father had sired halflings who were now threatening the woman he loved.

Outside his best friend's house, he greeted Kongur.

"Hello, friend."

"Don't hello friend, me. People see their friends," his familiar sulked.

"Aren't we too old for this?" Brynach scoffed. *"I've said I'm sorry."*

"It's possible to love someone without liking them. What do you need?" the large draft horse huffed.

"I need Ceiren to come to Alex's. Can you let Lidris know?" His familiar would alert his brother's snow leopard. The two familiars couldn't communicate, but they'd found a way to understand each other. Ceiren would know where to find Brynach, it was the one place in Faerie he felt safe.

His familiar didn't respond but Brynach knew he'd relay the message. He thanked Kongur and then lifted a hand, knocking on Alex's door. The large wooden slab swung open, and Alex greeted Brynach with open arms. When Ceiren sifted in behind him, Aindrea, his wife, eyed them suspiciously.

Not because Aindrea didn't love Brynach, she did, but because she had a newborn baby to protect. Nothing was stronger than this woman's love for children, including the eight fosters she currently had at the house.

"Don't you bring any trouble to my door, Brynach. I'll not thank you for it," she warned.

"I would never," Brynach promised and kissed her cheek before accepting the sweet warm bundle that was Joeigh. The child was perfect. A slight purple tinge to their skin and dark blue hair accented by the rosy pink of their cheeks made Brynach's heart melt.

Brynach sat at the table and rocked Joeigh as he fed her a bottle and talked to Alex and Ceiren. Voicing his suspicions felt a lot like manifesting them into truths, but they needed to be said. "I'm not sure what to do with the information. I see a logical trail to Gabriel, but I need more proof."

"I'll see what I can uncover at the castle, but I'm not sure what I'll turn up. I've spent a lot of time wandering the archives and I've never seen mention of Gabriel's children." He paused and looked at Brynach. "Not even the ones we know he had."

It should have stung but Brynach wasn't surprised to be undocumented in the courts. He never expected to be listed as Tynan's son. That much had been made clear by his older half-siblings. Being marked the bastard son of a cheating Queen seemed unlikely. He shook it off. Brynach wasn't fazed by his brother's lack of confidence.

"Which tells us the chances of him having more un-documented children is high. If anything, you can track his movements, associations, or affiliations, prior to becoming the Bloody Hand? His life didn't begin at murder."

"Actually..." Ceiren trailed off. "I've done a little bit of digging already, cause it's always good to know the monsters sleeping under your roof. His mother died in childbirth."

Brynach shook his head. "Wow. Okay. I'll process that later." Ceiren stared at the floor, probably realizing that was information he could have kept to himself.

Alex jumped into the conversation, "I don't know what I'm going to uncover with my inquiries but I'm happy to help. I still have plenty of connections with the unaligned. Between Ceiren and myself I'm sure we'll come up with something." Alex took his sleeping daughter from Brynach's arms and lowered her into the cradle in the corner of the room. "What are you hoping to do with the information once you have it?"

He ran a hand through his inky hair. "I'm not sure. But if he had children with Peggy, we need to know. That woman already murdered at least one person. She may be responsible for Maggie's death, too. If Gabriel and her had kids...I don't want to think about what they'd be inclined to do."

Brynach addressed Ceiren, "We need our mother off the throne, so he doesn't have a direct line to power. She lets him sway her too often. It's never been wise, but I won't tolerate the threat it presents any longer."

His brother nodded. "It's one of the reasons a lot of the Unseelie have deflected. Not all, but a good number. They don't trust the throne. But what you're asking for won't be easy."

"I've already spoken to Rainer. Put pressure on him. Help him strategize. We need to get the wheels in motion," Brynach encouraged.

Aindrea interrupted their talk, sidling up to Brynach and putting an arm around his shoulder. "Are you hungry? I can bring you something?"

Alex glanced at his wife and then the cradle in the corner as if the whole world was contained in them. Brynach's urge to get back to Aisling was strong. But so was his concern that he was involving his best friend in something dangerous.

"As much as I love your food, Drea, I have to get back home." Brynach smiled.

Eyebrows rose all around the table at his word choice.

"Oh, darling." Aindrea laid a hand on his cheek and Brynach smiled softly. "You're lost for her."

"Happily," Brynach admitted. "Walk me out, Alex?"

His friend followed behind him and even though he'd played this conversation out multiple times in his head, he was still nervous. Once they were far enough away to not be overheard by the Fae inside Brynach turned to Alex.

"I love you."

His friend quirked a brow. "What do you want?"

Brynach laughed, "I love her, Alex. I never thought I'd have this, a woman who makes me feel the way she does. This is real for me, and for her even if she has a hard time admitting it to herself."

"I'm happy for you, brother. We have earned our chance at happiness." Alex smiled at him.

"The wedding will be a political thing for most, but for me, it's the start of a new life. Will you stand by my side?" Brynach asked, anxious about his friend's answer.

"Happily. Proudly. Yes, of course." Alex embraced Brynach.

The relief that Brynach felt was palpable. "Thank you." He pulled back. "I have one last stop to make before I can get home to her. Off to the armory."

He sifted and entered the shop of the bladesmith. The custom order he'd placed was ready, and he was excited to see the finished product.

"Your Highness." The shop owner bowed.

"Enough of that, Tallis," Brynach dismissed the formality. "Let me see my wife's gifts."

Saying it aloud sent a thrill through him. The older Fae exited the room with a nod and returned with a wooden box that housed the blades he'd ordered for Aisling. When the lid opened, he grinned. He lifted one, testing the weight and balance. A single sapphire studded the end of each handle, a bird's wings creating the quillon. They were perfect. More importantly, Aisling would love them.

He thanked the weapons maker and sifted to the Veil, anxious to see Aisling.

CHAPTER 7

AISLING

T oday's a big day for you," Queen Branwyn commented from her seat. Her daughter stood next to her; hands clasped but face wild with excitement. Her sharp teeth flashed as she smiled and the wings, she hadn't bothered to glamour, fluttered happily. Corinna had been thrilled to get an invitation to join her today. And, of course, Aisling had wanted her there. The Princess had been a good friend to her during her time at the Seelie Court. She may annoy Brynach, but Aisling still had a soft spot for her.

Comparatively, Aisling's mother looked like she was going to burst into tears. "Oh, sweetie. This is a lot. Are you okay?"

Aisling didn't look to the Queen and Princess. She was sure the comment would anger them. "Mom, I love Brynach. This is what I want." She repeated to her mother what she'd had to remind herself of all morning.

Her mother had already embarrassed her on their way to the appointment by mentioning the need for birth control. Aisling had assured her they'd taken measures. They'd decided, collectively, that the pill would be effective for them with the addition of a tonic Dawn provided for Brynach and Riordan to drink each month.

Leave it to witches to provide a male alternative for birth

control. Her mother had blushed but been happy they'd come to an agreement among themselves. Aisling was still surprised her mother accepted the relationship between the three of them so easily, but she'd taken it in stride.

The Queen spoke, "I take it the Dark Prince has informed you of the power transfer?"

Aisling really did try to keep the surprise from showing, but she failed. The Queen huffed and even her mother shook her head.

"I'd like to say I'm surprised, but I'm not." The Queen sat back in her chair with her hands folded in her lap. "When Fae wed, they link themselves to one another. That means a sharing of their lifeforce. In simple terms, their magic. When it's one Fae to another it really doesn't mean much. But in your case, darling."

Aisling filled in the gap. "In my case, I get his Fae magic and he, what, gets my witch magic?"

Her mother nodded. "That's right."

Queen Moura sighed, "You'll get stronger and he'll, well he'll gather whatever benefits it is you have to offer, too, I suppose. Honestly, what is he thinking not talking to you about this?"

Corinna blushed. Aisling felt like an absolute idiot. Oh man, did she have words for Brynach when she saw him. This was a pretty significant piece of information he'd withheld.

The dressmaker came back into the room. "My lady, are you ready to try on another gown?"

Aisling was eager to leave the awkward silence hanging in the air. "Yes, please. This one isn't right." She followed the woman behind a screen and listened to her mother speak softly with the Seelie royals. Aisling had been surprised when they'd asked to be a part of her dress making process. None of the other women were particularly thrilled that Aisling had refused the idea of a white gown. But she was set on something less traditional.

As soon as she saw the dress waiting for her, she knew they were getting close. It was stark white at the top, blending to a deep rich black. Different hues of grey swirled like smoke from the bottom up. A perfect mixing of the Light and Dark, of her and Brynach. The cut may need to be adjusted, but the dressmaker was capable of that. At the delight in her eye the dressmaker smiled and helped her step into it. The mirror behind the partician offered her a full body view of herself.

"This is it," she whispered. Aisling turned to the dressmaker and then she walked into the waiting room.

Her mother took one look at her and beamed. "Oh, sweetie. It's not what I would pick but it's beautiful. You look amazing."

The Queen nodded her approval and Corinna ran to her, taking her hands and squealing, "Aisling, oh my Goddess, it's perfect."

She spun toward the mirrors, the dress moving with her. "I'd make changes, but the color and the fabric are exactly what I wanted. I don't want the sleeves and the neckline could be altered a little. I want the waist to come in a bit more and the skirt to be slightly fuller."

"See that the changes she wants are made, and we will be back to check on them in a week's time," the Queen ordered.

"Yes, your Highness." The dressmaker bowed and the Queen excused herself, calling Corinna with her.

As they left her mother approached her. "This is what you want?"

"It is. It's perfect. Right?" Aisling wanted her mother's validation.

The smile on her face said it all. "It is." Aisling turned to the dressmaker. "Let's talk about the changes. The dress needs to be full enough to hide blades on my thighs."

Both women looked at Aisling aghast as she smiled at herself in the mirror.

W e're going to need a larger bed," Aisling announced as she led Riordan and Brynach.

Her fiancé laughed and Riordan blushed. Aisling had given Brynach a talking to when she'd gotten home, and he'd apologized profusely. Of course, he was going to tell her, he just hadn't gotten around to it. And really, he'd assumed she'd known about the magic exchange. Even after he explained it to her Aisling wasn't sure what it really meant but he'd promised it was a good thing. She trusted him.

"Listen, I'm all for having more room with you, but as discussed, I'm not letting Fae Hulk over there defile me," Riordan joked and threw Brynach a wink.

"And defile you I would, Ravdi. You have no idea the pleasure I'm capable of bringing a male body." Brynach's eyes were so hungry on Riordan that Aisling was almost jealous.

She stopped the jokes because this was a big step for them. "I'm serious. I like the idea of us all being together. You two agreed you were comfortable sleeping in the same bed. If that's changed, I want to know."

Riordan knocked his shoulder into hers and grinned. "Nothing has changed. I'm just messing with Brynach. Nobody gets left out, remember. We're in this together."

Brynach made a sound that was akin to a deep purr. "That's right."

Riordan and Brynach were taking responsibility for the other's happiness. It had been Riordan, not Brynach, who had suggested that Brynach may need more time with them...in that way. And so, if Riordan was with Liam, Brynach shared her bed. When Aisling visited the apartment, she slept with Riordan. And when they were all together at the condo, it was snuggle-party time.

The agreement made the situation easier. Without their prior conversations, Aisling would have been a bundle of nerves right now. It wasn't every day you toured houses with your fiancé and Ravdi. The trip was supposed to also be for wedding venues, but she'd quickly been relieved of that duty. The ceremony would be held at the Seelie Court and the reception in the Unseelie gardens. A daytime wedding in the halls of the Light and a nighttime revel under the stars of the Dark.

Aisling had to admit, it was fitting, but even with the blooming relationship with Brynach, she still wasn't completely comfortable with the wedding. Not because she didn't trust or care for him. It felt too soon. Too rushed. Not to mention too many responsibilities and eyes on her. This should be about her and Brynach and when they felt ready, not when the royals told them they should be.

One thing that was non-negotiable was that they'd need a residence in Faerie. Aisling was a pro at house hunting now, but they all needed to feel comfortable. The housing market in Faerie was not traditional. You either got a house built for you or you settled into an abandoned one. There were plenty of stunning homes they could pick from, especially for a royal.

"You're pushing, Ash," Riordan said, but his voice was teasing and light. She hadn't expected Riordan to be left behind, but Aisling was surprised by his excitement. Aisling leaned into him when she felt the soft swirl of magic around her. Their bond didn't work in Faerie, but Riordan could still harness magic, and she could still pull from the stores in a non-bonded way. It wasn't as strong or controlled, but it worked. She loved that she could still have that with him while in Faerie.

"Please. You know my bed isn't big enough for even you and me, let alone Bry and me. And the three of us? I mean, if you want to continue to wake up pressed against Bry, I understand." She winked at her Ravdi who groaned but laughed.

"Remember, we can have something built, a stoirin. You don't have to pick one that we see today," Brynach said, hand resting on the small of her back. He was concerned about her happiness, but she was loving this. It gave her something she could control.

"Are you sure this place is inhabitable?" Riordan asked pushing branches out of his way. "Cause we don't want a house that's been overtaken by sprites and vines. There's secluded and then there's this."

"It's still better than us living at the palace...either of them," Aisling said as they pushed through the overgrown lawn toward the house. "Or that second house we saw? It was in the middle of such a busy trade area. The noise alone!"

"I don't know. The treehouse was kinda cool," Riordan mused.

"It had an outhouse! Absolutely not," Aisling gasped.

"Trust me, this walk will be worth it. And the upside is we didn't have to sift. So, enough complaining," Brynach joked.

Poor Riordan had gone green multiple times throughout the day. He still hadn't adjusted to Fae travel. Riordan parted the next set of branches and Aisling's jaw dropped.

"Oh my," she breathed and felt the rightness of the space.

"Wow." Riordan stepped to the side so she could see more. Brynach stood behind them, a hand on her shoulder.

"What do you think?" She thought she heard hope in his voice.

Aisling turned to look up at him as he gazed at the moss-covered A-frame cottage tucked into the woods. The facade was windowed, and she imagined the inside was bright with the light shining through the trees. She could picture smoke rising from the chimney as they cuddled, warm inside the small space.

It was perfect.

"I love it." Aisling moved toward the path winding to the house. "How is nobody in this?" She picked up the pace, jogging up to the front door and cautiously turning the handle.

The door opened into a bright, and surprisingly well aired, home. The wood paneling warmed the space and yellow lightbulbs added to the rustic feel. The countertop in the kitchen was a live edge piece of wood, all the metals in the house a brushed copper. A giant sofa graced the living room, a fireplace and two large chairs filled the space. It reminded her of their cabin getaway.

She took a deep breath. They could live here. It could be their own personal retreat away from it all. The kitchen had an exit to a deck overlooking a stream that ran through the back yard. A massive yard at that.

She passed a beautiful bathroom with a floor to ceiling window letting in light to the glass shower and rustic wood countertop. This wasn't her usual feminine aesthetic, but this was too fantastic not to fall in love with. When she exited the bathroom, she opened a door to a massive closet. It was strange to have that on the lower level but maybe the A-frame shape made closets upstairs too tricky?

"Well?" Aisling called.

"It's fucking amazing," Riordan answered. Aisling wandered through the house to where he stood under the skylights. He kissed her and she wished the bond worked here. Aisling was desperate to know if his excitement was for himself, not just her.

"Bry?" she called, not seeing her fiancé.

"Up here," his voice echoed from the rafters, and she looked up the staircase to the open loft. Brynach's handsome face smiled down at her, his hair falling forward. "Come on up and see the piece de resistance."

Aisling took Riordan's hand and ran up the stairs with him. When they got to the top, they both stopped, mouths hanging open.

"Holy shit. I thought the rest was impressive," Riordan said beside her.

Aisling wasn't sure what he was looking at. Perhaps it was that the entire upper part of the A-frame was one giant window to the forest outside. The light through the trees turned the space into a softly lit wonderland. Or, and this was the part she couldn't get over, the fact that the loft was one massive platform bed.

"I said I wanted a bigger bed. I didn't mean the whole house had to be one," Aisling joked. "Bry, this is magical."

Riordan's eyes traveled the room. "Actually, you're not wrong. It's positively steeped in magic."

"A stoirin?" Brynach moved to stand behind her, his hands going around her and pulling her flush to his front.

"It's perfect. Absolutely perfect." She turned and kissed him. Picturing a life with him here made her feel a certain way. "How did you find it?"

Brynach's body tensed. "Ummm, well."

"Bry?" She cocked her head at him. Aisling didn't trust that tone of voice.

"This isn't exactly an unexpected find. Your father told me about it." He waited.

Eventually, the pieces clicked. "This is it? This is where my parents lived?"

She surveyed the house with fresh eyes, imagining her mother hiding here and Nevan happening upon her. The giant bed wasn't quite as romantic when she pictured her parents...oh Goddess.

"It's really close to the Veil. It would mean Riordan doesn't have to sift to get here." Brynach hurried as if the new information would sway her against the home. "And I had the bed put in. This wasn't here when...you know...it's not where they... I know it was presumptuous, but I thought it could be a nice home for us. All of us."

Of course, Brynach had thought of Riordan. She kissed him again. "You're the best."

Just because she thought it was sweet didn't mean Riordan would, though. She turned to see how her Ravdi was handling the news of a shared bed. Aisling could see the moment of hesitation before he nodded.

"That means a lot to me. Thank you," Riordan said from a few feet away.

"It wouldn't be a home unless it worked for all of us," Brynach answered. "And you haven't seen the best part." He grinned and led them toward a door on the side of the A-frame bedroom.

"You mean it's not the massive fuck-fest bed?" Riordan asked. He winked and grabbed her ass as they exited. "Jesus, do the surprises in this place never stop?"

"Nope," Brynach answered, standing next to a sunken outdoor bathtub made of rock. Lanterns hung from the trees surrounding the deck. It was unlike anything Aisling had ever seen.

"This is really ours? You wouldn't torture me with this unless I could have it, right?" Aisling asked hopefully.

"Wouldn't dream of it, a stoirin. It's all ours. A gift from your father." Brynach smiled.

Aisling couldn't hide the excitement that swelled in her. She loved her condo, but this home was something else. Suddenly, having to spend more time in Faerie didn't seem like such a chore. Not with this to come back to.

"Riordan, you like it?" Aisling checked in with her Ravdi.

"It's amazing. And the lack of sifting is a bonus." He nodded.

"Unfortunately, we do have to sift once more," Brynach announced. "We have to go to the Seelie Court to see Nevan. I promised we'd touch base after we saw the house if she liked it."

Together they left, locking the door behind them now that it was spoken for. Nevan would have the key for them. The Unseelie servant who'd been helping them house hunt, met them outside.

"I really hate travel in Faerie," Riordan grumbled.

Aisling looked between her Ravdi and Brynach. Riordan would have an easier time sifting with the royal. She'd experienced the travel with multiple Fae and nobody was as seamless as Brynach.

"I do my best. Perhaps the royal would make for a smoother sift?" the aide suggested.

"You should take Riordan this time," Aisling offered. "He's right. It will be easier with you."

She could see that Brynach was about to argue but she really couldn't handle seeing Riordan this uncomfortable. The guilt ate at her.

"Please," Aisling begged. "I'll go with the aide this time. Take him to my father, please." Aisling could see the relief in Riordan's eyes. She moved to the aide, her mind made up. "See you there."

The sucking feeling and loss of space and time was rougher with the servant. He lacked the grace and smoothness of Brynach's sifts, but it wasn't too horrible. Her vision cleared as they settled on a cobbled stone path. It wasn't familiar to her. It certainly wasn't the Seelie Court entrance. Aisling turned to see a large gothic horror novel manor looming over her.

"Where are we?" Aisling asked, but the aide frowned and sifted away. "Hey! What the hell? I can't sift. Don't leave me here alone!"

What was she supposed to do now? She could walk, but where to? Aisling had no idea where she was. Fuck. Her stomach was queasy. Her head was spinning. Wherever she was, she did not feel well.

"Aisling, what's wrong?" Phlyren asked, his voice in her head worried.

She was about to answer when a hand grabbed her arm and ripped her backward. Aisling felt the thick blanket of a ward press against her. Her entire body stiffened at the feel of the magic. Every cell in her body screamed in pain. The uncomfortable feeling of stepping through magic, the thick spider web cloying sensation was nothing compared to this.

She never felt anything like it. Whatever that was,

whoever had made it, it was strong. Her head was spinning. She reached for Rin to answer his question and call for help but found nothing. She was met with a wall.

"What the fuck?" Aisling wondered out loud. Then she registered that the hand was still on her arm. Aisling stilled at the harsh grip. She braced herself to turn around and felt the harsh wash of magic roll over her. Then there was darkness.

A isling woke all at once in a bed she did not enter willingly. She sat up, ignoring how dizzy she was. The room she was in was bathed in darkness. On shaky legs she flew out of the bed and stumbled for the door. She had little reason to believe it would be unlocked, but she had to try anyway.

To her surprise, it turned easily, and the door opened.

When it did, she wished it hadn't.

"Hello, pet," the sickly-sweet voice on the other side said as the Fae moved toward her.

CHAPTER 8

Riordan

R eady?" Brynach asked moving up to Riordan. "As I'll ever be. Is it really easier with you?" He was skeptical.

"Should be," Brynach promised, and Riordan trusted him. "Thank you for being so understanding about all this. I know it makes Aisling happy."

"It's not only for her. It makes me happy, too," he admitted and put his arms around Brynach's waist. "It isn't fair."

"What isn't?" The large Fae asked and wrapped his beefy arms around Riordan's shoulders, holding him close.

"How fucking perfect you are."

Brynach's laughter was the last thing Riordan registered before the world upending feeling of sifting hit him. If he was being honest, it was easier with Brynach, but it still sucked.

"That was much smoother," Riordan said, though his voice still came out as more of a groan. He still felt like puking, but it was tolerable. A quick swallow and he was better. He glanced around for Aisling, not seeing her but spotting a small red face in the grass nearby. Riordan squinted to get a closer look, then Brynach spoke.

"Where's Aisling?"

"Maybe she's already in the palace?" Riordan offered, though it was unlikely she'd have gone without them.

The Dark Prince approached the stone birds that guarded the Seelie Court. "Has Aisling passed through these gates?"

The gravely voices of the sentient soldiers responded, "Not this day."

"She should be here." Brynach searched the wooded area. Above them, Phlyren squawked and rolled through the air, clearly agitated.

Riordan panicked. "Brynach, what's going on?"

"I don't know." His citrine eyes found Aisling's familiar as it dove at their heads. "I get it! We know something's wrong. Where is she?"

But the racket tailed roller didn't fly off. He didn't give them a direction to follow.

"Can you hear her?" Brynach asked the bird. "Land on my shoulder if you can."

"That's smart," Riordan commented, but the bird didn't settle. In fact, he became more vocal. Sprites yelled for him to quit the noise. "So, she went back through the Veil?"

"She wouldn't leave before speaking with her father or alerting us." Brynach's head pivoted, looking around and then back to Riordan.

"We have to look for her. I have to sift. Are you coming?" he asked, his voice high with panic.

"No. Go. You can move faster without me," Riordan assured him. "I'll wait right here. Just...come back, okay?"

"I will," Brynach promised and then sifted out of existence.

Riordan cursed and then screamed in vain, "AISLING!" No red-haired beauty ran to him, assuring him she was okay. Where was she? He searched the forest closest to the palace gates.

"Lost something, Ravdi?" a bark covered alate mocked.

"Fuck off," he responded, not tolerating the sprite's bullshit.

"You needed the easier sift. It's your fault she was trusted to someone else. You only have yourself to blame if she comes to harm," the alate threatened.

"What do you mean? What was wrong with her sift?" Riordan asked, moving to strike out at the alate.

Its laughter haunted him as it danced out of harm's way. "You were warned, Riordan Campbell. All of this could have been avoided."

Riordan screamed, loud and long, "Why are you doing this?" His hands dug into his hair, ripping. The rings on the chain around his neck clanging as he rocked back and forth, screaming until his throat felt raw.

"Your pain is insignificant. You are nothing. Your aunt was nothing," the voice of the sprite haunted his thoughts as tears rained down his face.

"Please. Stop," he begged. "Please, not Aisling. Oh Goddess, not her, too."

Riordan lost himself in the pain. The fear overwhelmed him. Time meant nothing. He didn't know how long he was on the ground, rocking himself, before Brynach returned.

Arms grabbed him and he fought them. "Get off me! Don't touch me!" He kicked.

"Shhhh. Riordan. Calm."

Logic had abandoned him. He struggled, but the arms didn't loosen. His body was lifted, settled into the lap of someone larger, and held so close that the broken pieces of himself pressed together, jagged and painful.

"Aisling. Please, not you, too. Please. Please," he cried.

The arms around him tightened, the voice in his ear soft and soothing. He felt the lips on his temple, on the top of his head. The hands that soothed even as the arms restrained him.

"Oh, Riordan," the voice was broken, lips against his closed and tearing eyes. "Sweet man."

Riordan stopped struggling and fell into Brynach's embrace. "Why is it always me?"

"We'll find her. I swear it," Brynach's voice was strong. Riordan had to believe him if he was going to continue forward.

"I can't lose her."

"Me either," Brynach answered. "I checked my court. She's not there. And I got confirmation she's not inside the Seelie Court. But both courts have sentries looking for her. We'll find her, Riordan."

"Faerie is too large, and I can't feel her, Brynach. I can't feel her here." Riordan clung to the large Fae. "Take me across the Veil right now! The bond will tell me if she passed through."

Brynach nodded and they sifted. Riordan already felt so nauseous that the sift didn't bother him. Brynach took his hand and pulled him through the Veil. They stood together while Riordan searched desperately for the bond. No matter how deep he searched, Aisling wasn't there.

"Nothing," he said, feeling hopeless.

"It's okay." But Brynach didn't look it. The usually tan Fae was pale, his eyes panicked. "Alright, let's go." He pulled Riordan back toward the Veil.

"No. I'll slow you down. I'll do what I can here. In case they bring her across, the police need to know. Her mother needs to know. Just...find her Brynach." He fisted the rings around his neck so hard they bit into his palm. He couldn't add Aisling to the chain. "Please, bring her home."

"I'll check in as soon as I can."

Riordan pushed the large Fae away. "Go!"

Brynach appeared torn, but turned and left, leaving Riordan alone. He saw a flash out of the corner of his eyes, spotting a red brown blur running alongside the tree line. Another fox? As soon as he reached the SUV, he dove for the glove box and unlocked his phone. He immediately dialed the number Loren had given him during the investigation of his aunt's death.

"Officer Loren Becker," he answered.

"It's Riordan. Aisling has gone missing." Now wasn't the time to mince words.

"How long has she been missing?" He asked, immediately gathering data.

Riordan didn't know. He'd lost all sense of time. "Today, earlier. I'm not sure how long. She disappeared during a sift in Faerie. Neither court has knowledge of her whereabouts. She lost connection to her familiar."

Loren was the only one in the department aware of Aisling's Fae blood. Not even the supernatural officers she worked with knew. It helped to have someone in the know when it came to situations like this.

Riordan continued, "When I got this side of the Veil, I couldn't find her either. No matter which side of the Veil she's on, she's in trouble." Saying it out loud made it too real.

"Okay. Explain what happened," Loren's deep voice was calm.

"I was struggling with the sifts, so she told me to go with Brynach and she'd use the servant from the Unseelie Court I'd been using all day. She winked at us and then she sifted. Brynach and I followed."

"Immediately?" Loren asked.

"After a brief conversation. A minute tops. But when we got to the Seelie Court, where we'd agreed to meet, she wasn't there." Already, it felt like a fever dream. "Then a sprite, an alate, it taunted me. I was losing it, Loren. Really losing it and it kept saying that it was my fault. That I had caused all this. I'd been warned and hadn't listened. They blamed me."

"What did it say, exactly?" A pen scratched across paper on the other side of the phone.

"That I was insignificant. That my aunt had been nothing to them. It circled me, taunting me, and reminding me that all these events were my fault."

"They're not, Riordan," the officer assured him.

"I don't give a fuck whose shoulders they're on! I want Aisling back. I need her to be okay."

"If you had to take a guess, how long ago would you say this happened?"

"An hour? It feels like a lifetime. They already tried to kill her once, Loren. We're not being dramatic. Please tell me you're taking this seriously." Riordan wasn't ashamed of the fear in his voice.

"You know I am, Riordan. I'll get the information to the PD and the surrounding areas. She's not exactly an average citizen, is she? It's not going to be easy to find her when we can't share all details. I'm going to have to fabricate facts to get this pushed up in urgency."

The thought hit Riordan and it felt like bricks had settled in his stomach. "Dexter. Do you have eyes on him? I swear if that son of a bitch touched her!"

"I'm going to investigate it, Riordan. I've got to get to work. I'll be in touch," Loren promised and hung up.

Riordan started the car and drove toward the apartment while dialing the number he dreaded.

"Mrs. Quinn, there's something you need to know."

CHAPTER 9

Brynach

L eaving Riordan was harder than Brynach expected. He'd never seen the man so broken and scared. Maybe he should have argued more for him to come to Faerie? Not just because Brynach would have felt better with him close but because Aisling would want him when they found her.

And they would find her.

But there was no denying that he would move faster without the Ravdi. Wherever Aisling was, and whoever took her, because she'd never have left willingly, they had a head start. He needed to move fast. Brynach had already been to the Unseelie Court looking for the servant who'd been assisting them. He hadn't been seen and somehow Brynach knew he wouldn't be again. Whatever he did, for whomever he did it, his job was done. He'd stay hidden if he had any sense at all.

Now he sifted to the Dark Court for an entirely different reason.

He was gathering troops.

"It's about damn time you put me to use," Kongur complained.

Brynach strode toward his familiar, took a handful of his silky mane, the same color as his own, and swung himself onto his back. He'd use no saddle. Just him and the large horse charging across Faerie, ripping apart the very world in search of Aisling.

Brielle was dwarfed next to his familiar's massive size. She was leading a battalion of unaligned who had answered the call for help. He was sure Ceiren had a part in rallying them. Their faction was growing and the unrest in their camps was still cause for concern, but he'd worry about that another time. Jashana stood in the distance with another Seelie officer trying to organize the Light Fae who'd be searching Faerie for Aisling.

Obviously missing were the Unseelie guards. Brynach had gone to his court for help and his mother had scoffed at him. His father's smirk told him they'd be offering no official orders to assist in the search. At least Levinas hadn't been around to revel in his pain. Some Dark Fae had answered the call for help, but they were already arguing with the Seelie. That wouldn't do.

"Everyone circle up," he barked and when nobody moved Brynach said it again. "Sit. The fuck. Down."

Slowly, they followed his order. Brynach sat atop his familiar, far above them.

"It should go without saying that I owe you neither explanation nor incentive to do your duty. You are blood sworn to your courts and, as such, their orders are beyond question."

He met the eyes of those around him, ignoring the grumbles. Brynach pressed on. "But I see unaligned here and I'm grateful to have you. I'm going to give you answers because you deserve them. I believe Faerie is a logical place to bring this particular hostage. She's more isolated in Faerie and we all know it's easier to find hiding places away from human law."

He met a few eyes. "Aisling of the Light has long been important to the Seelie Court, being both a friend and confidant to Princess Corinna and a royal ward. But she's also my betrothed and as such is under the protection of the Unseelie

Court. That should be enough to entice you to search for this woman."

He looked at the blonde wisp of a woman and addressed Brielle.

"You'll send updates as you search the eastern side of Faerie?" he asked.

"We'll cover as much ground as we can. We want to stay thorough, but there's no time to waste," she answered.

Brynach nodded toward the troops. "Get them moving."

Brielle uttered a single command that had the warriors sifting to begin their search. As he watched, the Seelie Court did the same. Unfortunately, before Brynach could nudge Kongur into action, Nevan made his way toward him.

"Brynach!" he called out as he neared. "Don't you dare be a coward and run from me."

Brynach jumped down from his familiar, wanting to meet the Regent on even footing. "Is this necessary right now, Nevan? We have other more pressing matters."

"It's pressing, Prince. My daughter was taken while she was under your protection. You failed her." Nevan jabbed a finger into Brynach's chest.

Brynach saw red. "You think I don't know that? That it's not eating me up?"

"It should be. You were sworn to protect her. How could you let this happen?" The anger seeping from Nevan was palpable.

"*Hit him. He needs a good rattle.*" Kongur was not helping matters. Above him, Phlyren swooped and cried out. He was eager to be on the move, too.

"I'm leaving. Follow me if you feel the need to keep screaming, but I refuse to waste precious time arguing with you over something I can't change." Brynach grabbed hold of Kongur's mane and before he was fully seated, his familiar took off.

Brynach gripped with his thighs and held on as they ate

up ground. Nobody knew exactly what to look for. Right now, they were looking for the Fae who had sifted her, Aisling herself, or signs of a struggle.

"It's not your fault," Kongur told Brynach.

"After all this time I thought we were past you attempting to soothe me with lies," Brynach sighed.

Overhead Phlyren soared alongside Breena's eagle hawk, Mayri. Their eyes were better than Brynach's. He was glad for their help. If Breena's familiar was here, it meant she wasn't far off, either. He'd be happy for her company.

Aisling was a fighter. She was a competent witch and a powerful woman. She'd be okay. If anyone could hold her own until they got to her, it was Aisling. If he let himself believe anything else, he wouldn't make it through this. Still, that didn't mean whoever took her wouldn't tire of her mouth and try and hurt her. She was too stubborn for her own good.

As he neared the unaligned campsite, he saw his brother and sister.

"We didn't find her. We've questioned the locals," Breena said. At Brynach's look she clarified, "nicely."

"The borders?" Brynach asked.

Ceiren answered, "They're checking them now. We're checking the houses if they let us in, but we can't force our way in if we're not welcome."

Brynach wanted to order that they enter with or without permission, but he couldn't. "You know what the servant looks like. You know their family ties. Question them. Find that man. And when you do, I want you to get answers. I don't care if you do it nicely, but he stays alive until I get my hands on him," Brynach ordered his siblings. "Is that clear?"

"Crystal." His sister grinned and fingered the end of one of her blades.

"If you find anything at all I expect to be contacted." He was micromanaging but now wasn't the time for miscommunication.

"We're not idiots, Brynach," his sister whined. "We know you want her safe. I do, too. The welp has grown on me."

"I'm making my way to the shores in case they're leaving by boat. I have no desire to journey the sea but if I have to..." He let his sentence trail off.

As he rode off it was hard to keep his mind from wandering to images of Aisling with a knife in her collarbone. To see her bleeding had destroyed him. Watching them sew her up, seeing how shredded her hand had been, had confirmed her mortality. Knowing he would lose her one day was hard enough. Imagining that day coming any time soon was impossible. He'd burn Faerie to the ground if she came to harm. And if his father had a part in this, any part at all, he'd see him dead before the day was out.

As they reached the nearest shore of Faerie, Brynach saw no ships on the horizon. Which could be a good thing, or a really bad one. Ships didn't last long in these waters. Taking to the sea was a desperate act, one he really hoped her kidnappers wouldn't resort to.

"I don't smell anyone," Kongur confirmed. *"But this close to the water and with this much air moving, that doesn't mean much."*

"I need to be sure." Brynach spurred the horse on. *"I'll look, you run."*

The shores of Faerie were not what humans were used to. Brynach never got used to it, to be honest. The beaches were rocky, full of bones and pieces of broken ships. Nobody was sunbathing on these beaches. As Kongur lengthened his stride and ran along the marsh grass dune, Brynach let himself look out over the waters.

The wreckage of ships lost at sea, sailors who lost lives to the monsters of the oceans of Faerie, were recognized annually. The Fae would gather, safely away from the water's edge, and sing a song of remembrance. The water offshore was dark and turbulent. Deep in the white crested waves and choppy ocean were creatures that hungered for flesh.

"*You're spiraling. Focus,*" his familiar scolded him. Kongur's hooves kicked up sand behind them, and his wide back was already wet with salty sea spray.

"*You're going to be disgusting after this ride. I'll make sure you get a proper scrub when we get back,*" Brynach promised.

"*We can worry about that later. There are a few cabins up ahead. You should check them.*" His familiar kept him on track and Brynach appreciated the centering.

By the time he hopped down off the draft horse's back his own hair was wind tussled and crisp with salt. Brynach caught sight of himself in a tarnished mirror inside one of the shacks and startled himself. He looked like a vengeful sea god.

"*You think too highly of yourself. Let's go,*" Kongur sounded irritated. Like that they were off to the next dwelling, and the one after that, all with the same results. Wherever Aisling was, it wasn't here.

CHAPTER 10

Aisling

"What have you done?" Aisling asked, backing up into the room.

Brynach's brother stalked into the room after her.

"Where am I?"

His laugh wasn't a friendly one. "Somewhere nobody will find you. Don't hold your breath for your Prince to charge in and save you."

It was her turn to sneer. "I've never needed your brother to save me." It probably wasn't smart to bait the Dark Fae, but he'd always had a way of getting under her skin. The skin that was crawling at his closeness.

The Fae yawned. "I don't understand why Brynach's so enamored with you. You are so pitifully common."

She put a hand to her chest. "Oh, I'm positively crushed. How will I continue to exist knowing I haven't met your standards?"

The slap came so fast that the pain began before Aisling registered that she'd been hit. Her cheek stung, her eyes filling against her will. She bit her tongue and refused to reward Levinas by putting a hand to the tender flesh. Aisling pushed her shoulders back, lifted her chin, and met his smug gaze.

His lips curled, his white teeth showing. "Now, that's the

most interesting thing you've done in a long time. By all means, keep fighting. It will be so fun breaking you."

Fear settled in Aisling's gut. She'd burn down the entire house before she let him touch her again. She reached for her magic, ready to go on the offensive and found it muted. It wouldn't be enough, not by a longshot.

"What's the matter, pet?" The corner of his mouth lifted. "Nothing to say? I'd hoped you'd put up more of a fight. Is that all it takes to silence you?" He let a finger trail down her naked arm and, though she tried, she couldn't stop the gooseflesh of revulsion from popping up along her skin.

Coppery warmth spread through Aisling's mouth as she bit the inside of her cheek to keep from screaming. She jerked her shoulder back.

"Get. Your. Hands. Off. Me." She punctuated each word.

He chuckled but removed his hand. "There you are."

Levinas moved to the chair at the end of the bed she'd woken in and took a seat. He swung his boot covered feet up and rested his arms along the back. His long blonde hair hung limp and dull around his face. He was all sunken hollows and sharp lines. Even his fingers ended in sharp nails. Something had changed since she'd last seen him. He was haggard.

"You've always been stupid, but I didn't realize you had a death wish. He's going to find me, Levi. Then there will be hell to pay."

Aisling didn't have to specify who 'he' was; Levinas understood. He had to realize Brynach would tear him limb from limb for this offense.

"You have always been blinded by him, Aisling. It kept you from seeing me and my potential." He stroked the fabric of the sofa. "That is a mistake I intend to remedy."

She swallowed against the bile rising in her throat. "How do you see this playing out, Levi?" Aisling didn't expect an honest answer, but it was worth a try.

"I have neither a death wish nor the patience for your

infantile questions." He approached her. "You're free to wander the house and grounds. They're secure, but I look forward to watching your failed escape attempts, because I know you'll try. It will amuse me to watch your spirit fade." His hand came up, fast. Aisling forced herself not to flinch. Levinas's fingers trailed lightly across the welt on her cheek. It stung like a son of a bitch, but she kept her eyes on his, unwilling to back down.

"It's in your best interest to mind your tongue, Aisling. I intend to break you but that doesn't mean I want to hurt you." His hand rested on her throat. "I will, mind you, but I'm not my heathen bastard brother."

Aisling's blood boiled. She spit in his face. "You aren't a fraction of the man he is. Holding me prisoner doesn't make me yours."

Levinas smiled at her and then his hand closed on her throat, cutting off her air. She refused to claw at his hand and fight. She'd turn blue before she begged him for anything.

"You must be under the impression that I give a fuck what you want. I don't. My brother tried to be kind and court you. We all know where that's gotten him." Levinas let go of her windpipe right as her vision started to swim. His fingers squeezed her face painfully. The red flesh on her right cheek burned. She tried to shake him off, but he held firm. "I'm not a patient man, Aisling. I'm not my brother. I take what I want."

Levinas made sure her eyes were on him when he continued, "If he'd been less patient with you, you'd be bonded, and I couldn't have taken you. Instead, he let you, a halfling child, dictate his life. He is weak and unfit to carry the title of Unseelie Prince."

Throat raw and face hurting Aisling laughed as realization dawned. Levinas dropped her face. "This isn't about me at all. You just want a way to feel superior to a man everyone knows is better than you. You're pathetic."

His hand was lighting fast as he matched the mark on the

right side of her face on her left. The slap rang through the otherwise quiet room. That is until her laughter joined it. She'd hit a nerve. She'd gotten under his skin. He wasn't nearly as composed as he wanted her to believe.

"You forget your place, Aisling. My feelings for you don't protect you from the consequences of stepping out of line," Levinas snarled.

She turned her back on him, dismissing him. "If you believe for a moment that I have even an iota of respect or deference for you, you are so fucking wrong. Get out of my room, Levi."

"You'll address me as Prince, Levinas, or sir. I'm done with your disrespect." He listed his names and titles as if she cared. "I expect you at dinner at six. The staff will be by to help you dress."

"I'd rather starve than eat with you."

"Don't test me, Aisling. It would bring me immense joy to watch you harm yourself out of spite. And I'm learning I may enjoy inflicting the harm myself even more." He eyed her red cheeks. "Continue to talk back and I'll do both."

Levinas stormed out of the room, closing the door behind him. Aisling sank to the floor. Her entire body shook, and she shoved her fist into her mouth to stifle the moan of fear that rose. What had she gotten herself into and why couldn't she keep her big mouth shut?

She touched her cheek tentatively and winced. Fuck, that hurt. If she couldn't access her magic she probably wouldn't heal as quickly, either. This marked the second time in way too short a time where her magic had failed her. Aisling didn't like the way it felt one bit. She wanted to crawl back into the bed and cry, but that wouldn't do.

Aisling needed to keep her wits about her if she was going to get out of this without Levinas doing something she wouldn't recover from. She needed to understand his strategy if she was going to counter his advances. And right now, nothing about this situation made sense. She pushed herself to her feet and moved to the other door.

Inside the bathroom she held a cold washcloth to her red cheeks and tried to gather her thoughts. She had to focus on facts. Somehow Levinas had convinced an Unseelie castle servant to turn rogue. Which couldn't have been easy because castle jobs were coveted, even in the Unseelie Court. For whatever reason, he also thought he could get away with this. He wouldn't have done it otherwise. Aisling had to believe he was working with someone else, because no way he was smart enough to carry this out alone.

She was in Faerie. Levinas was sure she couldn't escape, which made her nervous. But he was cocky and if there was a way, she'd find it. Which brought her back around to the ward. That was no regular magic. What she'd felt crossing through it had been excruciating. While she was positive, she could outsmart Levi, she didn't know how she was going to get through that ward.

To make matters worse, her connection to Phlyren and Riordan were cut off. She was alone, her magic felt weaker here, and she absolutely had to get home. She didn't know the time but out the window she saw the sun was past its peak. It wouldn't be long before dinner. He'd said the staff would help her dress and she shuddered to think what she'd be expected to wear. But at least there were other people here she could try and befriend. It couldn't be that hard, Levinas hardly evoked loyalty. She had to hope they'd turn on him.

He'd told her to wander the house and grounds and she was going to do exactly that. Knowing the lay of the land was vital. Information was key in situations like this. Right now, she'd get a better understanding of where she was being held and then she'd attempt to figure out what the hell that slimy Fae was planning. Aisling had to hope she was still valuable enough to keep alive, for now.

She ran the cold water again, applying it to her warm

cheeks, and winced. Aisling had never been hit in her life. Stabbed, sure, but never slapped or hit. Now she knew she most definitely wasn't a fan of that. Goddess help that sorry son of a bitch if he put his hands on her again. Regardless, he'd pay for touching her. And not only by Brynach's hands, although she was sure Brynach, Breena...hell even Ceiren and Rainer would have their brother's head for this. No, before they got their hands on him, Aisling would have her piece of flesh for this offense. And with whatever was left, the courts would exact their price. No matter how you looked at it, Levinas wasn't walking out of this.

She stared at herself in the mirror, hazel eyes determined.

"You're making it out of this. That cold turd will not best you. Be smart. Play the game. Move the pieces. Get your shit together, Aisling! There's a way out of here and you're going to find it," she scolded herself out loud.

Aisling didn't know what was on the other side of the door, but she had to find out. Whatever it was, she'd have to face it eventually if she wanted to escape. Aisling took a deep breath and turned the handle, prepared to be greeted by a guard or threat. But the hallway was empty.

The light was dim, and the halls were narrow. Arched black doorways with iron scrolls and ornate handles and locks decorated the hall. As curious as she was, she didn't open any of them. Whatever horrors lay beyond them weren't her concern. She needed to find the exit. It hadn't escaped her notice that the hallway was windowless. The air inside stale and still. The sconces on the walls had a nearly opaque glass in them, creating odd shadows through the space. The carpets bled a rich crimson and muffled her steps as she turned from one hallway to another. It wasn't nearly as labyrinth like as the courts, but it was still unnecessarily complicated and elaborate.

It was a gothic nightmare. Worse, it was so silent that the sound of Aisling's pounding heart seemed to echo off the walls.

Her anxiety spiked, the need to see light in the windowless hall making her lengthen her strides. Finally, she saw an opening and raced for a stairwell.

What should have represented an opportunity for freedom filled her with dread. The dowels at the top were topped with spikes. Was she in Dracula's freaking castle? Aisling started down the stairs, sliding her hand down the banister to ground herself. With all the adrenaline coursing through her it took a moment for the pain to register.

Aisling raised her hand to reveal blood speckled palms and a multitude of small lacerations. She held it to her chest and inspected the banister. It was a shining onyx snake's body, slithering toward the ground floor. The tail wrapped around the spike at the top of the staircase, blending in with the dark dowels so well she hadn't noticed at first. Her hand stung horribly as she inspected the scales, shining an oily black and carved out individually on the cylindrical spine of the serpent. A small thorny blade topped each individual scale.

Nobody could hold this railing and walk down without slicing their hand to shreds. What kind of horrific torture palace was this? Who the hell lived here? Levinas may be keeping her here, but this didn't scream of his aesthetic.

She hurried down the steps, making sure to keep her hands to her damn self. At the bottom she paused to make eye contact with the ruby red eyes of the serpent, its mouth open, and fangs extended to create the lowest arm of the railing. As horrendous as it was, it was magnificently crafted. However, her focus quickly shifted to the large wooden doors with multiple sliding locks. She glanced around the foyer but saw nobody. She rushed the doors, scrambling with the handle. Aisling hadn't expected them to be unlocked, but when she pushed, they swung open.

Bright light blinded her, the sun bouncing off the water molecules of the fog rolling across the land. In front of her was a massive stone walkway. Levinas had warned her that escaping would be impossible, and clearly, he wasn't afraid of her being outside, so she braced for the other shoe to drop. What was going to keep her here? Approaching the low wall, she saw that the stone pathway was a bridge that connected the house with a larger piece of land. Behind the house was a lush lawn, overgrown and uncared for, but probably a better chance of escape.

She took off for the back of the house through the waist high brush. Vines and moss covered the exterior walls. It was absolutely neglected. Aisling pushed forward even though her sight was impaired by the thick fog. Her feet wobbled on rocks and pits in the ground. She slowed her steps because escape would be a lot easier without a twisted ankle. Between one step and another her foot lowered and found...nothing.

Aisling threw herself backward, offsetting her forward momentum. Her ass landed hard on the grass, her leg still hanging into the nothingness. It was then that she saw, through the fog, that the yard dropped off into thin air. There was nothing. Just...an end. If she'd been running, she'd likely be dead right now.

Slowly, carefully, Aisling moved back until she was pressed against the rear wall. Only then did she continue around the house. Her fears were confirmed as she circled her new prison. On all sides except the front bridge, the land around the house disappeared. She was currently being held prisoner on a spike of land in the middle of the fog.

Having made her way around the house she decided the next move was to test the limits down the large stone walkway. But of course, she wouldn't be able to walk away from the house that easily. Aisling felt the spell as she approached what must be the border of the property. As she neared the end of the bridge, and other land became visible, she felt a pull on her energy. The closer she got to escape the weaker she felt.

The magic was strong, old in a way she hadn't experienced before.

This wasn't hurried work. It felt like energy reinforced year after year for longer than Aisling could dream of being alive. Whoever, or whatever, wanted to keep people on this island, they'd invested a lot of magic into ensuring nobody was getting out, or in.

Aisling couldn't take another step toward freedom. Her magic was gone, drained, and her body was shutting down. To escape would be to die. All hope of leaving without Levinas's help left her. She wanted to sink to her knees and cry but first she had to get away from this draining ward.

Carefully, she made her way to a door she'd seen on the side of the building. She entered without obstacles and even though she expected to see another Fae, none seemed present. She had no doubt if she called for them that one would show but right now, she felt alone in a haunted house. The abundance of taxidermy through the home didn't help. Beady eyes followed her wherever she went.

Aisling tried door handles, finding some locked and others opening onto bathrooms or in one case a room with a piano and nothing else. She explored a living room with deep sofas and a shelf stuffed with books and board games. It looked like it belonged in a house on the other side of the Veil though it was missing the television, which wouldn't work here anyway. The colors were brighter, out of place with the rest of the house, and Aisling had the odd sensation that she'd walked onto a set.

The strangeness of the room continued when she saw children's toys, the board games all meant for children, not adults. A table and chair set in the corner was child sized and covered in marker. Children had lived there once.

"You shouldn't be in here," a wide-eyed Fae said from the doorway, startling her. She rushed into the room and pulled Aisling toward the hallway. "Come on, we should lock this room up, again."

Aisling moved but asked, "Whose room is this? Are there

others like this?"

Once out of the room the Fae pulled out a keychain and locked the door. "These doors are meant to stay locked." It was impossible miss the fear in her voice.

"I'm not going to share anything with Levinas. It's okay to speak freely with me." She hoped her smile was a comforting one.

The Fae shook her head. "I came to dress you for dinner. You weren't in your rooms. It's best if we get back and get you ready. You don't want to know what Master Levinas is like when he's not obeyed."

CHAPTER 11

Riordan

"And you're sure this is safe?" Riordan asked for the fourth time. Sure, he had to keep himself busy, but even he had his limits. Everyone was busy looking for Aisling. The least he could do was his part. It wasn't like Brynach was coming back for him. Nobody was checking on him. He was so cursedly easy to leave. The Fae would never have abandoned Aisling as easily as he forgot about Riordan.

Perhaps he shouldn't be in the middle of such a pity party as he was storming into, what he hoped, was an abandoned warehouse. They'd uncovered a lead that Peggy and her kids had used the location once and were going to explore for clues.

"As a tetanus riddled metal structure can be," Liam answered.

Sean and Amber flanked the two of them. It hadn't escaped his notice that his brother orbited the witch. Riordan was happy Liam had found someone he was interested it. Maybe it would keep him around longer? For what it was worth, Amber appeared equally interested in him and she'd been adding a lot to the research team. It was cute but oh man, she was going to give Liam a run for his money. He smirked at the thought.

"Why am I here, again?" Sean asked.

"Because this is badass," Amber answered.

His brother tried to get everyone back on track. "Okay, we're looking for anything that can provide clues to Aisling's whereabouts, Peggy's motivations, or plans for the attack. Whatever seems useful, grab it. If it doesn't seem useful, grab it," Liam instructed.

"Grab it all. Got it," Sean answered, and Amber bounced on her heels.

"I'm so fucking ready." She pivoted, raised a leg, and delivered a side kick right to the handle. The door swung open with a metallic clang audible for miles.

"Jesus, Amber. That's a little aggressive, don't you think? Stealth is a thing," Riordan scolded without any heat.

She shrugged. "It's open, isn't it?" Everyone followed her inside.

"She terrifies me," Sean whispered.

"Isn't it sexy?" Liam muttered, staring after the witch.

What a group they made. They split up and searched the property. Riordan sneezed as they kicked up dust. After about the sixth consecutive sneeze everyone stopped blessing him. He was pretty sure they should have masks on. The dust and volumes of rat shit were not healthy to breathe. He loved Aisling, but damn it, this was disgusting. Riordan searched for anything that may lead them to more information about Peggy or her crew of horrific offspring. He needed to hold onto the hope that this would get them closer to finding Aisling. Especially since Brynach had been coming up empty-handed. It had been six days and they were no closer to finding her.

He picked up a piece of scrap metal and found nothing but more dust under it. A call rang from an office on an upper level and everyone made their way toward Sean. The path wasn't an easy one. Some of the stairs were rusted out, hanging loosely, making the walkways feel more like rope swings. It reminded Riordan of the Carrick-a-Rede bridge, which was absolutely terrifying, even if everyone swore it was safe.

"What did you find?" Riordan asked, out of breath from fear.

"The filing cabinet was locked but I got in. It's not much but I think it's related to Peggy and her kids." He pointed to the papers fanned out on a dusty old desk.

In front of him were drawings featuring four kids and one woman, unlabeled, but the landscape fit Faerie. Childish versions of sprites danced around a lawn of yellow flowers.

"These have to be pictures of Faerie," Liam commented. "That's jessamine. It grows here, but it's rampant on the other side of the Veil."

"How do you know that?" Amber questioned Liam, then looked back at the stack in front of her. Her head tilted this way and that as she studied the drawings. "Wait!" She held up a paper. "I need better light."

Amber moved to a frosted glass window, picked up a metal stapler, and hurled it through the glass. She used the sleeve of her jacket to push out more of the dirt covered glass and let sun in.

Liam was grinning ear to ear and shaking his head at Amber. Oh gosh, Riordan knew that look. Liam was going to fall hard for her. Eh, he could do worse. Sean, meanwhile, was wide-eyed in surprise.

"Yes! I knew I saw something. Come look," she called out, but looked directly at Liam.

Riordan and Sean stayed in place while Liam bent his head close to hers. "See here? There were names on this picture that someone tried to erase. You can barely make them out."

Amber rushed to the desk, rooting around in the drawers until she came up with an old pencil. "I have an idea." She laid the paper on the table and gently rubbed over the area. Grinning she went back to the sun and Liam made a celebratory sound.

"You're a fucking genius," he said.

"I know," Amber laughed. "Stavos, Callan, Sydney, and Victor. And then this one says Marny."

Liam shook his head. "I think it says mommy."

"Oh fuck! It totally does," Amber exclaimed. "We found something good, right?"

"We can use these pictures to try and identify where in Faerie they may have a house. Brynach might recognize the landscape," Riordan said. "Let's get out of here. My lungs can't handle all this dust."

As if on cue he started coughing. He needed a shower, badly. Plus, he was pretty sure he had cobwebs in his hair. The thought of spiders on his body sent shivers down his spine.

They got back in the car and conversation quickly turned to their latest task...Dexter. He was doing something super shady, but he'd covered his tracks really well. Sean was looking into him on websites that Riordan didn't want to know about. As in, he'd specifically asked not to know about them.

Amber was looking into him by more legal means, even if that did include asking people in the seedy underbelly of the town. The first lead came from Lettie, who thought she overheard a man talking about being in hiding from Dexter. It was further proof he wasn't dealing with things legally. They'd nail him but they needed more hard evidence. Riordan was desperate for it.

Once back at the apartment everyone got back to work. Riordan showered and left to go to see Aisling's mother. When he'd called to see if their appointment still stood, she'd said yes. He couldn't imagine this was going to go well, but he could use someone to talk to who got what he was feeling. He pulled into the driveway, noticing a fox scampering around the house. When the door opened for him at Mrs. Quinn's office, she opened her arms, and he fell into them.

Devoid of a maternal figure in his life it felt nice to be held and relax his shoulders for a moment. Since Aisling went missing, he'd been on edge, ready to spring into action. Now, he gave himself permission to breathe.

"How are you?" She led him to a large seat.

"Garbage. You?" He sat down.

"About the same. I still expect it to be her when the phone rings," the older woman admitted. "And Patrick and I..." She didn't finish the sentence.

"Patrick and you, what?"

The woman waved him off. "He hasn't been handling this well, or at all. I asked him to leave."

"I'm so sorry," Riordan offered. He'd seen them together a few times, but their relationship hadn't seemed strained.

"This isn't about me. How are you doing today?" She changed subjects.

"I can't believe how lonely it feels not having her with me, in my head. You know?"

She nodded. "And Brynach isn't around as much, is he?"

"No, and I didn't expect it, but I miss him. I'm angry," he admitted.

"At Brynach?"

Riordan sighed, "Yeah. I don't know. He left so easily. He didn't even try to fight for me to stay with him and look for her. I just thought that maybe..."

"He'd want you with him?" Mrs. Quinn finished. "It's got to be difficult to have feelings for him."

"It is and it isn't. It happened naturally. Being with him and Aisling is easy. A lot of things about Birchwood Falls has come as a shock to me, but being in a relationship with a man never even crossed my mind."

"Is that what you have with him?" Aisling's mother asked.

He thought for a minute before answering, "Yeah. I tried to deny it, but we're more than our feelings for Aisling. I don't know what 'more' means yet but, yeah."

She nodded. "And him leaving you hurts? Having both Brynach and Aisling gone while you're still coping with the loss of your aunt can't be easy." Well, she wasn't pulling any punches, was she?

Riordan groaned because it really would have been easier to focus on their shared fear for Aisling. Instead, he took a deep breath and dove into the emotional toll of feeling left behind by the people he cared for the most.

Apparently discussing his trauma made him hungry. When he was done with his session he parked on Main Street and made his way toward the diner. People were out walking, spiced lattes in hand in the crisp air.

He was gazing at the happy couples walking by when one pair caught his attention. His eyes must be playing tricks on him. Then the blonde man's head turned, and his lip ring caught the sun when he laughed.

"Trent!" He ran toward them.

A head turned, a face broke out in a smile, and Riordan smiled back. He reached his friend and embraced him.

"What are you doing back? I mean, I didn't know you were coming back," Riordan stumbled over his words.

Trent's face fell. "It was time." He turned to Ollie and Riordan acknowledged him with a smile and a nod. "I didn't come home when Lettie woke up but then I heard Ash was missing. Kidnapped. Liam Neeson-style fucking taken."

"You're spiraling, babe," Ollie commented.

"Right. Anyway, I had to come home. I was being selfish. It was nice being in our own little bubble and we both loved Scotland, but I couldn't justify ignoring all that was going on here anymore," Trent admitted.

"We wanted to help," Ollie said. "And we're really sorry about your loss."

Trent's hand on Riordan's arm tightened. "So sorry."

"Thanks." Riordan nodded. "Have you seen Lettie yet?"

"She was our first stop," Trent said. "So that means we saw Sean. Man, isn't that the oddest thing?"

"Nah. He's been really good for her. I can't imagine what she'd have done without him." Riordan's stomach growled. "What are you guys doing now?"

"Taking in the sites," Ollie laughed. "Why?"

"I was going to get a bite to eat. Want to join me and I can fill you in on things?" Riordan asked.

Ollie nodded to Trent who answered, "Lead the way, handsome."

Ollie pinched Trent's arm. "Don't flirt. From what we understand, he already has a man in his life."

Trent gasped, "Please start with the Dark Fae when you fill us in."

CHAPTER 12

Brynach

The mossy green glen was serene. Brynach wished he had the time to rest here a moment. It reminded him of a place he'd escaped to as a child in Faerie. The circle of his childhood had opened to the sky from within a cluster of ancient trees. It had been a magical combination of filtered sunlight or blazing stars. And within the safety of their towering forms, he'd found the only solace in his young life.

A memory swarmed into his mind of bringing a bruised and bleeding Breena here to rest after their father had tired of her questions.

"You have to be more careful," he scolded her.

"Why should I?" She spat blood onto the moss at her feet. "He has no business touching me. He oversteps. I'm a Princess."

Brynach shook his head, his hair just reaching his ears was knotted with twigs from his time on Kongur's back flying through the woods. "Don't be stupid, Breena. You know damn well Tynan isn't our father. We don't have his hair, his eyes, or his temperament."

His sister picked up a rock and hurled it into the trunk of a tree nearby. Her aim was getting better. "Appearances, brother. Mother doesn't want gossip and Gabriel knows that. He should be more careful."

"She won't stand up to him." Brynach rolled his shoulders. "She's never lifted a hand or said a word to stop our siblings from abusing us. She can't stop Gabriel."

"I don't need her help. I don't need anyone's help. You didn't have to sift me away. I can handle him." Breena picked up another piece of rock, deemed it fit for throwing, and spun, flinging the earthen blade into the trunk of the tree right below the first. "I'm getting stronger. One day, he'll have to fear me."

Brynach hugged her. She was stiff and then relaxed into his grip. "You're already fearsome but we need to be smarter, the both of us. I hate seeing you hurt."

She laughed, "I'm already healing. That bastard can't hurt me."

Brynach whispered into his sister's raven hair, "When you hurt, it hurts me. Please, Breena. For me."

He knew it was unfair. She'd do anything for him, even if it stifled her wild spirit. But he couldn't imagine suffering through life in the Unseelie Court without his only lifeline. She turned and kissed his cheek.

"For you. For now. But not forever." And then she sifted away.

Brynach came back to the present and acknowledged that this glen was nothing like his childhood one. It contained none of the magic or feeling of safety and seclusion. Nothing felt safe or magical with Aisling gone. And, if he was being honest with himself, without Riordan.

He'd pushed the Ravdi away when he wanted those he cared for close. It was a mistake and one he planned to remedy as soon as possible. Brynach was tired of doing everything alone, of denying himself joy. He took a moment to close his eyes, center himself, and then he opened his throat and screamed.

"AISLING!" The birds were scared from the trees, a few animals scurried in the underbrush, but no voices answered his own. Breena exited the abandoned house in front of him shaking her head.

"Empty," she confirmed. As beautiful as this place was, it wasn't where Aisling was hidden away. He almost wished it was. It would be better picturing her in a glade like this than all the scenarios his imagination had conjured. Every minute she wasn't in his arms was another that she could be in harm's way.

If he followed that train of thought, he'd become paralyzed by fear. Every time he closed his eyes, he saw her in horrific situations; bleeding and crying in pain. Again.

"Brother." Breena gripped his forearms. "Don't get lost in those thoughts. Feel it and move on. You've been through worse than this. So has Aisling. You've got to keep your head on straight."

Brynach nodded and sifted. Breena followed. They found themselves in a swampy area filled with wisps and a splash at the lake's edge indicated neapan were nearby. He most definitely didn't want to picture Aisling in their clutches.

"It stinks. Let's hurry up and get out of here." Breena screwed up her nose.

"Fine, but be thorough," Brynach warned.

She snorted, "Obviously." She sifted, showing up a short distance away, and began searching the high brush.

Brynach turned to the shore and, after acquiring a stick to poke around, began digging in the loose silt for bones or clues. He was relieved when his search turned up no charm bracelets or chunks of red-haired scalp. The neapan hadn't gotten a hold of her here. The sprites danced in the air around him and he swatted them away.

Breena appeared at his side. "Nothing that side of the shore. We've been at this for days, Brynach. It's time to take a break, and frankly, you need a shower."

Brynach frowned, but she had a point. The problem was that even though multiple squads of Fae were looking for Aisling, he didn't trust them like he did himself and his twin.

"You're not going to be any good when we find her if you're a giant ball of stench and anxiety. Come on." She took his hand and he allowed himself to be pulled along with her.

They arrived in the Unseelie kitchen, and the homely kitchen servant squealed. "How many times have I told you not to do that!" she said, hand to her heart.

"Sorry, Gaylene," Breena chuckled. "We were too hungry for a proper entry."

The woman shook her head. "You're filthy, the both of you. I shouldn't let you in my kitchen, but you look half starved. You are waning." Gaylene tsk'd and pinched Brynach's bicep.

He laughed. Nothing about him was small, but the kindly kitchen servant had been overprotective of him since his childhood. Brynach reached over and squeezed the woman's ample waist.

"I'm not in danger of withering away." He bit into a chunk of bread slathered in butter and jam.

She shook her greenish hair and turned back to the dishes. "You never did take good enough care of yourself."

Brynach smirked in the comfortable silence. They sat and she brought them plates, laden with meat, cheese, and potatoes. His mouth watered and then he dove in.

"Goddess, this is good," Breena exclaimed as wine dripped on her chin and she wiped it away with the back of her hand. "I was wasting away."

Brynach hid a chuckle as Gaylene turned and gave him an "I told you so" look. "Eat. We have to get back."

"A waste of time, if you ask me," a voice sounded from behind him.

It was through sheer force of will that his shoulders didn't stiffen. Breena stopped chewing and her right hand slid to her left wrist, pulling out a thin throwing blade.

"Levinas, you have some nerve showing your face." Brynach turned toward his sibling. He wasn't leaving his back to this asshole. Turning he saw bruises blooming across his brother's jaw. His eye was swollen nearly shut.

Breena huffed a laugh, "Let me guess, one of the squires beat you at sparring?"

Whoever had beaten him, Brynach was almost envious. Though who could have done it remained a mystery to him. Levinas wasn't one to tolerate being bested. It was surprising that he was showing his face before he was healed. Normally, Levinas would go to great lengths to avoid shows of weakness. If he was here now it was because he couldn't help but be seen. Levinas had clearly angered someone he shouldn't have.

Their brother put a hand to his chest, mouth open in shock. "Goddess, the two of you stink. Worry less about me and more about how putrid you are."

Breena spun, knife already hurtling through the air. Levinas was no stranger to her attacks. He knocked the blade to the side but in doing so didn't prepare himself for the second. Breena was on him, another blade at his throat. Brynach should get up and stop her, but he simply didn't want to. Seeing Levinas go still under her was too sweet a reward.

"I could do it, you know? Finish whatever the lucky bastard who did that to you started." She nodded to his face.

"Get. Off. Me," he enunciated each word through clenched teeth.

"Or what, you slimy bastard," Breena snarled in his face.

"I'm not the bastard here and you're out of line." Levinas spoke careful not to jostle the blade at his Adam's apple.

"That's quite enough. You'll not be spilling blood in my kitchen," Gaylene called, and Breena stepped back.

"Sorry," Breena offered, her eyes not leaving Levinas who was straightening his shirt.

"So dramatic. Is it that time of the month, sister?" Their brother smirked.

Breena lunged for Levinas again. Brynach didn't blame her. The smaller Fae sifted out of her reach, picked up a roll, and walked out of the room. Brynach had lost his appetite.

"The food was lovely, Gaylene. Thank you. I'm going to go clean up." Brynach left the kitchen and made his way upstairs to his suite of rooms. They'd never felt like home, less so now that he saw what a home could be like with Aisling and Riordan.

He threw himself into the shower, letting the warm water wash over his back. Brynach closed his eyes, his head rested on the wall against the cool tile. Images flashed behind his eyelids, memories of a dream that haunted him.

Him sinking into Aisling's silky warmth from behind while she kissed Riordan and stroked his hard cock. The three of them moving together in a fluid wave of taste and touch. Riordan's groan as Aisling took him in her warm mouth. The other man meeting Brynach's eyes over Aisling's bobbing head and licking his lips.

Brynach had followed that soft pink tip as it caressed a full bottom lip and the desire to taste the other man's sigh was overwhelming. He gripped Aisling's hips and pulled her back on him while she mewled around Riordan's cock.

When the dream had ended Brynach had been left with the memory of making love to the two of them. And once the images had taken root, they wouldn't leave. Of course, he'd wanted to stalk across her condo and demand to take part in the bedroom antics Aisling and Riordan enjoyed. But he'd never been invited and wouldn't presume to be desired. The dream felt so real he fought an erection every time it came unbidden to the forefront of his memory.

Brynach fisted his dick in his hand and pumped his hips, closing his eyes to capture the feel of Aisling's pussy again. He was desperate for the sound of her whimpers muffled on Riordan's flesh. He came on a ragged scream and fell back against the shower wall with tears in his eyes. Now was not the time for reminiscing, and it certainly wasn't the time for jerking off in the shower. It was time for action. It was time to bring Riordan to Faerie.

"It's about time you realized you need me, Hulk," Riordan said, as he packed his bag from the hall closet in the small apartment.

Brynach's shoulders hunched. "I don't know how else to say I'm sorry. You said it was for the best that I left you here, and I let myself believe it. I was wrong. The past few weeks have been awful. You belong with me."

Brynach watched the Ravdi's cheeks color. He clarified, "You belong in Faerie looking for Aisling. You should be with me when we find her."

Riordan slapped him on the shoulder. "You weren't yourself. Neither was I. But I know one thing, I'll be a hell of a lot better once we have Aisling back."

"How soon can you be ready to go to Faerie? I don't know when you'll be this side of the Veil again," Brynach warned.

Riordan thought for a moment, "Can you give me an hour to talk to Liam? I can't leave again without talking to my family."

Brynach agreed and went to see Dawn. He hadn't seen the witch in a while and wanted to check on her. Breena saw to her security most of the time, but with the search for Aisling in full swing, he was calling her away frequently.

Dawn was mixing spelled beauty products with her daughter resting peacefully in a shop that had recently been attacked, had seen multiple deaths, and still it felt bright. The earth witch had cleansed the space, and no negativity clung to the bubbly woman as she hummed to herself.

"Brynach! It's so nice to see you." Dawn wiped her hands on her "Magic is a matter of intention," apron and embraced him.

He moved toward the child. "She's perfect."

"Smart, too. She's got her daddy and I wrapped around her fingers. She's already showing signs of magic. Eves will be a wonderful witch."

A loud voice called from the back room, "Brynach?"

A woman who reminded him more of Breena than anyone else he'd ever met stuck her head through the beaded curtain into the shop. Liam stood behind her, eyes locked on the wicked-looking whip of a witch. Liam had found himself a companion.

"We need to talk. Let's go." She turned on her booted heal assuming Brynach would follow.

"Go." Dawn waved him off.

Back in the apartment Riordan spoke to his brother, his hand on his necklace. Amber, meanwhile, was standing legs apart and hands on her hips. "Where the hell have you been? We have shit you need to see. It may have something to do with Peggy's kids." She pointed to the old paper on the desk. "That's Faerie, right?"

Brynach focused on one part of the picture in particular. Faerie had plenty of lakes, streams, and waterfalls, but the one pictured was large. That narrowed down the locations if they could trust the scale and he said as much.

"We're looking at a child's drawing. Their perspective can't always be trusted. However, it gives us a starting place. That's where Riordan and I can start our search." Brynach's confirmation made Amber smile.

Their footsteps reached his ears before he saw them. This place was busier than a portal crossing. Trent, Ollie, Lettie, and Sean crested the top of the stairs. It was clear something was wrong.

Brynach turned to Aisling's best friends. "Lettie?"

The brave beauty bent her head and Sean moved to her side. Brynach respected the motion, it's what he would have done for Aisling. "I may have something else that can help. I was in Faerie with Trent and Ollie. I saw Aisling."

Gasps sounded and both Riordan and Brynach moved toward her. Sean stepped ahead of her, blocking them from advancing. Trent moved to her side and Ollie mirrored his boyfriend as though a tether connected them. Breena and Ceiren stormed up the steps to a room in chaos. Everyone had begun talking at once, asking questions and demanding details.

Sean called out, "You want to know what she saw, then shut up and listen."

"What the hell did I miss?" Breena commented.

Brynach shot her a look and she held up her hands. "The fuck?" she moaned but she shut up when Lettie began speaking.

"I have no idea what Fae I was seeing through. He didn't pass any mirrors. Before you ask, I don't know how to lead you to them, I only know that she's alive. The house she was in was dark. Not just a lack of natural light, though there wasn't much, but literally dark. It didn't look like a welcoming place."

Brynach could feel his pulse pounding in his ears. She'd seen Aisling. She was alive and she needed him. And here he was, letting her down. He wasn't even in Faerie looking for her. Damn it.

"Anything else you can tell us about what you saw? Anything at all that could help us find her?" Brynach asked in a fevered voice.

"Um. Dead things. Animals. And when he left it was bright out, lots of woods. They turned back to the house before I woke up. It was massive, gothic looking. It had spires and round turrets." She closed her eyes and tried to bring back the vision.

Brynach saw Trent move closer to his friend and squeeze her shoulder. Lettie met Brynach's eyes and continued, "They never let him into the house, but they were talking in the open doorway. The one I was seeing through was speaking to a male Fae. The two never addressed one another by name but the man he was talking to was promising him protection."

"From what?" Breena asked.

"He said that if he continued to keep Aisling's whereabouts a secret that he'd reward him with his protection. The Fae I was seeing through said that she wasn't supposed to know who had taken her. That she was supposed to be kept away from her betrothed but not in that house. He accused the other Fae of being reckless. The man in front of him got really angry, slapped him, and said he knew what he was doing." Lettie shivered.

"What did he look like, this man he was talking to?" Ceiren commented from the corner of the room.

Lettie closed her eyes when she answered, "Slim. Blonde. Really sharp features. Cold eyes."

Breena spoke, her voice a near whisper, "What color were his eyes?"

Lettie smiled sadly. "Lilac."

Ollie's head whipped to Ceiren. Breena shot Brynach a look and cursed. Brynach pushed back his shoulders, cracked his neck and knuckles, and clenched his fists. His pulse raced, his ears rang, and his vision danced. They'd fucking had him. Right in front of them and let him go.

Rainer got their mother's icy blue eyes, but Ceiren and Levinas had inherited the late King's soft purple eyes. It wasn't a common eye color, and the description fit Levinas.

"I'm gonna kill him. I'm going to fucking kill him," Breena said under her breath. Her beautiful face tilted toward the ceiling in anger. "I had my knife to his fucking throat. He's probably gloating right now at the fact we let him go."

"So, we know Levinas has Ash, but we don't know where. We find him and beat it out of the fucker," Riordan said, standing up and moving toward the door. He turned when he reached the stairs. "Why aren't you moving?"

"It's not that easy, Riordan. Come sit down," Brynach said, his fists tight at his side.

Breena stopped in front of Lettie and spoke softly to her, "Was Aisling injured? Was she scared, chained, or locked up?"

"Chained? What the hell do you think your brother is doing to her?" Riordan gasped.

"You don't want to know what he's capable of, trust me," Breena answered.

"Then again, I ask, why aren't we leaving?" Riordan was frustrated and Brynach understood.

"Um, she was kind of far away but she seemed okay," Lettie said.

"And you couldn't see any bruises or cuts on her, nothing to indicate she'd been hurt?" Breena repeated.

"Stop fucking asking that. She already said no," Riordan shouted. Ollie hugged Trent tight, and Sean soothed Lettie.

Brynach turned to his sister. "You're coming back to Faerie with Riordan and myself."

"Fuck yeah, I am." Breena rocked on her heels.

He turned to Liam. "Ceiren can stay here and protect the apartment and Dawn."

"I'll stay with them, too," Ollie declared. Brynach wasn't sure the Fae was capable of protection, but it was better than nothing.

Brynach bent his head. "Thank you."

Liam shrugged. "We still have people on the houses waiting to see if anyone comes back. We'll keep you posted if we come up with anything else." Liam paused and looked at Brynach with a rawness that nearly took his breath away. "Brynach, I will not stop Riordan from going with you. I couldn't if I wanted to, but you have to make sure he comes home. My brother is a priority, too. You understand?"

Brynach did. Riordan wasn't just important to his brother, he was important. Period. Hard stop. Nothing and nobody was going to hurt the people that Brynach cared about. Not anymore. Not again.

"You have my word."

CHAPTER 13

Aisling

"Miss, wouldn't you like to dress for breakfast?"

Aisling looked down at the nearly see-through nightgown she'd worn to bed the night before. It was one of the more modest offerings the drawers had to offer.

Dinner the previous night had been awful. She'd barely choked down any food and Levinas had enjoyed every moment of her discomfort. Her skin still crawled from the way he leered at her. She would not do it again.

"I will take my meal in my room," Aisling informed the housemaid.

"Master Levinas requests you join him in the dining room, Miss."

Oh, fuck that. She did not want to be at his beck and call.

"I'm not in the mood for company. My meal can be brought to me."

"I'm afraid that's not possible. Please, reconsider his offer." The fear in the woman's wide brown eyes was impossible to miss. "He doesn't respond well to being disobeyed."

"How he feels or what he wants is inconsequential. I don't want to look at his smug face. It ruins my appetite." Aisling refused to be moved on this.

The woman nodded and left the room. Aisling busied

herself looking out her window and wondering what her men were up to. They'd be going crazy looking for her. Time had started slipping away, but she'd been there well over a week. They'd be mad with worry by now. Aisling's stomach grumbled and she realized how hungry she actually was.

It took a while, but the Fae reappeared with a tray of food. She was moving to the desk to set it down when Aisling noticed blood on the woman's shirt.

"What happened to you?" Aisling rushed to the woman's side and relieved her of the tray. "Who bloodied your back?"

She smiled at Aisling. "The Prince doesn't like being disobeyed."

Aisling was horrified. Less at the fact that Levinas had abused one of his servants and more because she should have anticipated the action. "He punished you because I didn't listen."

It was a statement, not a question, and the woman didn't deny it. Aisling raged at the manipulation. She wasn't going to let anyone be punished on her behalf. "Are you well enough to help me dress?"

The relief in the woman's eyes nearly broke Aisling but she remained calm, head high. If she was about to walk into the lion's den, she'd teach him the true power of the pride.

"What can I call you?" Aisling asked as the woman moved gingerly toward her wardrobe.

"My name is, Gemma, Miss."

"Please, call me Aisling." She hurried to add, "And if your Prince doesn't allow such formality, please at least do so in my chambers."

Gemma nodded and smiled at her. Not for the first time Aisling was struck by how deceiving the Fae appearance could be. This woman was likely centuries older than her, but she appeared young still, more a peer than an immortal. She spoke past her too sharp teeth that crowded her mouth giving her a slight lisp.

The pink haired Fae was taller than Aisling, thin as a pin, and had what Aisling could only describe as claws in place of fingers. Still, she dressed Aisling with care and braided her hair carefully. She tried not to fidget but she was incredibly uncomfortable in the dress Gemma had chosen. That said, it was still the most modest choice. The black dress clung to every curve and revealed more leg and cleavage than Aisling would ever choose to share with Levinas.

Pushing her shoulders back she followed Gemma through the house, again noting the interior layout of the gothic palace. It had been cleaned but dust still clung to the tight corners of sculptures and the mirrors, though clean, were dull. She'd already determined it wasn't Levinas's house, but she hadn't uncovered any other clues.

No pictures lined the long walls or steep staircase, but what she did see was plenty of taxidermy. Stuffed animals of all varieties, all with beaded eyes that seemed to track her movement over the obsidian floors. She stopped in front of a large wolf, silver gray in a sea of darkness, and forever snarling.

"It was beautiful," Aisling mused, and Gemma backtracked to look at the animal with her.

"Yes, she was." Dismayed at the pain in her voice, Aisling turned to her.

"You knew her?"

The woman nodded, not looking at Aisling, and her hand came up to the haunch of the majestic animal. "She was my husband's familiar. She belonged to the pack the master's familiar leads."

Aisling was nauseated as the reality of the halls struck her. "These are...do you mean to tell me all these are familiars?"

"People go to extreme lengths to encourage loyalty," she deadpanned.

The killing of a familiar was one of the highest offenses in Faerie. The bond between Fae and familiar was sacred. No way the royal family knew about this place. Bonds were respected, whether familiar, romantic, or blood bonds. This was perverted. It was inexcusable.

"We shouldn't keep him waiting any longer, Lady."

Aisling followed, her eyes locked on Gemma's back. Seeing the brown blood stains on her shirt was still better than the horrors the halls housed. Gemma stopped at the doors to the dining room and gestured Aisling through.

Levinas sat at the head of the table, the only other place setting at his left. As she neared the table, she saw the large black wolf sitting to his right, camouflaged in the dark room. Its head rose as she approached and its intelligent eyes found her, lips lifting in an eerie smile. She suppressed a shiver at the thought of its pack member in the hallway.

"So nice to see you out and about, Aisling." Levinas lifted his glass to her. "I'm glad you changed your mind and joined me."

Aisling met his eyes, refusing to be cowed by him. "It appears you dole out beatings and take them." His face was yellow green with healing bruises. "I'm jealous."

She took her seat, and the servant moved from the back wall to uncover the cloche covering her food. Her stomach turned at the eggs, toast, and berries. The thought of sitting civilly with this monster after what she'd learned made acid burn up her throat.

"Some people remain shortsighted. I plan ahead. Not everyone agrees with my plans." Levinas stroked his cheek. "My mother never was good at keeping a leash on her pets."

Aisling nearly choked on her water. "Gabriel did that?" she laughed. "This might be the first time I agree with him."

The large wolf snarled at her and she rolled her eyes. She wasn't hungry but Aisling ate out of fear that her refusal may result in a chef or servant being hurt. The food went down like nails, scraping her raw, but she forced a berry into her mouth.

"I didn't figure you for such a dainty eater." Levinas picked up his fork and dug into breakfast meat chewing audibly through gristle. Aisling's stomach threatened to empty what little she'd managed to choke down. She didn't respond to him. She may have to be here, but she didn't have to talk to him.

Aisling wasn't playing it meek, she met his eyes and glared at him in disgust while she sipped her water, again. She could get through this. She could do this.

"I saw your precious Brynach."

Aisling couldn't school her face quick enough. The hope, the desire, and pain on her face was enough to have Levinas smirking into his own goblet.

"I thought that might spark something inside those angry eyes. Aren't you going to ask me how I saw him? Or how he's doing?"

She remained silent and Levinas sighed, "I despise quiet meals. It angers me to waste opportunities for conversation with beautiful company and when I get angry, I lash out."

The wolf at his side sprang into action, lunging at the servant in the room and clamping down on his forearm. Its head shook viciously and Aisling heard the bone break. The Fae cried out but didn't try to fight the animal off. When the wolf released him, he raised himself to a formal standing position, cradling the broken appendage.

The Fae's quick healing would see them mended before too long but a break that nasty, an attack that vicious, had to hurt. Still the Fae stood, eyes averted, waiting for the next order, or the next abuse.

"Still not compelled?" This time Levinas flicked a finger and a soot colored sharp alate sprang from where it had been hiding in a centerpiece of dark flowers and rushed her. It stopped short of her face. "I'd hate to bloody you, darling."

Like hell he wouldn't. The insecure Fae wanted what he couldn't have, and he couldn't have her. She belonged to and chose Brynach. It ate at Levinas. While she was here, she might as well remind him why he coveted her. It might keep her unbloodied a little longer. Aisling straightened, crossing her legs and arms, which inevitably presented her breasts to the Fae. She stared Levinas in the eyes and licked her berry red lips.

"Well played, Aisling," he laughed and shook his head, lowering his hand and calling off his alate. "How about this, you engage in pleasant conversation with me, and I'll give you information on your precious men."

She'd have no way of knowing if he was being truthful, but the tradeoff was too good to pass up. For information on Brynach or Riordan she'd smile prettily and chat with the devil.

"You look lovely this morning," Levinas attempted conversation again.

She huffed a laugh, "As if you hadn't hand-picked every skimpy outfit in that room."

"In fact, I didn't. The room used to belong to a woman who enjoyed dressing like the lady of the manor. Regardless, it suits you." When Aisling didn't answer, he continued. "You act as though you're being mistreated. The servants know to obey you. Ask for what you want, and it shall be provided."

"And if I no longer want to look at you?" She couldn't help herself.

Levinas tapped his fingers on the table. "Your stay doesn't have to be unpleasant, Aisling. We could get acquainted and enjoy one another's company." His eyes slid over her body, and she swallowed hard. It would be a cold day in hell before he touched her.

"Where did you see Brynach?"

He didn't skirt the question. Levinas answered quickly, "Yesterday at the Unseelie Court. He was taking a break from scouring Faerie for you. If I'm being truthful, he doesn't look good, darling."

Aisling bit the inside of her cheek to keep from weeping.

Brynach would be tearing himself apart with worry and guilt. "And Riordan?"

Levinas threw a hand out. "I'm sure I don't know. I wouldn't bother myself checking on the Ravdi. I didn't even want to see my bastard brother. That was an unfortunate run in."

"Riordan wasn't with Brynach?" She didn't know why they weren't together but neither would stop until she was found. She had to believe that.

A Fae hurried into the room, a piece of paper in his hand. Levinas read it and then turned to Aisling. "If you'll excuse me, I have business to attend to."

Like she gave a shit if he left. The large wolf left the room and Levinas rose, leaning over her chair. His face was close to hers, but she refused to look at him. With a huff he kissed her cheek. "You'll warm to me eventually, pet."

She held still, waiting until he'd left to rub at her face. Aisling was pushing her chair back to go to her rooms when raised voices sounded in the hall. Quietly, she slid her shoes off and crept barefoot to the doorway to listen. She didn't recognize the other voice, but the words being exchanged had her covering her mouth.

Safe or not, she had to confirm her suspicion. Aisling arched her neck toward the light streaming through the large front doors. On the threshold was Dexter's missing informant. What was he doing here? How did he know Levinas? Her brain was having trouble comprehending what was being said. Just as she refocused herself the informant spotted her. Aisling ducked back into the dining room, waiting until the door shut and Levinas walked away before exiting.

Aisling fought to calm herself in the dark hall. If she was stuck here, then she'd make the most of her time. She'd find out what the fuck Levinas was up to so that when she got out, she had concrete proof to take to the courts. It was time for her game face. She had asked her father to be a player at the table of Faerie, and now she had a chance to join.

She made her way up the stairs to her rooms, determined that the next time she saw Levinas she'd have an advantage. Luckily, she found exactly who she'd been looking for.

"Sorry, Miss. I didn't think you'd be back so quickly. Was everything okay?" She worried her bottom lip with her sharp teeth.

"Fine, Gemma. Levinas had business to attend to." Aisling thought for a moment. "I was wondering, can you help me find other clothes?" The woman didn't bat an eye as she answered affirmatively.

If Aisling was going to go to war, she wanted to look the part. She'd never be on even footing with that slimy High Fae looking like she did. Aisling knew just the raven-haired vixen she needed to borrow from.

Aisling let the woman know where to go and what to bring her. "Don't forget the shoes." She ignored the wide-eyed panic in the Fae's eyes. "Don't worry. She won't mind and if she does, I'll take the blame."

An hour later the woman returned with two men behind her, all weighed down with clothing. "That wasn't as easy as one might think."

"It will be worth it. You can put it in the wardrobe, please. I won't be needing those clothes anymore," Aisling instructed from the desk where she was writing down notes.

"Yes, Miss," they answered and swapped out the clothes for her.

Aisling moved to peruse the selection once the men had left and only Gemma remained. The other woman eyed the clothes like they would come alive and lunge for her throat. Aisling didn't blame her.

"Are you sure this is wise, Aisling?" Gemma asked, comfortable with her now that they were alone.

"He wants someone fitting of this prison, he's going to get it. I'm not some doll he can dress up," Aisling answered as she thumbed through the hangers. She smiled and picked a pair of black leather leggings and a deep red sweetheart neckline corset with black lace trim. She leaned down and chose a pair of black heels before standing and smiling.

"These should set the right tone."

Gemma didn't look convinced, but she helped Aisling dress without comment. By the time Levinas called Aisling down for lunch, she was ready. The outfit of a seductress was gone. In its place was a woman who wasn't going to be intimidated by anyone. Aisling had to keep her face schooled into a stiff resting bitch face to avoid a full-blown grin as he nearly choked on his drink.

"What are you wearing?"

"Do you like it?" She spun knowing that her curves were lusher than Breena's. That the leather and the corseted top lifted and hugged in ways they couldn't on his sister's more muscular frame. All the same, it was clear these were Breena's clothes. The look on his face was worth the risk the staff had gone to in order to get them.

His face was red, but he kept his voice level, "They don't suit you."

"Oh? I think they're wonderful. Isn't this what you wanted? If we're going to play house, I should look the part of the goth mistress." Aisling sat and accepted a napkin for her lap before picking up her fork and diving into her food. She ate happily while Levinas glared at her.

"What are you playing at coming down here dressed like that?"

Aisling glanced from his cold purple eyes to his lap. "What's the matter, Levi? Finding it difficult to get a hard-on when I'm dressed like your sister?"

His familiar snarled at her and she laughed, "Your puppy is grumpy. Have you walked him lately?"

"Watch your tongue, Aisling," he spat through clenched teeth.

"Or what? We both know you're not going to really hurt

me, and the staff seem used to it. You'll abuse them whether I'm here or not. Whether I "behave" or don't."

"Think really hard before you continue to push my buttons, Aisling."

"Tell me what you want, Levi? Do you want me plaint and willing? Your brother is man enough to handle me at my toughest and yet you get flustered." She took a bite of meat and chewed.

"Brynach isn't fit to be called High Fae. He's an embarrassment to our court." Levinas's knuckles were white around his glass.

"And yet he has things you never will. People's trust and admiration, loyalty that's freely given, and a power that doesn't require boasting." Aisling sat back casually.

"There's more to power than muscles, pet. He's got brawn but no brain. I'm a planner and I am steps ahead of you. You won't loosen my tongue in anger with your games."

"You're slipping, Levi. We both know I'm not staying here forever. I hope you've got a really good fucking plan in place for when I get out, or when your brother finds me, because he's going to tear you limb from limb."

Levinas shook his head. "Don't you worry about me. I have a backup plan for my backup plan. You think I did this at the spur of the moment? That I acted out of lust or jealousy? Aisling, you are insignificant. A tiny piece in a larger puzzle you can't even begin to see. You'll be alone for dinner. Do try not to miss me too much."

"How ever will I survive?"

The Fae Prince didn't respond, he simply turned on his heel and left the room. His familiar growled in her direction before following him.

Aisling allowed herself a deep breath. She'd taken a risk today. Not just with the outfit but with her back talk. He'd hit her for less before. She had come down prepared for the same today. But he held himself in check. Aisling had needed to know where the line was, but it seemed to move, often.

Gemma entered the dining room and moved toward her. "I saw the master leaving. I came to make sure you were okay." She looked at where Aisling was relaxed and eating. "I see you are."

Aisling smiled. "Thank you for worrying. I'm perfectly fine." She paused a moment. "Gemma, this is not a house meant for children, not with wards and stairs with razor blades. This is not a family home. Who would raise children here?"

She didn't really expect answers, but she had to ask.

"Do you like to read?" Gemma asked.

"I do," Aisling answered.

"Follow me." The housekeeper led Aisling on a labyrinth like journey. It ended at two ornately decorated wooden doors. It was hard in the dim light to see what was etched into them. "You may enjoy this room. The books are well-loved, though the material may surprise you. Some have been read more than others. When you're ready to leave, keep making left turns and you'll find yourself back near the main stairs."

"Thank you, Gemma," Aisling said, walking into the room. She was unsurprised to see a library, a dark one, but a library all the same. A part of her relaxed in a space filled with books, but as she perused the stacks, she realized these weren't your average novels. The titles boasted ways to torture, poisons that paralyzed, and histories full of violence. She found tomes on weaponry and even medical journals.

One spine in particular caught her attention, a copy of a book titled *The Gate to Honesty* that looked like it had been read countless times. The crimson binding was frayed to the pale cream of the glued pages. Aisling reached forward to remove it, pulling from the top to slide it from between its neighbors.

She shouldn't have been surprised when the shelf slid back and to the right, revealing a hidden room. Still, she snatched her hand back and screamed. A wall lamp had flickered to life when the door opened, even though it was barely lighting the room. If she was going to learn about the owner of the house it would probably be in their secret lair.

She'd seen enough movies to know she had to hold the door open. No way was she getting trapped in there. Before she stepped inside, she grabbed a book off the shelf and wedged it in the doorway so it couldn't close behind her. Aisling allowed herself to survey the hidden space. It wasn't a secret lab, no desk or mad scribbles on the walls. Aisling wished that's what she'd found. Any of those things would have been a relief compared to what she saw.

The room was bare save one chair, made of metal, sitting in the middle of the round room over a drain. If that wasn't ominous enough, the walls were decorated with meticulously arranged weapons. Despite their intended gruesome use, they were all polished and clean.

Aisling had stumbled upon somebody's torture chamber. This wasn't the room of a novice criminal. This was the room of somebody who wanted to inflict pain and who wanted to be good at it. As lovingly organized as the implements of torture were arranged, this was someone who took pride in their "craft". Sincerely twisted shit happened in this room.

All the tools of the trade were lined up: whips, prods, knives, clubs, and other assorted items Aisling couldn't even begin to understand the purpose of. Suddenly, the dark flooring was less like a continued part of the house's aesthetic and more a necessity to cover the horrors inflicted within these walls. She covered her mouth, looking at the chair with its clamps at the ankles and wrists. It was too much.

She'd learned all she could, and she wanted out of the room, immediately. Aisling exited, lifting the book from the door jam and closing the secret door. Could anyone work in this house and not know about the horrors that took place behind that wall? The sounds, the screams, must have been impossible to ignore. She left the library following Gemma's instructions back to the main staircase.

She rounded the last corner, panic at being in the restrictive hallway lessening as she entered the open space. Aisling sat on the stairs and tried to get her breathing back to normal.

"I take it your time in the library was informational?" Gemma said sneaking up on Aisling.

"It confirmed my assumption that a crazy bastard lived here. Why can't you tell me who it was?" Aisling frowned. "What kind of life could those children have had here? What chance did they have of growing up to be normal people?"

"I'm no stranger to raising children, miss. Some make it through and others cave to darker tendencies. In my experience, children are resilient." Gemma guided her back to her rooms. "Master never had a lot of guests, but he liked it that way. He was prone to outbursts of anger but never toward us. I'd been caring for him since he was a child, since his parents were killed in a rogue attack by the unaligned looking to establish land for themselves."

"Master was a youngster, but he fought back. He'd managed to kill two of the unaligned before my husband found him. He was covered in blood, shaking, and screaming over the corpses, with a wild look in his eyes. After that he was never the same and who could blame him?"

It was impossible to be unmoved by the horror that had befallen the owners of the house. Nobody should have to live through something like that, especially not a child. Still, Aisling couldn't forget what the house had become. Whoever lived here wasn't innocent and while their past had been tragic, nothing would excuse the future they had built in this place.

Gemma continued as they entered Aisling's rooms, "One day he showed up with a pregnant young girl and said that we were to treat her kindly, to see to any of her requests. It was clear that Peg loved him, her eyes followed him, and she brightened under his gaze. Her pregnancy wasn't an easy one and the delivery was even harder, but she was determined to not go across the Veil and get traditional medical help."

"We knew Peg was a witch, of course. She wasn't Fae, but she was strong. I curse myself for not seeing the signs, but anyone who could love him would have to be a little bit off. She wasn't a bad mother, but she wasn't much of one, either. Once the kids were born, she wanted little to do with them. I raised them, me and the other help, and tried to give them a normal childhood."

Aisling let the silence hang, afraid to interrupt and stop the story even though so many questions resided on her tongue.

"Over the years there were more children, Peg kept his interest as long as she could. Still he tired of her. He hadn't want to be a father. He humored her. The boys were like their father, rough and cruel. Not that they ever spent time with him. Still, the similarities were uncanny. Peg was always angry with the children. Maybe it was because they reminded her of a man who didn't love her the way she wanted? The girl was different. She was kind and shadowed the staff, but we couldn't protect her forever. When the youngest was around seven Peg took them from the house and Faerie. We never saw them again."

Gemma looked up at Aisling. "We've been here tending to the house even though nobody has lived in it, that is until Levinas told us to expect company."

"The murdered familiars, that wasn't Levinas?" Aisling hypothesized.

"No."

Aisling whispered her next question, "Gemma, whose house is this?"

"It's Master Gabriel's."

CHAPTER 14

Riordan

"Tell me what I need to know and then we need to get back to Faerie." Riordan understood his brother's distress, but the questions Breena had asked terrified him. If she thought her brother was capable of harming Aisling to that degree, they needed to move.

"We have to be really sure before we do anything, Riordan," Brynach's voice was low and slow. He was trying to soothe him. Riordan didn't want to be calmed.

"Up until now we have assumed that Aisling was kidnapped by someone who wanted to keep her safe so she could be used as leverage. But none of you seem convinced your brother cares for Aisling's physical well-being." He took the time to look them each in the eyes but none of them argued. "So, please explain to me why caution is necessary? We should be finding her and getting her away from him, immediately." Riordan expected the large Fae to agree, but he shook his head.

"We should talk before we go back." Brynach sat at the table, pulling out a chair. "Sit."

Riordan ran his hands through his hair and huffed out a breath. If Brynach was telling him to wait, then it was important to listen. "Can we at least make it fast?"

"It's complicated, Ravdi. Sit down and listen up," Breena

said spinning a chair around and sitting on it backward. Everyone gathered around the table, and she started talking again. "I'm not sure how much you know of Fae law so I'm going to break this down for you."

Riordan bounced his leg under the table, his fingers sliding the rings on the chain around his neck back and forth. Next to him Brynach placed a hand on his knee and squeezed. Riordan stilled under the other man's hand and breathed deeper when the hand stayed solid on him. When had the hulking Fae become a comfort?

"Despite attempts to solidify their bond Brynach and Aisling have not been legally claimed by one another in Faerie. This means that any transgressions against Aisling are fair game," Breena continued.

"If I were to challenge Levinas, or accuse him of wrong-doing, and we didn't have proof, it would be cause for a blood tithe," Brynach explained.

"A blood what now?" Amber chimed in.

"A blood tithe," Ollie answered, surprising them all. Trent was ghostly white by his boyfriend's side as he spoke. "If Brynach were to slander him, Levinas has the right to challenge him to a fight. The duels in Faerie don't end with the drawing of blood. He'd bleed Brynach, perhaps not to death, but it wouldn't be pleasant."

"But you'd win," Riordan deadpanned turning to Brynach.

"Obviously," Breena barked. "Fighting within the royal courts is unheard of. It would bring shame to the Unseelie."

"Then that would fall on Levinas for demanding the blood tithe, not Brynach," Trent commented.

"No," Riordan answered for the Fae. "In the Unseelie Court if blame is placed, it goes to Brynach. They'll find a way to make it his fault."

The large Fae gave him a small, sad smile. "And the court balance is already perilous. The unaligned are gaining in numbers, and I've heard whispers we won't be able to hold power."

"Who the fuck cares? My best friend is being held captive by a fucking animal," Trent yelled.

Riordan didn't disagree, but as much as he loved Aisling, he cared for the man at his side. He didn't want to rescue one to lose the other. "What do we do?"

"We go back, and we look for her. What we don't do is confront Levinas, not until we have proof," Breena said, standing from her seat and patting her body.

It took Riordan a moment to realize she was counting her weapons. "Do I need any of those?" he asked, more a joke than anything else.

"Yes," came her answer. "The first place we go when we get to Faerie is the armory. It's unacceptable that you've traveled to Faerie recently without a way to defend yourself." She huffed, "And my brother says he cares for you. If he did, he'd be training you in your spare time."

Brynach snarled at her, "Don't tell me how to protect what's mine."

Riordan blushed when Liam's head swiveled between the large Fae and his baby brother. When he caught his eye Riordan shrugged and Liam's face split in a grin.

"I sure as shit never thought I'd see this day." His laughter lightened the mood in the room. "Only you could swear off magic and then land a bonded witch and a Fae partner, Rory."

Brynach followed Riordan's lead. "No attacking Levinas, but that doesn't mean we can't look for Aisling. We've calmed down. Nobody will make any rash decisions in Faerie. It's time to go."

"Rory?" Liam hung his head.

Riordan looked into his brother's eyes. The rich brown mirrored in his own gaze. A gift from their mother, whose own eyes used to warm when she smiled. He nodded and embraced Liam. "I'll be back this side of the Veil with Aisling before you can miss me."

Amber moved to Liam's side. Riordan offered her a small smile before releasing his brother and turning to Brynach and the other Fae. Around the room people started walking for the door. Riordan hugged his brother one more time and then joined the Fae as they made for where the Veil bisected the town. He'd done it enough that the subtle "walking through cobweb" feeling didn't bother him. The sifting, however, that still sucked out loud.

Brynach's golden eyes gazed down at him. "Ready?"

One moment he had feet on the ground in the bright sun of Faerie with the sweet berry smell assaulting his senses, and the next they were in-between. His molecules stretched thin, and organs compressed as they spun through space and time. At least he didn't embarrass himself by throwing up as they settled back down on solid ground.

"You're getting better at that," Brynach said, arms still around Riordan.

A part of Riordan's brain, the toxic masculinity that had been beaten into him, wanted to dissect what it meant to be comforted and comfortable in the Fae's arms. And maybe he'd unpack that one day, but not today.

"Yeah, well, I kinda had to. I guess your sister wasn't kidding?" He was surrounded by walls of weapons.

"No, she wasn't. We may not want to engage in an all-out confrontation but that doesn't mean we won't find one anyway. You must be ready." Brynach pulled down a few blades. "Let's see what works best for you."

"I have no experience with knives. Or weapons of any kind, really," Riordan admitted.

"That's okay." He handed Riordan a blade, handle first, and Riordan grasped it. It was light in his hands, the leather grip warming to his touch.

"And I'll know how exactly?" Riordan asked following Brynach outside.

He pointed across the yard toward a rough target.

"Oh no." Riordan shook his head. "I'm not making an ass

out of myself." He started to walk away.

"Do you want to join the others in trying to find Aisling, or not?" Brynach asked. "Because I'm not taking you out, now that we know for sure what we're up against, until I know you can defend yourself."

Riordan stopped and turned on the Fae. "Don't threaten me. If you won't take me out, Breena will. She could care less if I get home safe."

Brynach barely hid his grin. "She will do no such thing. She may not care about you, but she loves me, and she knows I'll skin her if you come to harm because of her negligence."

"Could you care about me less and Aisling more?" Riordan asked in a huff. They were wasting time.

"We're not wasting time," Brynach said, and Riordan's head snapped up. "No, I can't magically read your mind. I know you better now. They're out looking for Aisling and we'll join them as soon as you can do so safely."

"Fine. How do I throw this thing?" Riordan asked gripping the tip of the knife and pulling his hand back to throw it.

"Not like that!" Brynach yelped and moved toward him, carefully removing the blade from his hand. "Like this, by the handle." He wrapped Riordan's hand in his own, both around the leather grip. He positioned himself behind Riordan and reached forward, taking his wrist and raising it.

"Bring your hand up and then arc it down, but do not release," Brynach instructed, and Riordan did as asked.

He tried to put the feeling of the large man's warmth at his back out of his head. Brynach's arms wrapped around his body.

"I assume at some point I have to let go?" Riordan asked to break the tension.

"The blade will travel downward naturally. You release above the target on the downswing."

Riordan let the blade go on the next downward swing and it fell, pathetically, to the ground.

"Well, that didn't work." And this is why he didn't try things he wasn't sure he'd succeed at. Frustration gnawed at his gut. "This is stupid."

"No, it isn't. Try this one. Same action. You're doing well," Brynach said, placing a different blade into his hand.

Riordan closed his eyes, took a deep breath, and pulled his arm back before releasing. The blade sang through the air and the satisfying thump of the blade on wood sounded through the yard. Sprites that dared to flit around the training ground scattered from where the blade still vibrated in the wood. Eyes wide with surprise, he turned to Brynach.

"Did you see that?" he exclaimed. He was nowhere near the bullseye, but he'd at least hit the target.

"Looks like you found the right blade. I'll get a few more and then we'll take off." Brynach offered warm praise, "Good job."

Riordan couldn't fight the audible groan as his eyes landed on the large black draft horse. "We're riding on Satan's steed?"

Brynach laughed and clapped Riordan on the back. "It's that or sifting. Which do you prefer?"

With a resigned sigh Riordan moved toward the horse. By the time he got help up from a Fae stable hand and settled onto the back of the massive beast, Brynach was by his side.

"Ready?" Brynach wasn't looking at Riordan when he asked. He was stroking the thick neck of his familiar. When he got no answer, he locked those citrine eyes on Riordan's and quirked a brow.

"Sorry, were you talking to me?"

Brynach's lip curled. "If I was speaking to Kongur I wouldn't be speaking out loud. And just so you know, he likes you. You're perfectly safe. Relax. Enjoy the ride. We have to visit the Veil first, and then we're going to find our girl."

Riordan sat atop a living weapon and tried to breathe through his anxiety. Letting his vision slip, he saw the swirling magic of Faerie and wondered at the beauty of it all.

CHAPTER 15

Brynach

Brynach waited with Riordan on the other side of the portal crossing for Lettie, Sean, and the others. Kongur was growing impatient, and Riordan kept throwing him very hesitant glances. He'd done better than Brynach had anticipated on the ride over, but that would be the calmest of the rides to come.

"Your friend doesn't like me," Kongur commented.

"He's not used to animals as majestic as you," Brynach soothed with a hint of sarcasm. The large draft horse huffed a laugh, startling Riordan. Brynach turned his attention to Lettie and Sean as they presented the necessary paperwork and passed under the giant metal archways of the border crossing.

Immediately upon entering Faerie, Lettie closed her eyes. Brynach was about to move to her, but Sean was already by her side. His Fae hearing allowed him to eavesdrop. The overwhelming presence of the other Hive members had lessened because fewer people in Faerie had been involved in the curse. He was happy she had a small reprieve from her trauma.

"When I came over with her before, it was the first time I'd seen her take a deep breath," Trent commented, and Riordan agreed. "How fucked up is that?"

"She's had a rough time with all this. With Aisling being missing. With her changes. She's strong, though," Ollie commented, hugging Trent close to his side.

Brynach saw the smaller man tense before leaning into his partner. Faerie was a vast land but in this small space, it felt crowded. How had so many people from Aisling's mortal life ended up this side of the Veil? Logically, he knew the answer. Trent was here because Ollie was helping them sift people around Faerie and because after being away so long, he wanted to be near his friends. Lettie was here to see if she could help find Aisling with her access to the Fae Hive and Sean had worked an invite alongside Liam to discuss the possible disturbance in technology when the Veil fell.

"Bry?" Riordan spoke beside him, "When can we go?"

"So eager to be alone with your hulking Fae," Trent joked.

The thought of Riordan being anxious to be alone with him had a warmth spreading through Brynach. One that settled somewhere it shouldn't, especially not when they should be focusing on finding Aisling. Or when they were sitting atop the same horse, pressed together, and his erection would likely terrify the Ravdi.

"We're going to make sure Lettie is okay and then we'll continue on. I want to make sure she gets to Trixie and Corinna. If we find Aisling and she learns we put her friends in danger." Brynach doesn't get to finish.

"She will have your balls." Trent nods. "Ollie can transport them once the welcoming committee is done with their introductions."

With that Brielle and Jashana walked up, ready to take over the task of keeping the humans safe. He was glad to have Aisling's guard back in favor with her court and working again. Brynach had already sent word about their assignments. As everyone gathered near them, a little further from the crowd of the crossing, Brynach spoke, "Welcome to Faerie." He swung off his familiar.

"It takes getting used to," Riordan commented as they watched Lettie try to take it all in.

"And you'll have time to explore a little. I've made them promise to show you around and not force you to work non-stop," Brynach promised. "But there is work to do. Liam and Sean, you'll be going with Brielle to discuss options with the elders. Lettie, you'll be with Jashana visiting the Unseelie and Seelie Courts to talk to Trixie and Corinna."

Around him, heads bobbed in agreement. "If you need anything, Brielle and Jashana know how to reach me. Riordan and I won't be joining you, but we will be in touch."

Lettie looked up to Riordan. "Be careful."

Riordan smiled down at her and at Sean. "You, too. Both of you. You'll be together at night, right?"

Sean nodded. "We arranged for a room at the Seelie Court together."

Ollie clapped his hands. "Alright. Good plan. Now, who needs a lift?"

And like that people were heading off and Riordan was shifting atop Kongur. With a grin Brynach swung up onto his familiar.

Something about Riordan sitting astride his familiar filled Brynach with a possessive pride. Having him close had brought Brynach more peace of mind in this short time than he'd felt in far too long. He fought a smile at how stiff the Ravdi was holding himself. Eventually, as they traveled through Faerie, Riordan let himself ease into Brynach's arms.

He watched as Riordan took in the sights and sounds of new parts of Faerie.

"I forget how little I know about this realm," he commented as they rode through.

"It's not a place easy to see in a few trips," Brynach agreed and pointed out different things as they continued their search.

"What's that?" Riordan asked, the awe in his voice clear.

"That's what you'd call a tree of life," Brynach answered. "It's an old tree, one of many in Faerie." Kongur stopped so Riordan could observe the large, gnarled tree decked out in metallic appearing bronze leaves.

Riordan stared at the tree, his eyes pivoting all around it. "There's so much magic."

Of course, there was. Anything that old in Faerie was bound to draw power to it. "It's a concentration of magic, yes."

Riordan gasped, "I'm such an idiot!" The Ravdi smacked himself in the forehead.

Brynach's instinct was to reach up and still his hand. He didn't want to see the man come to harm, not even by his own volition. "Care to share?"

"Magic. It's all around us."

"Yesssss," Brynach drew out.

Riordan turned his neck to look at Brynach. "It's not the same as the other side of the Veil, but I can still see the magic. It still answers my call."

Brynach watched as Riordan scanned the area around them. "I can find her! If she can't communicate with Rin, if she can't get herself out, then a concentration of magic must be blocking her. And if anyone can locate a concentration of magic, it's me!" He stilled atop the large horse. "Finally, something useful I can do."

Brynach opened his mouth to argue but Riordan held up a hand. "You know what I meant. Let's get going."

"The man has a point. We should keep moving," Kongur pointed out and stomped a hoof.

The massive black Percheron took off and a yelp from Riordan resulted. It wasn't easy sitting astride a horse as large as Kongur. It was made harder because he wouldn't tolerate a saddle. Brynach was used to riding bareback, but Riordan most assuredly was not. The Ravdi's hand was curled in his familiar's mane. Kongur wasn't a fan.

"Squeeze with your thighs, you're pulling on his mane too hard," Brynach reminded him when his familiar shook his head angrily. "Here, lean back into me."

Brynach wrapped an arm around Riordan and brought his back flush against his own chest. "You can brace against my thigh if you need to. It'll be more comfortable than leaning forward, for you know, your groin."

Riordan was stiff in his arms and Brynach released him, gently taking Kongur's hair in his hands so the other man was in the circle of his arms, safe from falling off. Slowly, Riordan relaxed into his chest and Brynach took a deep breath at the trust he was being gifted.

"Let yourself look for the magic and we will do the rest." Brynach hoped Riordan could find Aisling this way. But, at the very least, it was a start.

"Who is this we you speak of? I'm doing all the hard work. He's a feather. You're a stone," Kongur complained playfully. He was more than capable of bearing their combined weight.

"How will we know if the others find something?" Riordan said, his head on a swivel as the horse's long stride ate up ground.

"Don't worry, if they find her, we'll be alerted before anyone acts."

He nodded against Brynach's chest. "I need to be there. I want us to be the first people she sees."

Brynach's voice was quiet as he whispered his agreement into Riordan's ear, "We will be." He didn't miss the shiver that ran through Riordan's body as his breath hit his neck.

"Focus, Brynach!" Kongur scolded.

"Do you see anything?" Brynach asked the quiet Ravdi.

"Normal amounts of magic, more around homes but nothing that could hide someone as strong as Aisling," he answered.

E ventually, they agreed that getting Aisling home was more important than being the ones to find her. They'd contacted Breena and sent her back across the Veil to gather any Ravdi who were willing to come to Faerie and help search. Those who answered the call were paired up with Fae and were sifting around the kingdoms. That had been hours ago.

"To the castle," he told Kongur. And before Riordan could question the change of direction he told him, "We're heading in. You need a break and food."

"Bullshit. I need to find Aisling. I'm fine," Riordan complained.

"It's non-negotiable. Kongur needs a break and so do I." Brynach couldn't run his familiar that long and hard. They pulled into the Unseelie stables and Brynach swung himself down before turning to Riordan.

"Want a hand?"

The man laughed, "No, I want to free fall off a seven-foot-tall horse. Yes, I want help!"

Brynach reached out as Riordan leaned down and easily distributed his weight to set him on the ground.

"Jesus, my ass hurts. How do you do that?" Riordan complained.

"I'm used to it, I suppose." Brynach turned to a stable hand. "See that he's fed and check his feet. We're leaving again shortly."

Riordan followed behind him as they approached the side entrance of the castle. The Unseelie sprites swarmed the Ravdi. Riordan still didn't trust them, and their taunts were triggering to him. He didn't need Riordan on edge right now. He cursed them away and most listened.

"I'm right here, Riordan. They aren't going to mess with you," Brynach promised. "You'll be fine. We aren't going through the majority of the castle, just to my suite of rooms and the dining hall."

"No offense, but any time spent in that place is too much time." Riordan's whole body was tense. "At least being on your horse we didn't get bled by stone vipers."

"Spiders," Brynach said offhand. "This side of the castle they're spiders."

He watched as a shiver ran the length of Riordan's body. "Oh fuck no."

"Listen, before we go inside, you have to swear to me that you'll hold your tongue. I can't promise that Levinas isn't in there. Do you understand?" Brynach stopped walking and took Riordan by the shoulders. He waited patiently until the other man met his eyes. "I can't keep you safe if you don't keep quiet. We both want the same thing. Aisling will be back with us soon. But I don't want her safety at the cost of your own. Do you understand?"

"Head down. Mouth shut. Temper under control. Got it."

Brynach squeezed his shoulder one last time. "Let's go. I'm hungry and I want a shower."

They entered the castle to little fanfare and made their way to Brynach's suite. As they reached his rooms, he tried to view it through Riordan's eyes. The dark wood and rich fabrics, and the scent of sweet blooms on the air, intoxicating. How many times had Brynach imagined red-haired Aisling spread out against his dark navy sheets, the moonlight cascading across her opalescent skin?

Brynach moved to the bathroom, prepared to show the Ravdi around. There was a distinct lack of footfalls behind him. When he turned the other man was staring at his bed.

"Has Aisling ever been in here?" Riordan asked when Brynach cleared his throat.

Brynach arched a brow and smirked. "No. You beat her to it."

"Good," Riordan said, and walked toward the bathroom.

"I'll get clothing sent up. You're about Ceiren's size." Brynach's arm across the open doorway stopped Riordan. "If and when Aisling visits this room, you'll be as welcome as she is."

At the shock on Riordan's face, he laughed. "I'll be shower-ing next door in Breena's room. Don't be too long. I'm hungry."

Brynach was still smiling as he traveled down the hall. He was turning the corner, the dark marble familiar and almost comforting. Lost in thought, he didn't see the bundle of blonde hair and lanky limbs throw themselves at him. His legs were locked up and he barely caught himself before falling.

"Beatrix, you nearly bested me," he whooped and leaned down to lift his niece for a kiss. "What kind of trouble are you up to?"

"Aslan told me you were here." She squirmed, and he put her down.

"Oh, did he? What a nosey little cat." He poked fun at her familiar. Honestly, the sleek tabby was the best spy the castle had.

"I came to see if you found Auntie Aisling?" Her head was cocked to the side. "Daddy said I could call her that. I know she's not yet, but she's going to be. Right?"

A sharp pain lanced his heart. "That's right."

"You'll find her soon?" she asked, long lashes wet with unshed tears.

"Of course," he promised. "I'm off to Aunt Bree's rooms. Can I trust you with a top-secret mission?"

The young girl perked right up. "Nobody's sneakier than I am."

Brynach sent her off to raid Ceiren's room for clothes and drop them off for Riordan. She'd be in and out of both rooms before Riordan finished in the bathroom, he was sure of it. Then he continued to his sister's suite, desperate for a shower. Breena's bathroom smelled of lavender scented soaps and had more toiletries and fresh flowers than anyone would guess.

He stripped his clothes and threw his tired body under the warm stream of water. Self-care, like eating and sleeping, had stopped when Aisling went missing. Brynach still couldn't believe that his brother was responsible. He wasn't sure what he'd do if Levinas showed his face here today.

Rage boiled up and he balled a fist, punching the tile repeatedly until a knuckle cracked and he bled pink into the water. Tears spilled down his face, and he forced his breathing to even out. When he calmed himself, he washed his body and hair and then slung a towel around his waist.

He left wet footprints on the marble as he traveled back to his room. Brynach entered his suite to the sound of water and steam rolling from his bathroom. He grinned at the pile of clothes on the end of his bed. Beatrix truly was a miracle.

Brynach dressed quickly and finger combed his hair before going into his office. He left the door open enough that Riordan would see he was back but still have privacy. Not that he'd mind seeing the man naked, not at all, but when and if he did, Riordan would know it was happening.

He began a checklist of things to do for the rest of the day. Riordan was smart to search for magical concentrations, but they needed to be more strategic. He checked off areas they'd already been to on the map in front of him. Brynach needed to reach out to the others to make sure they didn't waste time searching the same places.

The water shut off and the door to the bathroom opened.

"Clothes are on the bed," Brynach called out and Riordan mumbled his thanks. A few minutes later he was standing, hair hanging wet around his face and barefoot at the door to Brynach's office. He was beautiful.

"They fit well," Riordan said running a hand down the soft tunic like shirt and pants. He'd never appeared particularly Fae to Brynach but right now he could pass for one.

"Ready for food?" Brynach rose.

"What were you doing?" Riordan filled the room as if he belonged. His long strides eating up the distance between door and desk. Brynach drank in the sight of the Ravdi in his space, one few saw. He wanted to remember Riordan like this.

"Brynach?" Riordan asked, now beside him.

"Strategizing. We need to be smarter about where we travel. The pictures from the warehouse show water, specifically a waterfall. We'll hone in on that after we eat," Brynach explained pointing to a map of Faerie spread across his desk. "But first we should probably get shoes for you."

"My socks stink. I didn't see any in the pile." He shrugged. Brynach pulled a pair out, tossing them to Riordan. "You need food, but we may have to sift, so for all our sakes, don't overindulge."

Riordan groaned, "Whatever finds Aisling the fastest." Luckily, the meal was just the two of them and a very excitable Trixie who entertained them while they ate. Riordan stuck to a lot of bread and butter and protein but nothing with sauce or spice. Brynach made a note to pack heartier snacks for the rest of the day.

When they finished, Trixie hugged Brynach. "Go find Auntie Aisling. I love you."

Brynach caught Riordan's eyes over the mussed curls of his niece and saw the resolve in his gaze. This was it, a turning point. They weren't resting again until they had their girl back. "I can sift. Whatever is fastest."

"We can ride to the basecamp first," Brynach said. "Up you go." He lifted Riordan easily onto the back of Kongur.

"I will never get used to this," Riordan commented as Brynach settled behind him. "You know, now that we know Levinas is responsible for this, Aisling must be in the Unseelie lands. How many large waterfalls are there in your court's territory?"

"More than you'd expect," Brynach answered. But there weren't as many that were isolated.

"Are you thinking what I'm thinking?" Brynach asked his familiar as they trotted from the barn.

"That the Ravdi is smarter than both of us combined?" Came the reply. But the horse banked, turning to the left.

CHAPTER 16

Aisling

The news that the house belonged to Gabriel should have come as more of a shock to Aisling, but it settled into her mind without dispute. After seeing the torture chamber behind the library wall, a part of her already knew. Slowly, the pieces fell into place. Brynach had told her he suspected Gabriel fathered Peggy's kids. That asshole son of hers had called him brother before he blew up in his jail cell. And now she was in a hidden house where children had grown up. Children that were not Brynach or Breena. Children that needed to be kept secret.

What remained unknown to her was how Levinas came to be in control of Gabriel's home? And what did the two have to gain from one another? Gabriel couldn't possibly benefit from the bumbling and cock-sure Levinas. But Levinas believed he had outsmarted everyone. The informant said he wasn't supposed to reveal himself to her. She was to be kept away from Brynach. She didn't understand why, but Levinas had been tasked with keeping her captive.

The answers could wait for another time. Right now, Aisling had one goal and one goal only. To get out of this fucking house without costing anyone, or their familiar, their lives. She had to get back to the men who loved her, who she loved. Aisling needed to escape before Levinas did something she wouldn't be able to come back from.

"Miss, the Prince would like you to accompany him for a meal." Gemma stood at her door. She'd stopped ringing her hands, but you could still see her fidget.

Levinas hadn't been around the night prior, holding to his promise to be gone for dinner. The meal was the best she'd had since her arrival. She'd been surprised when she was spared being called for breakfast, but of course her luck would run out.

"Help me dress," Aisling instructed and turned to the wardrobe.

"Of course, Miss. What would you like to wear today?" She pulled out a dress, but Aisling shook her head.

"No, not that." Aisling moved to the hanger and pulled out a top that was more leather and metal than anything else. She could see Breena wearing this in a dungeon, her recent lover at her feet, and a whip in her hand. "This will do just fine, but I'll need help getting into it."

At Aisling's nod she helped pull on the skintight spandex and leather leggings. The black pants were crossed with straps held tight with buckles meant to house knives. Aisling wouldn't have any, but the message was clear.

She took off her top, unselfconscious as she stood bare breasted in front of the Fae. Aisling put her neck through the collar at the top of the shirt and her right shoulder through the lone arm. Then she waited for Gemma to circle her and lace the corset that would cinch her waist in black leather. It was unforgivingly stiff, the spikes at Aisling's hips promising nobody would put hands on her.

"Are you sure about this, Miss?" Gemma asked as she tugged the laces tighter

"Positive," Aisling confirmed. Once she was inside the corset Gemma came to her front and buckled the silver clasp over her left breast. "The boots, next." She nodded to the low healed black combat boots that they'd managed to snag from Breena's closets. After offending Gemma by asking if she could French braid her hair—of course she could—Aisling accompanied the Fae down to the dining hall.

"You're going to anger him," Gemma whispered as they made their way to the dining room.

"I can handle him." Aisling kept her head high and her back straight, not that she had a choice given how tight the corseted armor was. "Stay out of his way. I've got this."

Aisling strode inside. The long table was set for two with Levinas already at the head. It was silent but for the rubber soles of her boots on the ground. How she wished she could have worn heels. The tapping would have been more satisfying. But for what she had planned, she'd need efficient footwear.

"A little extreme for a pleasant meal, isn't it?" Levinas mused when he saw her. With a smug smile he sat back and watched her approach.

Aisling ran a hand down her body. "I'm so often outmatched by your witty banter. It couldn't hurt to protect myself from your scathing words."

At her sarcasm the large wolf in the corner growled and though she didn't take her eyes off Levinas, the soft pads of its feet and sharp nails clicked on the marble floor. Not even Breena's battle garb would protect her from the familiar's powerful jaws. She should be more careful about what she said to Levinas, but she never had been good at holding her tongue.

"That's enough, Ardan," Levinas said to his familiar. "And quite enough out of you, too, pet. Have a seat."

Aisling moved for her chair but Levinas tsk'd her and his wolf snarled.

"Not there." He pushed his chair back and Aisling felt the bile rise in her throat. "Humor me for a moment."

Aisling didn't see a way out of this as his familiar nudged

her legs toward the Dark Fae. Crap. She moved to him and sat stiffly on his knee, as far from his body as possible.

"Now that hardly looks comfortable." Levinas pulled her back against him, ignoring the spikes she'd hoped would keep him at bay. "More wine."

Servants hurried to fill his glass and with eyes cast downward they handed one to Aisling, too. She waited for Levinas to drink before she did.

"So cautious, pet."

"I'm not your pet," she muttered between clenched teeth. Aisling thanked Breena's heavy armor-like clothing for creating a barrier between her body and the hand that Levinas had palming her stomach. "What do you want, Levi?"

His hand fisted at the base of her neck and yanked her head back. Levinas's teeth were on her neck, sharp and damn near close to breaking skin. "I've corrected you once about the way you address me. I won't do it again." Using the hand still in her hair he threw her forward and she stumbled to the ground. The wolf huffed in her face and then bared its teeth.

Aisling picked herself up and sat in her chair, determined to not let him rattle her. The fucker got under her skin, though. She fought the full body shiver of revulsion that threatened to overtake her. Instead, she brought a roll to her lips and ripped a chunk out with her teeth.

"So dignified," Levinas said with a sneer. "I see you've been making friends among the staff."

Aisling kept her breathing even, not wanting to betray her worry for her housemaid. The casual shrug of her bare shoulder hopefully portrayed nonchalance. "It's boring sitting alone in my room. I'm not fool enough to believe anyone can be swayed from their allegiance to you."

"And yet you convinced them to enter the palace and steal my sister's clothes?" The way Levinas leaned back in his chair, long blonde hair draped over his shoulders, and his eyes intent upon her was unnerving. If you didn't know what a deplorable person he was, he could be considered attractive. Instead, his gaze on her body made her skin crawl.

"You told them to see to my needs. I wasn't happy with the wardrobe I was provided. I asked for a new one." Aisling cut into her meat and placed it in her mouth, chewing while Levinas watched.

"You are pushing boundaries. Do I need to restrict you more? Of all the things I believe of you, ignorance isn't one of them." He reached over and put a hand on the head of his familiar.

"What is it you think of me?" Aisling asked as she continued to eat.

Levinas's chiseled jaw clenched as his lips thinned. He took a steadying breath before he answered, "You're beautiful but you need to be broken in. You're too stubborn and you believe yourself to be above your station. Nothing good comes of women who try to climb to heights they haven't earned."

Aisling ripped through more bread to keep herself from saying something she'd regret. After swallowing she said, "Your own court found me adequate enough to wed."

"To a bastard," he barked out his response. "That's what you were worthy of, a useless waste of royal blood. He shouldn't even be able to claim royalty as tainted as it is."

Aisling's blood heated at the way he spoke about Brynach. "And yet here I am. So unworthy, and yet you covet me."

She saw the guard go back up and Levinas shook his head. "I like a challenge. Like I said, you'll be fun to break."

The food threatened to exit as her stomach churned. "Better men have tried and failed, Levinas."

"Who, Brynach? He's hardly a better man," he laughed, not taking the bait. He picked up his knife and cut into his meat.

"And yet here you sit, dining at the head of his father's table," Aisling accused.

Levinas's laughter ended abruptly, "Aren't you smart?"

"You always underestimate me, Levi. You'll never be half the man your brother is, no matter what bloodline you claim. You're a joke."

Levinas pushed back his chair and rounded on her. His hands connected with the dowels at the top of her high-backed chair and spun it toward him. He stepped into her, rocking the chair back on two legs. His face was in hers, close enough that his breath stirred the baby hairs over her ears.

She bit her bottom lip but couldn't hide the smile on her lips.

"Something funny?" Levinas spat in her face. "Will you respect me enough to use my given name if I put you in your place? Is that what you need, Aisling?"

She hadn't realized the knife was still in his hands until it was at the strap over her breast. He worked it under the leather belt and tugged with the flat of the blade.

"Will this make you respect your betters?" He asked, his lips on the side of her exposed neck. The knife sawed at the leather but didn't cut through.

"I haven't seen one of my betters since you kidnapped me," Aisling said, and jerked her neck away from his mouth.

Knife be damned, she wanted distance from him. She tried to turn away from him but when she did her arm connected with the wet snout and teeth bared snarl of his familiar. Aisling forced herself to take a deep breath, to ignore the cold blade at her chest, and the angry Fae in front of her.

She met his eyes. "Does it drive you mad he got something you want when he's not even a full-blooded heir to the throne?"

The legs of the chair lowered to the ground. Their thump on the marbled floor coincided with the crack of his hand across her cheek. The backhand surprised her, knocking her head sideways.

"You'd shut up if you knew what was good for you." Levinas's hand gripped her tender face and forced her to look into his eyes. "You think you're so clever showing up in that bitch's clothes. As if that's what keeps me from your room at night. If I had wanted you, you'd already be mine. You think they didn't offer you to me first?"

The shock must have registered on her face because Levinas smiled, thrilled to know something she didn't. "Brynach was the only one who would have you, and even he had to be coerced into accepting you."

It was a lie. Brynach had told her he'd chosen her. Aisling trusted him. Levinas was trying to get under her skin. She wasn't going to let it happen.

Aisling raised her hand and pushed his arm away. "Get your hands off me," she said in a voice deep but quiet. When Levinas laughed and sat back in his chair Aisling took a sip of wine and licked her lips. She tasted blood. He'd pay for that.

"Whatever you think is going to come of this, you're wrong." She looked him in the eyes.

"Indulge me, pet." He rested his chin on his steepled fingers. "What will happen?"

"There are consequences for actions like this, Levinas. I hope you're ready for them because I am."

CHAPTER 17

Brynach

"What the fuck?" Riordan gasped, grabbing Brynach's legs for stabilization.

"You gave us a good idea. We need to check somewhere before we head to camp. Keep your eyes open for magic," Brynach called over the roaring wind. His familiar was racing, his heart pounding as his legs pumped under them.

It was exhilarating, riding the back of an animal let loose. If the cursing from in front of him was any indicator, Riordan felt differently.

"I'm never going to be able to have kids. My nuts are going to be so bruised I'll be sitting on ice for weeks. Goddess," he cried.

Brynach put an arm around the man and called out instructions, "Turn around."

"Excuse me!" Riordan exclaimed turning his wide brown eyes on Brynach.

"Turn around and face me. You can sit on my legs and your manhood won't hurt as much. He's not going to slow down," Brynach explained.

In front of him Riordan shook his head and cursed, "This is ridiculous. You want me to ride your fucking lap?"

Brynach shrugged behind the Ravdi. "It's not about what I

want. It's about whether or not you want a working member when we rescue Aisling."

"Damn it," Riordan cursed, again.

Brynach kept the smile off his face, but just barely.

"I swear, if I fall off this fucking horse!"

"You would never. Kongur wouldn't allow that, and neither would I," Brynach assured him.

He felt the Ravdi take a deep breath and then try to turn. His entire torso was twisted, but he refused to lift his leg over the large horse's back. "I will absolutely fall off," he announced.

Brynach put his arm around the other man's waist. "No, you won't."

Riordan shook his head and then swung his leg over and climbed into Brynach's lap. His thighs rested against his own, his legs wrapped around his back for balance. The Ravdi was keeping as much distance between them as possible, but to be securely seated he was going to have to belly up to Brynach. Riordan closed one eye, analyzing him.

"Did you plan this?"

Brynach gasped, "I would never. This was your choice, Riordan. You can try to go back to riding the other way, but I'm not slowing Kongur."

"Fine, but I swear to all that is holy, we never speak of this!" Riordan's cheeks flamed.

Brynach held him tight and kept his eyes over Riordan's shoulder. "Wouldn't dream of it." Brynach tried to school his face as Riordan slipped his hands around his back and clung to him. He only hoped that the Ravdi couldn't feel or hear his heart pounding over the thundering of his familiar's hooves.

"It's impossible for me to look for anything facing your fucking wall of a chest," he complained with no real heat to his words.

"That's okay. We're close." Brynach was upset that this would be over so soon. He couldn't pretend it was Aisling in his arms. Riordan's muscled back against his forearms was different from her lushness. The tight thighs that gripped him would never be mistaken for his fiancée's, but they were thrilling all the same. The Ravdi was new to physical touch from men, but Brynach wasn't. Aisling would always be enough for him, but that didn't mean he didn't desire Riordan.

Thanks to his familiar's speed they were already nearing the waterfall. It was rarely visited by Fae, Unseelie or otherwise, because of the concentration of neapan. The water sprites often left the water to drag victims into their dens and hence most avoided the area. It was exactly the kind of nefarious shit hole where his brother would set up camp. He'd want the extra protection of the dangerous sprites to keep people away.

When the horse came to a stop, panting and shaking with exertion, Brynach thanked him and then lifted a weary Riordan from his lap and set him on the ground.

"Never again!" the Ravdi said bending down and stretching his legs. "That was fucking nuts."

Brynach swung down and walked away from Riordan. He took in the massive waterfall, the dense brush around the water's edge hiding murderous sprites, and the mist swirling off the water. He didn't want to stay here any longer than necessary.

"Do you see anything?" Brynach asked, his eyes scanning for threats. "Riordan?"

He turned and saw the Ravdi's eyes locked on the top of the waterfall. His head whipped toward Brynach.

"I see something up there. Something big and powerful."

They had the army of soldiers sifting to them almost immediately. They'd climbed to the top of the waterfall, away from the neapan, where Riordan had pinpointed the concentration of magic. Brynach marshaled the forces as

Riordan tested out the magic with a few of the Ravdi who had come this side of the Veil. Their heads were bent together in intense conversation. Riordan had already given him a run-down of what they'd found.

Whatever was keeping Aisling in wasn't just hiding her, it was draining her. The closer to the border Riordan got, the more magic was pulled from him. If he was right, Aisling was trapped on the other side and weakened every time she tried to escape. They'd sent Fae back across the Veil for Ravdi and witch pairs who could help them break through. More solo witches came to work with the Ravdi already there searching Faerie. They had about twenty pairs gathered.

Spurred on by the very real possibility of finding Aisling, Brynach worked with Brielle to organize the rescue once the spell was breached. They had no idea what was on the other side of the ward but whatever it was, they'd be ready.

"How many do we have?" he asked the winged assassin.

"A little over one hundred. Not as many as we hoped for but one of me is worth twenty of your trained guard," Brielle bragged.

"Levinas won't have an army waiting. He's too cocky to consider needing one. We won't be met by opposition," Brynach theorized.

He looked to where Riordan was briefing the witches and Ravdi. Brynach was impressed at the way the Ravdi was conducting himself. He knew what Riordan was capable of, but he was proud of him none the less.

Riordan was listening to their advice and taking their opinions to heart. Together with the other witches and Ravdi they had come up with a plan that they thought could help rescue Aisling. Magic this side of the Veil worked a little differently. They couldn't utelize bonded pairs the same way they could in the other realm. But they could make something work. There were no promises, but Riordan's pushed back shoulders and take-no-bullshit tone meant he'd die trying.

Brynach wouldn't let that happen.

Brynach wasn't just proud of him, but proud to have Riordan's name linked to his own. Their relationship was hazy. They were stuck somewhere between friends and lovers but felt very much like partners. It was a situation Brynach hesitated to define, not because he couldn't, but because defining it wasn't only up to him.

Right now, seeing Riordan with the sun of Faerie on his hair and the scent of cedar and citrus that was uniquely his carried on the winds of his home, felt right. He was lost in thought when a hand landed on his arm, and he met eyes so like Aisling's, he nearly cried out and grabbed the woman.

"Mrs. Quinn?"

She followed Brynach's previous gaze to Riordan and turned back to him with a smile. "I heard you were looking for witches. No way I going to miss being here when you found my daughter," her voice had the same stubborn ring Aisling used far too many times.

Brynach nodded. "We're happy to have you. Riordan can fill you in on the role of witches and Ravdi. He knows more than I do."

Mrs. Quinn had a hand on his arm. "How are you?"

"I'll be better when I have Aisling in my arms."

She paled as she eyed the waterfall. "I've never seen magic like this before. Riordan explained how the ward drains him. The effect is different on me than him. If I get close it takes my store of magic and replenishes the spell with it. It strengthens the wards."

"That's brilliant but terrifying," Brynach commented. Only a truly twisted mind would come up with something like that.

"Which means that if the Ravdi are going to siphon magic from the spell to us to create a gap large enough for you to get through, the witches can't be too close to it. It's going to complicate things," Mrs. Quinn explained.

"Siphon?" Brynach asked.

"Stay with us, oh Dark One," she joked. "It's the best way to weaken the defenses. He'll pull from the ward and direct the magic to us. Then we'll release it back into Faerie. But, we need to be far enough away that the spell can't feed off us. That's not an easy task, not for magic this strong."

"How long will we have to get through?"

"Not long," she admitted before returning to the crowd of witches.

Brielle was at his side as soon as he was alone. "Brynach, a quick reminder. We're going in, getting Aisling, and leaving. I don't need you going on a revenge bender. Your girl needs you. Even if Levinas is inside, you ignore him. Got it?"

He ran his hands through his hair, pulling it back into a quick bun. "Fine, but if he comes at me, I'm going to lay him out."

"Obviously," Breena commented.

Riordan joined their small group. "We're good to go if you are."

Brielle nodded. "We're ready."

She turned and lined the reserve troops next to the witches, who waited further away from the spell. Brynach didn't understand shit about the kind of magic that Riordan and Aisling could touch. Magic was like breathing for him. It was always waiting for him to use when he needed it, no calling it, no containing it. He was trusting Riordan to guide them right now.

Brynach grabbed Riordan's wrist. He waited until they were alone before he spoke.

"When I go through the spell, I will go straight for Aisling. No matter what happens, I'm bringing her back for you," he swore.

"No, you're not. You're bringing her back for us. Go get her, Bry." Riordan turned to leave, but Brynach hadn't released him yet. "Was there something else?"

"Please be careful. I want Aisling back, but I need you safe, too." Brynach was very aware of Riordan's pulse under his fingers and the way the other man held his breath. He sent out a silent prayer to the universe that he hadn't pushed too far.

Riordan opened his mouth and closed it again saying nothing. He gave a quick nod and walked away. Before he'd gone far, he turned back to Brynach. "Both of you come back, okay?" He didn't wait for a response.

Brynach joined the first wave of Fae behind the Ravdi. Liam moved closer to Riordan, his hand on his brother's shoulder for a moment, before dropping. Brielle joined him with a nod. Breena danced beside him, twirling blades in hand with a subdued Ceiren at her side.

"Are you ready?" Riordan called. An affirmative answer came from the witches and Fae behind him.

For the first time in his life, Brynach physically saw magic as it appeared in the air in front of Riordan. Bright gold, dark blue, and rich red strands of the spell dissolved from the larger tapestry of the ward and wove toward Riordan, Liam, and the handful of other Ravdi.

They stood in the swirling riot of magic. As Brynach watched, their backs arched and they cried out before the threads crawled across the space toward the witches. The spell was absorbed by the witches who in turn fed the magic, now filtered to a pure glittering white, into the earth. Trees reached for the sun, flowers blossomed, and leaf litter danced on a magically called wind. They were feeding Faerie with ill intended magic turned clean.

"Are you okay?" Brynach called out to Riordan.

"It's working but the spell repairs itself when we pull this slowly," he cursed. "Ground yourselves and get ready for the influx of magic! Bry, when I tell you to, you need to charge the space directly to my right. Do you understand?"

Brynach answered, "We understand."

"Then let's do this."

Brielle motioned the troops to the side of the Ravdi, ready

to run. The anticipation of battle thrummed through Brynach's veins. His sister had murder in her eyes and Ceiren looked worried. The Dark Fae Prince prepared himself for the charge.

His blood lust was too close to the surface. He wanted justice but Aisling was his sole focus right now. He was so lost in thought that he almost missed the show. Breena's gasp sent his attention back to the man in front of them. Riordan screamed to the other Ravdi and then a serious amount of magic was pulled from the ward and flung over their heads to the witches. A scream rang from them and then Riordan turned to lock eyes with Brynach.

"GO!"

Without hesitation the Fae charged through the gap the Ravdi had created.

Passing through the spell was horrible. It felt like he'd run straight into a wall. Brynach spat blood from his mouth as they crossed, the toxic taste of twisted magic lingered on his tongue. He kept running, making room for the wave of Fae still breaching the gap. Brynach had no time to register what he was seeing in front of him. His brain struggled to take it all in.

A massive castle was isolated on an island in the sky beyond a large stone bridge surrounded by mist and fog. It was beautiful in its darkness. Together with Brielle and his siblings they ran toward the front doors. No battle cry announced their advance.

Maybe he got off on the whole savior thing, but he was looking forward to carrying Aisling away from here. All Brynach wanted was to be a safe space for her. He hadn't stopped her being taken but he'd damn sure be the one to bring her home where she belonged.

"We're getting close, Brynach. Any plan for the door?" Breena asked.

Brielle answered, "We have a battering ram if necessary."

Brynach grunted as he ran and then a wild cry from Brielle stopped everyone in their tracks.

"HALT!"

Immediately, the soldiers stopped. Silence fell without their thundering footsteps. Brynach, Breena, and Ceiren continued to run but even their steps eventually faltered. Brynach made it an extra step or two before he stopped and laughed loudly.

The large doors had opened and to everyone's surprise, and Brynach's amusement, Aisling was striding toward them. Alone, she walked down the cobblestone bridge, unhurried. His heart swelled with pride. His girl didn't need saving but he was damn glad to be here none the less.

"We still move forward!" Brielle called and the rest of the troops rushed up the walkway toward the castle where she'd handle whatever was inside.

Brynach had eyes only for Aisling. He moved toward her, and she ran to him smiling her welcome as he swung her up into his arms.

CHAPTER 18

Aisling

S he let the rage, the anger, and the fear of the past days flood her. Aisling pulled on the longing for Brynach, and Riordan to fuel her. Her magic may be lessened within the ward, but she was far enough away from the physical border that it wasn't actively draining what she did have. If Aisling had learned one thing, it was that her magic was its strongest when her emotions were high.

Aisling was done letting this man put his hands on her. She had no more patience for his games. Whatever she had to learn from him, she had. Enough was enough. She called the magic to her, the magic of Faerie, wild and unruly. She took from the raw power of the waterfall and the frightened magic of those who resided in this prison. Aisling pulled from within herself and around her, taking all that she could. It wasn't much and it wasn't easy.

It hurt. It didn't come freely. The wards made gathering magic feel like her skin was being stripped from her body. Aisling had been using magic for as long as she could re-member, but in this space, it felt like a punishment. Of course, Gabriel would make utilizing magic a form of torture within his halls. It didn't matter. She'd known the magic would fight her, but she'd fight harder. She wouldn't have the strength to do this again. This was her shot.

"Aisling, what the hell are you doing?" Levinas didn't sound so sure of himself now.

The doors to the dining hall slammed open and a wind blew into the room startling Levinas. A low growl sounded from his familiar and Aisling turned to lock eyes with the Dark Fae, a smile on her lips. She'd have a welt on her face. Aisling could feel the split in her lip pull as she grinned, felt the warmth of blood as it trickled down her chin when she did. Aisling wished she could see herself through his eyes. Whatever he thought he was getting when he kidnapped her, he'd been so damn wrong.

"What's happening?" His eyes shot to his familiar who was standing next to him, tail between its legs.

"I'm happening, Levi." Aisling toppled her chair and moved toward him. It was a testament to how unprepared they were for her anger that his familiar backed away from her. With access to her captor, she leaned in. "You made a mistake taking me. A bigger one when you laid hands on me. And a deadly one when you thought you could control me."

She smirked when she saw her blood speckling his white shirt. Then she delivered the final blow. She turned her back on him, finalizing that she didn't see him as a threat. Aisling still wasn't sure if it would work, but with anger fueling her, she might be able to wiggle through the ward. She wasn't going back to her room willingly.

"Where do you think you're going?" Levinas yelled after her.

Aisling didn't bother to answer him. She pushed open the doors to the hallway and was met by Gemma's panicked eyes.

"Miss?"

"You should get out of here. Now. Get the others and get out a back door. Hide. It's going to get ugly," Aisling warned her.

"Don't do this. Please!" She tried grabbing for Aisling. "The wards won't let you out. If you get hurt, Brynach will never forgive me."

Aisling smiled at her despite her strange wording. "I understand the wards, Gemma, but it's never dealt with someone like me. Stay safe and thank you."

The exchange was fast but not fast enough. Aisling didn't have time to spare. Levinas would no doubt be running after her momentarily. She had to move, and she needed to do it while her emotions were rioting. Aisling had to cling to that rage to fuel her magic. Levinas caught up to her quickly and grabbed her. Before he could register the movement, her fist connected with his chin, snapping his head back. Her magic sung on her skin, shocking him.

"You will never touch me again," Aisling spat, ignoring his now angered familiar's returning growl.

She ran for the front doors, but before she reached them, she felt a searing pain in her leg. With a scream she saw a wolf's muzzle clamped down on her calf. Fuck, that hurt. Levinas lurked behind his familiar.

Aisling kicked out with her booted foot, landing a solid blow to the animal's shoulder. Its dark eyes met hers and a growl rumbled through its body. Her vision swam and her ears rang. She managed another kick but the vise like grip on her leg didn't loosen. She scrambled back on her hands, pushing against the animal's bite. But she could feel her flesh ripping. She couldn't break free and the injustice of being so close but so far away was intense.

"Stop this silliness and I'll call them off," Levinas said from above her. "You're only hurting yourself." He sounded bored. She wished she felt the same. Instead, she fought a scream at the red hot pain.

Aisling refused to answer him. She kept fighting. With a stretch of her body, she reached the handle and thrust the door outward. Aisling sucked in a deep breath as the sun hit her face. It may not be much, but she was one step closer to getting out. Now she needed to get Levinas's wolf off her leg.

The Fae Prince sucked in a breath. He was staring over her, his eyes wide. Then he was gone and his familiar chomped once more before following after him.

She didn't know where they'd gone or why. She didn't care. She used the adrenaline to force herself to move. Aisling tapped into her anger, keeping it blazing, so that she could push herself to her feet. She was getting out of here.

Aisling turned and began to walk toward the bridge and paused as her brain caught up to what her eyes were seeing. The noise, the movement, and the sheer beauty of what was in front of her floored her. She nearly fell to her knees with relief. A rushing army of Fae charged toward her. Brynach and Breena's dark hair leading the pack alongside a tiny Brielle proved they were friendly Fae. Or, at least, friendly toward her. Levinas better hope he got far from the castle real fast.

Aisling locked eyes with Brynach and saw his face light in a smile. He staggered toward her and then her legs were pumping, moving her to him as Brielle and the rest of the Fae ran past her. She ignored the pain in her leg and the soreness in her cheek as she grinned.

"Good to see you, kiddo," Brielle called out as she charged past with Ceiren and a group of warriors.

Aisling didn't pause long enough to answer her. She didn't stop at all until she was in Brynach's arms. She leapt into them, wrapping herself around his large frame.

"I was coming to rescue you." His breath was hot on her neck.

"Of course, you were." She smiled against his cheek.

Aisling had a moment to prepare herself before his lips came crashing down on hers. His fingers left her face and cupped the back of her head. Before Aisling could lose herself in it, the kiss was over.

Brynach pulled back and scanned her. She saw the moment he noticed the marks on her face. His entire body stiffened.

"You're hurt."

"I'm fine," she assured him.

With a curse he dipped his mouth back to hers as he kissed her again. This time Aisling was ready. She fought for dominance, nipping, and tasting. A part of Aisling's mind was aware they were being watched but as his tongue swept hers, she couldn't find a good enough reason to stop him. Her lips tingled from the raw passion leaking off her fiancé.

A cough sounded at their side and Brynach growled, "Fuck off, Breena."

"Brother, there are other things you should be doing right now. You promised Riordan you'd keep your head and bring Aisling home. He can't hold the ward open forever."

That sobered Aisling, immediately. "Hold the ward open? Riordan is doing that?" She looked toward the gap in the spell. "Take me to him," she demanded and did her best to ignore the hurt that flashed in Brynach's eyes.

"Let's go," Brynach said, putting her down so they could walk to the ward.

Aisling ignored the burning in her calf, and the blood running down her leg. It would heal once she was outside of the spell.

Breena fell into step beside them. "You're bleeding."

Brynach turned on her. He saw her leg, and the blood at his hip. "Damn it, Aisling. Why didn't you say something?" He lifted her into his arms and moved for the gap in the ward.

"Brynach, put me down. I can walk," Aisling protested.

Breena cocked her head, finally noticing. "Why are you wearing my fucking clothes?"

"Trust me, I needed them. They kept him out of my bed even if it didn't stop him from smacking me around," Aisling admitted.

Brynach cursed and his hand on her back clenched into a fist.

"Hey, I took care of myself. I knew you'd find me and until

then I made the best of it. I'm okay, Bry," she promised.

"He's still dead when I get my hands on him." Brynach stepped up to the ward like it was nothing. Being this close to it made Aisling want to vomit.

"I'm not sure I can get through," she admitted as the force of the spell got stronger.

"I've got you." Brynach kissed her. Aisling buried her face in his chest and tried to breathe through the pain as he stepped through.

The passing left her feeling weak. The spell tried to fortify itself with her magic and left her dizzy. She barely had time to register the relief of being through before the comforting scent of amber and sea air surrounded her. Riordan's arms wrapped around her, and he pulled her from Brynach. Aisling went to him happily. His lips found her face and covered it in kisses while he clung to her. Her hands were busy in his hair, along his face and shoulders. Their reunion was short-lived as her mother ran screaming toward them despite the wall of magic that weakened her as she neared.

"Mom!" Aisling called, and together the two stumbled away from the spell and fell to the ground, hugging one another while crying.

"You're back. You're here. Oh, my baby! I was so scared."

Aisling was so wrapped up in her mother's arms that she didn't notice when her father sifted in and approached the two.

"Aisling!"

Watching the Regent for the Seelie Court fall to the ground with them must have been a sight for the others. She met Riordan's red eyes. He looked awful. He was still the most beautiful thing she'd seen in weeks.

He mouthed "I love you" to her, and she returned the words. Then he joined the other Ravdi, maintaining the gap in the spell.

"I have to go help them," Aisling said, trying to stand from her parent's hold.

"Like hell you will," her mother said with venom in her voice.

"I'm glad you're back safely, Aisling. You can move into the castle. We will protect you," Nevan offered.

"No, she will not. She's going to the other side of the Veil as soon as we finish up here," her mother demanded.

"She'll be safe, Regent. I'll be there, as will her Ravdi," Brynach answered, appearing at their side.

"You were both with her when she was kidnapped, if I'm not mistaken," her father accused with heat.

"It was hardly their fault. They couldn't have stopped it. Besides, I'm right here, and I say I'm going home," Aisling said, finally disengaging from the pile of limbs and standing up.

"You know, we were all pretty worried about you. You could afford to be gentler with them," Phlyren scolded. *"It's good to have you back, Aisling."*

Her familiar swooped down onto her shoulder, and she nuzzled her cheek against his soft head. *"I missed you. Stay with me?"*

"Always," Phlyren responded, carefully gripping the leather strap of her shirt with his talons.

Aisling's mother moved to her side. "Please, Aisling. Come home for the night. I need to know you're close."

She felt bad, but it wasn't her mother she needed to be with right now. And from the way the men in her life looked at her, they'd fall apart if she left them. She knew where she wanted to be. "I love you, but I'm going to my place. Besides, you'll have Patrick."

Something flashed across her mother's face that Aisling couldn't place. But her mother nodded and kissed her cheek before turning away. Nevan followed after her, taking her by the elbow and leaning to talk in her ear. Aisling was used to her mother brushing Nevan off but instead she leaned into the Fae. Interesting.

Aisling reached for Brynach, and he led her right where

she needed to be, to Riordan's side. When they reached him she carefully took his hand. He released magic into her, and she stored it, happy to have it back again.

"It's time to go home. The rest of them will figure this out," Aisling's words were soft, but the result was immediate. He disengaged and together they left.

"One quick stop," Brynach said, pulling them toward the tents set up further away from the action. Breena was standing outside one of them.

"I'll make sure nobody bothers you," she said with a wink. Phlyren detached from her shoulder and took to the air above the tent, keeping watch as well.

As soon as they were alone her amazingly strong men broke. Riordan took a shaky breath and then fell into a chair. Brynach, the strongest man she'd ever known, fell to his knees.

Aisling wasn't sure who to go to first, but the lost look in Brynach's eyes made her choice for her. She knelt in front of her sweet Fae. She took his face in her hands and kissed him softly.

"It's okay. I'm okay," she promised him quietly. With a speed that stunned her his body hit hers, knocking the air from her lungs. "Shhh, it's okay." She stroked his hair as he held her.

"You're really here?" he asked as his hands wandered her body.

"I'm right here," she confirmed in his ear.

"How?" Riordan asked from their side.

"You doubted my ability to outsmart an idiot? I'm hurt," she joked and tried to turn her head to Riordan. Brynach's arm shot out and then Riordan was squeezed as tightly to Brynach's massive chest as she was.

"Our girl is back," he crowed loudly. "You absolute marvel."

"She's also covered in spikes, which are digging into me

right now, big guy," Riordan groaned and pushed away. He didn't go far, though. Aisling leaned over and kissed him. Oddly, kissing him while being held by Brynach didn't feel strange at all.

"You look like Breena. I hate it." Riordan screwed up his face.

"I heard that," the Dark Fae Princess called from outside the tent.

"I'm going to kill that son of a bitch," Brynach snarled, his fists tight against her back.

"Hey, Ash is back. The rest can wait." Riordan soothed her fiancé.

Brynach stood and kissed Aisling. Riordan turned her and did the same. The world was still spinning when Brynach turned to Riordan and placed a kiss on his lips. She gasped and watched Riordan's cheeks color. His hand ran through his hair, and then he met Aisling's eyes, waiting for her reaction.

"How much did I miss?" She looked between the two men.

Together, the three of them laughed.

CHAPTER 19

Riordan

"How'd you get out?" Riordan asked as he pulled her down onto his lap in the chair. He couldn't stand the thought of her out of his arms. Plus, touching her gave a reason for the butterflies in his stomach that didn't include the firm feel of Brynach's lips on his.

Currently, the large Fae was kneeling at Aisling's feet and checking her leg wound. She'd be okay but the amount of blood was alarming. His whole body shook, and his head swam when Brynach removed her boot and blood sloshed out of it.

"Fuck. I really hate blood."

"Are you going to be sick?" Aisling asked.

"No. I can look at all the blood in the world so long as you're okay." His arms tightened around her.

"They're barely scratches," Aisling soothed. She was such a liar.

Brynach assessed her leg. "Who was it, Aisling?"

Riordan understood Brynach's need for confirmation.

Aisling was nervous. "Bry, you have to promise not to leave me. I'm serious. If you sift out of here, I'll never forgive you."

Riordan watched the large man's fists clench. The same

ones that soothed him these past weeks. The same ones that held him atop that hell beast he called a horse.

"A stoirin, don't ask that of me. Please," his voice broke on the last word.

"There will be time for retribution, but right now, I need you." She turned to Riordan. "Both of you."

"Wouldn't dream of leaving you, Ash," he promised. Then they waited until Brynach gave a small nod.

"The servant from the garden sifted me to Levi," Aisling confirmed. "He's not smart enough to be doing this on his own, Bry."

Riordan met Brynach's eyes, but the Fae shook him off. Now wasn't the time to tell her they suspected Brynach's father. If they could protect her right now, they'd do it.

Aisling leaned down and put a hand on Brynach's cheek as he tied a piece of his shirt around her leg. The Fae's teeth were clenched so hard Riordan's jaw hurt looking at him. Mr. Large and in Charge was barely holding on.

Aisling must have sensed it because she tugged his face toward her and buried her hands in his hair, holding him. He watched as Aisling took a deep breath and Brynach mirrored her without hesitation. She repeated the process a few times and then nodded to him.

"Better?" she asked.

"I'm always better when you're touching me, a stoirin." The Dark Fae grinned at his fiancé.

"Then you should wear me like a fucking fanny pack before I unleash this next bit of information," she joked.

Riordan saw the light in the large Fae's eyes before Aisling did. She hadn't uttered the first syllable of his name when he hoisted her in the air. Aisling wrapped her legs around his waist and shook her head.

"I was kidding."

"I wasn't," Brynach said, his voice steely. "Objections?"

He wasn't asking Aisling. His head swiveled to Riordan. "Please, continue."

Aisling rolled her pretty hazel eyes. "Fine. That place your brother was holding me at wasn't his. It was your father's."

She waited for the bomb to drop but both men stayed silent.

"You already knew?" She sounded a little put out. "Okay, fine. Well, did you know that it is also where Peggy hid their love children?"

Again, she was met by silence.

"Fuck! Really?" Aisling threw her hands up. "Do you know everything?"

Brynach shrugged. "Tell us what else you learned."

Aisling huffed, "Levinas was staying at Gabriel's house. It's staffed with terrified people and the halls are lined with stuffed animals. Worse, they're not just animals, they're the dead familiars of Fae that crossed your father. And I found his torture room. Or pleasure dome, I don't fucking know."

"What!" Brynach's voice was darker than Riordan had ever heard it.

"Ha! One thing you didn't know," Aisling cheered, clearly not reading the Fae correctly.

Riordan moved to take her from Brynach's arms before he squeezed her too hard.

"Aisling, that's horrific," Riordan commented. He met Brynach's eyes and held out his arms. He saw the Fae clench Aisling's thighs before nodding and passing her to him. "You're telling me he killed familiars?" Riordan asked when Aisling was safely away from the angry Fae.

"A lot of them," her voice wasn't victorious anymore. "And every time I disobeyed him or talked back, he'd slap me around. A real winner of a guy, that Levinas."

He wished he could sift Aisling away, instead he retreated quickly to the corner of the tent. Brynach moved to the desk Riordan had been sitting at and splintered the chair with his bare hands.

The Dark Fae was panting, chest heaving as he stalked

toward them. He took Aisling's face in his hands and stroked a thumb over her cheek. Even though it was covered in dried blood, the cuts already looked better.

"Fae healing," she murmured. "He wanted me scared and submissive. He doesn't know me very well."

"You're amazing," Riordan said. "I'm so proud of you."

"Me?" Aisling scoffed. "You brought down that ward! It was strong, Riordan. I couldn't get near it without feeling ill."

She pushed out of his arms and Riordan let her go. All he wanted was to hold her but after having her freedom taken away from her, he wouldn't force it. He released her even though not touching her made him ache.

"Can we go home?" Aisling asked. Brynach took her hand. Riordan did the same.

T he bond had snapped to attention as soon as they passed through the Veil. Riordan nearly wept in relief. He hadn't realized how much he'd missed it. He felt the contentment and joy Aisling was experiencing through the bond. They hurried to the condo where, once locked inside, Brynach relaxed.

Now Aisling was on her fiancé's phone talking to Lettie. Hers was being retrieved from the castle in Faerie and would need a charge, no doubt. Seeing her pace through her bedroom was comforting.

His own phone rang, and he picked up his brother's call. "Wanted to let you know I was back this side. Mrs. Quinn came with me."

Riordan breathed a little better, knowing his brother was this side of the Veil. "Thank you, Liam. I'm going to be out of touch for a bit. We need sleep and I want time with Aisling."

"Love you, Rory. Glad she's home," his brother said before hanging up.

Riordan turned to where Aisling was standing by her bed,

clawing at herself. Now, with the bond open, her emotions felt so raw and vibrant. He struggled to get to her fast enough as her pain struck him.

"What is it?" His voice was panicked enough that Brynach came running.

"What's wrong?" her fiancé asked, rushing to her side.

Riordan held up a hand and the large Fae stopped dead in his tracks. Cautiously he stepped up to Aisling but didn't touch her. He wasn't sure she wanted that right now.

"Aisling?"

"I can't be in her clothes anymore. I need..." She was crying so hard she could barely talk. "Get me out of this!"

Riordan turned to Brynach and nodded. Together, the two men undid buckles and straps. When prompted, Aisling lifted her arms and Riordan carefully pulled the top over her head. Without a word, Aisling left the men and turned into the bathroom.

They let her go.

Both men stared at the door their partner had closed, completely powerless to help her. He should have expected the crash. The excitement of her rescue couldn't have lasted long before the trauma and reality of the situation fell on her.

"How do you want to move forward tonight?" Brynach asked.

Riordan ran a hand through his hair. "I know you need to be near her as badly as I do but I don't particularly want to share her. Which is selfish, I know. Aisling gets to decide," Riordan answered turning to look at Brynach.

"No, not just Aisling. You can't deny that the last few weeks have changed things between us. I know what I want, Riordan." His voice was soft, making it feel like he was leaning in toward Riordan even though he hadn't moved. "Do you want me?"

Riordan ran a hand over his face. With Brynach's yellow eyes on him, the memory of his body under him as they rode through Faerie, and the taste of his lips so vivid it was harder to deny his growing feelings.

"You don't have to answer that if you aren't sure. It's something we can talk through. But I assume it's not a hard no?" Brynach spoke with a tentative hand on Riordan's arm, bringing it away from his face so the large Fae could study him.

"Not a hard no," Riordan admitted.

Brynach nodded. "In that case, and assuming Aisling is okay with it, we would both be her lovers. We will continue to check in with one another and determine what makes us happy. But we don't need titles and we don't owe anyone clarification."

Riordan played with the rings on the chain at his neck. "Okay. But only if it works for Aisling."

As if his saying her name called her into being the door to the bathroom opened and draped in a towel, she crossed the room. Her eyes were as red as her hair as she smiled weakly at them.

"I really want to hold you right now but I'm not sure if that's okay." Riordan moved toward her but left distance between them. "Do you want me to get you clothes?"

"No." Aisling moved toward her dresser. "I want to pick my own."

"I'm going to make food for us," Brynach said and gave Riordan a nod toward Aisling. "Come on out when you're ready."

Riordan moved to the bed and sat, waiting for Aisling until she'd chosen her outfit. If he guessed correctly, it had been too long since she'd been able to choose what she wore. Anger surged in him, again. He couldn't wait for Levinas to pay for what he'd done.

Aisling crawled up onto the bed, snuggling into the pile of pillows against her headboard.

"Come hold me a bit," she asked, and Riordan gathered

her in his arms.

It was the most natural and welcome distraction from the emotions roiling inside him. He could feel through the bond that she was struggling.

"Riordan?"

"Mmm." He pulled her in tighter.

"Things are going to be complicated. It's going to be messy and violent and all kinds of crazy. And my mind is racing imagining all the repercussions." He hated how unsure she sounded. Fuck that man for causing this.

"How can I help?" He wanted to ease her anxiety.

"I'm not sure you can. I want to keep you safe and I'm afraid I won't be able to." She raised her face to his. "I understand how Lettie feels now. At least a bit. Being helpless doesn't suit either of us."

"You're not helpless. Neither is Lettie. You're the strongest women I've met."

"Could you kiss me?" Aisling asked biting her lip.

Riordan lifted his hand, tugging her lip from between her teeth. He'd have given her anything she wanted in that moment. A kiss, that was easy.

When their lips touched, electricity sang through their bond. The little minx had coated herself in magic. Her fingertips left a blaze of heat up his back and into his hair. Goddess, he'd missed her touch, but when her tongue flicked out to lick his lip, he nearly lost it. His hands clenched at her hips, and she angled her head so he had access to her mouth. He saw she needed to be in control right now, but he was struggling to not take over.

He could feel her frustration through the bond alongside her passion. He moved his hands to her side as he brought down the intensity of the kiss.

"Shhh, it's okay. Neither of us are going anywhere. We don't need to rush." He pulled back because getting lost in her touch wasn't what either of them really wanted.

She rested her head over his thudding heart and together they listened to Brynach in the kitchen cooking. The smell of food was filling the condo, but Aisling didn't rush to leave his embrace. Instead, they laid together. This was home. He was home. As long as they were all safe, whatever came next would be manageable.

CHAPTER 20

Brynach

B rynach woke in a tangle of limbs to the soft snores of Aisling and the cedar smell of Riordan. In other words, he woke happy. Or rather, as happy as he could be with the two people he cared for when he really wanted to be in Faerie ripping his brother limb from limb.

He slid out of the bed carefully and placed a call to Liam. As soon as Aisling woke, she was going to ask to be filled in on what she'd missed. He needed to be sure of a few things before then.

"Brynach," Liam said when he answered. "Didn't think I'd be hearing from you so soon."

"What happened after we left?"

There was a slurp of what Brynach assumed was coffee before Liam answered, "Sorry, haven't had much sleep. Um, the castle was empty. Your brother must have sifted out when we breached the spell. They did find a few of the staff and they're being held for questioning."

"Did you find a housemaid named Gemma?" Brynach interrupted. Now wasn't the time to tell Aisling that the woman who had helped her had been his saving grace as a child. Looked like Gabriel had used the same nursemaid for all his children. If anyone could have protected Aisling, it was Gemma.

"Not that I recall, but I can inquire."

"Please do." Brynach asked his next question carefully, "What else did they find?"

Liam paused a moment. "The spell was held open long enough for Brielle to get her Fae back through. Whatever happens, we aren't going back any time soon. You'll have to discuss with her what she saw. I was busy with aftercare for the other Ravdi."

"Aftercare?" His stomach dropped.

"Brynach, please tell me you took care of my brother! After something like that he's going to feel horrible. We aren't meant to function that way," Liam sounded horrified.

"I, I didn't know." Brynach turned toward the bedroom where Riordan still slept with Aisling. He should have, though. He should have checked in with Riordan after seeing him work that hard. Hadn't he heard the man cry out as he siphoned the magic from the ward? And yet, he'd stormed past to Aisling and then back out without checking on him again. Shame and guilt gnawed at him.

"Where is he?" Liam asked, his voice terse.

"Asleep."

"Get him a drink and aspirin. Feed him and for the love of all things sacred, force him to rest today," Liam demanded.

"I will. I promise." Brynach was already searching through the cabinet where Aisling kept medicine. "What else do I need to know?"

"Um. Well, things aren't going too well in your court. Your sister kind of stormed in and accusations were thrown around," Liam was hedging.

He'd meant about Riordan's aftercare, but those words sent a chill through his blood. Brynach stopped what he was doing and braced a hand on the counter. "Is she okay?"

"She used careful wording but from what Ceiren tells me, it was a bit dicey. It would probably be best for you to check in at home soon."

"I will. Thank you," Brynach said, shaking two aspirin from the bottle.

"That's not all," Liam continued. "While we were away, we had a breakthrough on Peggy's daughter, Sydney. She turned herself in. It seems she isn't a fan of what Mommy Dearest has been up to and wants to testify in the trial. I don't have her full story yet but as soon as I do, I'll update you."

"Thank you. And Liam, well done." Brynach gave the man the praise he deserved.

"Take care of my brother, you idiot," Liam said without heat and hung up.

Brynach let his head hang, eyes closed. His sister knew better than to run her mouth at court. What was she thinking? If anything had happened to her... No, he wouldn't let himself go down that path.

"I thought you'd left." Aisling surprised him.

He turned and pulled her into his embrace. "Why are you awake?"

"Bad dream," she admitted. "I didn't want to wake Riordan."

He bent and put an arm under her legs, scooping her off her feet and carrying her across the room. Brynach sat, extending his legs down the length of the still too short full-sized sofa. He laid her on his chest and practically purred when she snuggled into him. With one hand, he pulled the blanket off the back and over them while the other held her tight.

"How is your leg?"

Aisling shrugged. "It's sore, but the worst of it is healed. I'm relieved that mutt didn't snap it."

Brynach felt the growl start in his chest and quelled the anger before he frightened Aisling. "He'll pay for putting his hands on you. In case I didn't say it enough yesterday, I'm so proud of you."

She didn't answer him. He didn't expect her to.

"You kissed Riordan." Aisling's voice was sleepy. He loved it. Brynach could feel her smile against his chest. Her cheeks rounding against him as she grinned.

"I did, didn't I?" he said in wonder. "Even I didn't see that one coming."

"I bet you saw it coming long before Riordan did," she joked.

"What about you?" He was curious what Aisling thought about his feelings for her Ravdi.

"Oh, I saw that coming before either of you. The sexual tension was palpable." His fingers combed through her hair. "Anyway, I think it's sweet."

"Two grown men, very attractive and well-built men, may I add. Whose kiss is sweet?" He poked her side.

"It's hot as fuck, but I get to say that because you're both mine. Anyone else says it and they're gonna have a fight on their hands," she laughed and squirmed away from his tickling. "Are you okay?" Aisling kissed his throat, and he tightened his hold on her.

"My sibling kidnapped you and then held you prisoner in my father's house. My other siblings spread a curse that nearly killed your best friend. Literally everyone involved in this whole fucked-up situation is related to me." He kissed her head. "I'm so sorry."

"You aren't your family, Bry. You never have been. None of this is your fault."

"I have to go back," he broke the news. "I know you want me here, but Breena ran her mouth at court. I don't know if she confronted our father or Levinas, but I have to make sure she's okay." He couldn't stop himself from touching her. His hands ran the length of her back, her arms, her hair.

"I won't ask you not to go, but I wish you wouldn't."

"I'd love nothing more than to stay by your side, a stoirin, but I can't protect you properly if I'm distracted. I'll call in a backup until I return. It won't be long."

"It's not my safety I'm worried about, Bry. I need you with me. Hurry back to us." Her breathing evened.

Brynach's heart jumped at her choosing him, wanting him. He didn't miss her inclusion of Riordan. He held no misconceptions of his family, not before all the recent events and not now. He had never expected loyalty or love from them. Finding it in Aisling and Riordan was a blessing, but one he didn't feel worthy of. Not when his bloodlust was so close to the surface.

Even now, holding her on the sofa, he wanted to be in Faerie hunting for Levinas. He dreamt of his brother on his knees before him begging for mercy and then denying him. The feel of his bones crushing under Brynach's fist, his hot blood coating his knuckles, would bring him joy. How could a monster capable of that also be worthy of someone like Aisling?

"He's awake," Aisling said, raising her head from his chest. "Something's wrong."

Brynach was on his feet, setting Aisling on her own, fast. Damn it! He'd let himself get so wrapped up in his self-pity and Aisling's warmth that he'd forgotten Riordan.

"He needs pain meds. I'll get them. You go run him a shower," Brynach said, and sent her off with a pat on the ass.

He rushed to fill a glass. By the time he reached the bedroom Aisling was already in the bathroom with the water running. Brynach moved to Riordan's side.

"Take these." He held out two pills, which Riordan took and placed in his mouth without question.

"How'd you know?" he asked after he accepted the water and swallowed the pills.

"Your brother schooled me on aftercare and Aisling sensed you. I'm sorry I didn't check in with you yesterday. I didn't know and Aisling, well she was distracted."

"I'm not angry at either of you. I should have taken better care of myself. It would be worse without the food you made,"

Riordan said and placed a hand on Brynach's shoulder. "Thank you."

Brynach still wasn't used to the casual touches from the other man, but he accepted them for what they were. Inclusion. Affection.

"Aisling has the shower ready for you. It'll help," Brynach said nodding toward the bathroom.

As soon as the man left the room Brynach let his head fall to his chest. He needed to get back to Faerie, but he wasn't leaving until he did something he'd been nervous about for far too long. He wouldn't go home until Aisling was safe and he knew one sure way to secure her safety.

"Bry?" Aisling's voice called him back. Looking up he saw her in the doorway to the bathroom.

"Yes?" Even to his own ears his voice was shaky.

"Riordan is going to need clothes and he doesn't have anything here. Can he borrow something of yours?"

"Of course." He walked to the guest room.

While he was there, he reached into the recesses of the top drawer until his fingers connected with a pouch made of soft leather. He pulled it out and stuffed it into the pocket of his jeans before returning to Aisling's room. She was sitting on the bed looking more than a little lost.

"I should have taken better care of him last night." She was beating herself up and he couldn't allow that.

"We both should have. But we're correcting it now."

Brynach knelt on the floor in front of her and she put her arms around his shoulders, drawing his head to her stomach. He rested there, safe between her legs, and gathered in her arms.

"I love you, Aisling. You know that, right?"

She shifted back and moved a hand to his cheek. "Yes."

He nodded to the bathroom. "That idiot loves you, too. And I'm rather fond of him. We want you. You want us. Am I wrong?"

His brave woman refused to drop her eyes as she answered, "No."

"That's okay, a stoirin."

She groaned, "It's selfish. More than that, it's unfair to both of you."

"That's bullshit!" Riordan called through the open doorway.

Brynach shook his head. "He's right. Love doesn't have rules, Aisling. A relationship like ours wouldn't create even the weakest of breezes in the gossip circles of Faerie. Riordan understands his value and place in your life."

Aisling glanced at the bathroom. Brynach pulled her face back to him. "I've talked to him. He knows I'm doing this." He waited for her nod and continued, "I desire you. I admire you. I respect you. I won't treat you unkindly. I will always take your needs into consideration and your opinions to heart. I want to build a life with you."

Aisling bit her lip and he desperately wanted to taste that sweet mouth.

"I want you to choose me, Aisling. Marry me because you want to, not because you have to," Brynach begged. He was unashamed of the need in his voice. He'd never wanted anything more than this.

His heart stuttered in his chest, and he held his breath, waiting for her answer. When her mouth opened, he prayed to the Goddess it was what he wanted to hear.

"A part of me has always wanted you, Brynach. And for as long as I've wanted you, I've believed myself unworthy of you. No, let me finish," she said when he opened his mouth to object. "I know my worth. I am not saying that to put myself down. But when your bonds are either forced or arranged, you question if people want to be with you or have to be."

She ran her hands over his bare shoulders and into his hair. He let his eyes close as her nails scraped over his neck and scalp. When he opened them Riordan was leaning in the doorway.

"I don't know how to do this. How to love and be fair to you both." She looked from one to the other. "But I want to try."

Brynach reached into his pocket and pulled out the leather pouch. Aisling gasped as he removed a thin silver band of woven vines and leaves that cradled a teardrop shaped dark blue topaz. Brynach's heart pounded in his chest, his large hands trembling around the delicate ring.

"Then I'll ask again. Aisling Quinn of the Seelie Court, will you spend your life as my partner? Will you marry me?" He gazed into her hazel eyes and waited.

This time she didn't look to Riordan, did nothing but nod her head and smile as the tears finally broke free of her eyes. Brynach took her hand in his and slid the ring onto her finger before kissing her.

It wasn't a shy kiss. It was a claiming and a promise. Brynach kissed her like a man deprived of air who finally broke the surface of the water, because that's how he felt. When he pulled away and rested his forehead on hers it was to whisper his thanks.

"Congratulations," Riordan offered before hugging Brynach and then Aisling. "What are we doing to celebrate?"

He sighed, "I'm going back to Faerie and the two of you are staying here and resting."

"Bry, no." Aisling shook her head.

"I don't want to leave you, but I have stayed as long as I can. There are matters that require my attention."

Brynach looked to Riordan for help and was relieved when the other man nodded.

"He's right. It's time to let Brynach handle things in Faerie. We can work from home today, but mostly, rest," the Ravdi said rubbing his temples.

"Teaming up against me already. I see how it is," Aisling joked. "I wish you didn't have to go, but I understand. Hurry home to us."

Brynach gave her another kiss, running his thumb over the ring on her hand. "I will." Then to Riordan he said, "Keep her safe. I'll send Jashana over."

As he neared the Veil at the back of her property, he took a moment to compartmentalize. The pride and joy still resonating in his chest at the sight of his ring on Aisling's finger had no place in his court. All of that needed to be washed away before he entered.

The switch inside him sat waiting, as he parted the Veil and sifted to the gates, it had already been flipped. Brynach raised his lips in a snarl and stalked into the castle ready to demand answers. He was making his way directly to the throne room when he was slammed into, bodily, by his sister.

"Brynach, no!" She pushed him through a doorway and into a, thankfully, empty room. "I understand, brother, but don't make the same mistake I did."

His chest rose and fell under her hand. "Fill me in. Fast."

"Levinas is in the wind. He tried showing up and acting like he was innocent. That man can't act for shit. He tried for ignorance, and was outraged when I confronted him. Ceiren acted as my second and spoke against him."

Brynach seethed, "It should have been me. I should have been the one to bring charges against him."

"You had more important things to tend to, Brynach. He threw around some disgusting bullshit about Ceiren not being a reliable second and accused us of having a romantic relationship. Obviously, nobody believes that. Levinas took off. He hasn't been seen since, but I have eyes out for him. He won't show his face here again."

"That's not helpful. We need him here to punish." Brynach paced, his hands in his hair.

"He'll be brought in. Nobody can pass up a royal bounty," Breena paused and broke eye contact.

Brynach quirked his head. "Breena! What is it?"

His sister didn't hem and haw over difficult things and she

certainly didn't spare feelings, even his. If she was avoiding his eyes, it wasn't good.

"Levinas may have thrown accusation our father's way," she admitted.

Brynach laughed, "Probably best he's in hiding, then. What did he say?"

Breena's twin citrine eyes met his. "He was smart. He didn't bring charges, but he said nobody would believe he could use Gabriel's homestead without the Bloody Hand's permission."

"Mother's reaction?" Brynach asked as he made his way to the door.

"Obviously, siding with our sperm donor." Breena joined him in the hallway. "Levinas has never been her favorite."

"She has a favorite?" Brynach barked a laugh. "Since when has she cared for any of us?"

Breena shrugged. "She was at least fond of Rainer before Britt."

Brynach straightened his back, rolled his shoulders, and fixed his expression before pushing his way into the throne room.

"Here is my wayward son," the Queen called. "It's about time you showed your face. All this mudslinging and you're hiding on the other side of the Veil, returning after your dirty work is handled."

Brynach bit the side of this cheek until coppery blood slid down his throat. "Mother, it's a pleasure to see you, as always."

She dismissed him with a wave of her hand. He looked past Moura's shoulder to his father. Gabriel scanned Brynach and then turned away. He cursed himself for not changing before coming, but jeans and boots are what they were getting.

He approached the dais. "Mother, this won't end well. Levinas must be brought to justice. It's my right as her betrothed. The wedding is approaching. Nothing has changed. Levinas knew exactly what he was doing."

Queen Moura sighed, "She's back, isn't she? And she was unharmed, yes? I fail to see why everyone is so up in arms about this child. Levinas behaved rashly, but he didn't hurt her."

"He kidnapped her, held her hostage, and struck her. By Fae law retribution is mine to exact," Brynach's voice didn't waver.

"It is," his mother proclaimed. "However, if the court were to look too deeply into your brother's activities, they may uncover other unsavory events. I cannot allow that."

At this, Brynach bristled. He kept his voice low when he continued, "Are you calling your Bloody Hand being complicit in Aisling's kidnapping an unsavory event? Or perhaps it's the fact that he has a brood of homicidal halflings with a witch who is hell bent on bringing destruction to the other side of the Veil? Which one are you referencing, Mother?"

Breena moved forward, her hand fisting in the back of his shirt and her warning low, "Brynach, stop."

Gabriel stepped forward, his hand on the hilt of his sword. "Mind your tongue."

"Or what? You'll massacre my familiar and stuff it for your halls?" Brynach cursed at his father. Breena pulled him back.

The Queen gasped, "Brynach, enough! How vile."

Clearly, his mother had no idea who she shared a bed with. When Brynach met his father's gaze again a cruel smile adorned his lips. Oh yes, he didn't mind at all that Brynach knew his little secret. He was guilty of one of the highest crimes in Faerie, positive that he was untouchable.

"You won't sit on this throne forever, Mother. And once you are off it, I hope you know you'll be held accountable for all the actions, and inactions, committed while on it," Brynach said before relenting to his sister tugging at his arm.

CHAPTER 21

Aisling

As soon as Aisling entered the apartment Lettie ran into her arms.

"Lettie?"

"I'm okay. Give me a second. You have no idea how hard it was to not kick down your door when I heard you were back," Lettie admitted.

"I told her I'd lend Ollie, he's quite strong, you know," Trent joked but his voice broke at the end. Aisling threw herself at their best friend.

"You beautiful man! I've missed you," Aisling cried into Trent's neck.

Riordan had told her he was home, but she hadn't realized how much she missed him until he was in front of her. Trent squeezed her tight.

"Oh doll, I missed you."

"I'm not strong enough to take on the men who were guarding her inside that condo. I don't have a death wish." Ollie winked. She was glad Trent hadn't been alone through everything, so far away home.

"I needed rest and time with the guys. But I'm so glad you're back. Never leave again." Aisling kissed Trent's cheek. "Promise."

Trent twisted his pinkie with Aisling and held his other hand out to Lettie who linked with them. The three smiled at one another. They were back together. They were okay.

Aisling pulled back her hair, wrapping it in a messy bun and biting her lip. "You have quite the setup here."

The tech was more advanced as Liam and Sean worked in tandem with Faerie. Riordan's brother waited until she moved away from her friends, then wrapped her in a hug. She rocked side to side with him, happy that her partner's brother cared for her.

"What's going on and how can I help?" Aisling asked when Liam let her go.

Liam pointed to the boards full of frantic handwriting. "Sydney is in witness protection. You know we brought her in, right?"

"She was the first to turn. In exchange for testimony against her brothers, she's not getting charged. Yeah, I know. I missed a lot while I was away."

Trent huffed, "You say that like you were on holiday."

"You got kidnapped, Ash!" Lettie cried. "Is it still kidnapping when you're an adult? It doesn't fucking matter."

Aisling squeezed Lettie's hand. "I'm back now and it sounds like I have you to thank for that. You know you're kinda badass."

"I'm not the one breaking magical forcefields and escaping captors," Lettie deflected. "Besides, it's about the next step, not the ones behind us."

"Right!" Aisling clapped her hands. "Which is why you're going to come with me to see Sydney."

"I am?" Lettie asked.

"She is?" Sean's head poked up from his computer.

"Riordan will be with me, and we will wait for Jashana. If I'm right, seeing Lettie will loosen her up," Aisling paused. "We can't afford to have her clam up. Facing a victim will force her to confront her actions. But only if you're comfortable with it."

It wasn't fair to ask. Lettie would do it if it helped Riordan find peace. It wouldn't be easy, but Aisling wouldn't ask if she didn't think it would work.

"Okay. I'll go."

G etting to Sydney was far harder than convincing Lettie to come with them. It involved a car change and identification checks.

"Will her own brothers really come after her?" Riordan asked from the front seat.

"Can't be too careful," the agent answered from the driver's seat.

"We need all the information we can get. Riordan will have his phone recording the whole time, but make sure to get consent on record. I don't trust any of us to remember everything," Aisling reminded them.

Riordan opened the bond and streamed magic to her. She scanned the safehouse for any ill-intentioned magic. Finding none, she followed the agent further into the home. When they entered the living room and saw a nervous Sydney pacing the room, she took control.

"Let's all sit down," Aisling suggested, and everyone found somewhere to sit. To absolutely nobody's surprise, Riordan sat next to her, his hand on her thigh.

"I'm sorry. I never wanted this," Sydney started.

"No, I'm sorry," Aisling's words startled the other woman. "I spent a fraction of the time in the prison you grew up in, and I can't imagine what that must have been like. I don't know if your father was around, but for your sake, I hope he wasn't."

"Not often, but that was enough," Sydney spoke softly. "It's no excuse for what we did."

"No, it isn't. And I don't think Gemma is too pleased with you," Aisling continued as Sydney wiped a tear from her cheek. Now that Aisling had time to study her, the resemblance to Brynach and Breena was clear. She had their same coloring, and while her black hair was curlier and her eyes were more hazel than yellow, the bone structure was the same. Gabriel may be a sadistic asshole, but he had good genes. She was beautiful.

"I don't excuse your behavior, but I understand that nature and nurture play a role. It's not too late to do what's right," Aisling reminded her.

"She wanted me to do unspeakable things. Things I've spent so long trying to forget and forgive. But what she did to you." Sydney turned to Lettie. "I can't make up for that."

"No. You can't," Lettie deadpanned. "And you can't unfuckup your childhood. But, like Aisling said, you can do something about it now. You think I'm happy to be in the position I'm in? No. But I get up each day and choose to look at how I can make the best of it. Stop feeling sorry for yourself!"

From the doorway Jashana sucked her teeth and Aisling saw her give Lettie a nod of approval.

"My mother raised us with the mindset that we had just as much right to the title of royal as Brynach and Breena. In her mind, Gabriel was the King." She shook her head. "She had this crazy theory that he'd marry Moura, take over as King, then come back for her."

"He would never share power once he had it," Aisling gasped.

"She was in love. She'd wander around that house pretending she was the lady of the manor. And then one day she realized we were preteens who'd never seen the world, and she was getting older. Gabriel had stopped visiting and the staff had stopped listening to her. She had no power, and she really didn't like that."

Sydney paused to take a drink. "Then we came this side of the Veil and mom started working with the Firinne. Anything to gain power and prestige. Of course, we were still in hiding and incredibly inept socially, so I only had my brothers for company."

Aisling interrupted. "What is the goal of this curse your mother is spinning with the help of your siblings?"

"I'm not sure."

"Bullshit," Lettie exclaimed.

"No, really. I have theories but they stopped sharing around me when they realized I wasn't the team player they wanted."

"Then you're useless to us," Lettie cursed. "And what's worse is you're wasting our time."

"No, I'm not! This isn't easy for me. Cut me some slack. Goddess!" Sydney paced. "I'm turning on my family for fuck's sake."

Lettie lunged at the woman, grabbing her by the tops of her arms. The glass Sydney was holding fell to the floor, shattering and spraying Lettie's legs with water. Aisling turned to the Fae in the room and held up a hand. Whatever was happening right now, Lettie had to do this.

The older woman paled as Lettie yelled in her face, "Do not ask me for mercy. Do not ask me to cut you some slack. Do you have any idea the hell I went through? That I'm still going through? You put me in a prison, isolated and listening to the screams of others, for nearly a month. And for what? So mommy could feel big and bad?"

Aisling could see Lettie shaking, feel the anger radiating off her always happy friend.

"I suffered. I'm not a fucking witch. I'm not a damn Fae. I am a human girl who didn't want anything to do with magic. It wasn't my world. And do you know what I have now?" Lettie asked as she pushed the woman against the wall, shaking her so her teeth rattled.

"I have people in my fucking head. I can't go home in case I give a criminal access to my family. I can't trust my own senses because they may belong to someone else. That's the legacy of your mother's madness. You're fine, you stupid bitch. You have magic. You have power. You cursed me to a life I didn't want. You're evil."

Lettie pushed the woman one last time and then let her go. Sydney slumped to the ground, her hands over her face as she cried.

"Get the fuck over yourself." Lettie didn't look at anyone before stalking out of the room.

Aisling nodded to Jashana and the warrior followed Lettie through the front door she'd slammed shut. Knowing her friend was taken care of, she turned back to Sydney.

"She's more understanding than I am." Aisling was still seated. She waited for Sydney to pull herself together. "Do you get the necessity of your help now?"

"I always did," she mumbled.

"Sydney, we need information that will help us find your brothers. And we need to know more about the curse you put on people and the resulting magic left in them. We need it now."

"I wasn't lying. I don't know where they are. Their distrust of me increased toward the end and they didn't tell me all the plans. I can tell you names, birthdates as I know them, last names we used. But I can't tell you where they are." Sydney wrung her hands.

Riordan got out his phone and began recording. "Tell us what you know."

Aisling listened with barely restrained anger to the woman who calmly described the men who had terrorized so many people. Who were likely responsible for the murder of Riordan's aunt in some way. And they sure as hell had the blood of Firinne Blakely on their hands. Riordan's emotions were rioting, and Aisling had one question she was still too nervous to ask. But she would.

"The Hive, was that intended?" Riordan asked.

Sydney shook her black curls, her hazel eyes wide. "No. Goddess, no. We would never." She took a moment. "I would never. My mother, maybe. But it's never something we discussed."

Aisling turned to Sydney. "You took part in weaving the curse." It wasn't a question.

The other woman didn't deny it. "We all did. She didn't leave us a choice. I knew they'd wake up. I convinced myself they were just sleeping, resting." She held up a hand. "I know that's not what it was. If you think I haven't beaten myself up for it, you're wrong. But keeping them locked up was never her intended goal. It was a means to an end."

"What end?" Riordan and Aisling already had their theories, but having recorded proof would help their case.

Sydney took a deep breath. "Growing up, my mother always told us we were better than. That we were stronger. That we deserved more than we were getting. When you hear that day in and day out, you believe it. Especially when you're isolated from the outside world. Eventually, she got it in her head that we couldn't live in Faerie with the power we deserved, but we could take it here on this side of the Veil."

"Because you're not just a witch," Riordan led.

"You know I'm not," Sydney's voice was tight. "Because we are part Fae and part witch, magic was always at our fingertips. More so in Faerie, but even here, we were stronger than our peers. Mom said if the other kids weren't as strong, that was their problem. And when she saw us excel, she wanted more."

"Did she ever get threatened by you?" Aisling asked.

The other woman's eyes lowered. "Sometimes. We avoided that at all costs. Things didn't end well for us if we overstepped our roles. But when she put this plan into place it was with the intention of scaring the humans. If we could convince them they weren't safe, create fear, and then come in and wake the victims, if we saved the day..."

"People would worship you. If you took out the Dorcha, and that is what you were trying to insinuate was behind it all, you'd be the heroes," Riordan finished for her.

Sydney went still. Too still. Aisling saw it and her heart dropped to her feet. No, it couldn't be. Riordan sensed her horror and turned to her. He took her hand and she squeezed it before turning to the other halfling. "Sydney, were you behind the Carnlough attack?"

Riordan stiffened beside her, and she heard his swift intake of breath. Across from them Sydney avoided their eyes. The blood in Aisling's veins went cold and red-hot anger flared from Riordan.

"You've got to be fucking kidding me," he screamed.

"It wasn't us!" Sydney was quick to say. "It wasn't us, but I overheard enough to know that it wasn't a supernatural power. My mother made up the whole Adair aspect of the curse. And that attack, the Dorcha, was a planted theory by the Firinne. She had insinuated as much. That wasn't her to the best of my knowledge. At least nothing I was involved with."

Riordan's voice was tight when he asked, "How is Dexter Ruiz involved?"

Sydney shrugged. "I don't know how deep he is, but I know he met with my mother and brothers. I was never invited to those talks. I don't know if either of them is involved in your aunt's passing. I swear it, Riordan."

"Can you go check on Lettie. I think we're done here for the day." Aisling sent her Ravdi out of the room and a guard followed him. Sydney's eyes were wet.

"I have one last question," Aisling started. "It can be off record. Riordan took the phone with him. But I have to confirm once and for all. Your father..." She let the question hang in the air.

Sydney closed her eyes and then opened them, meeting Aisling's. "Gabriel, but you already knew that."

Aisling admitted, "I did. But I had to hear it from you. All your siblings?"

The other woman nodded.

There was nothing left to say. Aisling left the room.

CHAPTER 22

Riordan

"She'll be okay," Riordan reassured Aisling for about the fifth time since leaving the apartment. They'd filled Liam in over the phone, wanting him to start investigating leads immediately. Sean had overheard and by the time they got to the apartment he was on the curb, bouncing nervously, so he could gather Lettie.

"Yeah, I know," Aisling whined as they drove to the police department. "I know it wasn't an easy visit for you, either. I'm sorry I put you through that. I pushed you both too hard."

"No, you didn't. We're both adults. We understood what we might hear. Besides, it gave Lettie closure and gave me information that may help put Dexter away. What we did today mattered. After a long time feeling helpless, in a weird way, I feel better." He rubbed Aisling's back as he steered the car into the busy parking lot.

As they got out of the car Aisling soothed him through the bond, preparing him for whatever they faced inside. Riordan reached down and took her hand, linking their fingers. He never got used to the love and warmth that flooded him when he was with Aisling. She was his anchor, filling a hole he'd ignored too long.

Before they reached the door Riordan pulled her up short.

"Come here." He reached out and took her by the loop of her jeans. He needed to ground himself in her feel and taste before he took one more step. Her hands circled his waist, holding him close. It was exactly what he needed.

"Better?" she asked when he let her go.

"I love you."

Aisling grinned at him. "Are you ready for this? He may be in there."

Riordan slumped. "No, but they need this recording. Let's avoid him if we can."

Heads turned as they entered the precinct. The whispers and shoulder nudging were things he could ignore, but Aisling tensed at his side, and he felt red-hot anger on her behalf. Together, they made their way through the maze of desks toward the office at the back of the room. And they almost got there before they were stopped.

"Nice to see you back," Pilson offered, putting a hand on Aisling's shoulder.

"Thank you, Jim." Aisling smiled at the older cop.

"You be careful, yeah? I've heard rumblings about an internal investigation. Some of the guys aren't thrilled about it," he warned, and Riordan moved closer to her side.

"I'll watch my six," she promised. "Captain in?"

Pilson nodded. "I believe so. Check with Sammy."

They approached the desk outside the captain's office and Riordan nodded to the Ravdi, who worked as his secretary.

"Hi, Samantha. Can I talk to him?" Aisling asked.

The woman's smile was genuine. "He said you'd be coming. Loren is in there."

Riordan opened the door after Aisling knocked. The large African American man smiled and embraced Aisling. Loren's relief at seeing her was obvious. Riordan remembered when the larger man had intimidated him. Granted, Aisling had a knife in her chest when they'd met. He liked Dawn's partner and he liked how protective he was of Aisling.

"Glad you're back, kiddo. Dawn told me you'd stopped in to see her earlier. Thanks for that. She felt better once she saw you." Loren squeezed her arm and nodded to Riordan.

"Of course." Aisling looked at the captain. "Riordan has something for you. Can we get a tech guy in here to copy files?"

Loren snapped to attention. "You got her to talk?"

Riordan laughed, "Did you doubt her?"

The captain picked up the phone and issued a request to Samantha before turning back to them. "Will it help us?"

Aisling shrugged. "It's going to shake shit up."

Both officers sighed and rubbed their foreheads. Riordan understood their frustration, but it was their job to right wrongs. And these were epically fucked-up wrongs they needed to address.

Captain spoke, "Okay, break it down for me. We'll get the audio, but I need the cliff notes."

"Sydney wants to help us, but she's scared. She knows what her brothers are capable of, and they worry her more than her mother does. But she gave us a list of aliases, birthdates, and a few addresses we should check out," Aisling summarized.

"You did good," Loren commented.

"That's not all. She also admitted to us they've used hired hitmen, one of whom is Dexter's dead informant. And the missing one, he's working with them, too." Aisling waited while the captain registered.

"Proof?" He grumbled.

"I saw him in Faerie talking to my kidnapper. Sydney described him for me. It's all on tape. The description and time frames match. She said the guys avoided any trouble because he had, and I quote, 'a guy on the inside'. Which means that Dexter had ties to the killer, to my kidnapper, and to Faerie." When Aisling delivered the information the mood in the room changed.

Riordan interjected, "So is it that much of a jump to assume he may have had a hand in the sprites that threatened me and started the fire that killed my aunt? We also have Sydney on tape saying Dexter was either involved or complicit in their plans as a whole."

Loren cursed and the captain ran a hand through his thinning grey hair. "Fuck." It seemed to be a favorite word of his.

Aisling nodded. "Yeah, it's not going to look good for Dexter or the PD. It means an internal investigation and the department under scrutiny. I'm not sorry."

"Did I ask you to be?" The door opened, and he nodded toward the gentleman who entered. "I'll handle Ruiz. Go with him. He'll get the files."

Riordan took her hand as they turned for the door. Before they reached it the captain called out, "Good work."

The file transfer was quick. The verbal consent and details were all there. All they needed to do was turn over his phone and wait. Riordan's knee was bouncing, his fingers on the chain at his neck while Aisling checked her phone. A quick glance showed a lot of texts from Trent.

"He missed you," Riordan commented.

"I missed him, too." Aisling sighed, "Is it wrong that I just want to spend time with you and Brynach, though? I should be catching up with Trent and Lettie, but I'm so drained I don't want to right now."

The officer returned the phone. Riordan offered a hand to Aisling. "It's not wrong at all," he said as he helped her up. They ignored whispers on their way to their car. "If that's what you want, that's what you get."

T he condo was empty, which meant Brynach hadn't returned. Jashana was posted up at the door, having refused to come in. They were alone for the first time in he couldn't remember how long.

Aisling entered the bedroom and began to remove her clothes.

"Ash, what are you doing?" Riordan tried not to wince at the squeak in his voice. Real smooth, buddy.

She turned to him, unbuttoning her jeans, and pushing them over her hips. "We're alone and I've missed you. Will you take me to bed?"

Sweet Goddess, it was nearly all he'd thought about. Hell yes. He wanted to lose himself inside her, but she'd been through a lot. "Are you sure? It's okay if you need more time." He moved to her, cradling her face. She leaned into his touch.

Her hands moved under the hem of his shirt, her slim fingers tracing his flesh where it met his jeans. "I'm sure."

"Thank the Goddess!" Riordan swore and lifted her into his arms.

Aisling's laughter rang through the condo as Riordan laid her on the bed. As he began to explore her body, his hands pressing firmly as he massaged up her legs, her entire body shook with need. Her breath caught in her throat and Riordan couldn't ignore the way her hips rose hoping he'd touch her where she ached. But Riordan didn't want to rush this. He wanted to give her time to get used to his touch again and to let himself believe she was here. She was home. As his hand rounded her hip and his thumb ran lazy circles on her stomach, she met his gaze.

"Are you okay with this?" He stilled his touch.

"I need you to touch me," Aisling's voice was as shaky as the muscles on her belly.

"I am." He watched his hands clench on her flesh.

Aisling shook her head and took his hand in hers, moving it down her belly and between her legs.

She was so wet for him. Like that, his restraint was gone. He sucked in a breath and prayed he'd last long enough to make this good for her. The way he needed her right now terrified him. His fingers parted her, his palm cupping her as he slid through her folds. Aisling moved against his hand, hips rolling in the desperate search for friction. Riordan's stomach tightened as her nails skimmed over him, down toward his zipper.

"You're distracting me, Aisling."

If he didn't get his cock away from her warm hand, he was going to lose it. His desire to get Aisling off first, to taste her, had him sliding down her body. Goddess, she was beautiful. He worshipped her, his tongue flicking across a pebbled nipple before sucking her breast into his mouth. Aisling gasped, and her hands threaded through his hair. He plunged two fingers inside her warmth, curling them and searching for that tender spot that drove her wild.

Aisling's back arched as she cried out, "Riordan."

"That's it. I love hearing my name on your lips," he told her.

Aisling reached for him, but he angled his hips away from her as he kissed his way further down her body. He licked at her stomach, feeling the way her body quivered beneath him. He loved the way she rode his hand, how she brought herself pleasure using him.

Riordan bit at the skin beneath her ribs, down to her hip bone. He pushed her legs further apart. "Need to taste you," Riordan informed her before his tongue darted out and licked the length of her. Aisling raised a leg and pointed her knee outward, opening herself to him. His left hand wrapped under her thigh and back up around so he could hold her open while he ate her out.

He licked and sucked at her, his tongue swirling around her clit while two fingers of his right hand found the soft fleshy nerve endings that had his bonded making the most beautiful mewling moans. He could get off on the sound of her alone. His cock ached and the desire to bury himself inside her, to remove all the time and space between them, overwhelmed him. But not until she came. Aisling held him in place while she rode his mouth.

Riordan growled his approval, humming around her clit while he fucked her with his fingers. She was so close, her legs trembling and closing around his head. Riordan needed her to finish so he could get inside her. His fingers flexed, he bit lightly at her clit, and Aisling fell apart. He drank her in, greedy for her.

"Riordan, Goddess, that was," Aisling managed, pulling him up her body.

Riordan kissed her and she hungrily tasted herself on his tongue, sucking it into her mouth with a groan.

"I need to be inside you." Riordan reached for the bedside table. "I want to feel you shuddering around me when you come again."

Aisling's hands cupped her breasts and her hips rolled. "You had your tonic, didn't you?"

Riordan couldn't take his eyes off her as he rolled the condom onto his cock. "I was late taking it while I was distracted looking for you. You clearly didn't have your pill with you. We need to be safe," he reminded her.

There was no finesse, no kisses, and gentle easing into her body. With one thrust Riordan seated himself inside of her. The heat, the grip of her pussy, nearly made him lose his mind. Nothing felt as good as being inside her. Riordan forced himself to take a few deep breaths and calm down. He couldn't blow his load already. Fuck.

In an effort to last longer, and to ensure she was okay, Riordan leaned his forehead against hers for a moment. "I love you," he told her.

"I love you, too," Aisling answered and opened her magic to him. "I thought of you every day," she told him, holding him tight to her. Then her hips started moving and she begged for him to fuck her.

Riordan pulled out only to sink back into her, over and over. The electricity of her magic sang across his skin, sparking anywhere she touched. And oh, did she touch him everywhere. As he stroked back into her, he nearly came at the sensation surging through his cock.

"Did you?" he had no words.

Aisling smirked at him. "Did I make my pussy magic?"

"You really will be the happiest death of me." He kissed her, his mouth bruising, and claiming. They loved one another with affirmations and bodies. With every kiss, every caress of his fingers Riordan was leaving his name on the deepest parts of her.

He'd known intimacy before, hell, he'd even known love. But he had never experienced anything like what he shared with Aisling. With the bond so open he knew the moment her mind began to wander. He leaned in, speaking into her ear.

"I'm right here, Ash. I'm not going anywhere," Riordan whispered as he tasted the sweat on her neck.

"Swear it," she panted as she moved against him in a desperate search for release.

He cradled her thigh and lifted it to his side angling her hips and stroking into her with a sureness that nearly sent him over the edge. He wasn't going to last much longer. He rubbed her clit in hopes she'd finish again, but tears welled, and she shook her head.

"I need..."

"What? Whatever it is I'll give it to you," he swore.

"I need to be in control," she admitted.

Riordan didn't question it, he simply rolled with her until she straddled his hips. "I love you like this, Aisling. You look like Diana on a wild hunt."

He felt her drawing power from him, and he freely fed her. Aisling's hair rose on a wind she'd created, and the jasmine in the corner that had died off while she was gone bloomed back to life. The sweet smell, her moans, and the feel of her overwhelmed him. Riordan's eyes closed.

"You feel too good. I won't last," he choked out.

He reached to where their bodies met, where she was grinding down on his cock and thumbed her clit. She clenched around him, and he lost it, bucking up into her while she pushed against him. When Aisling found release, she did so with his name on her lips, and then he gathered her to his heaving chest. She squirmed and he pushed a hand down on the dip of her spine.

"For the love of the Goddess, please stay still." He was still trying to settle himself and his cock inside her was so damn sensitive as the aftershocks of her orgasm pulsed around him. She giggled but remained frozen on top of him. Aisling played with the rings under her cheek.

"Don't ever leave me like that again. I can't lose you," his voice broke at the end of his request, but she wouldn't judge him.

Aisling leaned over him, clutching the chain that held his rings and kissed him. "I'm not going anywhere, Riordan."

He nodded but didn't say anything. A single tear slid down his cheek and she chased it with her lips, kissing the salt from his face.

"I love you and I'm yours. We're a team," her words soothed him.

They stayed like that for a moment, just being together and letting some of the wounds from their time apart heal. Then he had no choice but to get up and dispose of the condom. When he came back to bed, he pulled her right back into his arms.

"So, you know your mother started planning our bonding ceremony before you were...before," Riordan said into her hair. It was tradition for the witch's family to plan the ceremony. Her mother had reached out to him about having it as planned.

"She asked me the other day if we'd want to go forward

with it now that you're back." The question was clear. Riordan felt his heart stutter in his chest, waiting for her response.

"Of course, I do! As soon as possible," Aisling said.

"Good," Riordan answered. "It was supposed to be tomorrow..."

"I'd lost track of time. I can't believe I was gone that long."

"If it's too much we can wait. Personally, the sooner it's in place the better I will feel," Riordan admitted.

"Then tomorrow it is. I'm ready, Riordan. I want this." She kissed him, melting into his touch.

"I hate to interrupt," Brynach said from the doorway. "Actually, that's a lie. I'd have loved to interrupt a few minutes ago."

Riordan scrambled for the blanket, covering himself and Aisling. His bonded laughed, though the laughter died on Aisling's lips when Brynach licked his. Riordan fought a full body shiver. It wasn't just Aisling the Fae was gazing at hungrily. He felt the blush rise on his cheeks and cursed his lineage and pale complexion.

"Did you really have to come in right now?" Aisling scolded without heat.

"I could have come earlier and watched," the Fae dead-panned.

Riordan didn't know how he felt about that idea, but it was nowhere near revulsion. "We have another talk coming. Soon," Riordan stated, clearly picking up on Aisling's feelings in the bond. He sat up and pulled her close. "You might as well tell us what's going on."

Brynach moved into the room and sat at Aisling's desk. Riordan didn't miss the way his nose flared, and he breathed deep. When those predatory eyes opened again, they found his and Brynach's lip quirked.

Riordan muffled a laugh, "Real subtle, friend."

Brynach gave an unapologetic shrug. "I have news. You should probably dress before I share it."

Aisling nodded and made to get up, but Brynach wasn't leaving. "We're not dressed," she stated.

"Yes, I'm aware. Like I said, you should both remedy that." He crossed an ankle over his knee and ran his tongue over his canine teeth. "A quick shower may be in order. You two smell of sex. It's distracting."

Riordan wanted to take his eyes off that tongue, he really did. He'd just spent himself, but he was getting hard again. Suddenly, he wanted to feel those teeth on his skin or those eyes on him as he fucked Aisling a second time. At the spike of lust in the bond Aisling dug her nails into his thigh and he groaned. Damn it.

Riordan nudged her shoulder. "Let's go. I want to know what he's got to share." It was clear the large Fae wasn't going anywhere so Riordan gave Brynach a good look at his naked ass as he walked to the bathroom and started the shower. He fought to not react when a low growl sounded behind him.

Great, now getting hard-ons for Brynach was a thing.

With a resigned sigh Aisling lifted the blanket and slid out and joined him. Their shower was quick, and before long they were getting dressed. Without any modesty at all he and Aisling dressed, unhurried, while Brynach watched them. Riordan was secretly pleased to be teasing the Fae.

"This is not how I imagined the first time I saw you both naked," Brynach commented.

"What had you imagined?" Riordan asked as he pulled on his shirt.

Brynach grinned. "I'd hate to scare you."

Riordan barely held back the shiver at the promise in the Dark Fae's words. Aisling emerged from her closet in a long tunic sweater and a pair of leggings. Riordan was seated on the bed facing Brynach who was still lounging with a far-off look in his eyes.

"Enough daydreaming, Bry. What's going on?" Aisling asked sitting next to Riordan and taking his hand.

"Your brother was able to dig up more dirt on Dexter based off the information provided by Sydney. He's started working with Pilson already because they found out the brothers are at one of the addresses Sydney provided. They're sending a S.W.A.T. team over now."

Aisling looked between the two men. "That's good news. Once they're locked up, Sydney will be safer and when Peggy realizes all her kids are either in jail or have turned against her, she'll have to give up."

"That asshole has to pay." Riordan scrubbed a hand over his face and then worried over the rings on his chain. There was one less than usual, but Aisling hadn't noticed. He'd taken the raw amethyst from Maggie's charm to a jeweler to be reset in silver. He planned to give it to her at their bonding ceremony.

"So, what do we do?" Aisling asked. "Sit and wait for news from the arrest? I'll go crazy."

Riordan agreed. Luckily, Brynach had a few ideas. Of course, those ideas included dragging them along on visits in Faerie. Riordan had to admit, he was starting to get used to the place. The reality of the situation was that after their wedding Aisling and Brynach would spend more time in Faerie, which meant he would, too. He was glad that it was beginning to feel less foreign.

So, for the rest of the day they burned themselves out on manual labor. They moved Brynach's things into the cabin. They all took clothes and items they'd want with them. And since they were back and forth through the Veil, they could check in frequently.

"Are you nervous about tomorrow?" Aisling asked on one of their trips to Faerie.

Without the bond he could have lied to her, but he didn't want to. "A little. I'm committed to you, but the ceremony is a big deal. I know it doesn't change anything between us. But you've thought of the ceremony for a long time. I want it to be perfect for you."

Aisling smiled and kissed him. "Even if my mother royally screws it all up, I'll be officially bonded to you and nothing about that will be less than perfect."

Riordan's chest swelled with love and pride. He wasn't sure how she always knew the perfect thing to say. For that matter, he didn't know how the large Fae understood exactly what they all needed to distract themselves. But setting up their home together, planning their future, was a great way to focus on what they could control.

Later, sitting at the small table in Aisling's condo eating dinner together, he said as much. Brynach brushed off the compliment.

"It's my job to make sure you're happy," he said. Then he met Riordan's eyes. "Both of you."

"We should have heard something by now. I'm calling the precinct," Aisling announced standing and putting the phone to her ear.

Riordan barely contained himself while he waited for the update. Of course, Brynach would be able to hear the conversation, no problem. Damn Fae hearing. He didn't know he was chewing on his hangnail until Brynach gently pulled his hand away from his mouth. The large man's thumb grazed Riordan's lip and heat zapped through him.

His wide eyes met Brynach's, and the other man dropped his hand. "Sorry."

Riordan wanted to tell him it was okay, but before the words could leave his lips Aisling's voice rose.

"What do you mean? How is that possible?" She turned to them. "You had eyes on the place. You mean to tell me you weren't sure before you went in?" Aisling said a few more choice words to whoever was on the phone and then hung up.

Riordan stared at her, giving her a shake of his head and raised eyebrows. Was she really going to make him ask? Thankfully, she took a deep breath, then spoke.

"Not all the brothers were there when they breached the house. They got two of them, one remains at large. There was a shootout. An officer got grazed, but he is going to be okay. One brother had a superficial wound treated at the station."

"And the runner?" Riordan asked.

Aisling shook her head. "I'm sure he'll turn up eventually."

"Or they pushed him further into hiding and we never see him again," Riordan grumbled. Suddenly, he didn't want to act like he was okay. "I'm going to shower and turn in."

He felt the concern in the bond, so he hurried to add, "Just want to be rested for tomorrow." Then he left, not wanting to infect them with his bad mood. He'd sleep it off and tomorrow would be better.

"Today's the day! Let's go, sleepyhead." Aisling popped up, immediately chipper. How did she do that? She took her phone with her and put her mother on speakerphone as she dove into her closet. "I know you have the dress, but do I need shoes, hair accessories...tell me something!"

Riordan would get dressed at her mother's house with Liam's help, so he didn't have to prep much. After a quick breakfast, they left for her mother's house. As they pulled up, he saw a few familiar cars. It was more people than he'd anticipated. He hated the ideas of that many eyes on him. But for Aisling, he'd do anything. And he wanted this, he reminded himself.

"Lettie!" Aisling screamed and leapt from Brynach's truck.

Riordan had to admit he felt better this morning. Watching Aisling and Lettie across the yard made him smile. He and Brynach rounded the house and joined everyone else. Cait floated through the yard helping where she could, Kareem following quietly behind his girlfriend. Riordan smiled at his friend who clapped him on the back.

"Congrats, man! This is a big deal, isn't it?"

"Yeah. I'm glad you could be here. So, you and Cait?" Riordan said with a hint of warning in his voice.

"We gonna do this?" Kareem asked with a shake of his head.

Brynach nodded and Riordan answered, "Yup. Ash has been through hell, Lettie's been through the same, and Cait is important to both of them. If you hurt Cait, you hurt Lettie, and by proxy you hurt Ash. Neither of us are going to be okay with that. So, don't."

"That was the most unnecessary talking to. You've met her, right?" Kareem asked gesturing to where Cait was bossing people around as they set out chairs and vases of flowers. "She'd kick my ass before either of you got the chance."

Brynach laughed at his side and Riordan joined him. He put an arm around his friend's shoulder. "Come on, you can help me get ready."

Riordan was glad to have Brynach and Kareem with him to ease his nerves as he got dressed. Mentally he rehearsed what he wanted to say to Aisling even though the words would likely abandon him when he needed them. Both men left when Liam entered the room.

"Dad would shit himself if he could see you right now," Liam said by way of hello.

"Yeah, well." Riordan shrugged.

"Oh Rory, I didn't mean to be an ass. It's just, they'd love this, seeing you with Aisling. They'd be so proud of you."

Riordan found something interesting in the corner of the ceiling away from his brother. He was not going to cry right now.

"I wish I could tell them I know I was wrong. If I'd known it was going to be Aisling... I gave them such shite," Riordan mused.

Liam closed a hand on Riordan's shoulder and pulled him into a quick hug before saying, "Rory, they knew. They were smart, our parents, and they trusted you'd get here. Aisling is good for you. You're a better man with her in your life."

He tried not to fidget under Liam's gaze as he straightened the collar of his shirt.

"I'm glad I'm here today." Liam checked his watch. "Almost time. I'll give you a few minutes alone. I'm proud of you, Rory."

He didn't wait for Riordan to respond before leaving him alone in the bedroom. Riordan didn't know what to do with himself. His thoughts were spiraling, and he really didn't want to be sad right now. He looked out the bedroom window to the yard below.

The flowers were picked from Mrs. Quinn's garden. The chairs were a mismatched collection of folding chairs that people brought with them. It was perfect. As he watched, Dawn used magic to make the trees around the yard shine like fireflies had settled in them, even though it was mid-morning. Loren stood to the side with their daughter in his arms smiling at his partner.

Alates danced through the yard, landing on flowers, and flitting away when people approached them. Riordan saw a few air sprites dancing among the lights in the trees, and he felt his chest tighten. He wondered if the sprites who had attacked him, who had killed his aunt, were present? He shook away the thought, determined to focus on the positive.

The seats filled with their friends and family. He let his gaze sweep over them and couldn't help looking for Aisling even though he wouldn't find her. They'd walk out together. Which meant it was time to head down the hall and find her. Riordan smoothed a hand over his button-down shirt, stopping to rub the worn rings around his neck. He took one last deep breath and opened the door.

Aisling had her fist raised to knock. She lit up when she saw him. He drank her in. Her hair glistened in a brilliant cascade of red curls. She wore a sundress so pale yellow it was almost ivory, her feet bare, and her face radiant.

"You look wow."

"I look wow?" Aisling smirked at him.

"Yes. You are wow," he laughed.

"Why, thank you. You're pretty wow yourself. You should dress up more often." Aisling fingered the collar on his shirt after she'd pinned a sprig of flowers to his chest. With Aisling smiling at him he felt like the luckiest man in the world.

Aisling pushed him into the room and shut it behind her. She reached into the pocket of the dress and pulled out a small box. "Gifts are traditional and when I thought of what I wanted to get for you there was one thing that felt right." She reached up and toyed with his necklace. "I know I'm going to be Brynach's wife, but I wanted a way to show you and the world that you're mine."

She handed him the box and he froze. He hadn't been expecting anything that came in a tiny box. Also, he hoped she hadn't outdone him in gift department. At her nod he lifted the lid and saw a stunning bright silver and brushed metal Celtic arrow knot band.

"You got me a wedding band?" Riordan gasped.

His girlfriend laughed, "Not exactly. More like an I love you forever ring."

"A wedding ring." He nodded.

"I wanted everyone to know you belong with me no matter what. I figured you could wear it or add it to your necklace. I don't care if you put it on your left or right hand, Riordan. Either way, I'm not leaving. I'm here. I'm yours," she promised.

The knots represented eternity. He didn't have that with her, but he wanted as long as he did have. Riordan placed it on his right hand. Through the bond he felt Aisling's joy that her gift was accepted.

"It looks good," she whispered.

"I love it. Thank you." He kissed her. "I have something for you, too." He turned and brought the flower crown he'd asked

Aisling's mother to make to her. It was full of large blooms and fragrant jasmine.

"Will you?" she asked, ducking her head so he could place it on her.

"There's more." Riordan held her hand and played with the ring that Brynach had placed on her left hand. "Before we walk down, I want to swear myself to you."

"That's what we're doing, Riordan." She seemed confused.

"Not as your Ravdi. As a man who loves you." He pulled the ring from his pocket. He held it in front of him, the silver band held the now polished amethyst. The jeweler hadn't been able to get a piece without some crackle from the heat of the fire. Riordan thought it made it even more beautiful. He'd briefly considered melting down his mother and father's ring to make hers, but he couldn't bring himself to do it. Plus, witches preferred silver.

"Riordan?" Aisling's eyes were wide.

"Breathe, babe. This isn't a proposal. One fiancé is enough," he choked up. "It's Aunt Maggie's amethyst."

"Oh, Riordan." She pushed her fist into her mouth.

"Will you wear it?" Riordan asked.

She lowered her hand, her eyes shiny with unshed tears. "Of course, I will." She held her hands out and he placed it on the pointer finger of her left hand. "It's beautiful. Thank you."

Riordan watched as her thumb rubbed over the gem. "I don't deserve this."

"Why would you say something like that?" he asked, putting a finger under her chin and raising her hazel eyes to his.

"I failed her. The charms didn't work." Her chin shook. If she started crying right now, he'd never forgive himself.

"No, Aisling. Goddess, no. I gave it to you because, well, I have little by way of heirlooms. There are no centuries old jewels in my family. Just these." He held up the rings. "And now, that amethyst. Maggie loved it. And she really cared for you, even before me. She told me so. And I want you to have something with more meaning than a mall jewelry case."

Man, he was really fucking this up. He'd thought she'd understand all that without having to say it and here he was going on about fucking heirlooms. Aisling must have sensed his panic in the bond because she placed her hands on either side of his face and forced him to look at her again.

"I'm sorry. I was insensitive. I love it. It's beautiful. And it doesn't make me sad. I didn't think you were giving it to me as a punishment or reminder. It's my own guilt that I projected. Riordan, I love you. I love being your bonded. You are so much more than I dreamt up when I thought of my Ravdi as a young witch. I couldn't have imagined anything this amazing." She leaned in and kissed him.

Riordan let himself really sink into her words and the feel of her lips, sweet and soft beneath his own. His hands gripped her hips, tracing the lines of her through her dress. Before things got out of hand he pulled back and rested his forehead against hers.

He reached for her hand, and she gave it to him. They linked fingers. "Do we have to go down right now?"

Aisling shrugged. "They can't start without us. Why?"

He winked at her. She blushed and bit her lip. "Seriously?"

"I mean..."

Then Aisling got that look in her eyes, the one he loved but meant he was in trouble. The beauty that was his bonded sank to her knees and reached for his zipper.

"Ash, that's not what I mean," he argued.

"I want to. Trust me, it's as much for me." She licked her lips and he fought to remember why he didn't want those big eyes staring up at him while her hand stroked him.

Aisling wasted no time getting him hard and sliding him into her mouth. Fucking hell. Riordan looked over his shoulder to the window and the people down below. This was downright dirty, and he loved it. His girlfriend cupped his balls and let her drool slide down over them, tugging gently.

"That's it, babe. Take me deeper," he coaxed, and she obliged. He wanted nothing more than to fist his hands in her hair, but he couldn't. Not without messing it up. Damn it, this was the hottest thing he'd ever seen. His girl on her knees with his cock in her mouth.

"Your mouth feels like heaven, Aisling."

She hummed, smiling around his tip. Her hand stroked him as she relentlessly sucked at him. He was going to come in no time flat but considering their rush that might be a good thing.

"Ash, can I come in your mouth?"

She looked up and winked. The woman winked. Through the bond she asked for magic, pulling slowly and then funneling back to him. The feeling was intense. Then his dick started to vibrate. She had coated her tongue in magic!

"You look so fucking sexy, Aisling. So beautiful. You're perfect," he groaned. "I can't hold on anymore."

She took him deep and held him there as he rode his orgasm, hips bucking. Aisling sat back on her heels and grinned up at him while tucking him into his dress pants.

"That is not what I meant when I asked if we had time," he scolded and pulled her up for a kiss.

"Yeah, but it's what I wanted. You can't say no to me on my special day."

"Our special day, Aisling. You wicked siren." Riordan kissed her nose.

She smirked. "Ready now?"

"Absolutely." He took her hand, again.

Aisling practically floated down the stairs in her dress. He still couln't believe he got to love her. They paused at the back door and she looked at him.

"Last chance to run."

"Wouldn't dream of it. You're stuck with me," he kidded.

"Happily."

Together they stepped out into the bright sun.

They walked down an aisle made up of their closest family and friends. Just the two of them, hand in hand, until they got to the front. When he turned and looked at her every word he'd rehearsed fled his brain. His entire world narrowed to Aisling and the way she was looking at him.

"Aisling Quinn. Riordan Campbell. You're here today to swear in front of friends, family, and Firinne that you are dedicated to your bond. The relationship between witch and Ravdi is sacred and a union that shouldn't be entered into lightly," the Firinne official stated. "Do you, Aisling Quinn, enter this bond intentionally and willingly."

She smiled at Riordan and squeezed his hand. "I do."

The same was asked of Riordan and he didn't hesitate before answering affirmatively.

"The bond between witch and Ravdi is one filled with respect. Together you work for the benefit and happiness of one another. The sharing of magic, the union, works best with communication and trust. Do you as witch and Ravdi vow to never harm one another and to always keep each other's best interests in mind?"

"We do," they answered together.

The next part was the one that made Riordan nervous, but he had prepared himself for it. "As a bonded pair, your magic is significantly strengthened. By joining you increase one another's potential for greatness. As members of a bonded pair, do you promise to come to the aid of other witches and Ravdi when needed? To be a contributing part of the larger magical community?"

And there it was, the vow that led to the inevitable death of his parents. The clause that said you had to show up and fight, to help, and go to the aid of others. Aisling whispered his name. He gave her the slightest of nods and she grinned back at him.

"We do," they answered again.

"Have you prepared anything to say to one another?" The Firinne looked at them expectantly. Aisling said yes.

She locked eyes with him and spoke. "Riordan, I vow to always remember that your presence in my life is a gift freely given and happily accepted. Thank you for opening yourself to me and filling a void I never knew existed before I met you. I promise to continue to work to be a witch worthy of your magic. Thank you for completing a bond with magic, life, and love that I was missing."

She was absolute perfection. Of course, her words were exactly what he needed. Riordan could feel the sun beating down on him as he panicked. He couldn't get this wrong. Still, the words found him.

"Aisling, against all odds I've found peace inside our magic. I swear to honor and strengthen your gift. No matter what is thrown at us, and I know you well enough to know it will always be something new and exciting, I find such joy in knowing we'll face it together. Above all else, you are my center, my beacon of good in this world. I trust you, Aisling, and I believe in us."

For the last part of the ceremony the Firinne official presented them a dead flower. With their hands forming a bowl Riordan locked eyes with Aisling. Then he harnessed the magic surrounding them and directed it to Aisling who smiled at him and directed it to the bloom. The brown petals blossomed a vibrant pink, full of life.

The official announced them bonded in the eyes of the Goddess. Riordan kissed Aisling gently to cheers from their friends and family.

It was both that simple and that life changing.

They were swarmed by family congratulating them. No matter who came up, Aisling offered no more than a one-armed hug. She kept a tight hold on Riordan, and he didn't mind at all. Not even Brynach could pry her away from his side and for that he was thankful. His brother thumped him on the back and, if he wasn't totally mistaken, his eyes appeared red. Amber by his side smiled and nudged Liam with her shoulder.

"He's a big softy," she teased.

"We can't all be underground brawlers, Amber." Riordan gave it right back to her.

"Hey, I'll have you know I stopped doing that." Liam had already told him. His brother had been shocked that she did it to begin with and worried about Amber enough that she'd stopped. Turns out having loud and wild sex with his brother was enough of a thrill for the witch these days.

Lettie immediately noticed the new ring Aisling was wearing and fawned over it. Trent stole her crown proclaiming that it suited him more. Riordan disagreed but didn't argue as Aisling laughed and twirled her friend. She ran off with them and Brynach switched his attentions to Riordan.

"You did well, Ravdi."

"Not like I had to do much," he deflected.

"No, just put aside biases and trauma and accept a bond with possibly the wildest witch we've ever known. Nothing, really." He clapped a hand on Riordan's shoulder. "She couldn't have found a better Ravdi."

"Thank you, Brynach." The Fae didn't have to say stuff like that. It meant a lot that he did. It wasn't everyday a brooding Dark Fae complemented you. When they did, you accepted it for what it was. A gift.

People started to gravitate to the tables with plates of food and drinks. Mrs. Quinn really had done a great job with the party. Riordan's stomach grumbled. "Ready to eat?"

"Always," he answered. But before they could reach the buffet style food table Mrs. Quinn found them.

"Riordan, you look handsome," Mrs. Quinn commented hugging him. "That was beautiful."

Her cheeks bore tear stains and Riordan hugged her back. "Thank you for arranging this. It means a lot to us."

She waved a hand. "Oh, this is nothing."

"Stop being humble, Lydia," Nevan scolded as he approached. "It was a beautiful affair."

Riordan hadn't been around Aisling's father often and he was no less intimidating now than he'd been other times. He nodded to the royal Fae, who deemed him worthy of a nod in return.

"You realize this means I task you with Aisling's safety to the same degree as Brynach." Nevan wasn't asking. He was stating a fact.

Brynach chose that moment to walk over and put an arm around Riordan's shoulder. "Now, that's hardly fair. I'm significantly stronger than Riordan. Cut him some slack, Regent."

"Hey!" Riordan began, but the two Fae started laughing and Riordan recognized they were teasing him.

Nevan sobered. "Her happiness is your responsibility now, son."

Riordan nodded. "Yes, sir." He turned to Brynach, "Let's go find our girl."

When they were out of earshot he admitted, "That man terrifies me."

"He's not that bad," Brynach said.

"Maybe for you," Riordan sighed. A raised eyebrow from Trent and Ollie by the drink table made him very aware that Brynach's arm was still comfortably draped around his shoulder.

Brynach must have felt him stiffen because he pulled his arm back. Riordan immediately felt bad. "Sorry. This is new to me."

"You have nothing to be sorry for. Now, let's find Aisling."

Before they got very far, Brynach stilled and even Riordan heard the gasps and raised voices. Riordan stopped beside Brynach. This could not be happening. Not today. Next to him Brynach cursed, and Riordan saw the large Fae's hands clenched at his side.

"Aisling!" the voice called out again and around the yard voices quieted.

"How do you want to play this? Cause I'll gladly kill him, even with all these witnesses," Brynach growled under his breath.

He didn't fucking know. His eyes shot to Liam. Amber was physically restraining him. Aisling! Where was she? Then he saw her. Of course, Aisling didn't stay hidden and safe. No, she stalked, barefoot and ethereal, toward Dexter.

"Fuck!" He was moving immediately.

They both rushed to catch up to her.

"What the hell do you think you're doing?" Aisling accused, stepping up to the man and poking him in the chest. The officer swayed back at the jab. "You have no right to be here. This is private property and you're not here on official business. Get out of here, Dex."

"He's drunk," Brynach commented as they moved across the lawn.

Kareem had moved to Riordan's side, his hands in fists. This man had nerve coming here today, or anywhere near him for that matter. Riordan felt the blood rushing in his ears, his vision narrowing to the smug face of Dexter Ruiz.

"You bitch," Dexter slurred at Aisling. "Do you have any idea what you've done? This is my career, not some stupid cunt's hobby. You had to open your slut mouth." Dexter was stepping into her, and they were still too far away.

Brynach surged forward and Riordan followed a half a step behind. Before they could reach him, Aisling had pulled back her fist and cracked it into his nose. Blood sprayed her buttercup-yellow dress and she shook out her hand. Riordan stopped and Brynach looked at him, a grin on his face.

"Goddess, I love her," the Fae laughed. Riordan had to agree. Then Brynach was at Aisling's side checking her hand.

Riordan should have done the same but instead he stalked up to Dexter. Without comment he punched the man again.

He didn't defend himself, not with one hand pressed to his face and his eyes glazed over. It was a cheap shot, but Riordan didn't care. When Dexter fell to his knees in the grass, Riordan planted a foot in his chest for good measure.

He was vaguely aware of hands on him, of screams. In the last remaining logical part of his brain, he recognized he was ruining a perfect day, but this man, this murderer, had to pay.

"The fuck?" Dexter garbled through a split lip on the ground. "You're assaulting an officer."

"Not for long," Riordan spat and gave him a kick to the ribs.

It was Aisling who brought him home. Aisling who stepped between him and the curled-up form on the ground and took his face in her hands. Then Brynach pulled him away. He struggled but his bonded broke through the red haze.

He blinked and shook his head. "I'm sorry," Riordan whispered. And then all the energy left him, and he slumped into Brynach's hold.

Loren moved to Dexter and pulled him up. "Get up. You're trespassing on private property. I'd call this drunk and disorderly. I'd also say this stands as verbal assault."

Dexter spat blood, "What about the physical assault?"

Loren shrugged. "I saw you trip and fall. Anyone else see something different?"

All around the yard nopes sounded. Riordan would have mustered a smile if he could. Fuck that guy. Loren carted Dexter off and Riordan moved out of Brynach's arms and into a chair.

Mrs. Quinn turned the music up and reminded everyone of the food and drinks. Slowly, people resumed conversation. Aisling knelt by his side.

Riordan saw Liam standing next to him.

"I'm jealous I didn't get my turn. You alright, Rory?"

He shook his head. "I shouldn't have done that. What if that comes back to bite our asses in trial? I was stupid."

"No, you were human." Aisling's hand found his. They were both a bit bloody. What a pair they were.

"Your hand." He pulled it to him.

"Yours, too."

Brynach huffed, "Both of you up. Let's get you cleaned up."

The group moved inside, but only he and Aisling went into the bathroom. She knelt before him, a warm washcloth in her hands, and cleaned his bruised and bloody knuckles. He raised a hand to her cheek and wiped away her tears.

"I'm sorry I ruined our day." He lowered his head.

Aisling raised those hazel eyes to his, pinning him in place. "You have nothing to be sorry for, Riordan. Besides, in case you missed it, I broke his nose long before you got your hands on him."

CHAPTER 23

Brynach

B rynach was used to blood lust. He spent most of his day concentrating on keeping the need for violence in check. He was ever aware that with one lapse in focus, he could do something he'd regret. But Riordan wasn't like him. The Ravdi was a good man and a gentle one at that.

The night had been a hard one. Once they were home Riordan had broken down. Seeing Riordan cry had hurt Brynach. Not only because the man's tears felt like Brynach's failure, but because he'd been owed that pound of flesh. If anyone should have been able to knock Dexter on his ass, it was Riordan.

Nothing was worse than taking the revenge you so desperately wanted and still feeling empty. The soul broke when you realized nothing was going to bring back your loved one. And that's where Riordan had been.

Brynach sent Breena to keep an eye on the drunk. Dexter had been arrested, but he didn't trust the police to not discharge him on drunk and disorderly and have him show up at Aisling's condo. He couldn't have that. The need to protect them was strong. He watched Riordan and Aisling sleep.

He was sure he had made no noise, but Riordan's eyes opened and found his.

"How are you?" Riordan asked.

Brynach moved toward the bed. "I'm well. Not as good as you, though."

"Not even Aisling fixes everything, Brynach. I'm still fucked up," Riordan said sadly.

Aisling stirred at his side, and Brynach reached across Riordan to run a hand over her cheek. She nuzzled into his palm, and Brynach sucked in a breath. Even in her sleep her trust in him was a miracle.

"We all are," Brynach answered.

"What if I'm not enough for her?" Riordan wondered aloud.

Brynach's long black hair moved in silky ribbons over Riordan's chest as he shook his head. He watched the other man's eyes fall shut. "You're perfect for her. And I'm happy for you. I'll let you two sleep. Goodnight." He straightened to leave.

"Bry, wait," Riordan called, careful not to raise his voice and wake Aisling. "You can stay in here tonight, can't you?"

The invitation meant more than Riordan could know. Being alone in the other room hurt him, but he understood.

"I appreciate it, and I'll take you up on that another time. It should be about you two tonight."

"Why? We've done it before," Riordan pointed out.

Brynach leaned against the wall. Riordan was right, but this was a big moment. The other man had to be sure.

"Yes, when Aisling asked for it. She's asleep. She's not asking for the comfort," Brynach stated.

The Ravdi understood the meaning behind his words. Sharing a bed was nothing new but it was always for Aisling. This wouldn't be.

"I'm asking for it, Brynach. I could use the comfort, too." Riordan's cheeks reddened prettily. Damn, he was handsome.

In one quick motion he reached behind his head and pulled his t-shirt off. He kept his eyes on Riordan. He needed the

Ravdi to know it was him he was getting into bed for, not Aisling.

"Riordan?" Brynach's voice was soft as he neared. "What do you need from me tonight?"

The other man adjusted Aisling, so she was lying on her side and spooned her, making room for Brynach in the bed. Riordan motioned him to the other side of Aisling. "Just be with us."

Brynach shook his head. "I will join you if I have permission to hold you tonight. It's you I want to comfort."

Riordan's warm brown eyes looked up at him. He waited, silently asking to be allowed close to the other man. To be trusted. For Riordan to accept him.

"I don't want you out there alone," Riordan admitted.

"That's not the same as wanting me with you." The Fae frowned.

"You're right, it isn't. I don't know what I want yet, but I know you not being with us feels wrong. Can that please be enough for tonight? I'm tired," Riordan sighed.

Brynach wanted more but he wasn't going to push. This was a big step for Riordan. "Alright. If I do something you aren't comfortable with, you'll tell me?" He slid into bed beside him.

"I will," Riordan promised as Brynach settled behind him.

Brynach could feel the stiffness in Riordan, and he closed his eyes against the sting that caused. Slowly, he put an arm behind the other man's head, circling him until he was resting a hand on Aisling's back. The Ravdi finally let his shoulders relax, his head resting on Brynach's upper arm.

For now, this was enough. He was with them.

He woke first in the morning, surprised he'd slept at all. He glanced across the bed to where Aisling was smiling at him. Brynach threw her a wink, and her shoulders shook as she chuckled. Her mouth formed the silent words, "thank you" and Brynach nodded. Riordan stirred and Aisling placed a kiss on his nose.

"Morning, babe," she cooed.

Brynach felt Riordan stiffen when he realized who he was sleeping on. Slowly, he withdrew his arm. "I'll make a quick breakfast." Excusing himself was the best for several reasons. Firstly, the Ravdi probably needed time to come to grips with his feelings. Secondly, Brynach had a raging erection and doubted Riordan would be able to handle that. He palmed his dick through his boxers and tried to steer his thoughts away from sex.

From the bedroom there was a rustling of sheets as he started a pot for oatmeal. He could make out their conversation. He probably shouldn't listen, but he did.

"You invited Brynach to bed."

Riordan responded, "I did. Is that okay?"

He heard the soft sound of a kiss and then, "It's perfect."

Brynach smiled and breathed a sigh of relief. He'd never put the responsibility of his happiness on either of them, but he needed to be with them more than they realized.

Last night hadn't been an easy one for anyone. It should have been a time to celebrate Aisling's bond to Riordan. Instead, it had ended in them being upset and bruised. Brynach didn't mind holding them, but he hurt for them. It wasn't what they'd hoped for.

After breakfast, he followed Aisling into her bedroom for the sheer pleasure of watching her put on her makeup. With a smile, she caught his eye and continued her conversation with Lettie. It was clear from Aisling's side of the talk that they were discussing the wedding.

Their wedding.

Watching Aisling apply mascara, the sun glinting off his engagement ring, thrilled him. He moved into the room and after she removed her ear buds, he scolded her gently, "Those things are not safe."

"Good thing I have you then, isn't it?" Aisling winked.

Blood surged to his groin. Yes, she had him. She damn near always had. His tongue found his canines as he smiled, and Aisling's eyes locked on his lip. He moved toward her, letting her watch him and anticipate his arrival. It was all the preparation she'd get. He pulled her to him.

"Now that I'm yours, what do you want to do with me?" He swept his hair back with one hand and lifted her to his chest with the other. Aisling took the heavy length of it in her hands before reaching over his shoulders and tying it up with the hairband on her wrist. "Why'd you do that?"

She tilted her head up to his. "Because I like seeing your eyes darken as you lean in to kiss me."

He quirked a brow. "And you think I'm going to kiss you?"

"I was hoping you would." Flirty Aisling was one of his favorite Aisling's.

Brynach dipped his head to hers in the briefest touch of lips. Then her arms wound around his neck, clinging to him as she sought a deeper kiss. He wouldn't deny her; would never deny her. He swept his tongue over her lips until she parted for him and then he tasted her.

"I'm never going to tire of this," he swore against her mouth.

"Never is a long time, Bry," Aisling's lilting laugh made him smile.

"Not long enough," he promised as he kissed her again before he broke the news. "We have to go to Faerie today, a stoirin. We can't avoid the courts any longer."

She kissed him one more time and then wiggled. Even though he didn't want to, he set her on her feet. "That changes what I wear today."

"Wear what you want to, Aisling." Brynach was nervous about their visit to the Unseelie. He wasn't looking forward to facing his mother again. Unfortunately, it couldn't be helped.

"I know it shouldn't matter but it's the first they'll see me since the kidnapping. I want to look strong." She flipped through her hangers and Brynach wondered at her resolve. "Should Riordan be with us? I can call him back?"

Her Ravdi had left to be with his brother and see what he could learn about the case against Dexter, Peggy, and her children.

"No, let him do what he needs to do. I'll tell him we'll be back later." Brynach took out his phone and sent the text. Riordan's response was fast and short "keep her safe".

Aisling exited the closet in tight jeans, a black sweater, her brown leather jacket, and a pair of boots. She pulled her hair up in a high ponytail before strapping a leather holster to her thigh, over her jeans, in which she sheathed her throwing knife.

Brynach nodded his approval. "Which court are we visiting first?"

"My father's, I suppose." Aisling had seen him multiple times since being rescued from Levinas and he had become strangely smothering. Still, they had to see the King and Queen for their blessing before the wedding. "Frankly, I'm not ready to face your mother."

Brynach didn't blame her. Once in Faerie, Aisling moved gracefully into his arms so he could sift them to the gates. The large sentries announced their arrival to the royals inside and he was unsurprised to see the young Princess run outside to greet them.

"Aisling! It's so good to see you." Corinna embraced his fiancé and then spared him a nod. "Prince."

"Hello, Princess Corinna. It's nice to see you up and about." Brynach offered a small bow.

The Princess waved him off. "Oh that. That was nothing. Though, I suppose I should thank you."

He had rescued her, but who needed thanks? Aisling kept pace with the practically skipping young Fae. She was talking so fast that Brynach had relinquished her voice to background noise. He let the sights and sounds of Faerie comfort him, already feeling stronger being this side of the Veil.

Sometimes he had to remind himself that Aisling didn't feel like this. She didn't gather strength from other Fae or from the land itself. She felt as powerful on the other side, if not more so with Riordan around. But here in Faerie, Brynach felt a swell of power flood his veins, fortifying his own magic.

"Welcome home, friend," his familiar spoke inside his head.

"We'll be visiting there next. Everything okay?" A heads up never hurt when visiting the Dark Court.

"I don't think I'll be the one to share the latest news. Find me before you leave again," Kongur commented before going quiet.

Brynach wanted to ask more questions, but they were entering the court and he wanted his wits about him. The halls were long and uncarpeted, not unlike the Unseelie Court. Most Fae moved soundlessly on the floors, but not his fiancé. She walked the halls as though she owned them, chin up and chest out. He loved her all the more for it.

The doors to the throne room were shut, which wasn't entirely unusual, but the line of guards weren't standard practice. He turned to the Princess.

"What is this?"

"New precautions. I'm sure you understand." She waved a hand and the guards shifted to allow her passage. She danced toward the King and Queen.

"I understand no such thing," Brynach practically snarled. He softened his voice when Aisling's hand found his.

"Something is wrong. Stay calm," she whispered so only he could hear. "Whatever it is, we need to know. Please, for me, don't cause a scene."

He sent a quick message to his familiar that this was his last chance to share what he knew before he got real mad.

"You'll find out soon enough, friend," Kongur answered.

"Aisling, darling," Queen Branwyn greeted her, but didn't open her arms to Aisling. In fact, both royals sat rather stiffly in their seats, pushing their daughter behind their chairs next to Ellasar.

They were nervous. What would cause the royal family to be on edge, and why hadn't Nevan warned them if something was wrong?

"Thank you, my Queen. My apologies for being too long from court," Aisling's voice was syrupy sweet. They'd see through it, but it was smart to try and put them at ease.

The Queen smiled. "Nonsense. Your absence wasn't your doing. We heard of your capture and provided troops to aid in your rescue. We were positively distraught. Both the King and I are glad you were unharmed."

"I'm grateful for your help, your majesties. I won't take up much time." She stood with her hand in Brynach's. "We are here to honor our promise to the courts. Recent events have made us eager to solidify our bond. In fact, I've accepted Brynach's official proposal of marriage, happily and willingly."

King Kyteler wasn't moved. He nodded to the Fae waiting in a line at the side of the room. "We're glad you're well, but we can't always stop our work when you drop in."

"Of course not, your highness. We apologize. We're trying to get things in order for the ceremony and traditionally there are gifts we need from the courts. I thought it would be best to gather those in person." Aisling placating this fool bothered Brynach. It was all he could do to not charge the monarch and set him straight. But he'd keep a lid on his anger, especially since it was clear he didn't have the full scope of the situation.

The Queen motioned to a Fae at the side of her. "I will have a servant see you get everything you need. Given the current circumstances, our attendance at the wedding is still in question. It saddens us, truly it does. Hopefully, things sort themselves out before then."

Brynach gave Aisling's hand a squeeze before he spoke, "I'm sorry, your majesties. We've been preoccupied with Aisling's homecoming and bonding ceremony. We don't understand exactly what's going on."

The King managed to school his face quickly, but the Queen and Princess weren't as fast. "Then I suggest you visit your court and talk to them. Katya, please take the betrothed to the royal vault and get them what they need for their union."

The Queen added, "She's allowed three pieces. That seems fair. Nothing from the right wall."

The Fae at their side ushered them out of the room. "This way, please."

He saw Aisling look toward her friend, but Corinna didn't meet her gaze. What the hell was going on? Brynach and Aisling followed the servant through the winding hallways.

"I've checked with Phlyren. He's jabbering so fast I can hardly make him out, but your father's name keeps coming up. We need to hurry," Aisling whispered to him.

"Down here, please." Katya pointed down a flight of stairs illuminated by torches.

"Not at all ominous." Brynach ran his fingers along the damp stones.

Aisling bound down the stairs without fear. "I used to visit the vaults all the time with the Queen. It's fine. Come on."

Brynach had no choice but to enter the stairwell, the air within already musty. Oh, joy. Aisling waved to a guard at a massive metal door and then stepped through. Brynach was used to royal vaults but the ones in the Unseelie Court held weapons, interrogation rooms, and stolen artifacts kept secret from the Seelie.

What he saw was nothing like that. This was a room bejeweled in sparkling gems. It shone, floor to ceiling with display cases lit by lamps. The riches inside this room were, unfathomable.

"Aisling, she couldn't have possibly meant..." Brynach couldn't even finish the sentence.

Aisling bounced in the middle of the room. Then she began to wander around, ignoring the forbidden right wall.

Of course, that's exactly where Brynach went. Multiple beautifully crafted crowns adorned the walls. His mother's iron crown with blood red rubies paled to these. The Unseelie had no idea the Seelie Court held wealth like this. Then again, they'd never trade their torture chambers for scepters.

"What do you think?" Aisling asked and he turned to see her draped in a silver necklace positively weighed down by sapphires. It was decadent but still somehow dainty. The sapphires were set to look like flowers blooming across her chest. It was beautiful.

"Piece one, down," he confirmed and moved to the back wall. "Um, Aisling?" He reverently picked up a crown, smaller and less ornate than the others, but no less beautiful. It was a silver singlet woven like vines with small sparkling diamonds and sapphires set throughout. It would sit beautifully atop her curls.

"Oh, Bry, it's perfect. Will you?" She smiled at him.

"You shouldn't, my lord. It should be placed on her head when's she's announced your wife, not before," the Fae blurted moving forward quickly.

He shrugged. "You'll have to wait, a stoirin."

"Luckily, not for long. Now, to find something for you." She continued her search.

"Me?" Brynach asked in wonder.

"Of course. You need something from my court for our special day. The King and Queen will demand it, I'm sure. But more than that, I want to pick out something nice for you." She grinned and popped over to kiss him. "Do you want jewels or something more conservative."

"Surprise me." He leaned in the doorway, arms crossed and eyes on his fiancé.

Aisling chewed her lip, picking up and putting down pieces. Would she pick an obsidian piece, dark and lacking depth? Maybe she'd pick a jeweled blade, something to remind him that he had potential to be a killer? He tried not to let himself dwell on the meaning of the piece. Whatever it was would have nothing to do with her feelings for him.

"I found it." She smiled and blushed. "But if you don't like it I can pick something else."

"I'm sure I'll love it." He waited and then raised a brow. "Can I see?"

She brought the item out from behind her back and Brynach didn't bother trying to keep the emotions from his face. He trusted Aisling with them. She had chosen a beautifully crafted cuff that mirrored the crown he'd chosen for her. The woven vines had slivers of both diamonds and dark sapphires so deep they were almost, but not quite, black.

"Do you like it?" She was biting her lip again.

Brynach reached out and tugged her lip free, leaning down to kiss it. While his hand was still on her face, she opened the cuff and locked it around his wrist, closing it with a snap.

"It fits," she whispered against his lips.

"That it does. Thank you, a stoirin."

Aisling pulled back a little. "I assumed you'd have a crown from your court."

"I will, and I'll wear this with pride." Brynach pulled back from her and turned to the Seelie servant. "Can you please see that they find their way to our house?"

"I'll make sure they arrive safely." Katya nodded.

"Thank you," Aisling said, hurrying to take the jewels off and handing them to the waiting Fae. She gave Brynach a wide-eyed look and rushed out of the room.

"What is it?"

"Rin. He's panicking. We need to get outside the court walls and sift." She ran down the halls and Brynach kept pace with her easily.

"Her familiar talks to her! What aren't you telling me? I swear, I'll have your hide if you let us walk into danger," Brynach warned Kongur.

"So long as you come directly to court and don't mess around in the wilds, you're fine. And you really don't want to hear it from me. Breena is waiting at the south gates," Kongur answered haughtily.

As soon as they were outside the gates, Brynach swung Aisling into his arms and sifted to the south gates of the Unseelie Court. As promised, Breena was waiting.

"Oh, brother, shit has hit the fan." She stated as they offered their hands for the bloodletting. "Levinas has been officially charged with treason and conspiring to harm Aisling."

"We knew that was coming," Brynach said, grabbing Aisling's hand and hurrying after his twin.

"Were you aware that the accusations didn't stop there? Levinas brought charges against our father. He's been officially charged with treason and crimes against Fae, including but not limited to the murder of familiars," Breena informed them as they approached the castle doors.

Brynach stopped dead in his tracks. "What!"

"You've missed a lot. Mother is not happy."

"Is there open war?" Brynach asked, knowing his father wouldn't take that lying down.

"Not war, no. However, the Seelie Court put a bounty on Gabriel's head and demanded justice for the offense to Aisling, the Seelie, and the alliance with the humans. And Levinas has fled with a bounty on him, as well." Breena hurried through the gardens.

Aisling gasped. The thought of somebody putting a bounty on a royal's head, or the fucking Bloody Hand, was unheard of. But the issuing of an edict like that from one court against the other, it hadn't happened in Brynach's lifetime.

"Is it safe for Aisling to be here right now?" Brynach pulled her closer.

Breena scowled. "Would I lead you in if I thought other-wise? We'll keep her safe. We have bigger problems right now." She turned to Aisling, "No offense."

Aisling waved her off.

"The unaligned will use this against us. They'll take advantage of the distrust between the courts. We can't know when, but I'm sure they'll make a move for power," Brynach theorized.

Breena nodded. "Rainer has moved Trixie out of the court to a safe house where she can't get caught in the crossfire if anyone attacks."

Brynach thought a moment as they stepped into the great hall. "She needs to renounce Gabriel. If she holds him and Levinas accountable for their actions, it will go a long way."

"That will never happen." Aisling shook her head.

"Where's Rainer?" Brynach asked his sister as pieces fell into place.

"I was hoping you'd ask. Let's go!" Breena led the way.

Together they ran the treacherous halls to Rainer's suites. It was a veritable war room, full of Fae. Brielle winked at Aisling, and then gave her attention back to Rainer.

"Brother, I'm here to help!" Brynach called out.

Rainer nodded to Aisling and offered her a rare smile. "We're moving now while she's distracted."

"Moving?" Aisling whispered.

The King continued, "I have numbers, not a majority, but we won't face much opposition. It has to be now."

Brynach's entire body was tense. This is what he wanted, but Aisling was here. Damn it, it wasn't safe.

"Oh my god," she gasped when it finally clicked for her.

Brynach squeezed her hand then moved to his brother's side. He needed to know the details. Aisling wouldn't be a problem. She wasn't going with him. She could be angry with him later, but at least she'd be in one piece.

Breena laughed from his side, "This is going to be fun!"

Ceiren was next to Rainer and Brielle, a solid hundred other Fae were surrounding the room. He noticed quite a few of the royal guard.

Rainer didn't pause to give him the rundown, Ceiren did. "We'll have a few problems but without Gabriel around, mother is defenseless. This shouldn't be hard."

"We move now," Rainer announced, and Brielle rallied the troops in the back of the room. "When she's removed from that throne it's me that unseats her."

Brynach rushed to Aisling. "You are staying here!"

"Unprotected in the usurper's quarters? I think not!" She pulled her knife and smiled. "I go where you go."

"When we bond, you'll share my strength, but until then you're too fragile." Brynach kept a hand on her arm, getting swept up in the tide of bodies and unfortunately taking her with him. Damn it, where could he hide her?

"Brynach, it's not that I don't look forward to sharing our magic, but I want nothing I haven't fought for. Let's go earn a throne for your brother," she said with a wink.

Why was she so stubborn? Breena grinned at his fiancé, and he saw the respect for his future wife in her eyes. With a smirk, his twin handed him a sword and they fell into line behind Rainer.

"Be careful," his familiar cautioned.

"You damn well could have told me this!" Brynach countered.

As they neared the throne room, Rainer, Brynach, Aisling, Breena, and Ceiren fell toward the back. They let the guard and other Fae warriors storm in first. Breena was groaning next to him.

"I thought we'd get to be in on the fun," his twin whined.

"We wait until the room is secure," Rainer explained. "We are royals. We have no need to bloody ourselves."

The clash of swords rang from within the throne room. The screams of the common rose and one of the guards opened a door further down the hall and ushered some out. Brynach watched them flee. News of the takeover would spread fast.

"Fuck this," Breena cursed, "I'm going in."

She charged down the hall and in through the open door. Ceiren followed her with a roll of his eyes. Brynach wanted to, but he wasn't leaving Aisling. Breena would be fine. If Rainer planned this right, the fighting would be over soon. He highly doubted anyone was particularly loyal to their mother. With Gabriel gone they'd have no problem turning on her. Especially not once they realized Rainer was going to win the throne.

Beside him Aisling fidgeted, hand on her knife. The doors closest to them opened and Fae streamed out. Rainer froze, unable to tell friend from foe. Brynach moved to stand in front of Aisling without thinking. It should have been his brother he protected. It didn't go unnoticed.

He raised his sword and opened his stance. Aisling did the same, and Rainer called for their advance into the room. Inside a few smaller fights took place, but most of the remaining Fae stood against the wall behind Rainer's loyal men. One of whom came forward and bowed.

"The throne is yours, Your Majesty."

Brynach watched his brother take a deep breath, push back his shoulders, heavy with a regal-looking cloak, and walk ahead of them toward the throne. Brynach sighed, "Keep your weapon out."

They followed Rainer directly to where their mother still sat. Brynach and Aisling were met with a frustrated Breena and resigned Ceiren before they reached her.

"There was hardly any blood to draw," she complained. "Look, my blade is hardly dirtied."

Aisling shook her head at his sister and Brynach turned his attention to his eldest brother. Rainer held out his hand to his mother. Rainer kept his voice low as he spoke to her. Queen

Moura's jaw worked but she eventually nodded, placing her hand in Rainer's and rising from the throne.

As soon as she was up Rainer passed her to the guards and she was taken into custody. Rainer turned to the room where the remaining civilians gathered watching him.

"The reign of Queen Moura has ended. Heretofore, I am your King. An official coronation will follow, but for now, rest assured that I am ready to lead this court into better days." Then he sat on the throne as the King of the Unseelie Court.

Brynach wasn't sure if he was proud or sad. His brother was a father, a good man, and he feared what the crown would do to him. He saw healers tending to the injured, a few guards removing the causalities, but there weren't many of either.

"He looks good," Aisling said from his side, nodding to Rainer. "Also, that was...boring."

Brynach laughed, "My brother overthrew the sitting Queen and became King. And it was boring? You amaze me."

The room quieted as Brielle approached the throne, bowing deep. When Rainer told her to rise, she did, with something in her hand. Brynach's breath caught. She approached him and gently sat the crown upon his head.

Then Brielle addressed the room, "The reign of Moura of the Unseelie has ended."

"Long may King Rainer reign!" roared the Fae in the room.

Rainer held up a hand, his face stoic. Brynach's heart hurt at the role his brother would have to play now, but it was time.

"Your allegiance as Unseelie is to me now. My first official edict as ruler is to denounce by brother Levinas and the former Bloody Hand of the Unseelie, Gabriel. They are banished from our lands. Anyone found harboring them will be charged alongside them."

Around the room chatter started and cheers rose. Brynach held his breath, but nobody confronted Rainer on the matter.

"Come on. We'll get gifts from the court another time. Let Rainer settle in," Brynach said pulling Aisling away.

"You can't seriously want to leave right now," she protested as he pulled her arm.

"Oh, but I do," he promised as they exited the room.

"Bry, it was just getting interesting," Aisling's voice was high, annoyed.

He pulled her quickly through the gardens where Fae celebrated their new ruler. Nobody seemed too sad to see his mother out of power. As soon as they were outside the Unseelie gates he swept Aisling into his arms and sifted them to the Veil.

"I said to come see me," Kongur complained.

"And I told you to warn me," Brynach threw back before parting the Veil. He still carried Aisling as he walked across her lawn to the condo. He opened the door with his keys and shut it with his foot. He took a moment to lock it before walking down the hall.

"Where are we going?"

"Bed. I'd like to hold you, if I may?" He set her down and when she nodded, Brynach stripped down to his boxer briefs and slid into bed. Aisling removed her knife belt, boots, jacket, and pants before joining him in her sweater and underwear.

When she snuggled into his chest, he closed his eyes and forced his thoughts away from the softness of her body. Her hand began exploring his shoulders. Brynach swallowed a groan as her padded fingertips gave way to the light scrape of nails as her hands wandered from shoulders to pecs and over the hard nub of his sensitive nipples. If she went any lower, he was going to lose his mind. He trapped her hand in his, stilling it over his hammering heart.

"Aisling, I beg you to take pity on me."

"Sorry," she whispered, and her hand flattened under his. He busied himself scraping his own fingers over the crown of her head and down her hair. She purred against his chest and curled deeper into him before her breathing evened out.

"I love you, Aisling." Brynach kissed the top of her head

and closed his eyes.

That was the last thing he remembered before swatting at the gnat buzzing next to his head. He woke in Aisling's bed, her soft breath cascading over his chest.

"Turn the damn thing off," a very grumpy and shirtless Riordan growled from beside Aisling. Then he picked up the pillow from under his head and threw it at Brynach and Aisling.

"He's a gem in the morning. You get used to it," she grumbled.

Riordan disagreed, "No, you don't. You just love me enough to tolerate it. Who is making coffee?"

"I will," Aisling offered, lifting herself and leaving the two men alone in bed.

"I like waking up with both of you," Brynach said turning his head toward the Ravdi.

"Even when I'm moody?" Riordan asked, batting his eyelashes in jest.

"I love you enough to tolerate it," Brynach parroted the man's words back at him before standing. "You coming for coffee or not, Sunshine?"

"That will not be my new nickname!" Riordan yelled from their bed.

CHAPTER 24

Aisling

"Y ou have a dress maker. Totally normal," Lettie joked as she thumbed through the racks.

"Having people make you clothes is kinda normal," Trent commented from the chair in the dressing room.

"For you. Nobody makes clothes for me. Curvy girls get shafted," Lettie complained.

"Since when do you whine about getting shafted?" Trent quipped and earned a smack on the arm.

"Gross," she yelped. "So, if you have your wedding dress, what are we doing here?"

Aisling smiled at her friends. "The dress is stunning but I need another for the reception. It was fine to have my mom and the Queen help me pick the wedding dress, but I want you guys for this one. I want it to be sexy, but it has to work with the custom weapons garters being made for me in Faerie."

"Weapons garters?" Trent asked, eyes wide. "As in, actual stabby weapons?"

"Mmmhmm," Aisling answered scanning racks of dresses and blushing remembering Brynach's wedding gift. He'd knelt before her and gifted her the most beautiful, bejeweled throwing knives. She would proudly wear them to the wedding. "We're still not completely sure the unaligned won't attack the ceremony. It's better to be prepared."

Lettie exclaimed, "And yet you invited me to stand with you. Real nice." She winked but it didn't ease Aisling's worry.

She'd already considered that it was selfish to invite her family and friends to the wedding. Aisling wanted them there but if they got hurt, she'd never forgive herself. She couldn't imagine Lettie not standing with her. Each time she thought about the day it made her smile. Sure, it also made her stomach flip, but mostly, it was from excitement.

"She's kidding." Trent nudged her. "We wouldn't miss it for the world."

Aisling nodded. "Okay. I need something bridal but not formal. Ethereal but sexy. It has to make a statement," Aisling explained.

"Got it." He pulled Lettie up. "Let's go find a dress."

When they returned Aisling had already pulled another dress and the showroom employee was helping her into it. She was walking out as they returned, dresses draped over their arms. Both of them stopped when they saw her.

"Oh, Aisling!" Lettie sighed, "You look beautiful."

She moved to the mirror, and she had to admit it was stunning. The dark plum fabric draped off her shoulder and it was long enough to hide her thigh harness. It was pretty, but it didn't feel like a wedding reception dress.

"Of course, she does. But that's not it. Go get it off. Try these." Trent handed her an arm load of dresses. "It's one of those or they don't have it here."

The employee hung the dresses in the fitting room. "Your friend has great taste. Which one first?"

Aisling pointed to the one knee length dress on the rack. Brynach loved her legs, and she liked the idea of driving him wild. She stepped into it and let the attendant zip her up. Aisling purposefully avoided looking in the mirror. Her friend's reactions would tell her what she needed to know.

She stepped up onto round dais facing her friends. Trent

smiled and nodded, and Lettie's eyes got teary. For a moment, she could almost pretend things were normal, like the past year hadn't happened. Lettie wiped at her eyes and waved a hand.

"Stop looking at us. Turn around and look for yourself," Lettie ordered then turned to Trent. "Everything looks so damned good on her."

Trent smirked in agreement and nodded to Aisling. He mouthed the word "turn", so Aisling did. Under the lights of the store, which absolutely held some kind of magic, she glowed. Her pale skin looking somehow tan against the ivory dress.

Aisling was relatively sure that Brynach would want her no matter what she was wearing but this, she knew he'd love. The skirt was nearly weightless but held a deceptive number of layers. Aisling twisted to see them swirl around her thighs. Moving in this dress was a dream.

"It's perfect," Lettie gasped as she watched the light sparkle off the dress.

It looked like a thousand stars shone from the skirt. The light caught the small crystals woven into the fabric and danced. The moon in Faerie would light them up.

But it was the rest of the dress that sealed the deal. Aisling appreciated her bare shoulders, the band tight around her waist, and the deep neckline. Lace formed a thin strap over her shoulders and merged with the neckline that concealed her breasts and little else. Her back was bare, a slight curve at the top of her ass showing.

"Brynach is going to swallow his tongue." Trent raised a pierced eyebrow with a cocky grin.

Was it too much? Did that matter? Her wedding dress was stunning, but this was the perfect party dress. She'd be able to dance, and move, and still drive her husband wild. Aisling wanted him to be proud of being hers.

"Oh, my god. You're really getting married," Lettie gasped.

"I'm getting married," Aisling mumbled. "I'm going to be a wife."

Trent and Lettie were at her side in a flash, telling her to breathe. She didn't remember stopping, but she must have because she was crouched on the platform in front of the mirror.

"Everything okay over here?" the attendant asked. "Did you want to see another dress?"

"I thought I dropped something. Luckily, it's so easy to move in this dress." Aisling smiled. "I love it, but let's try the others to be sure."

An hour later she confirmed she could have stopped after the dress Trent chose. Aisling ordered it, very secure that she was going to knock Brynach off his feet.

"Seriously, Aisling, he's going to lose his shit," Lettie reassured her. "You know, I'm really struggling to balance the fact that I originally wanted to sit on his face with the fact that he's going to be your husband."

Aisling laughed, "Apparently, I'm still coming to terms with it, too." They got in her car, and she drove them to her empty condo. Riordan was staying with Liam for the night, and Brynach had gone back to Faerie. Which meant she could have a sleepover with her best friends, like old times.

"I can't believe how different this place looks. You upgraded and I approve," Trent said when he saw the new entertainment center.

"Bry's in love with tech now. If he had this way, we'd be giving your set up a run for its money. This was our compromise," she said, standing in front of the new 55-inch television and gaming setup in her living room. She still thought it was too big for the space, but Brynach and Riordan had convinced her it worked.

"There's a guitar and amp in your living room, Ash." Trent's jaw was slack. "What happened to you?"

"I fell in love," Aisling shrugged. The condo she meticulously decorated had changed to make the men in her life feel at home. She wasn't the least bit upset about it. Aisling loved the mix of everyone in the space.

"You guys get into comfy clothes. I'll preheat the oven and get food started." Aisling grinned at the note on the refrigerator.

Have fun! I'll miss you. Call if you need anything. -R

What he said. I'll be back tomorrow morning, early. I have eyes on you, but they'll stay away. -Bry

Aisling was humming as she prepped the array of appetizers on a tray. While she waited for the oven to heat, she went into her bedroom where Lettie was exiting the bathroom in her pajamas. Aisling smiled as her best friend moved in for a hug. Trent came in from the guest room and wrapped his arms around them.

The oven beeping broke them apart.

"I'll put the food in," Lettie said. "Get changed."

Aisling nodded and her friends left her room. She wasn't sure how tonight was going to go. A lot had changed since the last time they were all together. Aisling wanted the easy comfort of her best friends, but she wasn't sure they could slide back into it after all that had happened.

Trent yelled from the kitchen, "Aisling, you have craft beer in here! What the fuck happened while I was away? You hate craft beer."

Then again, maybe it could. "It tastes like licking a pine tree, but Riordan likes it. While I was getting stuff for tonight, I picked up a six pack from a new brewery for him."

"Oh, girlie. You have it bad," he joked and handed her and Lettie a drink.

Aisling didn't bother arguing. She also noticed that Lettie

didn't open her beer. When she gave her the "what's up" look she shook her head. Alright then, she wouldn't ask.

"Where's the beautiful terror that doubles as your familiar?" Trent asked settling on the sofa and curling up like a slinky cat.

"Um, he's in Faerie. Voluntarily acting as my eyes and ears. I go to the back of the yard and pop into Faerie and get updates each night," Aisling admitted. Not even the guys had noticed that her familiar was gone, but of course Trent would.

"That's really smart!" Lettie said. "Sneaky as fuck, but smart."

"Yeah, well, I'm tired of getting information from unreliable sources and I'm worried about Brynach. Things are going to shit, and I want to make sure he's safe," she said. "But enough about me. I need a highlights reel. Give me the most interesting thing that happened to you this week?" Aisling said settling on the sofa.

"Jashana hit on me when she followed me outside the other day," Lettie said with a grin. "I didn't hate it."

"How did Sean feel about that? Ollie would have been pissed if someone hit on me when they knew I had a partner." Trent leaned his head against the wall behind the sofa and groaned. "I cannot believe I just said that."

"I didn't tell him. It's a non-issue. I'm not willing to hurt Sean." Lettie hugged Trent's side. "It's nice seeing you in love."

Trent pulled his lip ring into his mouth, before answering, "I'm terrified I'll fuck it up."

"You won't. I know you, T," Aisling assured him.

"How did I become a one Fae man and you're over here with two," he joked.

"Hey, I'm a one Fae woman! I also happen to be a one Ravdi woman." She leaned into him.

The timer sounded and Aisling checked the food.

"You know, I couldn't help but notice that the guest room is pretty empty." A hint of a smile was in Trent's voice.

Lettie laughed, "And, um, my recently very astute observational skills led me to recognize different sizes of men's shoes and clothing in your bedroom. Not to mention the three toothbrushes and men's grooming supplies in the bathroom."

Aisling hid her face in the oven, hoping she could blame the blush on the heat.

"It's almost as if, and I know this is crazy, but it's almost as if both Riordan and Brynach are staying in your room." Lettie was clearly fucking with her now.

Trent clutched invisible pearls. "Oh, my heavens, how scandalous! What will the townsfolk say?"

"Oh, stop it!" Aisling laughed as she set the timer for another ten minutes. "So, you and Sean, huh?"

Both her friends laughed. "Don't try to change the subject. We all knew Lettie and Sean were going to be a thing eventually. That's not news." Trent waved a hand in the air.

"Wait. What do you mean everyone knew?" Lettie turned on Trent. "I didn't know!"

"Oh, sweetie. That man's been crazy about you for a while." Trent kissed Lettie's forehead.

Lettie sighed, "I'm not sure I could have gotten through the last months without him. But I don't want to use him, either."

"You're not," Aisling assured her. "If you're worried, talk to him. Communication is key."

Trent winked at her. "Is that how you make things work with your Ravdi and Dark Fae fiancé? I need to know your secrets! How did you convince them to have a menage a trois?"

Immediately Aisling was defensive. "Don't you dare, Trent! I won't let you debase our relationship like that."

"Sorry." Trent was genuinely apologetic. "So, clear up misconceptions. What's going on, Ash?"

Lettie licked her lips. "Details are welcome." She held out her hands. "But like, not in a creepy invasive way...but also, details, please."

Aisling laughed, "It's not as sexy as you're imagining. And it's so much work making sure they're both satisfied. But they work hard to make sure I'm taken care of, too. Plus, they're so sweet with one another."

Trent closed his eyes and listened.

"They bicker like brothers, but then I wake up in the morning and they're all tangled together or spooning while I'm wrapped in all the blankets and they're trying to stay warm." She let herself smile and shake her head. "I've been researching a lot about polyamory, and we've had these really beautiful talks about what we need to be happy. It's nothing I would have expected for myself, but it works so well. We don't put rules on our relationship except those we want. They're so fucking perfect," she admitted.

Her friends hugged her. "You deserve it," Lettie said.

The timer beeped and Aisling got up to get the food. Lettie followed her grabbing paper plates and a bottle of water for herself.

Trent carried food to the table while Aisling cut the pizza. "Please tell me you've taken the Dark Prince to bed," he begged.

Aisling laughed, "Not yet."

"Waiting for your wedding night?" he joked.

She didn't want her friends laughing at her, but she loved the idea of not sleeping with Brynach until they were husband and wife. The idea of a virginal wedding was out, but they could save that for themselves, still.

"Actually, yes. Besides, we still have to work out the dynamic before I bring sex with Bry into the mix," Aisling admitted.

"But you're going to. I mean, of course you will," Lettie said.

"It's all very fluid right now. I'm with both men romantic-ally. What they decide about their relationship is up to them."

Trent groaned and Aisling rolled her eyes. "Don't sexualize

my future husband and Ravdi."

"I can't help it! Just because I'm with Ollie doesn't mean that's not one of the hottest things I've ever heard," he complained.

"And you all share the bed, like always?" Lettie was leading her.

"When we're all together, yes." Aisling blushed and took a sip of her beer.

Trent grinned around a bite of pizza. "Look at us in healthy relationships. Go team!"

Aisling high fived the hand he was holding up and laughed. Time with her friends had been far too sparse lately and having them with her filled a hole in her heart she hadn't realized had been aching so badly. When they'd finished snacking, they got comfy on the sofa, again. Trent rested his head in Lettie's lap, and she played with his blonde hair.

"Give us the highlights of the trip. Ollie seems pretty devoted to you," Aisling wanted to celebrate her friend's happiness.

"He is." Trent blushed. "And I love him. I didn't want to, but I do. He prioritizes me. And he's so strong. Like, the man can toss me around. And the sex. Holy hell. I mean, Fae in general have stamina but he's insatiable. But that's not all it is. He wants to help me toward my dreams. And he asks all the time about you guys and stories from growing up."

Lettie shot Aisling a look. "That's sweet. I think?"

Trent blushed. "It is a little intense, isn't it? He's like that, though. He's...passionate."

Aisling smiled down at Trent which is why she saw when his eyes widened. She turned to Lettie and realized she'd gone stiff beside her. Aisling moved back a bit and Trent sat up.

"Is this? Is she?" Trent's voice shook.

"Yeah. It's a sensory experience. She'll come out of it soon." Aisling couldn't take her eyes off Lettie. Trent's hand found hers and gripped, hard.

"How can you watch her go through this?" His voice was soft.

"Because I don't have a choice. I've given her the charms and wards. I've taken away what I can, but sometimes the strong ones still get through," Aisling explained.

Breena entered the condo, most likely hearing their conversation through the door.

"Is she okay?" Breena nodded to Lettie.

When Aisling shook her head the Fae Princess opened the balcony doors and motioned to her familiar who took off from her perch on the railing. No doubt Brynach would be arriving shortly. Through the bond she felt Riordan, his concern. He'd probably arrive soon. If Lettie was being taken under, while inside Aisling's wards and through the protections on Lettie herself, this was a strong one. They'd need everyone here when she woke. She kept that to herself, so she didn't freak out Trent.

"Is it normal that it takes this long?" Trent whispered as if his voice could stir Lettie.

"No," Aisling admitted. But then Lettie's eyes fluttered, and she turned her head to Aisling. "Hey, sweetie."

Tears streamed down Lettie's face. She shook her head and then, to Aisling's horror, she went back under.

"What the fuck is happening?" Trent yelled, standing up.

Breena moved to answer the knock on the door. Riordan and Sean arrived. "We were together," Riordan said, moving to Aisling. Sean was already at Lettie's side, his arms around her still body.

Brynach was the next to barge into the condo with Brielle on his heals. She saw the concern in her fiancé's eyes.

"She was under for a while, started to wake, and got pulled back under," Aisling told the room.

Sean looked at Aisling. "That's never happened before."

The concern in the room was palpable. But nobody could do anything but wait for Lettie to wake up. It had been minutes since Lettie had gone into the second vision. Aisling had been away for a while, but from the concerned faces around the room, she could assume that this was not normal. Sean's eyes were wide and worried. That told her all she needed to know.

"Lettie, sweetie, it's time to come back," Aisling spoke as Sean rocked his girlfriend. It didn't have the magic effect she hoped it would. Damn it, Aisling, of course. "Riordan, please."

She felt her Ravdi funneling magic to her and put her hands on Lettie. She reinforced the wards and protections on her. She didn't throw it her friend's way, instead easing it onto her and slowly waking her from the visions.

Lettie blinked, taking in the room, and then buried her head in Sean's shoulder.

"Are you okay, L?" Trent asked.

Brielle spoke from the wall, "What did you see, Oracle?"

Oracle? Aisling looked to Brynach who shrugged. She'd be asking the Fae about that later. Her friend was shaking, and the questions didn't stop.

"What's wrong with her?" Breena asked, none too quietly.

Sean's head raised and his anger was barely concealed as he addressed the room, "Shut up, all of you. I swear, you're all so damn ignorant. Can't you see the trauma she's dealing with? Do you have any idea how hard this is for her? Shut up and wait until she's ready to talk. Fuck."

"I'm sorry," Aisling offered. "It's going to be okay."

"It's not," Lettie said from the circle of Sean's arms then scanned the room in a daze.

"What do you mean, babe?" Sean asked.

Silent tears streamed down her face.

CHAPTER 25

Riordan

R iordan took his phone out and moved away from Aisling. When his brother picked up, he made his request quick. "Get eyes on Sydney and confirm everyone tied to Peggy is still behind bars. I'll explain later."

"She's dead," Lettie whispered.

"Who?" Brynach asked.

Lettie shook her head. "I don't know. It was a Hive vision. I was moving around with her inside her kitchen, making lunch for her family. She was in and out of the refrigerator and then one time she shut it and there was someone behind it. They were taller than her, wider, and dressed all in black. She was so scared."

Riordan tore his eyes from her to look around the room. Everyone seemed as horrified as he felt.

"No. No. NO! She screamed. I screamed. Her family was home. She needed them to be safe, to be okay. All I could hear was the drumming of her heart in my head. She begged. Whatever they wanted, they could have. Don't hurt her. Don't hurt them." Lettie gasped for air.

His skin crawled but if Lettie had to live through this experience, he could handle hearing about it.

"And then the sun caught on the metal barrel of the gun.

The sound. Oh, Jesus, the sound was so loud. The last thing we saw was a man running into the room and another loud crack." Lettie shook against Sean.

"Lettie, I'm so sorry," Aisling offered but Lettie held up a hand.

"That's not all. God, I wish it were. Right after that I was pulled into another vision." A shiver ran through her. "I was in the back of a store. I saw motion out of the corner of my eye. I told them, no customers in the back. A large figure dressed in black locked the door behind him."

"Goddess, no," Aisling whispered, her fist pressed against her lips.

Lettie didn't spare her a glance. "He begged, of course. Who wouldn't? But the killer said they couldn't allow loose ends. Then he looked right into our eyes."

Riordan watched as Lettie broke. Her shoulders shaking. The room waited, knowing what came next was going to be bad. Staring sightlessly, she spoke.

"Are you listening? Do you see me? Can you smell the piss on the floor? Can you feel the heart inside this man pounding? If you can, know we're coming for you. Then the gun came up. I was thrown back into myself before the pain set in."

Nobody said a thing.

Aisling wiped her hands on her pajama pants. "Right. Okay. You're going to let me blindfold you and put noise canceling headphones on you. It will be harder to track your whereabouts that way. You're coming with me to Faerie. Trust me, L, I'll keep you safe."

Sean raised his head. "Like hell you are! You can't just whisk her away."

"I can, and if she lets me, I will," Aisling's voice wasn't inviting discussion.

"It's smart. We can protect her, and the risk is less," Brielle pointed out.

Breena chimed in, "If they're hunting them down, then

Lettie stands a better chance away from here. Not to mention it would keep those around her safer."

That was all it took to break through to Lettie. "I'll go."

"If she goes, I go," Sean announced.

Aisling threw up her hands. "I don't give a shit who comes as long as Lettie is safe."

"Remind me again why we have to go to this meeting?" He wiped sweat from his brow. He was so damn nervous.

"Because we're the entire reason for the meeting in the first place," Aisling reminded him.

The past two weeks had been stressful. Liam and Amber had been trying to hunt down leads on the killings, which hadn't slowed. The Hive was on high alert, but it was hard to hide from people who could see inside your head. Aisling had gone immediately to Sydney for help after setting Lettie up in an undisclosed location in Faerie. Unfortunately, other than saying it was likely her remaining brother responsible, she couldn't offer much help. Aisling had dealt with a very angry Mr. and Mrs. Moore who disagreed with Lettie being taken away from them. Brynach understood her parent's pain but was not thrilled that they'd added to Aisling's stress.

Riordan had been back and forth with Brynach, getting Sean and Lettie's things to them. And despite all the mayhem the wedding was swiftly approaching. Which meant on top of all that, they had to prepare for the Veil to drop. He knew, logically, that what they were about to do today was the least dangerous thing they'd done in a while, but he still hated it. It felt so official.

Aisling moved to Riordan and wrapped her arms around his waist. "I know you want to keep me in a bubble, but you have to trust me on this one. This makes sense."

Her head was resting on his shoulder, and he wanted to

push her away and kiss her. Or take her to the bedroom and make her forget about any meetings she had for the day. It didn't hurt that the bed in their Faerie home was one of the most comfortable things he'd ever been on.

"It's not like I don't know this has to happen, it's just—if we do this it makes everything unavoidably real." Riordan ran a hand over his hair.

He turned to the living room full of Fae. Breena, Brynach, Brielle, Aisling, Nevan, and Rainer crowded the small space. He should have been intimidated by having the King of the Unseelie in his living room lounging with an ankle resting on his knee, arms across the back of the sofa.

"I'd rather present a united front when we sit down," Rainer spoke, his voice a pleasant growl.

"Obviously, that's ideal. However, I'm not sure that's possible. Not with so many Fae against the dropping of the Veil," Aisling pointed out.

"What's the point of the meeting then?" Ceiren commented as he entered their house without knocking.

Riordan spoke up, "If the Veil drops and we don't give humans a warning, convince them that their government can protect them, it will be chaos. It will be dangerous for both sides."

Ceiren nodded. "The buzz in the unaligned camp centers mainly around the prophecy. When the Veil falls, they'll disperse into the human realms and away from Faerie."

Nevan spoke as he paced the floors, "Brynach and Aisling will unite the two courts, creating a stronger Faerie. There's no promise of the fall. The unaligned may decide the new Faerie suits them."

"I wouldn't hold your breath," Ceiren commented.

Brynach moved until the three stood united. Aisling's voice was sure when she spoke.

"I believe in the prophecy. But even if nothing happens, I want to wed Brynach. Not for my safety, but because I love him." Aisling gazed up at the handsome Fae. Riordan could see how much her words meant to Brynach. It was impossible not to be happy for them.

"It's time to go," Breena announced. "Which is good because I'm starting to feel sick to my stomach."

Her gruff words lost their bite when she winked at Riordan before turning for the door. She was miserable most of the time, but she'd warmed to him. Slowly, Rainer rose to his feet and the Fae followed them out of the cabin.

Before they left Brynach hugged Aisling close and kissed her soundly. With a grin and a pat on Riordan's back he followed his family out the door leaving them alone.

"I know you hate this," Aisling started.

Riordan shook off her concern. "I don't hate anything that makes you safer or happier, Ash."

Aisling kissed him softly and he wished they had time for more. "We have to go," he whispered when he pulled back.

She kissed him once more. "Fine, but tonight you're mine."

He was hers, always.

"Alright, we've kept them waiting long enough. Let's go." Riordan took her hand and tried to clear his head. "As discussed, I'm going to keep you fully charged. I want you ready if things go south."

They stepped into the bright sun of Faerie and Riordan sneezed. He was starting to wonder if he'd ever get used to the overwhelming otherness of this land. Today they had no choice but to sift. They weren't heading to Aisling's condo. They were going to the government building that housed the governor and other state officials. There was a rumor that the President would have ears at the meeting. Riordan wasn't even an American citizen and that made him nervous.

Apparently, they had been recruited for a team concerning the safety and welfare of humans and ensuring a smooth transition when the Veil fell. They sifted to a new section of the Veil and passed through as close to the building as possible. A quick walk and they were heading up a wide set of steps. Once through the metal detectors they were shown to a conference room, around which government officials sat. Liam gave him a quick nod from beside the Firinne representative. The Fae began to settle in their chairs, Rainer on the right side of the table with Nevan representing the Seelie Court on the left. Breena stood against the wall behind Rainer while Brielle chatted with a member of the security detail behind Nevan.

"Miss Quinn, Mr. Campbell, and Prince Brynach, I presume?" A man in a power suit smiled at them and waved a cup of coffee toward three empty chairs at the head of the table. "If you will."

Riordan had a moment to let the panic show in his eyes before he masked it. He followed Aisling and Brynach to the space opposite where the government officials and advisor to the national security team would sit. Aisling's hand settled on his arm.

"The room is spelled," she whispered so Brynach, and he could hear. "I won't be able to use magic in here."

Riordan tested the waters, letting his vision slip and looking for magic. He found none. Or rather, none he could reach. They should have anticipated it. Of course, government buildings would be protected from magic users.

Aisling took a seat as did Brynach. If he couldn't aid Aisling as her Ravdi, why was he even here? Before he could continue his internal debate, the door swung open and a group of men and women with serious faces and very official binders in their arms entered.

Once seated, a man in a gray suit set his hands on the table. His eyes rested on each occupant for a moment before he spoke, "For those of you who don't know me, my name is Governor Settenfield. I appreciate you taking the time to meet with us."

Aisling smiled. "Thank you for having us, sir. As you're

already aware, there are hints that the Veil may come down soon. We believe it is in all our best interests to be prepared for such an event."

A shrewd looking woman sitting next to the governor spoke, "It seems to me that the prophecy is rather avoidable. Why are you actively pursuing such a catastrophic thing?"

Aisling sucked in a breath and Riordan stiffened beside her. It was a valid question and one they were prepared to answer. Whether or not they agreed with their reasoning was another matter. It was Brynach who spoke.

"The union of the Seelie and Unseelie Courts, even through less royal lineage like mine and Aisling's, marks an important time in the realm of Faerie. We have been discussing a unified Faerie with our people for a long time. We feel that now is the right time for such action," he began. "The ranks of unaligned are growing, unrest is building, and our marriage can help calm that. It just so happens that an old prophecy..."

"We are aware of the prophecy," the Governor interrupted.

"Right," Brynach continued. "Well, we can't know for sure what will happen, but I know that I will do whatever it takes to guarantee the safety of the woman I love. I won't postpone marrying Aisling or securing her place in Faerie. If the prophecy is true, it's a joining of two realms meant to be one. It's a healing, not a hurting."

Brynach either didn't care about the annoyance on the woman's face or wasn't paying attention. Riordan didn't believe it was the latter. "Also, I'm pretty sure your government has known for a while that the Veil is weakening. The merging of our people is somewhat inevitable, is it not?"

Riordan waited for shock or arguments, but there were none. Fae and humans alike seemed to know this was going to happen, either now or later. Beside him Aisling opened the bond a little, sharing her shock. At least he wasn't the only one caught off guard.

"It's my understanding that the prophecy, if it's to be believed, portrays a world where the Veil was never meant to exist. It's told our two realms and people lived together in harmony," Aisling added. "We have seen through the implementation of border crossings and Fae integration this side of the Veil that there are benefits to the merging. This can be a positive step forward for both sides."

"That remains to be seen, Ms. Quinn." The Governor didn't seem convinced. "Still, we need to prepare for the off chance that the Veil does come down. I have bulletins out to the heads of all Supernatural Police Departments. We are employing witches to spell all jails, prisons, and cells to hold supes," he announced.

"What we're concerned about are the unknown factors. Are you staying in your realm despite the Veil coming down? What can we expect from the influx of magic that your realm merging with ours will create? Should border areas be policed more heavily? Will the Veil drop everywhere or just in our area?" An unnamed man spoke from among the group.

Nevan answered, "With all due respect, we can't possibly know how the entirety of our realm will react. A large portion of our people don't fall under the reign of the Seelie or Unseelie courts. We can pass edicts to stay on our side, to leave humans alone, but to be fair, we can't promise that. Nor can we predict how magic will behave."

The governor sat back in his chair. "That is not what I hoped to hear."

"Let me guess, you'll employ riot gear, tanks, and military presence at all border towns? Air strikes into Faerie the moment the Veil drops?" Rainer's voice was more growl than anything else. Beside him Ceiren shook his head.

"What my brother is wondering is if you're planning to take action against our people preemptively?" Even reworded Ceiren's words were terrifying.

"The Fae have not been entirely trustworthy throughout history. Given free rein of our realm what's to stop you from dominating our government, overwhelming our military, and enslaving our people?" Settenfield asked, taking a sip of water.

"And that fear has nothing to do with the prejudice and over policing of our people? We have certain advantages that are inherent in our genes but that doesn't make us an immediate threat." Rainer was angry.

Riordan waited to see if the Birchwood Falls police chief would speak up. He wasn't overly surprised by his thoughts when he did. "You admitted yourselves that you can't control factions of your people. Can you promise they'll stay peaceful? Can you ensure control over your courts and their subjects?"

Riordan didn't even register that he was speaking until the words were out of his mouth. "Can you?"

Heads snapped his direction, but he continued.

"Can you promise that scared humans won't put bounties on the heads of Fae? Can you say that you have complete control over all American citizens? Or citizens of the world? Can you promise that the Fae aren't at risk from armed humans?" Riordan was leaning across the table.

Behind Rainer, Breena nodded to Riordan. Aisling moved her hand under the table and took his.

"If I may?" Aisling began and when nobody objected, she pushed on. "Distrust exists on both sides and people on each will use that to their advantage. There will be fighting and conflict. But how we present ourselves right now matters. If we go out together, show you with the King and the Regent, if we say we're excited about the unification, people may be behind us."

The governor nodded. "I had the same thought, young lady. We're going to spin this to our benefit. Tell them you're willing to share secrets to longer life and health, the cure for cancers, and all that."

"We don't have those," Nevan argued.

"Irrelevant." He waved a hand.

"We need people on your boards, making decisions that benefit both races," Rainer said.

"Fae cannot hold human offices," Mr. Settenfield answered. "That's not negotiable."

"The Veil coming down means that laws need to protect and benefit everyone. By our laws if someone touches someone we love we have the right to their blood. By our laws if a Fae moves into an empty home, it becomes theirs. By our laws our rulers have the right to sentence and execute those they see fit without trial." Ceiren was speaking calmly but nothing about his words were gentle.

Riordan waited to see how the humans felt about that little bit of information.

"Right now, all your laws are about keeping Fae in check, making sure they don't encroach on your lands. But there won't be any more "your lands". We need new laws that protect all of us," Brynach said, his hand on the table in Aisling's.

"And I suppose you have ambassadors in mind?" Governor Settenfield asked.

"My brother and his partners," Rainer said.

Oh, hell no.

"Brynach, Aisling, and Riordan represent the best of both sides of the Veil, a Fae royal, a witch, and her Ravdi. People will rally behind them." Rainer smiled at them, and Riordan felt like he was going to be sick. "We need representation in your defense department. We have several Fae in mind, Brielle being one of them." Rainer nodded to the small blonde by the door. "Of course, local law enforcement will need Fae as well. We have warriors and guards to spread out, but I can't promise all of them will want to leave Faerie."

"Will Faerie even exist anymore?" The woman who spoke had been quiet until now, taking it all in. Riordan could see magic around her, a witch, like the governor.

"We don't know," Ceiren answered. "Our world isn't like yours. We believe that will still be true when the Veil falls. Not all Fae will want to live away from lands they know. There are inherent issues with our immortality and being near our kind and our land. Some things we will wait and discover with time."

Settenfield nodded. "I want a list of your representatives and those willing to start immediately in aiding our police and justice systems. I expect discretion while we work out new laws and regulations. If the Veil doesn't fall, I don't want to cause panic."

"Of course," Nevan answered. "As we stated, this is an old prophecy and only time will tell if it has any merit."

The group rose. "I appreciate you giving us warning and allowing time to prepare. It was a pleasure meeting you, and I look forward to working with you to ensure the safety and interests of all parties involved."

Without waiting for a response, he walked out, flanked by his constitutes. It was then that Riordan was able to take a full breath.

CHAPTER 26

Aisling

"Are you okay?" Riordan asked from his position under her.

Aisling stretched against him, leaning up to kiss him. "No."

His chuckle vibrated through her. She had promised he'd be all hers after the meeting. Oh, had he been. They'd practically raced to the condo and with the bond wide open, they had loved one another. She should be happy. Instead, she was filled with worry. Lettie had messaged her she was tired of hiding and had returned home.

"I'm terrified Lettie will be hurt, and I can't do anything about it," she admitted.

Riordan made a noise somewhere between a huff and a grunt, "You can't keep her prisoner, Ash. She wanted to come home. All you can do is keep her wards strong and she will do the rest. She's being careful."

"It feels like it's my fault. I've always kept them safe and I'm failing them." She buried her face in his chest.

"They'd hate it if they knew you were beating yourself up about this." He kissed the top of her head and Aisling let the love pouring through the bond reassure her.

Aisling let the soft caress of his hand on her back and the steady rhythm of his heartbeat under her ear soothe her. She felt the heaviness of her body and sunk into him.

Sleep claimed her and with it, the dream began. It became obvious early on that this wasn't an ordinary dream. She was dreamwalking, though she didn't understand how. There were only a few Fae Aisling was linked to. There was no denying she was in the Seelie court. She'd know the corridors anywhere. At the end of a long hall was a very distracted Fae.

Corinna was peaking around a corner, her hands fluttering at her side. Aisling was about to reveal herself to her friend when she heard footsteps and Corinna hurried toward the figure in the dark.

"Where have you been?" she asked the shadows.

"Busy." A hand came out of the darkness, followed by a face Aisling knew too well. "Have you missed me?"

Her friend leaned into the man's touch. "You know I have. I hate being away from you. I don't like hiding."

The man's voice was soft when he answered, but Aisling heard the steal under the words. "You haven't told anyone, have you? I don't want to share you with anyone yet." He leaned in and kissed Corinna's eager mouth. "Soon, my dear, but once they know we'll never know peace."

She sighed, "But I worry about you. It's not like I can ask after you or come to you. I don't even know where you're staying."

"And you won't. It wouldn't be safe. But I will always find you," he promised.

And it would have been a sweet moment between Corinna and her suitor if Aisling's blood hadn't run instantly cold at the sound of his voice. Her heart hammered and she fought to control her urge to wake from this nightmare. She forced herself still so she could listen and learn as much as possible before waking.

"It's not true, is it?" Corinna's voice broke at the end of the question.

The voice that answered wasn't patient and soft like it had

been. "You know it is. We discussed this. There's only one way we both get to be together the way we want. I am doing it for you. For us. Don't you dare make me feel bad about that."

Corinna gasped, and Aisling saw a tight hand on her arm. The desire to surge forward and break that arm was strong. But she wouldn't defend the Princess. Their conversation ended when the man surged at Corinna, and they began making out. Aisling tore her eyes away and willed herself awake. That was something she most definitely did not need to subject herself to.

When Aisling woke it wasn't a gentle easing into mindfulness. It was a jolt. She sat up and seethed. Riordan was already awake and Brynach was sitting shirtless next to her waiting for her to wake.

"That must have been some dream," Riordan commented. "You were really pissed off."

Both men were looking at her, waiting for her to talk. Her head swiveled between them. "Can you guys like, move together? I am going to get whiplash looking back and forth."

With a chuckle Brynach shifted his hips and straddled Aisling's outstretched legs, paused to kiss her, and then settled next to Riordan. Maybe one day small gestures like that wouldn't awe her, today wasn't that day. She took a moment to smile at them and then shared her news, "I saw Levinas."

She felt the fear in the bond and Brynach snarled. She put a hand on each of their legs. "I'm okay. It was a dreamwalk. They didn't know I was there. They were, distracted, to say the least." Aisling fought the revulsion.

Riordan spoke first, "Was he this side of the Veil? Was it a Hive connection?"

Aisling bit her lip. "It was a dreamwalk. With Corinna."

"Why was Levinas with Corinna?" Brynach asked.

She wanted to know the same damn thing. The sting of betrayal finally set in. "They kissed. She was waiting for him in the hallway and Levi was spouting off bullshit about wanting to be with her but needing to keep it a secret."

"Hallway?" Of course, that's what Brynach snagged on. He was not going to like this.

"They were in the Seelie palace," she shared.

Curses rang through the room. Aisling knew what it meant. Levinas may want to keep things quiet between them but no way he was within the walls of the Seelie Court and the King and Queen didn't know. Not with the sentries at the gates. Which meant the people Aisling trusted had betrayed her.

"I'm so sorry, a stoirin." Brynach cupped her face in one of his large hands and she let herself nuzzle into it for a moment.

"She asked him if what people were saying about him was true. He said it was, that if they wanted to be together, he had to do it."

"What does kidnapping you have to do with their relationship?" Riordan looked entirely confused.

"I don't know. I also don't know what would make Branwyn and Kyteler throw their hat in the ring with Levinas." Aisling was pissed and she had questions that demanded answers. But she didn't know what to do next.

"You're sure they didn't see you?" Brynach asked. His hand had moved to her neck, rubbing at the knots.

"If Corinna felt me, she gave no indication of it. I was about to step out when Levi walked up. I ducked further into the shadows," Aisling confirmed.

She could practically see the wheels in his head turning. "Then we still have the element of surprise."

Riordan jerked his eyes toward Brynach. She lowered her brows and sent a question through the bond. Her Ravdi sent back worry and hurt while jerking his head slightly toward her fiancé. The hell?

"Bry, are you ok?" It was clear he wasn't, but she asked anyway.

His citrine eyes found hers. "Nothing about this day has been okay."

"What's going on?" Aisling asked, her hand on his thigh. Brynach let go of her neck and wound their fingers together. She found comfort in the warmth of his touch.

"I'd been coming to tell you they found my father," he whis-pered. "But then I saw Riordan's eyes all wide and worried and none of that mattered until I was sure you were okay."

"I'm fine." Aisling climbed into his lap and held him.

"What does that mean?" Riordan asked, placing a hand on Brynach's back.

"I'm not entirely sure. He's being held in the dungeons," Brynach shared.

Aisling didn't understand. "How the hell did they find your father before Levinas? Clearly, we need to question Corinna, but your brother is a fucking idiot. No way your father got pulled in first."

"We'll have a better idea of where Levinas is now that we have a lead. But I'm sure the King and Queen will protect themselves and their daughter. My father, he may be power-ful, but he doesn't inspire loyalty, just fear. I guess nobody would harbor him," Brynach reasoned.

He was hiding behind his hair. Aisling lifted her hand, removed the spare hair tie from her wrist and pulled his hair into a messy bun. "Bry? Look at me."

Slowly those citrine eyes she loved rose and locked onto hers. The pain she saw in them startled her. He looked scared.

"Talk to us. What can we do?" Aisling prompted.

Riordan put a hand on his shoulder and squeezed. "What-ever it is, we're with you."

Aisling's heart nearly burst.

"I have to go to Faerie," he announced.

"So, we go to Faerie." Aisling nodded.

"No. I have to go. You don't. You shouldn't." Brynach was shaking his head, his bun bobbing.

"Not happening, big guy. We're going with you," Riordan

answered for both.

"We've already wasted too much time." Aisling stood and Riordan mirrored her. She held out a hand to Brynach, but he didn't take it.

"It's still not safe for you. Not until after the wedding," he argued.

"The wedding is days away at this point. I'll be with you the entire time. You're not going to convince us to stay. Let's go." Aisling wasn't going to be swayed. He needed them.

Brynach hugged her, his chest heaving as he held her tight. One hand rested on the back of her head and the other on her lower back, cradling her to him. She felt safe. She felt loved. She was home. Aisling pulled back a little and whispered his name, waiting for his eyes to lock on hers.

"Kiss me and then we'll get dressed and go," she demanded, and he obeyed.

With that settled Aisling grabbed her bag, Riordan sent a text to Liam letting him know they were leaving, and then they were out the door practically sprinting to Faerie.

"What are we walking into?" Riordan asked.

"Likely Rainer sentencing my father to death. It won't be pretty, but I need to be present." Aisling had never seen Brynach quite so emotionless.

He split the Veil and they all stepped through. Immediately, her familiar was screeching in her ear that they needed to hurry. Brynach must have gotten the same message because he threw his arms out, pulling both Riordan and her to him. Like that they were sifting.

Riordan's recovery time was improving. They were able to immediately run for the stone sentinels. Without hesitation her Ravdi held his finger out for the bloodletting, and she did the same as soon as Brynach was done. He pushed the gates open, and they rushed through the gardens to the castle.

They charged through the halls, Brynach in the lead and Riordan safely between him and Aisling. Her brave fiancé didn't hesitate at the throne room doors. The fear that he was too late was evident in his urgency.

"Brother. I'm glad you could make it," King Rainer called from a black throne atop the dais.

"I came as soon as I could," Brynach answered, his pace slowing and his hand shooting back for hers. Aisling took it and quickened her pace to match his. She knew without looking that Riordan was at their back.

Gabriel was chained to the floor, his body stretched in what must have been an uncomfortable position. His arms were splayed to either side, fully extended. Metal cuffs around his ankles and his neck held him atop a carved rock that he'd used many times to separate head from body.

"I see the Bloody Hand has been sentenced," Brynach's tone betrayed no emotion.

"You weren't here to weigh in. Justice is yours, or rather, Aisling's. I will defer to your decision if you can agree to one," Rainer announced, and a murmur sounded through the hall.

A King deferring to anyone, especially a bastard royal, was unheard of. But the law was the law and the right to blood for offenses against Aisling was Brynach's as her betrothed or hers as the one he'd harmed. Still, a King giving a halfling the same right as a full-blooded Fae was worthy of the murmurs.

"He killed countless familiars, Aisling. Don't you dare go soft on us," Phlyren's warning came, angry in her mind.

Beside her Brynach turned his head toward his father, his body radiating tense anger. Aisling tugged on his hand until his eyes were on her. Those eyes she loved weren't seeing her anymore. His chest was rising and falling too quickly. She recognized a panic attack when she saw one.

"Your Highness, may we have a minute?" Aisling asked, looking past Brynach to his brother. Rainer nodded his head, and she pulled her fiancé until he followed her to a corner of the hall. She stepped to the window, sliding behind a heavy curtain to a hidden bench and taking Brynach with her.

Riordan followed them but didn't enter the curtain. His feet were visible under the hem of the heavy drapes. She loved him in that moment for knowing they needed time and guarding it.

"Brynach. Bry. Hey, look at me," Aisling begged, trying to keep the panic from her voice. She pushed on his shoulders until he was sitting on the obsidian slab. Aisling moved in front of him, between his spread legs, and pulled his head to her belly.

Holding him felt natural. Offering comfort and support right now was what he needed. She had to bring him back from wherever he was. Her fingers lightly tugged the tie from his hair, and she wove her fingers through his long inky locks. Aisling's small hand latched to the hair at the nape of his neck.

She took a deep breath and, praying she wasn't wrong, tugged on his hair, hard. With a growl, Brynach's head shot back, his eyes on hers alive and full of fire. His arms shot out, and in a flash, she was seated on his lap.

Brynach returned the favor and maneuvered her head using a fistful of her hair. His teeth raked across her neck before his mouth claimed hers. The kiss was not gentle. A rough hand groped at her breast, and she pushed into him. She couldn't stop the hungry sounds she was making. Aisling moved on his lap, enjoying being manhandled by her fiancé. His hips jerked up against her, the proof of his arousal pressing at her core. He swallowed the gasp that left her mouth before biting down on her lip.

She sighed his name. Her hands framed his face and she repeated it. "Brynach. Are you with me now?"

He nodded. "Sorry, a stoirin."

"You had me worried for a minute." Her body was still flush against his, their chests rising and falling together.

"What do I do, Aisling?" the Dark Fae whispered against her temple.

"I don't know, Bry. I can't make that decision for you." She wished she could.

"You have a right to weigh in. Even if he hadn't hurt you, you're my partner. What are you thinking?" His arms were wrapped around her so tight she was struggling to breathe.

Gabriel deserved to be brought to heel, to pay for his crimes against Fae and familiars. But death? She didn't know if she could sentence someone to that.

"I know I shouldn't care. I know it shouldn't bother me to see him dead. But," Brynach started.

"But he's still your father," Aisling finished.

His head shook violently. "No. That man is nothing to me. It's that it would be so easy to be like him, Aisling. So very easy to lose myself in hate and anger, in the blood and retribution. I'm scared of myself. Of how like him I could become if I let myself."

"Shhh." She kissed the top of his head because it was all she could reach. "You are nothing like that man. You are kind and you are loving. If your anger gets the best of you, or you are driven to violence, it is to defend and protect those you care for."

Aisling pushed on Brynach's shoulders until he was forced to loosen his grip on her. "I love you and you will never be like him."

Brynach lowered his chin, his eyes shying away from hers. She couldn't have that. She raised his face to hers. "Never."

His grip on her loosened and he nodded. She wasn't naive enough to think he believed her, but she'd prove it to him over time. Right now, they had an immediate issue to deal with.

"They're going to expect an answer from us," she prompted.

"I won't kill him." He shook his head. "I should, but I won't."

"Okay, what does that leave us with?"

"Banishment."

"He'll hurt people somewhere else." She dismissed the

idea.

"Permanent imprisonment," Brynach offered.

"Gabriel will convince someone to help him escape and then we're back to square one. Or he'll be murdered."

"Problem solved." Brynach raised a brow at her.

"No. There's got to be something else that prevents him from hurting others but keeps him alive." Aisling thought hard, but she didn't know what that other option could be. Brynach's eyes flared. "What is it?"

"We could strip him. It hasn't been done in my lifetime, but I've heard of it." When Brynach stood, Aisling was still wrapped around him.

She dropped her legs and Brynach took her hand. He pushed back the curtain and shared a quick look with Riordan before pulling her forward. She had a moment to lock eyes with her Ravdi in which he mouthed, "Are you okay?" Aisling lifted her shoulders and then nodded as she hurried after her fiancé.

"Have you come to a decision?" Rainer asked when they were standing in front of him once more.

Aisling could sense the room holding their collective breaths. The silence was deafening. Brynach's hair was a wild mess around his shoulders when he announced they had.

"Gabriel, Bloody Hand of Moura, is to be stripped."

Aisling's head spun, taking in the surprised looks, the covered mouths, and the horror on the faces of the Fae around her. Her head whipped back to Rainer who sat stoically.

"As you wish." Rainer nodded to where Gabriel was still shackled to the floor. "He will be constantly guarded while we prepare the ceremony. See to it he remains as he is."

The guards nodded, immediately at attention. Aisling had no idea what the ceremony entailed, but she assumed Rainer did. The King gestured to Brynach, who led Aisling in the new ruler's wake to his private chambers. This time, Riordan didn't follow.

As soon as the doors to the King's rooms shut, Rainer turned on Brynach, eyes wild and cape still swinging. "Have you lost your mind, brother?"

"No." Brynach didn't back down. "I won't kill him."

"You should. He's a menace and a pain in my ass." Rainer threw up his hands before schooling his features again. "This is the first big decision of my reign. How we deal with him sets the tone. I never thought you'd spare him."

Aisling spoke, even though she wasn't entirely sure she should. "You want a more united Faerie, right? Would it really hurt to set yourself apart from the way your mother and Gabriel handled things? Nobody is getting off without consequences, but a little leniency may go a long way in rebuilding trust."

"She's a good match for you, brother." He smiled. "You're not wrong, Aisling. I assume you want to perform the ceremony."

She felt the color in her cheeks. "I can do that?"

"We don't know how the ceremony works," Brynach admitted, and his brother shook his head.

"Of course, you don't. I have no doubt you'd be able to perform the ritual, Aisling. It must be done by someone the Fae has betrayed, but with good intentions," he explained.

"Good intentions?" Aisling wasn't so sure she qualified.

"Someone who wants to protect the interests of Faerie. Not seeking vengeance. Which is hard to come by, seeing as the one to perform the ritual must also be someone wronged." Rainer approached her. "But I warn you, it won't be easy, and it won't be pleasant."

"Fantastic. I was hoping you'd say that." Aisling rolled her eyes, a habit she still hadn't broken. "What do I have to do?"

The King thought a moment and then sighed, "Damn it. This complicates things. You're going to hate this."

Brynach moved closer to her. "Rainer, what is it?"

"She needs to draw from Faerie, from the people and the

land, and she needs to use the strength of the collective to reach for Gabriel's magic and strip it away, distributing it to the whole," Rainer's voice was slow and melodic.

Brynach turned to his brother. "Aisling can't access the magic of Faerie."

"Not right now, no. But when she marries you, she can," Rainer promised.

"Right, well I don't think we want to wait until then to handle this," Aisling answered, "So what now?"

"As King of the Unseelie, I can marry you. Nobody would need to know, and you can still have your wedding. But once your bond falls into place she'll share your power, Brynach. She'll be able to do it." Rainer's eyes were wild.

"No. I won't rush her," Brynach's voice brokered no argument from his brother.

"I'll do it. I want Riordan here, but I'll do it," Aisling said quietly.

Rainer nodded to a Fae by the door.

"A stoirin, no." Brynach took both her hands in his. "You don't have to do this for me."

"You silly Fae, haven't you realized yet that I'd do anything for you." She smiled at him and watched as his eyes filled. "I love you, Bry. I choose you. I don't care how or when it happens. I want to be yours. We'll have the big wedding, but I kind of like the idea of it being just us."

"And me," Riordan said stepping up to them. "So, we're having a wedding."

Aisling turned and saw her Ravdi smiling at them.

"You'll stand with me?" Brynach asked Riordan and Aisling's heart swelled even more.

"Hell yeah!" He clapped his hands together, entirely too chipper.

Aisling huffed a laugh and squeezed Brynach's hands. "Are you okay with this?"

"Am I okay marrying you so you're strong enough to strip

my father of his immortality?" His head hung back as he stared at the ceiling.

"No, Bry, are you ready to be mine?" she asked with a smile.

"I've been yours for longer than you know, a stoirin." He took her chin between his thumb and forefinger and kissed her.

"Will this bring down the Veil?" Riordan asked and they jumped apart.

"I'd forgotten about that." Aisling looked to Rainer.

"Don't look at me. I have no idea what constitutes fulfilling the prophecy. But if you want to strip Gabriel this has to happen," the King offered absolutely no reassurances.

"Right. Well, let's get you two crazy kids hitched," Riordan laughed.

CHAPTER 27

Brynach

A isling stood before him in jeans, a sweater, and low boots. She'd never been more beautiful to him.

"Not without me!" Breena called, rushing to Aisling with a bundle of black blooms in her hand. "From the gardens. Don't smell too deeply."

"Poison wedding flowers. Cool," Aisling laughed and then thanked his twin. "Will you stand with me?"

Breena shrugged. "I've got a few minutes."

Brynach marveled at the woman in front of him who could laugh in the face of such paralyzing decisions and consequences. He was the luckiest man in any realm to be hers. Behind him, Riordan put a hand on his shoulder and squeezed. Brynach felt his lips curl in a smile. Maybe he was lucky to be Riordan's, too.

"Ready?" Rainer asked from in front of Brynach and Aisling.

"Yes," they answered together.

Aisling hadn't wanted to know the specifics of the wedding ceremony. The more she knew, the more she had to worry about. But it was relatively simple. Rainer brought out a piece of rope and Brynach took a moment to breathe through his emotions. This isn't how he imagined this moment, but staring into Aisling's hazel eyes, he realized this is what it was always going to be. Just her. All else falling away.

Rainer held the rope and asked them to tie one knot for each promise they made to one another.

Aisling grinned and took it from him. "I promise to keep life exciting for us, but that within my arms you will always find love and acceptance."

Damn it, he was going to cry. She handed him the rope and Brynach spoke while tying a knot above the one she'd made. "I promise that my sole purpose in life is to love you, which means fighting for the life we want and supporting you in all you do."

The way Aisling smiled at him nearly stopped his heart. Rainer asked if they wanted to say anything else.

"A million things," Aisling answered. "But that's enough for now."

Brynach winked at her and nodded to his brother, who took the rope and tied their wrists together.

"You are bound to one another by word and action. You are hereby acknowledged by Fae law to be one. The happiness, pain, and pleasure of your spouse is now yours to protect."

The words were simpler than the ones exchanged in the official ceremony, but they settled in Brynach's chest with a joyous weight. He stared at his wife.

His.

Hers.

Eternity.

He whispered to Aisling, "It won't hurt."

She had a moment to tilt her head at him before Rainer set the rope binding them on fire. The Fae flames licked at their skin but didn't burn them as it dissolved around their wrists. Once the rope was ash they'd be bound.

Aisling's startled expression turned to wonder as she gazed at the flames and then back to him. Her eyes didn't waver, locked on his as the rope fell away. As soon as it was nothing more than ashes at their feet Aisling threw herself into his arms.

Brynach was vaguely aware of clapping and Rainer proclaiming them married. All he cared about was the feel of his wife against him as he lifted her for a kiss.

His favorite feeling in all the world was her hands in his hair and her mouth on his. If this moment could stretch on forever, he'd live a happy life. Aisling was his wife. Nothing could dampen his joy.

"It's time, brother."

Well, except for Breena reminding him that his new wife had to strip their father of his magic. Aisling pulled back from him and rested her forehead on his.

"We'll come back to this feeling. I promise. Let's go finish this." She wriggled and he set her feet on the ground.

The guards who had stood quietly by the walls, his twin, his brother, his wife, and his...well, his Riordan...walked to the doors that led back to the throne room.

"Congrats, you two. Way to elope," Riordan joked as he caught up to them.

Aisling's laugh vibrated in Brynach's chest as she took her Ravdi's hand and brought it to her lips. Before the doors opened, she was forced to drop it, and that broke Brynach's heart. They'd have to fix that.

Brynach straightened his shoulders, the cold calculated stare reentering his eyes. It was easier to slip into now that he trusted Aisling to bring him home. He needed to be this right now.

While they were still far enough away, his brother leading the way, Brynach whispered to Aisling, "Can you feel it? Faerie?"

Her answer was a small nod of her head. "It's beautiful."

Brynach stood to the side of Rainer's throne with Aisling by his side. He wasn't entirely sure how his brother was going to go about the stripping, or how he'd explain Aisling's new powers.

"Aisling, Child of Light, has agreed to strip Gabriel, former Bloody Hand of the Unseelie Court, of his powers. The decision to let Gabriel live a human life is a fate worse than death for one so used to power. May you always remember that it is by the mercy of Brynach and Aisling that you remain alive," his voice rang loudly in the room.

On the floor Gabriel remained silent but the twitching of his arms betrayed him. His father respected power above all else. Nothing would terrify him more than losing it.

"Aisling, come forward," Rainer called to her, and she was forced to let go of his hand and walk to the King.

He was proud of his wife, who was clearly nervous but held her head high.

"She looks different," Riordan whispered at his side.

"Excuse me?"

"She's my bonded, too. I can see the magic that swirls around her, the threads of her power. She's changed," Riordan sounded sad.

"She still needs you," Brynach assured him.

When Riordan didn't answer, Brynach spared him a glance and saw the way the Ravdi was staring at Aisling. When his eyes turned and met Brynach's, he felt something unfamiliar but warm.

"How is this possible?" Riordan gasped.

"Are you okay?" Brynach put a hand on the Ravdi's arm. "Riordan?"

The other man shook his head. "Later." He turned back to Aisling.

Aisling's magic whipped up a breeze. Her hair swirled around her as Rainer sat stoic on the throne. A few gasps sounded in the room.

"Are you feeding her magic?" Brynach asked.

"Nope," he answered. "That's all her."

From the throne, Rainer asked, "Aisling, do you understand your duty here today?"

"Gabriel has inflicted unforgivable pain upon countless Fae. He has betrayed his kind and for his crimes he will be stripped of magic. Not out of anger or hatred, but out of respect for that which was gifted to us. What was once his will return to the land," her strong voice resonated through the large space.

How had she known exactly what to say?

"The halfling doesn't have the power to strip one so old. This is foolish," came a call from amongst the crowd. It parted, leaving a lone Fae standing, head high in defiance.

"You have no idea the strength of a woman like Aisling. The land is getting stronger. The Unseelie are stronger with the poison of my mother gone. The gifts bestowed upon her are many," Rainer answered.

Riordan began to murmur, but Brynach silenced him by gripping his forearm tightly. He wasn't sure what his brother was playing at, but it sounded a hell of a lot like he was using Aisling as a political show of power. Brynach didn't like it and from the way Riordan ripped his arm from Brynach, her Ravdi didn't either.

Rainer nodded on his throne and instructed Aisling to begin. Brynach didn't need Riordan's sight to know that Aisling was drawing immense amounts of power to her. The air in the throne room cracked, charged with magic, and Aisling stepped forward. She descended the steps toward Gabriel with her hands palms up at her side.

Thunder clapped above them, lightning flashing outside the windows, and Fae heads throughout the room swiveled. The wind howled. Aisling's hair swung around her face, her sweater rippling in a wind that touched her alone.

"Goddess. What is happening?" Riordan mumbled.

"I don't know. Does she look okay?" Brynach asked, worried. He'd seen her like this once before and she'd tried to kill him. That had been a dream world. If he had to step in now, in this realm, he wasn't certain he'd make it out alive.

A clap of thunder shook the walls of the castle, a crack appeared in a large window, wind whistling through it. A Fae screamed and ran for the doors. They were followed by others. The guards around Gabriel stepped back, their weapons raised. If he had to fight them, things might not end well, but he wasn't letting anyone touch her.

Riordan stepped closer to Brynach and though it wasn't necessary he yelled over the noise, "It's too new for her. She's taking in too much."

Brynach agreed. Aisling didn't have experience drawing magic from Faerie, from the land or the people. What if she hurt herself? He'd never forgive himself. Would the land acknowledge her or fight her?

"This was a mistake," Riordan yelled, and Rainer's head snapped to them.

"Silence him," his brother demanded and Brynach turned on Riordan, blocking Aisling from his view.

"You have to trust her. If she needs help, we can bring her back, we always have. She's got this." Brynach forced the man to look at him. "I need you safe, so please, unless things have reached critical levels, stay silent."

Riordan nodded and then stepped around him so he could see Aisling. The Fae in the room moved against the walls, afraid to be caught up in the stripping. His father's head might be shackled but his eyes were raised to Aisling. Brynach could see the hate in them, but something else, too. Something he recognized because he'd seen it in the eyes of countless others in the same position.

Fear.

The doors burst open, and Moura screamed above the roaring wind for the man she loved. Their mother hadn't been detained in the dungeons, instead she was guarded in her rooms. Brynach was sure this outburst would have her freedom restricted even further. The guards held her back. Still, she struggled to reach Gabriel. But his father's eyes never left Aisling. Not for a single moment did they search for the old Queen.

The storm raged. Rainer remained seated and calm, but his guards moved closer to him. Breena stepped to Brynach, her hand finding his and their fingers twining together. It's the same way they'd weathered the executions they'd been forced to watch as children. He closed his eyes a moment and let himself be thankful for his sister by his side.

Lightning cracked along the room's ceiling, thunder shaking plaster loose. Fae ducked and Riordan moved slightly behind Brynach. Aisling took another step toward his father and held her hands out toward him.

Riordan gasped, "She's pulling it from him. I can see it."

Breena heard him as clearly as Brynach did and squeezed his hand. Her chest rose and fell fast as she watched Brynach's new wife strip their father of his immortality.

Gabriel's body jerked in the chains. His eyes rolled back in his head and his hair, once black as night like Brynach and his twin, was shot through with brilliant streaks of white. His back bowed in the shackles and then he stilled. The storm immediately quieted.

Brynach dropped Breena's hand and ran to his wife. He stepped between her and his father and brought her face up so he could see her eyes. They were a beautiful hazel.

"Are they okay?" Her voice was raw like she'd been screaming for hours even though she'd never said a word.

"Perfect." He kissed her. "You were amazing."

"Did I kill him?" she asked quietly.

Breena was at their father's side. "He passed out."

Aisling allowed herself to relax, falling forward into his arms. Brynach scooped her up and the Ravdi hurried down the steps to their side. Together the three of them left the throne room. Whatever else needed to happen could happen without them.

Brynach navigated the halls to his suite. Riordan recognized his rooms and rushed to open the doors. Once inside he registered the sound of the lock turning. Riordan was smart. Nobody would interrupt them caring for Aisling.

It concerned him she hadn't spoken yet. Her eyes remained closed as he laid her on his bed. Riordan lifted his shoulders. This was as new for him as it was for them.

"Aisling?" Riordan asked, climbing onto the bed with her. He picked up her head, resting it in his lap and running a hand over her hair. "Ash, can you talk to us?"

Brynach kneeled at the side of the bed, Aisling's hand in his. His thumb ran over the ring she wore, his ring. His wife. His everything. He'd pushed her too far. This was all his fault. He was a selfish ass. Why had he allowed this?

"Aisling, I don't know how you're feeling right now. I can imagine you're overwhelmed. But if you can hear me, you can heal yourself," Brynach kept his words soft. "What you did was a lot. But you don't always need to pull so much. You can absorb tiny amounts to restore what you used. Take from me, a stoirin."

Tears fell down her cheeks and Aisling cried out the words, "Why didn't I know it was like this?"

Brynach knelt at the side of the bed and rested his head on her hand. "Oh, Aisling. I'm sorry. I wish I'd had more time to let you get used to it. Are you hurt?"

Her fingers pulled from his hand, and he knew he deserved it. She had every right to hate him. But then her hand rested on his head, ran over his hair the way Riordan was caressing hers. She wove her fingers into it, massaged his scalp lightly and then tugged until his head rose.

"I love you. I'm okay. I'm just overwhelmed." She smiled at him. "Come here, husband."

She'd never have to say those words again. He never wanted to be far enough away from her for them to be necessary. They readjusted themselves until all three of them were comfortable and then they slept.

CHAPTER 28

Riordan

He'd known immediately that something was different, but it hadn't been the right time to share. Riordan didn't blame Aisling for not realizing it. She was busy stripping a killer of his magic, so you know, that was understandable. But now he was left not knowing how to bring up his theory. Of course, the hulking Fae called him out first.

"You've been weird the past couple of days," he accused.

"To be fair, the past few days have been really strange," Riordan deflected. It was the truth. They'd camped out in Faerie, nervous that the Veil hadn't immediately crashed down when Brynach and Aisling wed. They didn't want to risk her leaving Faerie in case that's what triggered it.

"Riordan, talk to me," Brynach demanded.

Aisling was warding their house, out of earshot. If he was going to admit his suspicions, now was the time. But once he voiced it, he couldn't take it back and a part of him needed the option of denial. Brynach placed a large hand on Riordan's shaking leg.

"Something changed after you married Aisling."

"Yes, I should think so."

"You're not making this any easier for me. What I mean is that Aisling got some of your magic, right? And you get some of hers, correct?"

"Yes, I suppose so," Brynach agreed.

"And what's a key component of Aisling's magic?" Riordan asked.

"I'm not following." The large Fae shook his head.

"Come with me," Riordan instructed.

Without question Brynach followed him out of the house and across their front path toward the Veil. He pointed to the area where magic concentrated. "Open it."

Brynach looked confused but did as he was asked. Riordan stepped through the Veil and held out his hand. "Come on."

The Fae stepped through the Veil and let it close behind him. His wide eyes rose from the ground to Riordan's.

"Oh fuck!" Brynach cursed.

Riordan nodded. "Aisling is my bonded. I'm her Ravdi, which means..."

"You're mine now, too." Brynach stared at him in wonder and Riordan could feel the panic and excitement through the bond.

They'd learn to close it but right now, new and untrained, Brynach couldn't manage that. To be fair, it was nice to finally be able to sense the big lug's feelings. Riordan put his hand on the other man's shoulder.

"You okay?" he asked.

Brynach stared at him in wonder and Riordan felt a rush of pride and affection in the bond. Oh wow. Okay. If he could be that raw and honest, so could Riordan. He let himself focus on his trust for the Fae and watched as Brynach's pupils got blown out.

"Riordan this is incredible. You. I mean, this is what it's like for Aisling and you?"

The way he was staring at Riordan made him want to look away, but he couldn't break the Fae's stare. "Pretty crazy, right?"

"I had no idea. It's. I mean, it's beautiful." The awe in his voice pleased Riordan. "Can I admit something?"

"Anything," Riordan whispered, very aware he was still touching the Fae.

"I'm honored and so happy right now." Brynach paused and licked is lips. "I like having a bond with you."

Riordan smiled. "Me, too."

Brynach's face fell. "Then why are you sad? I can feel...a hurt."

Riordan nodded. "Promise not to tell Aisling. I don't want to worry her right now."

The Dark Fae scowled but agreed.

"I knew right after you married her. When she was pulling magic to herself, I was watching for the threads. I could see the one that links her to me, and I saw a new one to you. I knew we had bonded, that we were connected. But," he forced himself to keep talking. "I could also see that my thread to Aisling was weaker. When she got your magic, she became a little more Fae and a little less witch. Our bond isn't as strong anymore."

He watched as the news struck Brynach and the reality of the situation finally really hit Riordan. He was happy he was right about his bond with Brynach, but the grief over the lessening of his bond with Aisling was real, too.

"Riordan, I'm sorry. I didn't know. You have to believe me."

He could feel the Fae's guilt and pain in the bond and tried to project understanding and forgiveness to him. Brynach's breathing evened a little as he felt it.

"I can't believe you agree to time in Faerie with her when it means losing this," Brynach wondered.

"You agree to time here without your bond to your familiar." Riordan shrugged. "It's not much different."

"Yes, it is," Brynach assured him. "You should tell her, but I won't say anything until you're ready."

He looked to the Veil and shook his head. "I should want

to get back to my wife, but I don't want to lose this, here, with you."

Riordan understood. "We have the rest of my forever, Brynach. It's okay. We shouldn't leave her alone. You go back. I'm going to check in with Liam since I'm here. I'll have Ollie bring me back."

"Are you sure? I don't like leaving you, either." Brynach rubbed his own arms. "I'm used to hearing a voice, but I can feel you. This is going to take getting used to."

"Imagine my shock when I bonded with Aisling," Riordan joked.

"I was pretty hard on you at the beginning, huh?" Brynach's guilt sang through the bond.

"Hey, it's okay. I wasn't the nicest to you, either." Riordan smiled at the Fae. "We're good now, that's what matters. I should go. Get back to our girl."

That shook the large Fae from his stupor. He left to go back to their home and Riordan grabbed his phone and keys from the condo. Before long, he was driving to the apartment, eager to see Liam and check in on developments this side of the Veil. The distance from Brynach and Aisling would be nice, too. Now that he'd confirmed his suspicions, he really needed to sit with the fact that a lot had changed. His life had taken a pretty serious twist with Aisling's marriage to Brynach.

He jogged through Dawn's garden, slowing after being scolded by the cranky alate, and continued upstairs. Riordan was glad to see Amber and Dawn upstairs, too.

"Ahh, my estranged brother. The hell have you been?" Liam complained.

"Oh, you know, reassuring my girlfriend and her fiancé that they're okay after stripping the Bloody Hand of the flipping Unseelie Court of his immortality," Riordan burst out. "Dude, there's a wedding tomorrow. Things are busy!"

Liam waved him off. "Yeah, yeah. Always with an excuse." But he was clearly joking.

Riordan shook his head and huffed, "How's it going?"

"We're doing all we can but having Aisling here would probably help." Dawn rocked her daughter.

"And she wants to be here, but with the wedding coming up she can't get away," Riordan made excuses for her. "In the meantime, we have to make do with what we have. I'd love to bring her an update. Any news on Peggy or her kids?"

"We had someone call in a sighting that they're checking out. The two sons are still locked up and Sydney gave an official testimony the other day. But the attacks haven't slowed since the two were brought in which means we may be dealing with hired help," Amber shared.

"Which is why we started shaking down her brothers," Liam chimed in. "We got the police to agree to a reduced sentence for the first one of them to talk. The younger one seems close to breaking."

Riordan made a mental note. "And Dexter?"

"He's been suspended pending investigation. The case is still building," Dawn answered. "Loren is pretty sure the internal investigation will turn out enough for a conviction. They found a lot of incomplete paperwork and missing evidence that resulted in a lot of bad people staying out of jail."

"Can I do anything to help?" Riordan asked as he gathered his things.

"The day before your girlfriend marries into Dark Fae royalty?" His brother tilted his head and gave him that "you're an idiot" look. "No, Rory, we've got it covered. Go back and we'll see you tomorrow."

"Don't be late," Riordan said and jogged down the stairs throwing an "I love you" back toward Liam before he got to the bottom. Anxious to get back to Faerie, he called Trent.

"Hey, man. You all set for tomorrow?" Riordan asked.

"You mean have I had a facial, manicure, and picked up my suit? Yes. Am I ready to watch my childhood best friend become a Princess? I guess. Although, I still think I'd suit Dark royalty better," Trent answered.

From somewhere behind him Ollie grumbled, "You have to settle for the unaligned misfit turned human realm resident. Sorry, love."

Riordan heard them kissing and blushed. "I need to borrow Ollie, stop making out."

A laugh sounded before Trent agreed to meet him in a few minutes. Riordan drove to Aislings to pick up a few last-minute things. When he came back down, the now familiar and expected flash of red darted between the trees.

"Hey, little guy." Riordan pulled the remains of an energy bar from his pocket and tried to coax him closer. "I won't hurt you."

The fox stared at him and belly to the ground crawled closer to Riordan's outstretched hand. Normally, befriending wildlife during the day was a bad idea, but Riordan liked the fox.

Trent and Ollie came around the corner, and the fox ran off, back into the cover of the trees. Ollie had been happy to offer his services for travel through the Veil. It was easier and faster than using border crossing lines. Riordan appreciated it more than the Fae knew. He hated waiting at the crossing and having to sift to their house.

Trent hugged Riordan tight and then handed him over to Ollie.

"Hurry back, sexy." He winked at his boyfriend. "Give Aisling a hug for me and tell her I'll see her soon."

Riordan promised to give her the message before Ollie parted the Veil and they stepped through. The bright Faerie sun and the citrus sweet scent of the air no longer made him sneeze. Still, he longed for the pine scent of the woods around their house and the feel of Aisling next to him.

"Here you are," Ollie said in a crisp, curt tone. Riordan didn't miss the change between when Ollie spoke to Trent, his voice soft and caring and when he talked to him, deeper and more rushed.

"Thanks for this. It's got to be a pain in the ass for you." Riordan didn't need a sift to their house, just the parting of the Veil.

"It's important to Trent, so it's important to me. I'm glad you came around and aren't making rude comments about Fae anymore," Ollie reminded Riordan of their first meeting.

"You know I didn't mean anything by that, right?" Riordan felt awkward.

Ollie shrugged. "Sure. I get it. I'm used to people thinking I have an ulterior motive for things. I left Faerie because I didn't feel like I belonged and even here I get the side eye. Guess it's my burden to carry."

Riordan was surprised by his words. "I can't imagine what it's like to feel that way, but I do know Trent cares for you. By default, his friends care for you. You're accepted with us."

Something crossed the Fae's face that Riordan couldn't read. Before Riordan could analyze it, Ollie grabbed Riordan and sifted.

Riordan was taken by surprise. "You didn't have to do that. It's not that long of a walk."

"This close to the big day we don't want to risk anything happening to you." Ollie smiled at him. Riordan fought a shiver at the cosmetically filed down teeth in the Fae's mouth. They'd once been razor sharp and a dentist may have blunted them, but it didn't make them look less inhuman.

"I don't have to rush off if you want to hang a bit," Ollie hinted. "I don't spend a ton of time in Faerie, but I'd like to have more friends here."

Riordan was grateful for the Fae, but they were all protective of their space.

"Thanks, but I have to catch Aisling up on a lot, and with the wedding tomorrow, things are hectic. But we'll see you there, right?" Riordan tried for polite refusal.

Ollie's face fell a little. "Yeah. Sure. See you then."

Before Riordan could stumble over another apology, the

Fae sifted away. He shook off the feeling of unease and moved to the house. Through the windows he could see crystals lining their windowsills. She'd already saged the space, and a tiny jar of rice rested by the door to absorb negative energy. Even in Faerie, Aisling was witchy. He loved that about her. He was opening the door when a yell came from the backyard. He changed paths and followed the porch around to the back of their home.

His girl was struggling, big time. This new level of Faeness wasn't easy for her and Aisling didn't enjoy being bad at things. Watching Brynach teach her to sift in their backyard was both amusing and sad. He hated seeing her frustrated, but she was learning, even if it wasn't at a pace she liked. Then again, he didn't mind it when Aisling ran to him for comfort.

"Fucking hell," Aisling screamed. Riordan sat in a deck chair and watched Aisling disappear from one spot to reappear in the stream that ran the length of the yard.

Brynach was laughing too hard to see Aisling summon the magic of Faerie and toss the cold water toward him. He didn't sidestep the chilly torrent of water. With a growl the soggy Fae Prince lunged, and Aisling was on her ass in the stream, a dripping Brynach looming over her.

Riordan barely stifled a laugh as he ascended the stairs to the master bedroom patio. He started running the warm water in the outdoor tub they'd all come to love. He didn't need to call down to them for them to know what he was doing. A moment later Brynach sifted with a sulking Aisling in his arms right to him.

"That seemed...fun?" He tried to hide his smile and failed.

"Don't you start with me, too," Aisling complained but softened when she saw the steaming water.

Brynach set her down and frowned. "I wish I could join you, my bride, but I have to go finalize the security details for tomorrow."

Riordan had gotten used to Brynach calling Aisling "his

bride" in private, but he hoped it reverted back to a stoirin when the novelty wore off. "I'll take care of her."

Brynach looked to him. Riordan may never get used to the intensity of that stare. Especially not now that the bond had shown him the depth of the Fae's feelings. "Of course, you will. I'll see you both later." He kissed Aisling. "Less than twenty-four hours until I have you begging before I bury myself in your pussy, Aisling."

Aisling bit her lip and Brynach sifted away. By the time Riordan turned back to Aisling she was naked, the bright sun of Faerie caressing her pale skin. He had a moment to appreciate it before she slid into the stone tub with a sigh.

"Join me?" She winked at him, and he stripped so fast he tripped over his pants. Aisling laughed, "Easy, tiger. I'm not going anywhere."

He dropped into the water behind her and cradled her to his chest. "Are you ready for your big day?"

She nodded, her hair swirling in the water. "It's not like it will change anything. We're already married."

"Yes, but nobody knows," Riordan reminded her. "And it's a lot of eyes on you."

"Thanks, that's really helping the anxiety." He could practically hear her eyes rolling. Her hand traveled his legs, nails on his thighs grazing higher and higher.

"Aisling?"

"Is it wrong to want you right now?" She squirmed against him, and he let his hand drop to her spread legs and stroked her softly.

"It's never wrong to want me. And it's never wrong to want Brynach. Just like it's never wrong for us to want you. When will you realize that?" Riordan purred in her ear.

Her hips rolled under his hand. "It's a lot of human prejudice to overcome, Riordan."

His teeth scraped her neck and she shivered. "You're not human, Aisling. You never were and you certainly aren't now that you're sharing Brynach's magic. Let yourself have what you want."

Aisling turned and grabbed a hold of his neck and Riordan felt the squeezing discomfort of a sift.

"Hey, that was pretty good!" he exclaimed at Aisling's successful sift. She'd gotten both herself and Riordan into their bedroom. Brynach would be proud. Although, he'd probably be pissed that their mattress was soaking wet.

"It's easier when I'm strongly motivated." She smiled, naked and beautiful from beneath him. "Make love to me, Riordan."

He didn't need to be told twice. Aisling's lips rose to meet his as Riordan lowered a hand and Aisling spread her legs for him, hungry for his touch. Her craving for him a powerful aphrodisiac.

"I love you," he whispered against her lips and then trailed his tongue down her soapy neck. "So much it hurts." He crooned as he rubbed her clit, applying pressure that had her arching her back. "And I love how you respond to me."

Their bond may not work in Faerie, but Riordan had learned about her body. He knew what her every sigh, gasp, and moan meant. He could read her reactions like no other woman he'd had the honor of taking to bed.

"I'll never tire of you, Riordan. I will always be hungry for you," she breathed as her hands stroked his back. Her breath caught as he captured a nipple in his mouth and sucked. His teeth scraped gently against a pebbled point and then closed harder around it.

Aisling gasped, her hips bucking. When her hand joined his own, her fingers added pressure and speed. "That's it, Aisling," he encouraged as she worked herself to orgasm. Her body was slippery as he kissed across her chest to the other nipple. Riordan waited, ever patient, until he sensed Aisling was on the brink.

She began to whimper. Her small cries and gasps had his

erection throbbing against her hip. He waited, waited, waited. And as he felt her hand go rigid against his own, he sucked hard on the side of her breast. It would leave a mark. It might heal before the wedding but he would still enjoy seeing it there. Aisling broke apart. Sweet Aisling. Strong, powerful woman that she was, absolutely lived for losing control.

"So beautiful." He kissed her mouth. Riordan couldn't wait anymore. He moved over her, sliding his cock against the wet heat of her pussy. Even so soon after finding release, her hips rocked against his length and she moaned when his tip stroked her clit.

Riordan's heart raced at the thought of her heat without any barrier. "I'm back on the tonic." He wanted this, but not without her consent.

"Stop playing games," she growled. "I am so empty without you inside me."

Riordan looked down at her flushed cheeks and messy wet hair and had never wanted her more. On his next stroke he seated himself fully inside her. It wasn't gentle, and Aisling's eyes rolled back in her head.

He pulled out, his tip circling her entrance again, and she clenched at the bedsheets. "Riordan!"

He marveled in the way her hips rose to meet his thrust. Aisling would have a bruised pelvic bone in the morning if she wasn't careful. He rested deep inside her, letting her warm and clenching pussy cradle his length.

His love bit her lip as her hands moved over his chest. "I love how full I feel with you inside me like that. The way you make me sore in the most beautiful way. Make me feel you, Riordan."

He cursed and started fucking her. The sounds of their love making echoed in their home, their wet bodies making a music all their own. Her sweet panting and cries of encouragement spurred him on.

"Like that. Goddess, you make me feel so good," she called

as Riordan pulled her legs up, angling her hips so he could stroke deeper.

Aisling purred, "I'm going to start stroking my clit. You have until I get off to find release."

His eyes went wide. "Wait. What?" Riordan stilled as Aisling's hand slid between them.

"You told me to let myself have what I want. This is what I want." Aisling smirked.

"Goddess, Aisling! Where is this coming from?" Riordan didn't mind, but damn.

"How do you want me, Riordan? Talk to me," Aisling encouraged.

"For fuck's sake get your hand away from your pussy and let me think!" he cried out, his hips moving but his mind racing.

"Get out of your head. I want you to feel. How do you want it?" Aisling was going to drive him wild.

"Damn it!" Riordan pulled out of her and lifted her off the bed. He pushed her against the floor to ceiling window, her breasts against the cold glass.

Aisling gasped at the contact. Riordan put his hands between her sensitive nipples and the window, holding them tight. He took a small step back and Aisling arched her back for him.

"Take it," she said, looking over her shoulder.

Riordan drove himself back into her and lost all logical thought. His hands took the brunt of the thrusts against the glass. Aisling's hands pressed against the window as she pushed back into him.

"Why this?" she panted. Her warm breath fogged the window.

"If anyone happens upon our home, I want to make it clear you belong to me," he said as his cock speared her.

Aisling bit her lip. "I'm yours, Riordan."

He leaned forward and kissed her, then dropped a hand to

stroke her. He was close, so close.

"Mine," he agreed and lowered his head to her shoulder.

"Yes, Riordan," she gasped as she came. Her muscles squeezing and his name on her lips threw him over the edge. Riordan was quick to pull out, making a mess on her back.

Aisling's breasts heaved against the window while he fetched a washcloth and cleaned her. Then he picked her up and took her to a dry part of their bed. Exhausted, they lay staring out the window at the darkening sky.

"Promise me this won't change tomorrow," Aisling whispered against his naked chest.

"Nothing will change unless we want it to," he swore. Although that wasn't entirely true.

She kissed his neck. "You feel further away lately."

"I'm right here." He held her tighter and tried to ignore the dread settling in the pit of his stomach. He couldn't hide the truth from her forever.

CHAPTER 29

Aisling

Aisling never had been good with other people's tears. If someone else cried, she cried. So, when her mother started to sob, she had to fight to preserve the makeup Lettie so artfully applied to her face.

"Don't you dare ruin my masterpiece!" Lettie's outrage made Aisling laugh.

"It's her fault!" She pointed at her mother through the mirror where she was being dressed.

Mrs. Quinn dabbed at her eyes. "You're so beautiful. I'm so happy for you, sweetie."

Aisling smoothed a hand down her custom-made dress. The fabric transitioned from a stark white that hugged every curve of her breasts and waist down to an inky darkness that swirled at the bottom like smoke. It was meant to symbolize the merging of the Light and Dark Courts. But lately, it felt more like a representation of herself. She had darkness inside her, but there was light as well.

She had debated over whether or not she'd wear the crown and jewels from the Seelie vaults after Corinna's betrayal. But Brynach had reminded her of the young Fae's naivety and how Aisling had always championed her. Apparently, she had to give the girl one epic fuck up, plus she looked amazing in the jewels.

Her mother clasped the necklace and made sure it was sitting correctly. The earrings were dangling from her ears and the crown was in the throne room, ready to be placed on her head. Aisling's charm bracelet remained on her wrist, but otherwise she looked nothing like herself.

Her mother hugged her. "I wish I'd been brave enough to accept your father's proposal. You're all I could have dreamt of in a strong capable daughter. I'm so proud of you for following your heart."

Aisling didn't know what to say. How do you comfort a woman who had split from her husband and mourned the missed opportunity to be with the Fae she'd loved? But knowing her mother was proud of her made her happy. What woman doesn't want to hear that on her wedding day?

"Are you ready to marry that fine piece of Fae flesh?" Lettie joked.

Her mother cackled and clapped her hands. "He's going to freak out when he sees you!"

Aisling grinned because she wasn't wrong. Brynach loved her no matter what she wore, but seeing her dressed up for him would please him endlessly. Knowing that she'd walk down the aisle to his smiling face and a future with him set butterflies fluttering in her stomach.

A part of her wanted to rush through the ceremony and get to the afterparty. Not because it wouldn't be beautiful, it would. But because Brynach had been edging her for too long. He wouldn't let himself touch her until the official ceremony was over, but the dirty things he'd been promising her still played through her mind.

"I'm ready," Aisling confirmed.

Lettie poked her head into the hall. "The coast is clear. I miss cell phones. A simple, 'Is Gorgeous Groom in place?' text to Trent and we could walk the halls without fear. But no."

Aisling laughed, "Rin already gave me the go ahead."

Her mother grinned. "Let's not keep your fiancé waiting

any longer than he already has."

"The man is immortal. It won't kill him," Lettie quipped but the three of them made their way out into the hall. Jashana and Brielle accompanied them through the palace to the gardens of the Seelie Court where the ceremony would be held. The two warriors were in formal wear, smiling at her. She accepted their praise at her dress and frowned because Corinna wasn't with them. Aisling hadn't confronted anyone about the Seelie Princess's betrayal and being in the castle felt wrong. She pushed that aside and focused on the reason she was here today, instead.

As they reached the bottom of the staircase a very energetic Trixie bounced out of her chair and ran to Aisling. "I stayed clean!"

Aisling kissed her cheek and squeezed her tight. "Yes, you did. I promise you can get dirty real soon."

"I don't even care about getting dirty. I got to see the gardens! And the sprites! And the castle! It's so pretty, Aunt Ash." The young girl was glowing. Her blonde hair braided into a crown and decorated with flowers.

Aisling took Trixie's hand and led her through the halls with their guards surrounding them. She was wearing a mirrored version of Aisling's dress. Dark at the top fading to white at the bottom.

Gemma held her hand and grinned at Aisling. She'd known the housekeeper had gotten a job at the Seelie Court and was happy to see her well. Aisling felt a warmth toward the Fae after Brynach had shared who the woman was to him. She owed her a lot.

"You look beautiful, Miss."

"Aisling," she corrected her. "You were sneaky, Gemma, but I'm so happy to see you well."

The maid lowered her head, "Thanks to you. I owe you. We should talk soon, Aisling."

She was about to answer that she would visit when the

music sounded from the garden and the Fae pushed her toward the doors. Nevan waited there, shoulders back and hair brushed until it shone. Aisling had decided to have her mother and her father walk her down the aisle. It seemed wrong to do anything else. Lettie moved ahead of them with a wave of her fingers.

Gemma bent to Trixie and gave her a basket of blooms to throw along the path. Another servant brought Aisling her bouquet, a balanced mix of flowers from each court. Dark and Light, sweet and more likely than not, poisonous. As they neared the glass doors, she saw the massive crowd that was gathered. She was immediately grateful this wasn't their real ceremony.

"Ready?" her father asked as Trixie began throwing flowers along the stone path.

Aisling nodded and they began the long walk to Brynach. The sun was bright, and music floated on the air. It was beautiful but the winding path meant she couldn't see her husband, yet.

"Slow down," her mother whispered.

Her heels on the cobbled stones threatened to topple her, especially with the weight of her veil. But all that mattered was getting to Brynach.

Then he came into view.

Dressed in a black suit the same rich color as the ends of her dress, his hair was loose and his eyes shone. Brynach made her knees weak. At her elbows her parents held her a little tighter. Then she saw a hand reach forward to pat Brynach's arm. Alex beamed at her, and when he nodded, she turned her attention to the rest of the waiting people at the front.

King Rainer was standing in front of Brynach alongside Queen Branwyn. Lettie was already standing in her spot. But all of that faded away as her father placed her hand in Brynach's. Only his warm gaze mattered now.

A tap on her shoulder had her handing her flowers to

Lettie and then turning back to Brynach. Aisling had been prepped about what the ceremony entailed, and they'd walk her through it.

Brynach mouthed the words, "I love you" to her and she repeated them back to him. Her fingers played with the intricate design of the cuff he was wearing from the Seelie Court while Brynach's played over her charm bracelet. Fae ceremonies didn't require them to do much, and she wasn't paying attention to the words the King and Queen were saying. Their wrists were bound again and like before, the Fae flame burned it away. Then Lettie and Alex linked arms with them and led Brynach and Aisling around the ceremonial table seven times.

It symbolized the Kings and Queens of old, the spirits, and the elements. That meant little to her but promising herself to Brynach in front of all of Faerie made her stand straighter. She was proud to be his wife.

As they stopped before the King and Queen one last time, they both knelt and were crowned. When they rose, they did so as husband and wife. Aisling rose as a Princess. Unlike last time there was no startling shock of magic sweeping through her. Brynach's large hands held her face, his fingers toying with the nape of her neck, and his eyes burning. Then he was bending over her, his mouth sweeping over hers. Small kisses that tugged at her heart. Goddess, she loved him.

When they ended the kiss, the crowd erupted in cheers. She gazed at her husband and his face split in the brightest smile. Aisling would never forget the way he looked at her. Treasured. Loved. Worshipped. She didn't deserve him.

There was a small squeeze on her neck and then they turned to the crowd. Aisling met eyes with her mother and father, with Trent and Dawn. She saw a forlorn but smiling Corinna, a clapping Ceiren, and even a grinning Breena.

She turned to Riordan and his smile was so genuine her heart ached. Lettie was trying to hand her the bouquet of flowers, but her husband shook her off. Brynach swung an arm around her waist, and they sifted out of the garden. Now that she could do it on her own it no longer unsettled her the same way it used to. Still, she hadn't been expecting it quite so soon. Aisling had assumed they'd at least walk down the aisle before sneaking away.

"Already?" she said when their feet found purchase on their deck.

There was raw hunger in his feline gaze. "Yes."

"Brynach, it's our wedding. We can't just leave." She smiled knowing exactly why they had come home.

"It's our wedding so we can do as we please. And right now, it would please me to have you moaning my name." His mouth found hers, his fingers loosening the veil and dropping it to the floor. She moaned. The relief was immediate with the heavy weight gone.

"Oh, that feels amazing," she sighed as she rolled her neck.

Brynach's breath was hot on her neck and the sting of his teeth was sharp but brief. "Do you remember what we talked about?"

It was all she'd been able to think about. The promise that their first time wouldn't be gentle, but a needy, fierce union. Leaving the wedding had been discussed. Their mutual desire to satiate the sexual tension had been agreed to. She shivered. "Yes."

"Good," his voice was a ragged sound in her ear. Heat pooled low, her body readying itself. They'd both waited so long. Too long.

"If you ruin this dress, I'll never forgive you!" she warned before turning so he could get to the zipper.

"You're stunning." His hands stroked her back reverently. The dress was snug, but he got a finger between it and her skin, teasing her.

"I'm not taking it off of you." He leaned over her, forcing her down with him. When she was bent at the waist toward the railing, he took her hands and placed them on the weather worn wood. "You hold on and don't let go."

Aisling had barely registered the growled command when her dress was lifted from behind and her underwear was torn to her knees. With her legs held together by the thin fabric, Brynach had just enough room to kneel and bury his face in her folds.

The air hissed from her lungs as his tongue and teeth found her.

"You're soaked."

What did he want her to say? Of course she was. She pushed back against him, wanting more. His hand clapped against her ass cheek before running reverently over the blades strapped to her thighs.

"These look beautiful against your pale flesh." He kissed her legs. "But don't forget, you're not the one in control right now," he reminded her.

"You're barely in control," she accused, which earned her another smack. She grinned and bit her lip as he rededicated himself to tasting her. His mouth was hungry on her and her legs shook as the tension in her belly grew to a fever pitch.

"So, fucking delicious," he mused. "I could feast on you all night."

"Goddess, no. Please, Bry." She'd beg if she had to. His mouth was damn near perfection, but she needed more. The cool air of Faerie caressed her hot flesh when he rose.

"You remember what I told you?" He growled in her ear as he licked her neck.

"Don't let go." She nodded, desperate to do anything that ensured he didn't stop. Aisling had anticipated Brynach's dominant side, but when he learned how much she enjoyed it, he'd really leaned into it. The man was a dream come true.

"That's right, a stoirin." He kissed her before murmuring in her ear, "Be a good girl and take me."

There was a whoosh of his zipper moments before his

hard length drove into her. He'd have filled her to the point of pleasant discomfort even if she'd been properly spread for him, but with her legs banded by her underwear, he was impossibly large. Aisling moaned and Brynach echoed it.

He pulled back and drove himself back home. "My bride. Mine."

"It's the other way around. You're mine," she reminded him in a ridiculous struggle for power when she was being taken from behind in her wedding gown, crown, and royal jewels.

"Oh, I'm yours. My heart, my body, and this cock. All yours, Aisling." He plunged into her.

"Your pleasure is mine." He slid a hand around to stroke her clit.

"Your pain is mine." He pulled a hand back and slapped her ass, hard.

"Your safety is mine." That same hand found her throat and applied gentle pressure.

All things they'd discussed she liked. All things she'd been waiting forever for him to provide.

"Yours. All yours," she promised as she repositioned her hands. They never left the railing, she followed rules, but they slid from the top where he'd placed them to the inside edge so she could use them to push herself back on him.

He angled his cock and hit her g-spot over and over with amazing accuracy. When her legs shook, he anchored her with an arm under her belly. "I told Riordan where I was bringing you. He knows exactly what I'm doing to you right now." His breath was hot on her neck.

Aisling blushed. Had he really done that? The idea that Riordan knew Brynach was deep inside her thrilled her. She moaned and swiveled her hips. That was the hottest damn thing she'd ever heard.

"And I promised him that later you'd be both of ours." He drove into her hard. "Would you like that? Being taken by both of us at the same time?"

"Yes," she cried out, so close to coming.

"That's my girl," he growled into her ear. "But right now, who is it bringing you pleasure?"

"My Prince. My love," she swore as her orgasm crashed down on her and her legs shook.

Brynach rode her through her orgasm, her body clenching down on him, with a curse. "So good for me, a stoirin. I've waited so long. I'll be gentle later."

Aisling recovered enough to throw her ass into him. "You're perfect. I love how you love me. Show me, Brynach. Come for me."

With a primal scream he pulled out of her. Aisling ignored his command and let go of the railing, turning around and dropping to her knees. Before he could be angry, he was in her mouth, and she was swallowing him down.

"I told you not to let go." He shook his head as she finished cleaning him off.

Aisling looked up at him, her skirts pooled around her, and grinned. "Somehow, you'll forgive me, husband."

"Damn right I will. You have no idea how perfect you look on your knees in a crown, Princess." He pulled her to her feet and fixed her underwear. Then his hand met her ass. "But you still need to be punished for not listening."

She fought a smile as he fixed the many layers of her dress and tucked himself back into his pants. Brynach's eyes held such love for her that her stomach flipped.

"Come here." Brynach held his arms open, and she pressed her face to his broad chest. "It won't always be that intense. Are you okay?"

"More than," she promised, her arms wrapped around him. "I may not have fought my attraction to you so long if I'd know it would be that good."

His chuckle reverberated in his chest. "That wouldn't have been nearly as much fun if I hadn't earned it."

Brynach put a hand on her cheek, tilting it so she was looking at him. The other still firmly gripped her ass through the dress. "You are beautiful. I will never forget the way you looked walking toward me."

"My husband." She smiled up at him and felt him harden against her belly.

"If you don't watch yourself, we'll never make our own reception." He stepped away from her. "I'd use caution calling me that unless you've cleared a block of time."

She was used to power but power over Brynach was a high Aisling could get used to. "I can't believe I am going to show up to my wedding reception with everyone knowing good and damn well we snuck away to have sex." She moved to the window, trying to fix her hair in the reflection.

Brynach grinned at her from over her shoulder.

"You could be less proud of yourself," she scolded.

"No, I couldn't." He winked.

"Did you really tell Riordan?" She followed him into the house. It wasn't easy navigating in a dress as heavy as hers was. The train made closing a door after yourself particularly difficult.

"I did. And I meant what I said earlier. We plan on having you tonight. If that's okay with you." He turned to her, a glass of water in hand. "Finish that."

She nodded, a little too enthusiastically, and drank the water. When she was done, she told him to wait and ran to the closet. It hadn't been easy hiding anything in a space three people shared, but she'd managed. When she came out Brynach was lounging in his suit, and he took her breath away.

"We won't go back if you keep looking at me like that," her husband warned.

Aisling blushed and moved toward him. "I know it isn't customary for Fae to exchange rings." She pulled her left hand from behind her back. "I know you gave me this as a part of my human customs. But I wanted to get you something."

"Your trust and love are enough, wife."

The way he said 'wife' had a shiver running down her spine. He saw it and grinned. She pushed on. "Then consider me jealous. I want everyone to know you're mine, Brynach. You're my husband, my heart."

She handed him the box and watched as he opened it. His cat like eyes narrowed and then widened. Aisling couldn't tell what he was feeling.

"It's black tungsten. It's a really strong metal, so it should last a really long time. Since, you know, you'll live a long time. And it can handle whatever abuse you put it through." She smiled at him. "You can clench those fists all you want, it won't bend."

Brynach's eyes met hers and she continued, "The wood on the inside of the band is from Faerie. I've been told it's enough to keep you strong when you're away from here. I want you to have a piece of it even on the other side with me. Or, you know, whatever comes if the Veil falls."

Her words were cut off when Brynach picked her up, pulling her into his chest as he kissed her. The moans Brynach released were nothing short of starved.

When he let her up for air she asked, "So, you like it?"

"I've never seen anything more perfect, except for you," he assured her.

He stared at her in wonder, and she grinned like a fool. Brynach shook his head, speechless for maybe the first time ever. Aisling's chest swelled with pride. She'd done well.

Brynach finally spoke, "I wish we could hide out here so I could show you how much I love being yours, a stoirin. But I'm afraid we can't avoid the Unseelie reception forever."

Her husband held out his hand to her and she took it, ready to face whatever was next with him by her side.

CHAPTER 30

Brynach

Even the blooms in the Unseelie gardens couldn't mask the scent of his wife. He felt drunk on the taste of her still lingering on his tongue. Brynach was happy to give Aisling whatever she wanted, and she wanted it rough and desperate. He'd have happily spent forever between her thighs. Being inside her was the closest he'd ever felt to paradise. It was all he could do to not find her wherever she was and plunge back into her.

As soon as they'd arrived, Aisling had left to find Lettie and her mother so they could perform witchy magic to her dress. He had learned enough about dresses to know they'd have to bring up her train so she could move around the gardens. With a grin he made his way toward Breena who was standing with Riordan and Ceiren.

A waiter provided him a flute of Fae wine, which he sipped though it paled to the taste of his wife.

"You reek," Breena teased.

Brynach didn't bother hiding his smile as he took another sip of wine and checked in with Riordan. Knowing a man was going to have sex with your girlfriend and him actually doing it were two different things. But Riordan was holding out his own flute to Brynach's in a toast.

"I'm happy for you. Both of you," Riordan offered.

"I'm happy for us," Brynach corrected and tapped his glass against the other man's. He leaned down to Riordan's ear, close enough that nobody could overhear. "If I'd known how amazing that would be, I'd have been more jealous every time I laid in bed stroking myself to the sounds of you having sex."

Riordan coughed around his wine. His eyes were wide, and his pupils blown out. "Welcome to the addiction." The Ravdi's eyes caught the ring on his hand. "I see she claimed you, too."

Brynach grinned. He'd been a little jealous of the ring Aisling had given Riordan, but he couldn't begrudge the Ravdi the symbol of Aisling's love. But he wouldn't deny he enjoyed having one, too.

"So it seems. Your kitten is territorial." Brynach winked. "I like it."

Breena groaned, "Honestly, enough."

Brynach turned to her. "Any breaches or threats I need to be made aware of?"

Brielle sauntered up to them in a tight navy dress. She hadn't bothered to glamour her wings, which fluttered a pretty iridescent behind her. "A few. They were handled quickly."

They'd known to expect problems with such a large gathering of royals. "Gabriel?"

Brielle shook her head. "Hasn't been seen since he was sent away from the court a human. No sign of Levinas, either. Though we do need to determine a fitting punishment for when he's found. And once you're done playing nice with the Light, their Princess has explaining to do."

Brynach didn't need to be reminded, and neither did Aisling. They'd all agreed that Corinna would be dealt with after the wedding. He was trying to be sensitive to the fact that Aisling wasn't ready to confront her friend for the betrayal, or acknowledge that the King and Queen had done the same.

Brynach understood that, but it didn't stop him seeing red as that two-faced bitch had proceeded over their wedding. If this had been their actual union, he wouldn't have allowed it.

Even now, looking over the crowd that was gathered, Brynach wanted to get justice for Aisling. Light and Dark talked amicably, some danced, and others stood in shadows whispering. Tonight wasn't the night, but soon those who had wronged Aisling would explain themselves.

"I don't need the bond to know you're tense," Riordan said. "And knowing what you just experienced, you should be pretty damn happy right now. Breathe, Brynach. Enjoy your wedding."

Music floated on the air, laughter and voices mingling with it. Brynach nodded his head. "Tonight, we celebrate."

Arms embraced Brynach from behind. He stiffened before he recognized the voice in his ear crowing their congratulations. "Have you not learned better than to sneak up on me by now?" Brynach growled and turned to embrace Alex. Having his oldest friend by his side earlier had been surreal.

"I wouldn't have had to if you hadn't sifted away with your bride so quickly. Real classy, my friend," Alex teased.

"Riordan, meet my oldest friend, Alex," Brynach presented his friend to Riordan proudly.

Without missing a beat, Riordan held out a hand. "You're the one Aisling lived with, right?"

"I am." Alex beamed.

"Thank you for taking care of her until we could," Riordan said sincerely and Brynach's heart clenched with love for the man.

Alex grinned at Brynach. "I see why you like him."

Riordan blushed and Brynach redirected the conversation to spare him more embarrassment. "Where's Aindrea? I want a dance."

"You have your own wife now, leave mine alone," his friend joked. "She's talking to Aisling. Quite a few tears were shed during the ceremony. We're so happy for both of you."

Brynach's eyes found Aisling and by default, Aindrea. Aisling's mother was standing with them, the two older women embracing while Aisling smiled. He could see his wife's head, her body blocked by other party goers.

"Well, it's time to grab another drink," Brynach said.

"A fine idea, brother," Rainer said walking up to the group. The Fae around him dispersed, even Breena excused herself, but Riordan remained at Brynach's side.

"You officiated beautifully," Riordan offered. "Again."

"If you thought that was good, wait for the speech." Rainer grinned.

Brynach tensed. "Brother, I don't know what you're planning but if you cause discourse at my wedding, we'll have words," he warned.

"No discourse, just a reminder. Don't worry, the Light have agreed to it," he assured Brynach. That didn't ease his concerns one bit. "Besides, why would you worry about me with a bride that looks like that to dote on?"

At Riordan's gasp he turned. Gone was the heavy gown from the ceremony, the one he'd forever see pushed up her back as he drove into her sweet pussy. Instead, she wore a short dress, legs on display, and heels so tall she'd likely meet his eyes. Brynach wasn't sure which was more mesmerizing: the long expanse of leg, her cocky smile, or the way the light played off her dress. She was a walking star, and all eyes were on her. Brynach's palms itch to touch her.

"Sweet Goddess above, she's stunning," Riordan crooned as Brynach moved toward his wife. His heart soared, pride and lust spiking his bloodstream in a way no alcohol ever could. He reached her, picked up her hand and kissed it, then spun her.

"Had I known we were changing outfits, I'd have planned something." He put an arm around her waist and pulled her tight to him. "You are breathtaking." The shiver that ran down her naked spine under his hand thrilled him. The gooseflesh that rose on her arms as he stroked them proof that she was as affected by him as he was her.

In her heels he could easily nuzzle her ear. "You knew exactly what that dress would do to me, didn't you?"

Aisling nodded against his cheek, and he felt his pulse quicken. She'd learn quickly that teasing him had consequences. If Brynach understood his wife, and he was sure he did, she'd known exactly what she was getting herself into. He leaned in close and licked the side of her neck, whispering softly.

"Well, wife, here's what is going to happen now. I'm going to lead you to our table, pull out your chair like the chivalrous husband I am, kiss you sweetly for the gathered crowd, and then you're going to spread your legs."

Her breath caught and she leaned her head back. He nipped at her earlobe, heavy with royal jewels. "You're going to stay quiet. Nobody will know that the Princess is being finger fucked by her husband."

Aisling moaned and he nearly lost it. "Brynach, they're Fae. They'll know."

He pulled back and shook his head. "I share with Riordan only. Make sure they don't."

With a quick kiss to her forehead, he stepped to the side and lead her their head table. Luckily, it was at the edge of the reception space, nobody at their back, and the closest table a decent distance way. Brynach was so hard it hurt but he'd never been happier.

Aisling had communicated that she wanted this kind of freedom and release. But perhaps he was pushing her too hard? When they got to their table, and he pulled out her chair she paused.

He bent and whispered, "You remember your safe word? If this is too intense, use it."

Aisling's fiery eyes met his. "I won't."

"You will! If you need to, you will," he ordered.

She arched her neck and kissed him, her tongue sliding into his mouth. "What I meant was, I don't want to," Aisling clarified when she pulled back.

Brynach swallowed hard. Once they were both settled in their chairs, the rest of the gathered crowd took theirs. He looked out over the people who had come to celebrate with them. Aisling had tables of family and friends all laughing and smiling at them.

Brynach was struck by how little family he had. Breena sat with Rainer, Trixie, and Ceiren. Brynach's mother had decided not to attend, instead stubbornly staying in her rooms. He'd have loved to see Gemma there, but staff would never attend a royal wedding. Seeing Aindrea and Alex helped soothe some loneliness in Brynach.

Aisling's hand rested on his thigh and held him tight. With a wink she slid her feet apart and cocked her head at him. Brynach smiled and raised his glass to accept a toast from the King of the Seelie Court while the other delved between her legs.

"Congratulations to the newly bonded. May your union be a blessing to yourselves and to Faerie. And may the long-awaited joining of our courts lead to a stronger and healthier Faerie." Kyteler was lying through his teeth, but for appearances sake he said what was required.

Cheers erupted and Brynach tapped his glass against his new wife's before taking a sip. The squeeze on his leg told him Aisling wasn't buying it, either. But soon she wouldn't be thinking clearly at all, not if he did his job right. As the King's voice rang out, he'd slid his hand to her core. The panties she was wearing were a joke, a tiny scrap of silky fabric already damp. She was so wet for him. He pressed his fingers against her over the fabric and watched her fingers clench around the stem of her glass.

"Behave," he reminded her as he slid the fabric aside and

slid two thick fingers into her.

Aisling sat smiling at the Seelie King while he plunged into her a few times. Her legs closed around him and he tsk'd her softly. Obediently, she spread her legs again and Brynach pulled his now lubed fingers up to stroke her clit. He wanted her to finish, but he wasn't looking to embarrass her. There was a slight gasp from beside him.

Then Rainer met Brynach's gaze. He held it, even though he was still thinking of Aisling. Of the way she was gripping his wrist as her jaw clenched. His wife was close, and he was determined to get her off.

Brynach leaned over under the guise of kissing her cheek and commanded, "Come for me before that bastard starts talking, Aisling. Give it to me. I need it."

He felt her thighs quivering and pinched her clit lightly. With a gasp Aisling fell apart, her body sagging in the seat. She lifted a shaking hand to her glass and raised it to him. With a smile on his lips, he tapped his glass against hers. "You're perfect." Under the guise of feeding Aisling a grape, he let her taste herself. His wife's tongue darted out to stroke up his finger. Brynach barely contained his own moan.

He distracted himself by eating a piece of fruit himself, the taste of Aisling and the fruit bursting on his tongue. Then he sipped his wine and buckled up for whatever bullshit Rainer was about to rattle off.

"Faerie has been blessed with strong rulers for as long as memory serves us. Today, I had the honor as the new ruler of the Unseelie to join my brother to the lovely Aisling Quinn. Some of you may have heard that recently Aisling stripped the former Bloody Hand of his immortality, a task impossible for one without pure Fae blood. But the land is strengthening, healing now that Fae are working together toward common goals. Some have wondered who I will appoint for my own Bloody Hand. It's logical for my brother to fill the position his father was forced from."

Brynach's blood chilled and Aisling's hand under his curled into a fist. How could Rainer do this? He wouldn't be a killer for his brother or anyone else. Aisling started to push her way out of her seat, but Brynach pulled her back down.

"But there's no need for the kind of cruelty our mother ruled by. Instead, my brother has agreed to become my advisor, the Regent of the Unseelie Court," Rainer announced. Applause sounded through the Unseelie garden.

Brynach didn't like this. The only reason Aisling could strip his father was because they'd secretly wed. Now his brother was claiming her strength was due to him. Not to mention, he'd never agreed to any role for the Unseelie Court. His brother was playing at something, but he couldn't argue it right now.

He glanced at Aisling and saw her smile was still plastered on her face. He didn't dare look at Breena. She'd be steaming. Riordan was absolutely stunned. All eyes were on them, and Aisling was playing her part, but he hated she had to.

"Tonight, we celebrate the union of not only Brynach and Aisling but of the Seelie and Unseelie Courts and present a unified front against any and all threats. Let us celebrate the future."

Brynach and Aisling sipped from their glasses. Rainer met his eyes once he was seated, the look on his face daring Brynach to argue. He wouldn't. Not here. Not now.

Nobody outside their immediate circle sensed the tension in the air and the revel began in earnest once the meal was over. The music began, people rose to dance, and Brynach and Aisling lost themselves in the swirl of activity and congratulations. Everyone wanted a dance with the new Princess or to congratulate the pair. Brynach hated letting her go, but custom dictated he allow others their turn on the dance floor with Aisling. Still, the only time he felt comfortable not having Aisling in his arms was when she was in Riordan's.

His wife had avoided the Seelie royalty as much as possible

while still being civil. Instead, she busied herself with Brynach's family or her friends and parents. By way of royal events, it wasn't bad. But in terms of how he'd like to celebrate his marriage to Aisling, well, he was glad this wasn't their actual wedding.

"What was that all about?" Breena asked as she came up to him in her black gown, a drink in hand.

Brynach was standing next to a table watching Aisling dancing with her friends. "I have no idea, but I will be visiting brother dearest tomorrow to figure it out," he assured his twin.

"Tomorrow? I figured you'd be in bed for at least a week." She nudged his shoulder.

"Don't tempt me." Brynach wished they had that kind of luxury.

Ceiren stepped up to the group. "You better get your wife and partner out of here before the Fae part of the revel takes over. It won't be safe for them much longer."

Brynach could always count on his brother to keep a level head. Looking around the party, he noticed the telltale signs of Fae frivolity. Clothes were starting to come off and the rest of the royals were long since gone. It would devolve quickly into an orgy and drinking on a level no human could maintain.

"Probably a good idea," Brynach admitted. "I'll go break the news."

Making his way to her took longer than he'd hoped as he was stopped by acquaintances and a few Fae he'd have rather avoided.

"Here's my hunky husband!" Aisling called out as he neared her. She'd stayed away from the wine after the toasts but was flushed all the same.

"As if she's not already spoiled with Riordan, she really landed the Prince of Darkness and has to gloat?" Trent joked. The Fae beside him stiffened. The others missed the quick flash of anger on Ollie's face, but Brynach hadn't.

Aisling wrapped her arm around his hip, pulling up close to him. Brynach spoke to the group, "Unfortunately, the party has ended for the mortals."

Most of her friends complained, but he saw the look of relief on both Lettie and Sean's faces.

"The Fae are getting restless. It's in everyone's best interested to head home," Brynach insisted when Aisling said she wanted her friends to stay longer. She immediately scanned the party for threats. "It's okay, a stoirin. This is to ensure everyone stays safe, not because they aren't.

"Thank you for watching out for us," Tara said, eager to keep her girlfriend safe. He was surprised to see Kara in Faerie at all.

Trent's partner nodded. "Thank you for the invitation and the good time. I'll make sure Trent gets home safely."

Aisling insisted they wait until all her friends were safely sifted away before they went home.

Home.

Seeing Riordan and Aisling walk up the steps to the cabin and knowing they felt safe with him released the tension in his shoulders. He'd been so worried something would go wrong today, but it had been wonderful if you ignored his brother's speech. Brynach picked up the pace to follow his wife and her partner into the house.

"Brother, we have a problem," Breena's voice was sharp.

He put a lid on his lust, with more than a little disappointment. When he turned he saw his sister wasn't alone.

"You might as well all come in," Brynach said to the crowd.

"I'm sorry, Ash." Lettie rushed into the living room. "There's literally nothing I want to do less than stop you from being manhandled by these two, but this can't wait."

Aisling blushed and stammered, "That's not. We weren't."

"Yes, you were," Breena confirmed, and Lettie barely stifled a smile. "But it's going to have to wait. Lettie, tell them what you saw."

"It's your friend, Aisling. I wasn't out of Faerie yet and maybe the wine weakened the wards? Either way, I had a vision," Lettie stammered.

"My friend?" Aisling looked confused. Both he and Riordan moved to her side.

"Corinna. I saw her in a vision. Levinas has her." Lettie pushed her fist against her mouth. He'd seen her shaken before and she only got like this if it was bad.

"Are you sure she didn't go with him willingly? The last time we saw them she appeared happy to be with him," Riordan's voice was cold.

She shook her head. "No. She was miserable."

"Good," Breena muttered.

Aisling linked her fingers with his, and Brynach knew without looking that her other hand was in Riordan's.

"Her dress was bloody and while I was watching Levinas hit her, multiple times. His familiar is guarding the room. I don't think she can leave," Lettie told them.

Aisling made a strangled sound at his side. Even if the princess had something to do with her kidnapping, Aisling was still too loyal to not care she was being hurt. "Could you see anything else in the room? Anything that could help us find her?"

"It was dark and if a room could look like a smell, I'd say it was damp and stale. I couldn't see any windows. And mice. A lot of them." Lettie shivered.

Aisling didn't share her horror. "That's good. She's not alone then. Her familiar is a mouse."

"It is?" Brynach hadn't known that.

Aisling's relief was obvious in the way her shoulders dropped and her breathing evened out. "Yes. And she'll heal fast."

Breena shook her head. "Who cares about the bitch's blood? This is the first clue we've had to Levinas's whereabouts. We need to find that neapan fucker."

Lettie added a theory, "I'm not the only one here who is

connected to the Hive. Someone else may have more information from other senses."

Brynach nodded and his twin exited the house and sifted.

"She'll check with Trixie, even if she has to wake her. Aisling, can you try dreamwalking with Corinna?" Brynach asked.

"I don't owe her this, not tonight." Aisling was hurt, and Brynach shouldn't push. Still, he wasn't surprised when she sighed, "I'll try."

Aisling placed a hand on his chest as leverage to reach his lips. She kissed him, then she took Riordan's hand and they moved upstairs to the bedroom. Brynach ran a hand through his hair, looking up at the loft. He didn't need more reminders that Levinas was morally corrupt. With each new piece of information, the blood lust rose. But Lettie needed to unburden herself, so he'd listen.

"He was talking, not yelling, talking, as he beat her. I couldn't hear, but she was at his feet, and he hit her over and over calm as could be." Lettie keeps her voice low.

"There's no excuse for the monster he became. He was sheltered more than Breena and me ever were and neither of us ended up that cruel." Brynach paced the room.

"She was asleep, but she had a 'dream' about a woman crying and loud water," Breena informed the room when she returned.

Brynach ran his tongue over his teeth. "At least she was spared the worst of it. Alright, we give Aisling a minute and then we go back to that fucking hell hole. That's where he'd feel safe."

"He's dumb enough to return," Ceiren agreed.

"Will I be safe going home?" Lettie wondered.

Breena positioned herself closer to Aisling's friend. "Probably not."

"You could come back with me. Be my guard." Lettie smiled at his twin, licked her lips, and cocked a hip. Beside her

Sean sighed.

Brynach watched his sister's cheeks flush. "You're tempting, darling, but I won't risk Jashana's anger. Not even for you."

Lettie shrugged and Sean looked pretty confused. I guess she hadn't shared the Fae's interest in her with her boyfriend.

"I've been wondering...about your marriage," Sean spoke up.

Brynach's eyebrow rose. "Oh?"

"I thought when you married Aisling the Veil would fall. I assume it hasn't," Sean commented and the three Fae in the room exchanged looks.

"Yes, I'd noticed," Brynach answered. "The short answer is the prophecy is old and there's a possibility it was translated or passed down incorrectly. The prophecy says that when the realms were ready to reunite a child would be born of both Light and Dark, of both magic and mortals. That child could heal the pain centuries of separation between the two races caused. They predicted a marriage of the realms, one denied them all those years ago by Kailyn and Larken. But marriage may have been symbolic and not literal. The marriage ceremony doesn't seem to have been enough to bring it down."

Lettie grinned. "And you fucking Aisling didn't either."

Brynach smirked. "Apparently not."

"And we feel how about that?" Lettie wondered.

It was complicated, that much was certain. A part of Brynach really wanted the Veil to fall. He'd never felt like he mattered to the world in large. Being a part of something so monumental made him feel useful, like everything he'd been through in his life had been for something. And he had to admit that he liked the idea of healing a rift that shouldn't have existed in the first place.

Breena spoke, "There are a lot of really good reasons to keep it in place but in my opinion, more to remove it. I've never been one for fairytales, but I'd be lying if I said I wasn't a little disappointed the wedding, or consummation thereof, didn't fulfill the prophecy."

"The humans have been preparing. We know about the meetings. They still think it's going to happen." Lettie's blue eyes were confused.

"Right, but how many groups have militarized? How many hate groups have become more vocal about the need for the Veil to protect their precious children and wives?" Ceiren asked in an uncharacteristic display of anger.

"A lot," Sean answered. "But others are excited to share the world with you again."

"It won't be that simple. It never is." Ceiren shook his head.

The conversation, though long from over, was brought to a halt when Aisling descended the stairs with Riordan.

"I did it." The wonder in her voice was clear but, Brynach had never doubted her.

"What did you learn, a stoirin?" Brynach moved to her, pulling her close.

"It's not your father's house. She said it's somewhere dug out and unfinished. It has a dirt floor and lamps for lighting. She can hear water, but he sifted her right into the space," Aisling told the room. "She hears howling and what sounds like dogs fighting. Her wounds are healing but she feels foolish for trusting him. She's sorry, not that it changes anything," she added.

"Her parents don't know she's with him," Breena pointed out.

"They must. He was in their castle. The guards and sentinels would know he was coming and going, or that she was," Ceiren wasn't convinced and Brynach agreed.

Brynach was already moving. "It's time we paid your father's court a call, wife."

"I'm coming with you." Lettie stepped to Breena, who was obviously going, and grabbed his twin around her middle.

"This involves me." Lettie refused to back down. "I'll go home afterward."

Breena's lips curled in what might pass as a smile and then she sifted away with Lettie. With a groan Sean moved to Ceiren muttering that he hated sifting. Brynach embraced Aisling and Riordan, and the three of them followed his siblings.

A guard startled at their approach, "What do you think you're doing charging in here like this?"

"Alert the King and Queen that I want an audience. And find my father." When the guard didn't jump to do Aisling's bidding, she ordered, "Now!"

A crack of magic disturbed the otherwise quiet hallway and the Fae jumped, eyes narrowing before he hurried away. Brynach fought the urge to adjust his hardening cock in his pants. Damn it, he loved when she embraced her power.

"They'd never listen to you in our court," Breena muttered. "Weak ass Seelie."

Brynach turned on his twin. "They damn well better listen to my wife!"

"Let the royal rumble begin," Sean whispered.

Breena snickered and everyone else ignored him.

"We should continue to the throne room." Aisling led the way. Once inside, an exhausted looking Lettie and Sean sat. Riordan nodded to Brynach and then tilted his head toward Lettie before walking over to her. Aisling sidled up to his side and together they listened in.

"I haven't properly said thank you," Riordan's voice had Lettie opening her eyes again.

"For?"

He played with the rings resting on his chest. "I know it's difficult finding yourself in a situation you didn't ask for. Believe me, I do. I'm sorry this happened to you and I'm sorry we continue to benefit from your pain. We appreciate all you're doing to help us despite not wanting anything to do with magic."

"But sometimes good things come from unfortunate circumstances. Right?" Lettie responded.

"And sometimes it sucks, and the bright side never comes," Riordan's voice dropped. Aisling wiped at her eyes, and Brynach hugged her tight to his side.

"The investigation on Dexter isn't over. Peggy's in jail and Sydney is fully on board. They can't hide the truth forever," Lettie reminded him.

Riordan started to say something but the doors slammed open, and the King and Queen glided in, flanked by Aisling's father and their advisor. As one, the group stood and waited for the inevitable fallout of demanding anything of the Fae royalty.

"What's the meaning of this?" Nevan's voice wasn't kind. His green eyes were burning holes in his daughter and Brynach felt immediately protective. What the hell was wrong with him?

"Silence, Regent," the Queen ordered, and Nevan bowed his head. "Someone explain why you are bothering us and on your wedding night no less."

Aisling's back straightened and she stepped forward, Brynach and Riordan stayed a fraction behind her. This was her confrontation but that didn't mean she'd do it alone.

"Levinas has been coming and going from this court despite being a wanted criminal in Faerie. You aided him. You hid him," she accused.

"We did no such thing, and you'll watch your tongue, child." The King stepped forward and the guards moved with him.

"So, you have a breach in your security? A way for him to evade and confuse the sentinels at the gates?" Aisling wasn't going to be gaslit by this asshole. Brynach barely contained his grin. Riordan let loose a soft chuffing laugh.

"I'd hate for the unaligned to learn of such a weakness,"

Breena said in a saccharine voice.

The Queen slashed her hand through the air. "Enough. Your threats don't scare us, Princess." The Queen continued, "Corinna was misled. She's young and impressionable. But don't mistake our love for her as weakness in the court, our security is as strong as ever."

"Then you knew he was here and did nothing. He deserves punishment for his crimes against me," Aisling's voice rose. Brynach hated seeing her this hurt by people she'd trusted. She turned to her father. "You should have wanted to see him brought to justice for what he did."

If the Unseelie had ever wondered who dominated the Seelie Court, the answer was evident in the King's silence. The Queen had easily cowed both him and Nevan. Bryanch watched her father actively avoid Aisling's gaze and noticed when Aisling's shoulders dipped.

"You may have enjoyed our protection and our lenience as a child, but Corinna is our daughter. As such, we will always protect her over you. You were a ward, a responsibility, not a royal." The Queen glared. "You've always been prone to theatrics. He barely touched you. So he held you for a while, away from your precious home and lovers. You're fine."

Neither man needed the bond to know the Queen's words hurt Aisling. They both moved until their bodies connected with her back. They didn't reach for her hands. They didn't speak for her. But Aisling would know they were there for her.

She finally played the ace up her sleeve. "And where's your princess now?"

The King and Queen exchanged a look. It was the King who spoke, "She is at the revel enjoying a night out."

"No, she isn't," Aisling informed them. "She's been taken by Levinas, who is currently torturing her."

"And you know this how?" It was Aisling's father who asked the question.

"I know because Lettie saw Corinna in a vision being

slapped around by Levinas. Then I was able to reach her via a dreamwalk."

"A vision?" the King asked.

It was Lettie who answered, "The Hive. The group of people who fell victim to the sleeping curse. The Princess is a part of it, linked to all of us. You had to know. Didn't you wonder what Levinas's interest in her was? He was using her, and apparently you, for information."

The idea hadn't occurred to Brynach, but it made so much sense. Levinas would need any tool he could get his hands on just to keep his head above water. He had to admit, it was smart of him.

"Where is she?" The Queen's voice was even, but Brynach saw her hands clench in her skirts. Oh, she was not happy.

"We're unsure." Aisling didn't ease up, "Frankly, after harboring my kidnapper, I shouldn't be helping you at all. Corinna isn't blameless in this, either. But she's young and naive. You knew better."

The guards moved forward, and both Riordan and Brynach moved in front of her. The Queen held out her arm and they stopped. Nevan glanced between Aisling and his King and Queen. He appeared torn, but he wasn't moving to his daughter. Any respect Brynach had for the man was gone instantly. The two of them moved back to her side.

"We don't owe you an explanation. We can entertain anyone we please," the Queen dismissed Aisling's outrage.

Brynach's low growl had Aisling placing a hand on his arm. Riordan moved closer to the large Fae's side until they were touching, too.

"You won't bring official accusations. Stop with the empty threats. You have my thanks for informing us of Corinna's situation. We'll handle it from here." The Queen turned and left the room, dismissing them.

The King followed her, and Nevan looked between their backs and Aisling. Brynach's chest ached when his wife called

out to her father softly. Nevan shook his head and followed his
King and Queen.

CHAPTER 31

Riordan

B rynach couldn't do anything to ease the hurt Aisling was clearly feeling. He'd never missed the bond more. Riordan didn't know what to do to help her right now. At least with the bond open he'd have some clue. Or at least, he thought he would.

They entered the house and Aisling let out a sob. She'd been crying since they left the Seelie Court. He hated it. It was well after midnight, but it was still her wedding day, she shouldn't be upset today of all days. She was still wearing her reception dress and even red eyed Aisling was stunning.

"A stoirin?" Brynach spoke softly.

"Rin is complaining about my father. He has choice words for him," she attempted a laugh.

"What can we do for you, Ash?" Riordan asked, giving her distance in case she didn't want to be touched right now.

"I want a shower and I want our bed."

"Is that all you want?" Riordan asked knowing she'd understand what he was really asking.

She looked at the two men in front of her. "No."

Brynach nodded to Riordan over her shoulder. Then he was standing with Aisling in his arms and the three of them were moving to the bathroom. He'd never ask for this, not when she'd been through so much today. But a part of him was relieved she still wanted them. Not because he was insecure that Brynach had been inside her earlier. Because honestly, he thought Brynach was a true Prince for the way he'd waited and protected Aisling. But Riordan needed this. Tonight, they'd start their relationship together, all three of them. He still hadn't unpacked why, but that was important to him.

Brynach undressed Aisling, setting aside her weapons and laying her dress out. She moved only when he instructed her to. Riordan quickly stripped then turned on the shower. Riordan pulled her under the warm spray and held her a moment. Over her head Riordan saw Brynach naked for the first time. No amount of blushing or rioting emotions, both of which he had in spades, could stop his eyes from wandering the man's body.

He took in the Fae's wide frame. His muscular arms and large hands taking such care with Aisling as he began washing her hair. The way the water slid down his chest, through the v-shaped muscles near his hips, and cascaded over his groin. His already sizable cock thickening under Riordan's gaze. Brynach spread his legs wider as he stepped into Aisling and reached for the soap.

Riordan wasn't insecure about what he was working with, but the sheer girth of the hulking Fae's cock was impressive. Fuck. He shook his head and looked back to where Brynach was soaping his hands and washing Aisling's body.

Brynach called his name and when he met the Fae's eyes. The vertical pupils burned into him. "She needs you, too."

He blushed and tore his eyes away from the Fae. Aisling was unmoving and staring blindly at the wall. Brynach was right. He needed to do better than this. A soft touch on his arm and Brynach smiled. "I love the way you look at me. But for right now..."

Riordan nodded and moved to Aisling. He took the soap

from Brynach's hand and washed down her arms and across her shoulder, still careful around the scar on her collarbone even though it didn't hurt her anymore.

"Tonight, we take care of you, a stoirin," Brynach informed her. "Understand?"

Aisling nodded and let them walk her out of the shower.

"Riordan and I have talked about tonight," Brynach said as he dried her body. Riordan smiled at her. Brynach stroked her pussy with the towel, effectively getting her attention. "Tonight, you'll do as I say. Because you know that my intention is our pleasure, all of ours. Because you trust me to take care of you." Brynach turned to Riordan. "Both of you."

He could feel Aisling's eyes on them, but Riordan couldn't look away from the Fae's strong gaze. Riordan had so many questions, but none he was willing to take the time to ponder right now. Not with the two of them naked in front of him. He turned to Aisling who was breathing fast and flushed.

"Oh, Goddess, this is happening," she murmured.

"A stoirin. Breathe," Brynach coaxed, and Aisling sucked in air. "We can get in bed and sleep. You've had a long day. We can revisit this later. Nothing will happen tonight unless you want it to."

"No." She met Brynach's gaze, a hand going to his cheek. Then she leaned back against Riordan, her other hand finding his cock. Riordan groaned and his hips bucked into her firm grasp. "I want this."

"And you remember your safe word?"

She nodded and then, as agreed upon, verbalized her consent, "Yes, I remember."

Brynach took her chin between his thumb and forefinger and raised her face to his. Brynach's lips lowered, his wet hair moving across her face and shoulders as Riordan watched. "Get in bed," he growled, and Aisling practically ran.

Brynach and Riordan followed. Riordan got on the bed next to her, but her husband stood. "You're tired. We all are.

But we won't let you go to sleep unsatisfied. Isn't that right?"

Riordan answered, "Never. It is our job, our pleasure, to share your bed."

Brynach smiled down at them. "If you so much as touch that hot pussy of yours, I'll tie you up so fast your head will spin. If you need something, anything, use your words and tell us." His citrine eyes pinned her to the bed.

"Understood." She nodded furiously and Riordan bit back a laugh at her enthusiasm.

"Riordan, hold her up so she can see herself," Brynach instructed.

Riordan kneeled behind Aisling, cradling her between his legs. Gently, he pulled her shoulders back to his chest and her hands went to his legs, holding tight to him.

"Feet flat. Legs spread," Brynach demanded, and Aisling complied immediately. "Look at yourself, a stoirin."

Aisling looked down at her pussy, pink and puffy with arousal. Her breasts bobbed on her chest as she fought to control her breathing. Riordan was mesmerized by her. She was so strong. So beautiful. So trusting.

Brynach lowered himself onto his knees, the mattress dipping under his weight as he prowled to her. Aisling watched him.

"I didn't tell you to look at me," Brynach tsk'd. "Look. Back. Down."

Against his chest her head dipped down, and they watched Brynach's hand slither up her thigh, flesh puckering where he squeezed. Riordan had memorized the feel of her and the warm scent of her arousal. He envied Brynach his position in front of her. Aisling reached one hand for him, and Riordan twined their finger's together as his erection pulsed against her back.

"Kiss her neck. Bite her. Make her squirm," Brynach ordered Riordan.

You didn't have to tell him twice. Riordan wasn't much for

being topped in the bedroom, or at least he hadn't thought so. But Aisling loved it, and Riordan was happy to play along if it gave her what she needed. Frankly, shutting off his brain appealed to him, too. Brynach gathered his long hair and swept it over his shoulder. A strand went rogue, and he pushed it back, again. Riordan pulled his hand from Aisling's and pulled off a spare hair tie, handing it to Brynach.

"Thank you." Brynach's eyes softened, and then he tied his hair in a quick bun while maintaining eye contact with Riordan. Then he lowered himself to Aisling's core.

Riordan stroked the long column of her neck, and his hand found her breasts, cupping first one and then the other. He ran his thumb over them, listening to her breath catch. His mouth found her neck, first tasting the skin there and then biting, as instructed. Aisling leaned more of her weight on him, and he groaned his approval as more of her body made contact with his erection.

Brynach used his fingers to spread her open. "You are so wet for us. Riordan, feel her."

Riordan lowered his hand to Aisling's pussy and slid a finger along her folds and then slipped it inside of her. His chest rose and fell beneath her. "Goddess, you're burning hot." He plunged in and out of her a few times, her body making lovely wet sounds.

"Did you know I fucked her with my hand under the table at the wedding?" Brynach asked. "I could taste her on my fingers as I ate afterward."

"Fuck," Riordan cursed as he continued stroking into her. "That's so damn sexy." He kissed Aisling's neck then sucked hard on it. She squirmed under him making lovely mewling sounds.

Her husband agreed and when Riordan pulled his hand away from her pussy Brynach grabbed it. His breath caught as Brynach locked those hungry eyes on his. The grip was assertive but not unbreakable, but Riordan didn't pull away.

Slowly, the Fae extended his tongue and moved toward Riordan's fingers, slick with her juices. So slowly that Riordan had time to object. He thought about it, but quickly realized he didn't want to stop him. Instead, he rocked his hips against Aisling's back as Brynach licked up Riordan's finger, from palm to tip without breaking eye contact.

Aisling moaned and tried to grind herself against Brynach, but he was focused on Riordan. He didn't mind that attention, at all. Against him, Aisling's whole body shook, and she whined her need.

"You're not allowed to get yourself off tonight," Brynach growled, eyes still on Riordan. "That's our job."

"Then do it!" Aisling whined.

Brynach winked at Riordan and damn it if his balls didn't tighten. Then the large Fae lowered his head and lapped at Aisling, the flat of his tongue pressing against her clit. When he looked up at her, face slick with her arousal, his eyes were vibrant. "How many times do you think I can make you come before you pass out?"

Tears formed and slid down her cheek. Riordan leaned down and licked them away. "Those are ours, too," he purred in her ear.

Brynach smiled his approval and then resumed his feasting. Riordan continued to whisper in her ear, "Let go, Aisling. Give us your pleasure. Relax and let yourself be loved."

Brynach linked the fingers of his left hand with Aisling while he feasted. His right searched and Riordan's pulse sped as he realized what he was looking for. Riordan reached down and twined his fingers with Brynach. With both of the Fae's hands occupied Riordan lifted Aisling onto the slope of his knees presenting her to her husband. Aisling sobbed her release as Brynach sucked at her clit.

Riordan curled behind a still quaking Aisling and Brynach moved in front of her. "You're amazing, Aisling," Brynach crooned in her ear. Then he lifted her leg up and over his hip.

"Make love to her," he instructed Riordan. Aisling rested her head on Brynach's arm while he whispered in her ear and Riordan stroked inside of her from behind.

"I love you," she panted. She didn't clarify who she was speaking to. Aisling meant both of them. "I don't deserve you," she cried as Riordan slid into her again.

Brynach's hand was lightning fast as it settled around her throat. Aisling gasped as he applied pressure to the sides. "Don't ever let me hear you say that again. Don't even think it." He met Riordan's eyes. "Pull out."

Riordan did as asked, his whole body aching with need. One second she was facing Brynach, the next she was facing Riordan. Brynach held her leg up with one hand, cradling her neck with the other but no longer applying pressure. Riordan kissed her and seated his cock inside her again.

"Do you see the hurt on your partner's faces when you say things like that?" Brynach asked. "I know you don't want to hurt us, Aisling. Have we given you reason to doubt us?"

She shook her head and Riordan fought to control himself. The hot feel of her wrapped around him, the hitch of her breath against his neck while Brynach rocked behind her, pushing her further on his cock was driving him wild.

"Use your words, Aisling. Are you happy, wife?" Brynach asked.

Riordan stroked deep inside her and leaned in to lick a tear from her face as she cried out, "Yes. So happy."

Brynach's hand dipped down to her ass and Aisling tensed. He met the Fae's eyes over her shoulder and damn if he didn't wink at Riordan. "You look so beautiful fucking Riordan. Do either of us seem unhappy to you, a stoirin?" he asked, his hand moving along the crease of her ass. Aisling gasped and pushed back against him.

Riordan grinned. "She likes that."

Brynach growled his agreement, "Damn it, Aisling. I'm trying to be angry with you and here you are practically begging me to play with your ass."

Aisling bit her lip and cried out. Riordan would have given anything to know what was happening behind her. Instead, he brought a hand to her breast and pinched hard enough to get her attention. "Do you want him inside you at the same time as me?" Then his mouth was on hers, swallowing her cries.

Brynach's voice was a barely controlled groan, "Is that what you want, Aisling? Do you want to be so full of the both of us it feels like you're being split open?"

"Yes!" Aisling screamed as she broke away from Riordan's mouth and a powerful orgasm surged through her.

"Goddess! She's squeezing the life out of me," Riordan groaned and tried to ride out her orgasm without blowing his load.

Aisling was panting and wild with want. Brynach reached down to stroke her clit as Riordan worked toward his orgasm. Fuck. The man's large hand couldn't stroke their lover without touching his cock as it slid itself home. The sensation of his knuckles against his hot, hard flesh shouldn't have been as arousing as it was.

Brynach hushed Aisling, "You did so good, a stoirin. But we're not done. You'll come again before Riordan finds his release or we won't touch you for a week. Give it to us, princess."

She shook her head. "I can't!"

Dear Goddess, he hoped she could. He didn't want to go a week without touching her. And he hoped she could do it fast because the Fae's dirty mouth had his balls tightening with desire.

"You can and you will," Brynach assured her. One hand fisted in her hair and pulled. The growl that escaped the Fae's lips had Aisling's body quivering. Then Riordan watched as he sank his teeth into their lover's neck. It wasn't a gentle bite. He could see the flesh turning white around the other man's teeth.

Aisling moaned, "Yes. Please. Yes."

Riordan stroked into her. Aisling's hand found the back of Brynach's head and held him to her. Between the feel of her hot pussy gripping him and the sight of Brynach and Aisling together he was losing control. Riordan leaned forward and sucked at her nipple.

"Harder," she cried. He didn't know if she meant biting or fucking. He did both.

"Aisling, my fingers may be on your clit, but my knuckles are brushing Riordan's cock every time he plunges into that hot pussy. He's slick with you. And his eyes are wild, a stoirin. We're both wild for you." Brynach's dirty talk burrowed into Riordan's brain and had the desired effect on his wife.

Aisling came, and with her pulsing around him, Riordan did, too. Panting and sweaty she fell into Riordan's arms. He stroked her through her orgasm as he bucked inside her. And fuck if it wasn't the hottest thing he'd ever experienced.

Brynach rubbed her back. "You did so good, Aisling. I'm so proud of you."

She closed her eyes, panting and slick with sweat against Riordan's chest. Her hair plastered to her cheeks and her body absolutely wrecked. She was marvelous. He kissed her sweaty forehead. The Fae's eyes were heavy with lust as he gazed first at Aisling and then Riordan.

But then it hit him. "Brynach, you haven't finished."

Aisling turned toward her husband. "Let's fix that."

Brynach shook his head and without a hint of embarrassment admitted, "I found my release watching you find your own." Then he winked. "We're going to have to change these sheets."

The thought of Brynach coming from watching him fuck Aisling was inconceivable. Aisling must have agreed because she complained, "Bry, that's not fair."

He kissed her. "Aisling, believe me when I tell you that I am satisfied. Off to the shower again, a stoirin."

Neither of them had the energy to argue.

CHAPTER 32

Aisling

W hen she woke, the bed was empty. When had they left? How awkward were things going to be this morning? Last night Brynach casually touched Riordan's cock while he was fucking her. Her husband shared her with her lover. Would they hate her, or each other, in the light of day? They'd talked about last night but actually doing it was another thing. Aisling felt fantastic. Last night was everything she'd wanted it to be, and she really hoped they still felt the same.

"There you are." Riordan moved to her and kissed her, hard. "We were worried we'd worn you out and you'd sleep all day."

She leaned into him, loving his fresh smell and the soft cotton under her hands as she held him tight. Brynach smiled at her from his place at the stove. He was naked save sweatpants he was wearing, the very opposite of Riordan in so many ways. "I'm glad you slept. You needed the rest."

Aisling blushed.

"Not because of that, wife. Because you've been through a lot." He shook his head.

She turned to Riordan. "You're okay?"

"I'm fantastic. Stop worrying. I'm not the one who has been through the ringer in the last twenty-four hours." He kissed her and then spun her around so Brynach, who'd snuck up on them, could do the same.

When her husband had his fill of her mouth, he stepped back, leaving her breathless. Aisling started her life as a wife and partner by eating breakfast with the two men she loved most. The sun was shining in through the massive windows, open to allow the sweet-smelling air of Faerie into their home.

"We have to talk."

Reality slammed into Aisling as she bit into a piece of sausage. "Damn it. Really, Bry?" She groaned, "I was having a moment."

"Sassing your husband already?" Rin laughed, *"Cut the guy some slack. I'm sure he'd rather be back up in bed with you, too."*

"I can't let him get used to destroying my marital bliss," Aisling retorted.

Even Riordan was giving him a dirty look, but Brynach shrugged those large shoulders. "It can't be avoided, a stoirin. You have never enjoyed being coddled. Should we start now?"

Aisling slumped in her chair. "So much for the honeymoon phase. Fine, I'm listening."

He started, "I have to go talk to my brother about his bullshit games. Your father was a disgrace last night, and it's clear the Seelie Court had an arrangement with Levinas. That may not stand after he smacked their daughter around, but I want to know why it existed at all."

"Any theories?" Riordan asked.

"I'm not sure. But if the Seelie Court is working with Levinas, and Nevan turned his back on Aisling, that's something." Brynach took a deep breath. "And it's time to address the Veil."

Aisling slumped in her seat and picked at her toast. "It's a stupid prophecy. I'm just a halfling, a powerful one, but it's too much to lay on my shoulders. I never said I knew how to bring that fucker down, or even if I was sure I wanted to."

"Nobody's blaming you, Ash. That's not what Brynach is getting at. I thought the Veil was supposed to...I don't know... disintegrate?" Riordan shrugged. "I didn't think you had to do anything more than marry Brynach."

"Maybe it's not about me?" She was both disappointed and relieved by that idea.

"I still believe it is," Brynach sounded so sure.

Riordan chimed in, "We've kept her from going through the Veil. Should we, I don't know, send her through?"

Her husband shook his head. "It can't hurt. We'll try it. But if that doesn't work, I might know what will."

Brynach turned to Aisling, and the look he gave her set off alarm bells. She held up her hands. "Oh, no you don't. Don't give me that look, Bry!"

"What look?" Riordan asked, his head swiveling between the two of them.

"The 'you're not going to like it but you have to trust me' look," Aisling said shaking her head. Damn it, she didn't want to have to do anything else. It wasn't fair.

"You won't be alone. I will be with you and so will Riordan. Every step of the way," he swore, one hand on hers and the other over his heart.

Aisling let her head fall back and stared up through the sky lights. She caught a flash of Rin as he soared happily overhead. "What are you getting me into this time?"

"An idea came to me when you stripped my father. If you can remove magic from a Fae maybe you can remove it from the Veil." Brynach's brow raised.

Riordan squeezed her leg. "You did destroy an entire soul prison."

"That was a fluke. I had no idea it would actually work," Aisling deflected.

"But it did. Your instincts were right. And you're stronger now, a stoirin," Brynach pushed. "You can part the Veil, that means the magic bends for you."

"It bends for all Fae!" she argued.

"Aisling, the soul prison held Fae." Brynach's voice lowered, slowed. He drove the point home. "Full-blooded Fae. Royal Fae. And they couldn't get out. They couldn't break the bonds that held them captive."

She tossed the toast on her plate. Why did he have to make so much sense? "It's because I'm part witch, too. Riordan helped me. We weren't in Faerie, but he could still reach me."

"Look, I just want to test the theory. Will you do that?" Aisling knew Brynach wasn't going to let this go until she said yes.

Biting her lip, she asked, "What do I get if I say yes?"

Riordan barked out a laugh. "We've created a monster."

Brynach grinned his approval of her appetite. "Whatever you want, my heart."

"I want to taste you. Both of you at once." Aisling was pushing boundaries. Brynach and Riordan had decided that for now they'd share her but slowly ease into their own relationship, whatever that looked like. But she wanted this, and she trusted them to be truthful with her.

Brynach waited for Riordan and her Ravdi flushed. His hand fidgeted on her leg.

"Yes, you can have that." Riordan's voice was husky. She knew that voice, she'd heard it often in the bedroom. She kissed him, her fingers weaving into his hair. Together they tugged and nipped, fighting for control playfully. Goddess, she loved him. Brynach put a hand on her back, and she pulled away.

"Thank you," she whispered against Riordan's mouth.

"We should go." Brynach's voice was as ragged as Riordan's had been. It wasn't jealousy, it was lust adding weight to his words. "If we don't now, we won't."

"Your fucked-up family or the Veil?"

"The Veil. We need that information before we go see Rainer."

That was not the answer Aisling had been hoping for. But, if she had to do it, she'd rather get it over with. They finished their breakfast and Aisling went to change. She was in their closet staring at her clothes when Brynach approached her.

"You okay?"

"No." She shook her head. "What do you wear to potentially end the world as you know it?"

Her shoulders shook as the weight of it all settled on her. Hot tears flooded her lashes and fell down her cheek.

"Oh, a stoirin, no. It's not ending the world as you know it. It's restoring what should have always been. We weren't meant to live like this." His words didn't reassure her, but his arms around her and his kisses on the top of her head helped.

"Even if it ends up being a good thing, it will be bad first," she hiccuped into his chest and inhaled his woodsy scent. "I don't know if I'm more worried that I can do it or that I can't."

Brynach smoothed his hand down to her back. She slowed her breathing to match the rise and fall of his chest, the tightness in her own easing a little.

"You've dealt with a lot lately. More than anyone should be expected to handle. You are loved and supported, a stoirin. No matter what happens, we'll be together, and that means it will be okay," Brynach promised.

She allowed herself one last moment in his arms and then leaned back. Brynach let her go and Aisling nodded. She plucked leather pants from the drawer and Brynach growled approval when she pulled them on and strapped twin knife holsters to her thighs. She'd fill them from the weapons locker on the way out.

Wanting to match Riordan, she turned to his section of the closet and shrugged on one of his flannel button ups. She did two buttons in the middle and then tied the ends up under her bra.

"You are trying to torture us, aren't you?" Riordan accused from the doorway.

Brynach shook his head, his hair swaying. "The problem is, she has no idea how fucking stunning she is."

Riordan murmured his agreement, making Aisling blush. Then she watched her Ravdi pull a hair tie from his wrist and offer it to her. "Braid it so it's out of your face. When you call significant magic it goes all crazy."

Aisling took it and pulled her hair over her shoulder, quickly braiding it as instructed.

"You need one, too?" Riordan asked Brynach, pulling another tie from his wrist. It hadn't escaped Aisling's notice that he's started wearing them for her and Brynach. It was incredibly sweet.

Brynach winked at her boyfriend. "I still have the one you gave me last night."

Riordan cursed, "We need to get out of this house. Now."

Aislng approached the Veil at the edge of their property and ran her hand over it. If she stayed in it the magic embraced her, sending goosebumps racing along her skin. "If it was this easy wouldn't someone else have tried it?"

Her husband huffed a laugh, "Nothing about it is easy. And no. Most Fae are happy with the way things are. And those that aren't may not be brave or strong enough to do what you can."

Riordan spoke, "At least try the easy option. Go through the Veil."

Aisling did as instructed. She stood on the other side with her hands on her hips. "Well, that didn't work."

Riordan held up his hands. "It was worth a try." Brynach called her back through the Veil, and she let it close behind her. "All you have to do is try a stoirin."

She closed her eyes and plunged her hand into the Veil between worlds and tried to pull from it, to strip it the way she had Gabriel. She'd been new to the power Brynach shared with her then, and now she had practice. Still, the magic swirled around her, avoiding her attempts to grab onto it.

Gabriel's magic had fought her, too. It had struggled and hidden and gripped to the foul man. But she had overpowered it. She plucked and pulled until every last drop of his immortality was gone. And she'd been joyful about it. There had been pride in protecting what was hers, in bringing peace to Brynach after all his father had put him through.

"And, she finally gets it," Rin chirped from the trees above. *"Motivation, darling. You have to want it."*

"But what if I don't? What if I don't want to be the one who brings the collapse of the Veil?" she argued with her familiar.

"You've come way too far to turn back," his voice in her head was a comfort even if his words weren't. *"You've known all along what the prophecy meant and now because it's a reality, you're scared. I understand. Do you think I'm not worried what it will mean when the Veil comes down? We don't know if we'll still be able to talk. And Riordan, that sweet boy, he hasn't told you that the Ravdi bond is weaker now that you're bonded to the Dark Prince."*

"What!" Her eyes swung to Riordan. *"He wouldn't keep that from me."*

"Wouldn't he? You can't change it and he wouldn't want you to feel bad. But the more Fae you get, the weaker your witchy connection to him gets." Rin's voice was sad and soft. The same he'd used with her as a kid when he was trying to soothe her.

Aisling turned to Riordan and held out her hand. He came to her, and she parted the Veil, sliding through. He paused at the edge of Faerie, his eyes sad. That look told her all she needed to know even before they'd passed through. He gave her a small smile and a shake of his head before locking eyes with her and stepping over. It didn't take long to confirm what Rin had said.

Tears sprang to her eyes. "Why didn't you tell me?"

"We can't change it." The sadness in the bond was going both ways. Riordan was as upset as she was.

The bond was still there but it wasn't as vibrant. She pulled on his magic, and it still came but it didn't fill her with warmth and color the way it used to. It was duller. It broke her damn heart.

Brynach, still on the other side of the open Veil looked at them with worried eyes. He reached a hand through and caressed her cheek then he stepped through. Aisling was slammed with emotion. Love, guilt, sadness, and acceptance.

Her head swiveled between Riordan and Brynach. Aisling's jaw dropped. "What is this?"

Neither man answered and she dropped both their hands and crossed her arms. "I'm serious, what is going on?"

The swirl of emotions was overwhelming but each of the men were grinning. She felt like she was missing something, and she did not like it. Someone had better start answering soon.

Riordan fidgeted. "Um, well, when you bonded with Brynach you became a bit more Fae and a little less witch, but Fae Hulk here became a bit witchy."

He let the statement hang and Aisling pieced it together. "You and Brynach?"

She turned to her husband who nodded. "Seems so. He's my Ravdi now."

"And I'm guessing since both of you are this side of the Veil the bond got stronger because all parts of it are this side," Riordan hypothesized.

Aisling tried to not feel hurt. "You knew about your bond with one another and didn't say anything?"

Brynach reached for her, and she moved back. "Aisling, how could we tell you that without telling you about the weakening of your bond with Riordan?"

"You should have told me!" She yelled, "I deserved to know."

"We didn't want to worry you. I love you. Brynach loves you. We're alright," Riordan assured her.

"And honestly, bonding with Riordan was beautiful and special and for a little while it was ours." Brynach reached for her.

"You like it?" she wondered.

He nodded. "I love it. I never knew." The awe in his voice was clear.

"This is a lot," she stammered.

"Which is exactly why we didn't want to stress you out with it. But I'm sorry I wasn't honest," Riordan apologized.

It was a lot to process, but that didn't mean it was bad. Brynach was right, it was beautiful, and a part of her was thrilled the two men had bonded. Perhaps nobody had lost anything, but rather gained. Now they were all linked.

"I have an idea." Aisling stepped away from the men and parted the Veil. "Bry, go into Faerie."

The large Fae moved past her and into Faerie. Riordan stepped up to her, but she held out a hand.

"You stay on that side. Both of you give me your hands." She stood in the Veil, a man on each side of her. "As long as I'm with Riordan on this side, he can funnel magic to me. Brynach, so long as I'm with you in Faerie, I can pull from the land and your strength. I can use the strength of both of you."

"Of all of us," Brynach corrected.

"You absolute genius," Riordan crowed.

This time, when Aisling tried to strip the Veil of its magic, it came to her. She threw her head back and laughed, and the men beside her smiled.

CHAPTER 33

Riordan

After Aisling determined she could strip the Veil, even a little, the three were on a high. Of course, that couldn't last long. No, not for them. The visit to Rainer didn't go as Brynach had hoped.

"I trusted Rainer to be a better ruler. I'm beginning to believe I was misled," Brynach complained as they left the Unseelie Court.

"I'm not going to lie. I really didn't understand a ton of what just happened," Riordan admitted. The brothers had fought, that much was clear. And he understood Brynach was pissed off that he and Aisling had been used as pawns. Rainer had dismissed Brynach, called him foolish and short sighted.

But they'd left without even mentioning that Aisling could weaken the Veil. Sure, they weren't sure she could strip it entirely, but it seemed like something they should have brought up.

"They've spent so long pushing Brynach and I together and now that we're married, it's clear they had bigger plans for us that we weren't in on," Aisling said.

Brynach nodded. "I talked to Ceiren and the unaligned are restless. He said that factions are moving away from the middle lands and toward the outskirts of the courts."

"Why would they be moving toward the Dark or Light lands?" Riordan wondered.

Aisling shrugged and they looked at Brynach.

"I don't know. They haven't moved in large groups in some time. But," he paused and ran his hand through his hair. "Kongur has a theory and while he's usually a little grumpy and dramatic, he may be on to something. He believes the unaligned were pinning their hopes on the Veil dropping when we got married. They got agitated when it didn't."

"That doesn't make any sense," Aisling said.

"Doesn't it?" Brynach asked. "When the Veil comes down how long do you think the two-court system will last? The unaligned want a united Faerie, no courts to pay fealty to. With the Veil down they could access the human realm, they could hope for the demise of an outdated, in their eyes, royal system."

Aisling seemed shocked and Riordan didn't blame her. It seemed neither of them had considered that angle.

"I really don't know what to do with that information," she said, squeezing her temples.

Riordan moved behind her and rubbed her shoulders. "You don't have to do anything. How they react to things isn't your responsibility."

"He's right," Brynach agreed. "For now, we don't do anything."

"Are we making the right decision still trying to bring down the Veil, Bry?"

The large Fae thought a moment. "I believe that we are. But you have to believe it, too."

Aisling sighed, "It's the way the world was meant to be, right? It may not be easy but it's the right thing to do. I think." She straightened her shoulders and Riordan was full of pride. She was so damn strong. But that didn't mean that this wasn't going to hurt. They were on their way to see her father even though nothing he said would make his behavior okay.

Riordan barely flinched when the stones asked for his blood. That, if nothing else, was a testament to how used to Faerie he was getting. They'd already agreed to head to the other side of the Veil after this and he was anxious to have the bond open. That brief moment with all three of them had been beautiful. He wanted it, again. But first, they had to face Nevan. Aisling deserved to get answers.

"We'll be right by your side," Brynach promised.

They passed through the gardens but before they reached the doors to the castle they were stopped by a guard.

"You're not welcome at court," he announced.

"Excuse me?" Aisling took a step forward. "How dare you. I want to speak to Nevan."

She made to walk around him but a sword across her chest stopped her. Brynach lurched forward and a second guard held up his weapon, stopping him. Aisling put up her hand and both men stilled.

"Can you send him out?"

"No, we cannot. It's at his request that you're denied access to the Seelie Court. Now, you can leave, or we can remove you." He advanced on Aisling and Riordan reached out and pulled her away.

"Aisling, let's go," he all but begged. She was numb, zombie like as he put an arm around her shoulder. They hurried her away.

She didn't let the tears fall until they were outside the gates. "He doesn't want to see me," she sobbed. She barely got the next words out between cries. "He's always been distant, but he's never flat out turned me away. How could he side with them?"

Aisling curled in on herself and Brynach looked at Riordan, feeling helpless as hell. He didn't need the bond to know Brynach wanted to hold her. He could carry her easier than Riordan could. He nodded. They needed to have a talk. He never, ever, needed to ask Riordan for permission to care for Aisling. He wouldn't allow the other man to ever hesitate again.

Riordan clung to the Fae, and they sifted to the Veil. Within moments they were through, and the pain nearly dropped Riordan to his knees. He wouldn't leave her alone with it. He let his love and support shine through the bond, and Brynach turned his head to him. Riordan felt the man's affection for him returned, even if the original intention had been to comfort Aisling.

"I never asked him for more than he could give. I made things so damn easy for him. Forgave so much. That asshole," she cried into Brynach's neck. "Why would he do that?"

"I don't know, a stoirin." Her husband made his way up to the condo carrying Aisling. Riordan hurried to open the door. Once inside Brynach sat on the sofa with her, and Riordan got a glass of water before joining them.

All they could do was let her cry it out. It absolutely killed him. Riordan was thankful the bond only worked between him and Brynach and he and Aisling because right now, the large Fae was so angry it was palpable. If Aisling could sense how close to losing it Brynach was, she'd be either worried or scared. As it stood, he wasn't sure her husband had the restraint to not go back to Faerie and murder her father.

Riordan rubbed circles on Aisling's back and with the other hand he took a risk. His hand found the back of Brynach's neck and in an attempt to distract the man, he rubbed there. He saw the Prince lower his lids and take a deep breath. Riordan fed him magic slowly, letting it seep through his fingers into the Fae's stiff muscles.

He felt the other man shiver and then lean into Riordan a little. Aisling must have felt the shift because she lifted her head. With a smile he sent her love through the bond, and she returned it.

"Are you two?" she questioned.

Riordan nodded.

"It's amazing," Brynach groaned.

A small smile crept onto Aisling's lips. "Yes, he is."

She leaned forward and Riordan kissed her tears and then her mouth, all the while funneling magic and rubbing on Brynach's neck. Aisling let magic leak through their bond toward him making his lips tingle. She wiggled on Brynach's lap.

"He likes sharing magic with you," she noted.

Riordan didn't need to look down to know the Fae was hard as a rock. He remembered what it was like the first time he'd shared magic with Aisling. It was an overwhelming full body experience.

"For fuck's sake," Brynach ground out. "Is it always like this? I feel like my whole body is on fire."

They laughed and Riordan answered, "Not always, no. But when it's good it is."

"I won't survive this." His hands fisted in Aisling's shirt.

Riordan laughed. "How you doing, babe?" She twisted the ring he'd given her, and he took her hand and brought it to his lips.

Aisling sniffed, "I'm not wasting any more time on that man. Come on, we still have work to do."

Brynach pulled at his pants, readjusting his sizable bulge. "Evil. You're both evil," he complained.

They still had to alert the Firinne, witches, Ravdi, and local police that they were going to try and bring down the Veil tomorrow. Which meant that in less than twenty-four hours the world as they knew it could change. No big deal. Riordan powered on his phone and warned his brother they were incoming. His response was fast and short, an "okay", which caused Riordan distress. His brother never answered with one word.

Brynach grumbled all the way to his truck but hopped in and drove them to Terra Bella without complaining. Though he did have plenty of questions about the bond and sharing of magic. Riordan and Aisling answered as many as they could before they got to the front door of the shop.

"You're home!" Dawn hurried around the counter and hugged Aisling and then Riordan, pausing as she turned to Brynach. He smiled and embraced the witch.

"What are you doing here? I mean, I'm happy you are, but I didn't think you'd be home so soon after the wedding. I took off early, but you seemed to be having a great time." She winked at Aisling. "I'm sure it only got better."

Color flooded Aisling's cheeks and Riordan shifted a little, but Brynach just chuckled. "We're here with news. We need to head upstairs but you're welcome if you want."

Dawn didn't need further prompting to switch the sign in the window, lock the door, and follow them upstairs. When they crested the landing of the apartment Riordan saw his brother and the smile on his face fell.

"What's wrong?" He dropped Aisling's hand and rushed to his brother's side. "Liam, what is it?"

"Bullshit. That's what it is. Complete bullshit," Amber cursed from behind him.

Liam shook his head. "He's gone. They had him under surveillance, and he's slipped them." There was no need to ask who "he" was.

Aisling's phone was in her hand immediately. No doubt she was calling someone at the PD, probably Pilson.

"Dexter got away?" Riordan was shocked. The man was guilty of Maggie's murder, they all knew it, and he'd somehow evaded being pinned for it.

"It looks bad for him," Sean piped up. "Nobody who runs is innocent. They'll find him. The man is too stupid to stay hidden for long."

"And the Hive is on it. They're keeping an eye out for him since we know he has engaged with people in it. If he's with them, we'll find out," Lettie added.

"Is he a loose end she wants cleaned up?" Brynach wondered out loud.

"I don't know," Liam admitted. "Sydney isn't either. I hope not. I want him brought to justice and rotting in prison, not dead. That's too good for him."

Riordan's whole body was shaking. Whether in shock or anger, he wasn't sure. Brynach moved to his side and put a hand on his shoulder.

"That's not why we came," Riordan started.

"Rory, didn't you hear me?" Liam stepped toward him, but Riordan held up a hand.

"It sucks. It does. But I don't have time to hunt him down and neither do you, so we're going to let the professionals handle him. We have bigger things happening."

"Bigger?" Amber questioned, stepping forward. "Bigger than finding your aunt's murderer?"

Riordan flinched at the words, and he saw Liam do the same. "Yes. Bigger than that. Life is more than my desire for justice. We found a way to take down the Veil."

The silence that followed was broken by Dawn's yelp, "I'm sorry, what?"

Aisling hung up the phone and answered the witch, "The Veil is Fae magic bent by a witch from so long ago that people forgot what to look for. But after I stripped Gabriel of his immortality, Bry got an idea. We tested it this morning. If the Ravdi and witches could break through the ward that held me prisoner, if I could break a soul prison, we figured it might work. With a combination of the different magics, we can do it. I can do it."

"Fuck yes!" Dawn cheered. "Sorry. I mean, of course you can."

"But should you?" Sean asked, and Lettie smacked his arm. "I'm serious. If it came down because of an ancient prophecy, fine. But to actively do it. Is that smart?"

Riordan got defensive, "It's not an easy decision for her. For any of us. But if the lore is correct, the worlds were never meant to be separate. What if the Veil falls and things get better?"

"We've seen Fae integrate into our society with success. They're contributing members of our communities and separation only leads to more misunderstanding," Dawn contributed.

Aisling brought the conversation back around. "Captain thinks we need reinforced charms at the station. I have to head in for a bit. Plus, I want to talk to them about potential places Dexter may use to hide this side of the Veil. He talked a lot while we were out together."

Brynach moved to her side. "I'm coming with you."

Riordan stayed put. He didn't want to leave them, but he had other things to arrange. He needed to recruit more witches, Ravdi, and Fae on this side of the Veil.

"I'll stay here and prep them," Riordan said, and then they were out the door.

"Prep us?" Lettie asked.

"Buckle up," Riordan said, and clapped his hands.

B y the time he was done describing what the Veil drop would entail, and the backup they'd need, the group was sufficiently concerned. But true to form, they all got started on their tasks. Liam called the Firinne, Dawn reached out to the witches, and Amber started texting her underground fighting buddies. Lettie was reaching out to Trent and via him, Ollie, to recruit Fae.

If Brynach was telling the truth, Aisling was running around like a mad woman enforcing wards and protections while also prepping the police force. Not to mention getting word out to other officials in other areas to prepare them for the fall. The world would never be ready, but they'd prepared as best they could for areas where the fall could cause more problems. Major cities didn't tend to form along the Veil, but extra protection had been moving toward the larger ones prior to the wedding anyway.

Liam walked Riordan out when it was time to go. "I'm going to be right at your side. But I need you to promise to be careful."

He hugged his brother. "Liam, I have more to live for than I ever anticipated. I'm not trying to put myself in harm's way. We will be as safe as possible while trying to dismantle the largest and most intense magical presence the world knows."

Liam laughed, "I wonder if Sydney could help. She's a halfling, too. I could be her Ravdi."

Riordan shrugged. "It's worth an ask."

"I'll check with her." Liam shook his head. "Where will you stay tonight?"

"The condo. We want to be accessible to any official before the attempt." Riordan tilted his head to the sky. "You'll stay safe tomorrow, too?"

"I'll be careful, and Amber will be close. You know I can't throw a punch for shit," Liam laughed but Riordan could see the lines creasing his forehead. He was scared.

"Never could. Luckily, you don't have to learn now that you have a badass girlfriend." He patted his brother's back. "I'll see you tomorrow, then." Riordan turned and began the walk to the condo.

He wandered the streets and wondered how much they'd change tomorrow. Would they be overrun with Fae, or would things still look the same? How long would it take for both sides to realize what had happened? And how long until the peace between them dissolved and chaos broke out?

Riordan wanted to have faith that the scales would tip on the side of better. While he supported Aisling and Brynach neither of them was truly at risk tomorrow. His stupid mortal self was. Now that he had Aisling, and Brynach, he didn't want to lose them. Not yet.

"We told you that you wouldn't like what happened if you continued down this road, Ravdi," an alate rasped in his ear.

Fucking hell. He swatted at it, connecting and enraging the others. He hadn't expected to hit it. The resulting scratches and bites weren't pleasant.

"Damn it! What the hell do you want from me? Haven't you done enough?" he yelled into the air.

"Don't blame us. You were warned. You have no idea what you're about to do," a smoking fire sprite hissed.

"So, tell me," he dared it. "If you know so much, fucking tell me."

Collectively they shook their heads. "That's not our place. What you do, or don't do, is of no consequence to us. We will continue to thrive. We aren't the ones in danger."

And like that they were gone. If he'd learned one thing, it was to pay attention to their warnings. He texted Liam and Brynach while the words were fresh in his brain. Let them try and figure it out.

And maybe he should have been surprised to see his fox friend sitting at the bottom of the steps, but he wasn't. "Hey buddy, I missed you." Riordan approached it slowly. The fox's tail slid between its legs and its belly hit the ground as it crawled toward him. What was he thinking petting wild animals?

Overhead, Phlyren soared. Riordan was sure he'd have warned him if the fox posed a threat. Slowly, the fox neared him and sniffed at his fingers. Riordan held his breath until the soft head bumped his hand and he felt safe lowering it to the animal's head.

"We don't have any food upstairs, buddy. We haven't been home in a while. I'm sorry. I wish I had a treat for you," Riordan whispered.

The fox cocked its head and regarded him before making a snuffling sound and trotting away. "Alright then. See you later, I guess," Riordan said standing and going inside.

He sat on the sofa and let his head fall forward into his hands. "What am I doing?" He asked to nobody at all. "Fall in love with a woman and commit myself to our bond? Sure. Love her husband and share her with him? Okay. But take down the barrier between worlds and merge the Fae and humans? We're out of our minds," he continued into the empty space.

He moved to the bedroom and was flooded with memories. Bringing Aisling home bloody and broken. Or finding her with Brynach wrapped up in her arms while he dreamwalked. The passion they shared on that bed. Good memories that he cherished and bad memories that fueled him toward caution and patience. He couldn't see her hurt again. Couldn't risk her being taken away from them.

He didn't want Aisling to be a part of this fight. He didn't want to face the possibility of losing anyone else he loved. Wasn't it his turn to be selfish? Riordan wasn't sure when he'd started to cry. But he knew when Aisling noticed through the bond. The phone rang and he picked up, knowing it would be her.

"Are you okay?" His girl was protective, and he loved her for it.

"I'm working through things in my head. I forgot you were in it," he admitted.

"I know it's different now, but we'll make it work," her voice softened.

"What if it doesn't work at all once the Veil is down? What if it becomes more Faerie than human and it fails completely?" He was terrified. He couldn't lose the bond.

"Hey. Breathe. It's going to be okay. I'll be home soon, and we will work through it."

"All that magic you absorb has to go somewhere. Where will it go? This is too big, Aisling," he panicked.

There was rustling on the other side of the phone, and heavy footsteps.

"We're on our way back. Stay on the phone with me." Riordan could tell she was trying to keep her voice even, but concern zinged down the bond.

"You're. Overreacting. I'm. Okay," he gasped. His anger over his reaction made his breathing worse.

"Bry, drive faster," Aisling ordered. "Babe, listen to me. I want you to get on the floor, okay? Lie down and put your legs up on the wall, the sofa, the bed, a chair. Anything. Get on the ground and put your legs up."

The ground? Yeah, that sounded like a good idea. He slid himself down the edge of the bed onto the floor, then dropped the phone and raised his feet. Aisling's voice sounded far away.

"Breathe like a baby. Deep in your belly, Riordan. Nice and slow."

That was easy for her to say. He was staring down the end of the fucking world. It was hard to take baby breaths and work your way through that one.

"It's getting dark," he murmured. Aisling's scream was the last thing he heard before the darkness took him.

CHAPTER 34

Brynach

Never in all his life had Brynach felt such panic as he did waiting for Riordan to come to. He wasn't sure which was worse, the crushing anxiety he'd felt through their bond or the nothingness of him passed out. Aisling may be used to sharing feelings with Riordan, but it was all very new for Brynach. Having to drive at breakneck speeds toward a man he could admit he loved while worrying over both his wife and Riordan was terrifying.

Brynach currently had the Ravdi's head in his lap and Aisling was over him, brushing his hair back. They'd found him on the floor, his legs up on the bed, but unresponsive. Aisling swore he was okay and would come around. Brynach tried to actively engage their bond, sending warmth through it. The feeling of safety and calm

Aisling's sharp intake of breath had Brynach looking down at Riordan's slow blinking eyes.

"There you are, handsome," Brynach said.

Riordan groaned, "How long?"

"Too long," Aisling answered. "The wards are in place. I was so worried it was another attack. I mean, it was, but a panic attack not a magical one."

Brynach put an arm around Riordan and helped him sit

up. "You scared us. But it's a normal reaction to the serious decisions we've been making," Brynach assured him.

He saw the way Riordan was avoiding Aisling's eyes. He could see his wife fretting, wringing her hands. He could feel how it was influencing Riordan.

"A stoirin, can you get him a glass of water, please?"

She jumped up to get him one and Brynach helped him stand.

"You have to know this is not weakness, Riordan. It's okay to be scared. We're scared, too," the large Fae whispered.

"You're fucking bulletproof. I'm not. The stakes are different," he murmured.

Brynach took Riordan's chin in his fingers and lifted it until their eyes met. Brynach loved the depth of Riordan's brown eyes. He felt the other man's fear and it broke his heart. "I will die before I allow anyone to hurt you. Do you understand? You're mine. I protect what's mine."

Brynach held Riordan's face as he nodded. The Fae gave him a small nod of his own and then at the spike of emotion in the bond his eyes dropped to Riordan's lips. He had time to move as Brynach's head lowered, the Ravdi didn't use it. Whatever was going on in that complicated brain, it wasn't doubt. He may be new to the bond, but he understood attraction.

Riordan's rough voice whispered, "Yes."

That's all it took to have him lowering his mouth to claim the other man. There was no power play, no passionate clashing of tongues. This was a slow exploration. Brynach placed his lips against Riordan's and plucked softly at his lower lip. He pulled back and slanted over his mouth the other direction. The hands on his face moved to cup his neck and tenderly hold him close.

Brynach kept a leash on himself. He wanted more. He craved more. But Riordan had to initiate that. The other man wasn't a submissive, not like their girl. He could damn well let

Brynach know what he needed and wanted. And right now, this seemed to be enough for him. Pride swelled in Brynach at the other man's trust in him. At his vulnerability and ability to let this happen.

The Fae pulled back. "Whatever happens tomorrow, I'm glad that happened first."

Riordan smiled at him and even though Brynach waited for it, there was no regret from the Ravdi. If it all ended tomorrow, Brynach would still feel like the luckiest man in the world. He'd heard Aisling walk up on them as they kissed but when he looked up from Riordan's brown eyes she was nowhere in sight. He loved her more for letting them have their moment.

They headed for the living room and there was no way she'd miss the blush still prettying Riordan's cheeks, or the way his chest was heaving. But his wife smiled at them, and he didn't need the bond to know she was happy for them.

"So, uh," Riordan began.

Aisling stopped him. "It's okay. You don't have to say anything."

"But I should. It's important to," Riordan continued. "We promised to always communicate. And right now, I'm terrified."

Brynach frowned. "I can tell it's not because of what just...what we. Man, this bond is strange. What's worrying you?"

"Tomorrow. And the next day. How this will change things. How much things have already changed," Riordan admitted. "We don't know how magic will react to the Veil coming down. And I want to be selfish. I don't want our bond to change any more than it already has." He turned from Aisling and looked at Brynach. "And Bry, we just got this, and I like it."

"I do, too." Brynach smiled. "And I understand the concern, but we can't predict what will happen. Worrying about it won't make it any more or less likely to happen."

Riordan ran a hand through his hair. "I know, but it doesn't stop the spiral of worry."

He had turned back to Aisling, and she moved to him. She was feeling what he was. The fear. The pain. And Riordan wasn't wrong. It was unknown. It was dangerous. Watching the other man's shoulders shake as Aisling hugged him hurt Brynach's heart.

"I'm happy," he cried. "I finally feel like there's hope for my future, a real chance at life without that pit of pain trying to suck me in."

"Hey," Aisling soothed. "Change doesn't have to be bad. It may be amazing."

Brynach moved closer. "Riordan, nobody can say what tomorrow will bring, whether there's a Veil dropping or not. Every day is a chance of pain or joy."

"Not helping," Riordan groaned.

The large Fae chuckled, "You didn't let me finish. What I was going to say is that whatever comes, you're not facing it alone. Regardless of how our bonds strengthen or weaken magically, the love and connection between us is strengthening."

Brynach felt an easing of pain in the bond and relaxed a little.

"What can we do to help you?" Aisling asked.

Riordan looked between the two of them. "I need to be near you guys. One last night together before things change."

He met his wife's beautiful gaze and saw the love there. Brynach nodded to her, and she kissed her Ravdi.

"We can do that. It's always us, Riordan. Us against whatever comes our way." Aisling looked up at Brynach before turning back to her boyfriend. "Tonight, I want both of you again. Is that okay with you?"

Riordan nodded his head and reached a hand for Brynach. The large Fae felt his heart stutter in his chest. He moved in and held the two of them in his large embrace. Brynach wasn't sure if they needed him to take control tonight. He would, happily, but this didn't feel like one of those times. Yes, they wanted a distraction, but they needed to be a team, unified, more than they needed a director.

His feelings were confirmed when the Ravdi wiggled from the group, and hand in each of theirs, pulled them toward the bedroom. The nerves in the bond were second to the trust. Brynach wasn't sure what he'd done to deserve that honor. In fact, he was sure he didn't deserve it, but he was selfish enough to take it.

When they reached the bedroom, it was Aisling who gently led the men. The love he felt for her, the love he felt from Riordan through the bond for her, was so vibrant. They'd worked to be able to close their bond, but Brynach couldn't imagine ever wanting that. It was beautiful.

"Bry?" Aisling called him back into the moment.

He looked down at her hands on his shirt and dutifully sat on the bed next to Riordan so she could pull it off of him. She stood before the two of them, Riordan's hand on her hip and Brynach waiting. He would forever sit at the feet of this woman if she wanted him to.

"I know, right?" Riordan said from beside him.

"No fair," Aisling whined.

Brynach chuckled, "Now you know how I felt, a stoirin. Don't worry, anything we are feeling for you is complimentary."

"Very," Riordan agreed.

She stood back from them and grinned. "Tonight, we'll do what feels right. If anyone gets uncomfortable, they'll speak up, no judgement. Nothing happens that we don't want to happen."

Brynach and Riordan both nodded and he felt a weight fall from his shoulders. To be loved by them and not have to be in control sounded fantastic.

"In that case, you both promised me something for attempting to siphon magic from the Veil," Aisling reminded them.

His heart sped and beside him he heard Riordan suck in a breath. She was right, they had.

It was her Ravdi, their Ravdi, who nodded to her. "We are men of our word."

Both of the men raised their hips in turn as Aisling stripped them of their pants. His wife knelt before them and licked her lips before she worshipped both their cocks in turn. First she took Riordan into her mouth and worked her tongue along his shaft before taking him as deep as she could.

Lust and love were swirling through his bond with Riordan. He knew how much the Ravdi was enjoying the show Aisling was putting on. She turned and bent over Brynach's lap. "I love you," she said a moment before her tongue made contact with his tip.

Brynach threw his head back, eyes closed, hands fisting in the sheets. "Fuck," he ground out. His wife's mouth was wicked but this side of the Veil, with magic, she was dangerous. "Goddess, Aisling."

He felt Riordan's amusement before his chuckle sounded. "She's coating her tongue with magic. Welcome to dark side, friend."

"I have been missing out," Brynach managed and then his hands found Aisling's hair. He didn't pull or guide, he just needed to watch. Aisling's hand rose to his and helped him tug. Brynach didn't need telling twice. He wove his fingers along her scalp, pulling from the root and then pushing her onto him.

As Brynach watched Riordan's hand wandered down his taunt stomach to his cock and he stroked himself lazily as he watched. But their girl had a prize to claim.

"Stand up," she ordered. Both men hurried to obey, naturally leaning their hips on one another, their cocks now side by side. Aisling smiled up at them and then kissed both their dicks before taking them in her hands and bringing them together.

The moment Brynach felt the smooth skin of Riordan's cock sliding along his own he nearly blew his load. He would crack a tooth if he clenched his jaw any harder. The Ravdi's hand reached out and took his, squeezing it. Brynach looked to him and saw his eyes heavy with lust, locked on his. Brynach moved a hand to Riordan's chest, over his beating heart, and held it there.

Aisling was squeezing their cock heads into her mouth which had both of them breaking eye contact to watch her.

"Fuck, Ash," Riordan cursed.

She pulled them from her mouth, her tongue swirling over both their crowns and Brynach vaguely acknowledged that his legs were shaking. His muscles taut as he tried to restrain himself. He was trying really hard not to cross any hard boundaries right now. Everything in him was telling him to demand from her, to take control of the situation, but he didn't. Instead, he let his wife enjoy her prize.

It was Riordan who broke first. "Ash, babe, this is amazing, but I really need you now."

And because his wife had the biggest heart he knew, and because she wanted nothing more than to be there for him in any way he needed, she stood and kissed him.

Brynach held out a hand to her and between he and Riordan, they undressed her. Riordan moved her to the bed while Brynach took off the rest of his clothes and joined them.

"I want to see all of you, Riordan." Aisling bit her lip and her Ravdi hurried to oblige her.

Brynach kept his hands on Aisling, stroking her arms, her belly, and her breasts. She was so beautiful it hurt. He bent and kissed her, the sweet taste of her flooding his senses. When he sucked on her tongue, and she moaned into his mouth, his cock hardened even further. Her hand reached for him and there was no shyness as she gripped him firmly.

"What do you want, Riordan?" Aisling asked, her voice a husky rasp.

"Sit on my face," her boyfriend's reply was immediate. He had situated pillows under his head and his arms were reaching for her.

Aisling moved over him and tugged Brynach with her so she could continue to love him with her mouth. He was desperate to bury himself in her, but he wasn't in charge. He envied Riordan the taste of her. Then his body tensed as a new sensation hit him.

Aisling, the minx that she was, sent a flood of magic to Brynach's cock and his hips thrust up. Her beautiful eyes watered, and he backed off but her hand under his thigh held him to her. Damn, she was amazing.

"That's enough, love. Face up," he let the authority drip in his voice. She obeyed immediately, her hazel eyes meeting his. "You are beautiful. You are perfect. But focus on yourself, a stoirin. Let yourself fall."

Brynach leaned in to kiss her, his hand caressing her cheek before moving to her breast and palming them. He rolled her nipples between his large fingers and let the tide of magic being shared between them tingle across his skin. If he kept contact with Aisling, he could feel it and sense it through Riordan. Aisling tried to dip her head but he tsk'd her and she met his eyes again, body shaking as she rolled her hips on her Ravdi's face and fell apart.

She was breathtaking. He wanted to feel her clenching his dick, pulsing around him. He hadn't been inside her again since their wedding day and he needed her. His need must have traveled through the bond, because Riordan gave her a sharp slap on the ass and instructed her to turn around.

Aisling tried to move on her shaky legs but failed, flopping with a laugh. Brynach lifted her and when Riordan abandoned the pillows, the Ravdi folded the top one in half and patted it.

He gently placed Aisling's belly on the propped-up surface, holding her by the hips. Her Ravdi kneeled in front of her, his cock dripping already. He was gorgeous.

Brynach met his eyes and let the emotions fill him. When Riordan reached down Aisling's back and met Brynach's hand, his breath caught. He would spend the rest of his eternity trying to convince himself he was worthy of the two of them. The moment stretched until Aisling moaned.

"I love you both, desperately, but can you fill me already?"

Brynach laughed and Riordan shook his head. "She asked for it," the Ravdi said, and moved closer to his girlfriend's face. The Fae slid his cock through his wife's folds. She was hot, wet, and ready. But still he let her coat him before sliding inside. Even ready, he'd stretch her. His cock tingled, electricity singing across his skin. Goosebumps broke out across his body, and his hips bucked against her.

"Aisling. Fuck! Don't do that." His hand came down hard on her ass and she laughed around Riordan's cock.

Riordan shook his head in sympathy. He knew exactly what their girl had done. Damn witchy pussy was going to kill him. If she wanted to play, he'd play. Brynach pulled back, lining up his tip with her opening, and thrust inside in one sure stroke. She cried out and he closed his eyes at the pure ecstasy that was her pussy. The squeeze of his hand had his eyes opening. Riordan smirked at him and then his hand left Brynach's and stroked Aisling's cheeks as she hollowed them out around his length.

Damn it, that was sexy. Unable to wait any longer, he began to move. Smooth strokes, feeling the grip and pull of her around him. It was heaven. He wanted to live inside her, like this, always. Brynach wanted to draw this out, for her and for himself. He angled himself, bottoming out inside her in a way he knew would be deliciously painful. Aisling quivered around him, and he pulled back, the tip stroking softly into her and then out to caress her.

"Damn it, Bry," she cursed him, and he gripped her hips tight.

He let himself sink deep into her again, holding himself there and rocking his hips against her. She tried to move herself away from him and then back, getting traction and controlling his thrusts. That wouldn't do. Brynach pinned her hips and held her still. Edging her was his new favorite pastime. So eager, his wife.

Riordan groaned and Brynach watched him spill into Aisling's mouth. She swallowed him greedily and then licked her lips like a pleased little kitten when he pulled free of her. Brynach reached forward and tugged at her scalp until her body lifted off the pillows and her back was flush against his front. He gripped her chin and brought her face around for a kiss while he slammed into her.

Maybe the Ravdi wasn't ready to let Brynach touch him but he damn sure could taste him. He swept into his wife's mouth and tasted their lover on her tongue. He sucked her tongue into his mouth and felt the rush of lust in the bond. Brynach calmed the kiss and his thrusts before he let Aisling's head fall forward.

"Delicious," he purred while looking in the Ravdi's eyes. He didn't miss the way Riordan's body shivered under his gaze.

"Is your husband teasing you, Ash?" Riordan asked with a cocky grin.

"Yes," she panted and tried to push back against him. "Damn it, Bry, I need you. Please."

"I like hearing you beg," he encouraged her.

Aisling tried to be stubborn but when he started to pull out from her, she caved. "Damn it. Brynach, please. Please, fuck me. I need it. I want it. Please."

He plunged back into her, taking her hard and fast the way she liked. His wife got what she wanted, but only when he was good and damn ready to give it to her. But who was he kidding? He was lost for her. He'd give her anything she wanted.

"You look so beautiful taking his dick, Ash." Riordan teased her nipples. "And it's a big dick. I bet he's stretching you to bursting, isn't he?"

"Yes. Goddess, yes." Aisling was a wet loose-limbed mess. Her hair was wild, sweat trickled down her spine.

"You should see him, babe. His eyes are rolling back in his head. And the way he feels. He's holding back. That's not his one hundred percent. I can feel how tightly he's keeping himself reigned in," Riordan whispered in her ear as he sucked at her neck.

"Give it to me, Bry. Let loose," she begged.

"Who am I, a stoirin?" He coached her.

"You're my husband, Bry. Take me."

Any sense of control he had was lost and he leaned forward, his teeth biting into her shoulder as he rode her hard and Riordan cushioned her against himself. Then there was a tug on his hair, and he looked up into the Ravdi's eyes. There was a moment to recognize the other man's intentions and then his mouth was crashing down on Brynach's.

This wasn't like their other kiss. Riordan demanded. He took. His tongue sought Brynach's mouth, and the Fae happily opened for him. Aisling moaned between them as Brynach continued fucking her and Riordan tore him apart with his mouth. Aisling cried out her release, quivering around him and when Brynach followed it was her Ravdi who tasted his groan.

Perfection.

They were perfection and they were his. Riordan pulled back, his face red, and his breathing ragged. Brynach could read the surprise on his face. Guess that wasn't a planned thing, but he was damn glad it had happened. Brynach lifted a hand and ran it through the other man's hair.

"Thank you," he told him before lowering his mouth to Aisling and kissing her.

They let their bodies fall in a sweaty heap and had no choice but to curl up close on the smaller bed. Eventually, they'd have to get up and clean themselves, but right now they were happy to lay there, satiated, and together.

CHAPTER 35

Aisling

In the morning Riordan groaned as he stretched. "I never thought I'd say this, but I want to get back to Faerie. This bed doesn't cut it anymore."

Brynach mumbled his agreement, and Aisling let herself enjoy the simple joy of the moment. Waking up beside her husband and her partner made the day to come more tolerable.

"Whatever happens, we're together," Brynach reminded her.

She knew it was true, but she also felt Riordan's apprehension in the bond. Brynach could, too. Nerves, uncertainty, and yes, love, was rioting around the condo. All too soon they were heading out of the condo and into town. They had opted to walk knowing that it would be too congested to get close in the truck. The extra time allowed them to hold hands and just be together.

Aisling shared magic with Riordan and if Brynach's wonder was any indicator, the two of them were sharing, too. It was sweet seeing the two of them explore their new bond. As much as Aisling wanted to grieve the weakening of her bond with Riordan, she loved that they had a bond of their own now. It felt right.

"Holy shit," Riordan gasped as they turned a corner.

"Oh, wow," Aisling agreed.

Brynach wasn't impressed. He was immediately alert, his hand on hers squeezing tighter. "We go right to the front. Don't stop to talk to anyone. Stay together."

The crowd gathered was larger than Aisling had anticipated. The police had constructed barricades and people seemed to be respecting them, but for how long? Brynach rushed them through as quickly as possible, skirting around the denser areas.

She nodded to an officer she recognized as they crossed the barricades toward the group of gathered witches, Ravdi, and Fae. The police presence was significant. She hoped it was enough. Brynach's grip on her hadn't loosened and Riordan was leaking anxious energy. Honestly, none of it was helping.

"I'm closing it down for a few. I need to think," Aisling told Riordan. Her Ravdi nodded and the connection dimmed even more.

It was time to focus. Too much was riding on her getting this right to be distracted. Almost immediately, they were swarmed by people all talking at the same time. Sydney was with Liam and Amber. Ceiren and Breena were with Brielle, and the captain's voice could be heard over all of them ordering his officers. She was moments away from covering her ears and screaming. She felt the anxiety she'd kept at bay for so long come crashing down on her.

It was great that everyone was here and apparently ready, but if she didn't ground herself, things were going to get out of control. Her mother and Dawn were making their way toward her, and her mother looked worried. Damn it, she needed to do this fast.

"Riordan," she moaned. "Help me."

He was distracted and she didn't blame him, but she needed him right now. She opened the bond back up and Riordan's head whipped toward her. Her Ravdi placed his hands on her bare skin just below the hem of her t-shirt.

His magic flowed over and into her. "Deep breaths, Ash."

She listened to his voice, blocking out all others and slowed her breathing. Aisling was fast about it. She didn't need anyone seeing her fall apart, and she was acutely aware of all the attention on her. When she opened her eyes, the Fae were walking toward her.

"They know about the drop," Breena said by way of hello.

"Excuse me?" Aisling shook her head.

"You didn't tell them. Thanks for that, by the way, that was fun. The Fae know what you're attempting today. Not everyone is thrilled," Breena answered.

Brynach put an arm around her waist. "It means we're starting a little sooner than planned. We want a head start before they show up."

"Alright, everyone. You know your tasks. Provide backup and protection for the those involved in the spell work. Prepare for hostiles if and when the Veil falls," the captain called out. "Anyone not essential to the mission is encouraged to get the fuck out of here. And those in need of more protecting, in other words those of you not heavily armed or immortal, would do well to stay behind those that are."

Aisling saw too many people ignoring the warning, but she couldn't do anything about that. He shrugged his shoulders when he reached them.

"I tried. You focus on your task, and we'll focus on ours, okay?" He nodded at her, his salt and pepper hair disheveled.

She gave a mock salute. "Yes, sir."

He shook his head at her and moved back to his men. Riordan and Brynach took her hands.

"We're doing this, huh?" she asked.

"Looks like it," Riordan answered.

As Brynach reached for the Veil, Breena put a hand on his arm. "I swear by all things holy, if you fuck this up or get hurt, I'll kill you my damn self." Then she hugged Brynach close. "I have your back, you fucking idiot."

Brynach smiled at her and then turned to Aisling. "Ready?"

"Let's do this," she said and stepped into the Veil after Brynach. He stood in Faerie, Riordan in the human realm, and her between, all linked.

The magic of the Veil swirled around her, raising the hair on her arms. The electric charge of it, the sheer power, took her breath away. Could she really do this? Sure, she'd pulled a little bit, but enough to drop the Veil? Everyone was staring at her, waiting for her signal to begin.

The bond, dulled though it was now that Brynach was in Faerie, was still open in the in-between. She let Riordan know it was time and he slowly fed her magic. Brynach on the other side supported her, and Faerie itself fed her. She saw Liam raise a hand to the witches and Ravdi behind him and felt their magic pull at her. Aisling called from the land, from the magic that dwelled there, with good intention and a pure mind.

If this worked the same way as Gabriel's stripping, her intentions mattered. Slowly, timidly, magic crept to her, and she released the tension in her shoulders and let it crawl over her.

This was how it began.

The end of the world as they knew it and the start of the new one.

Like before, she spoke to the Goddess, with eyes closed promising her intentions were true. Aisling let her into her mind to see the world she wanted to create. At least, that's what she imagined she was doing. And in the Veil, with magic swirling around her, it felt right. The crowd of magic users tugged at the magic, and she felt it gathering around her, trying to protect itself. The sweet citrus smell of Faerie mixing with the grassy scent of the human realm as the two sides swirled around her.

Riordan kept the stream steady, feeding her power. The pressure of Brynach and Riordan remained, but her body no longer felt like her own. She was a conduit, a lightning rod of magic. She pulled into herself, dragging from the Veil as she had from Gabriel.

The small tugs on the Veil from the other Ravdi and witches were miniscule but for the one gap that Sydney was creating. That girl had power, but it didn't rival Aisling's. Not now that she was married to a Fae and bonded to someone as strong as Riordan. This would still come down to her.

She took and took and fed back into the land, both in Faerie and in the human world. She pulled and plucked and distributed as safely as she could. But the rate that it was entering her was faster than she'd anticipated.

Suddenly, she was very aware of both Brynach and Riordan calling to her. Aisling opened her eyes and found herself several feet off the ground, her partners her anchors. But she wanted to fly. She needed to ride this wave. The magic called to her. It whispered and sighed across her body. It sang in her ear and caressed her spirit.

Aisling tore more magic from Riordan and the bonds that held her down broke. She barely registered the screams, and the clash of swords on armor. The fighting had begun. What did it matter to her when she had all this power? So much power.

It felt like coming home, this drowning in magic. She was made for this.

After all she'd been through, she deserved to be rewarded with this power. She pulled more, drinking in the Veil. Consuming. Aisling wanted to hold it all but there was more to take.

She flung it away from her to make room for more. The Veil shimmered in her skin and crawled through her veins. The magic, old and steeped in power, was hers. Warmth spread through her, radiated out of her. She shared it, throwing it from her only to be filled again. Over and over, she repeated the process. For how long she couldn't be sure, all logical thought had stopped long ago.

Aisling opened her eyes when the noise became too loud to ignore. Below her she saw necks strained in screams that didn't reach her ears. People ran from one side of the Veil to the other, with weapons held high. Aisling witnessed it all as an impartial observer, detached. Her job wasn't done yet and their fights weren't her problem. What had been started needed to be finished.

The Veil still existed, weak but present. The magic left was the oldest, the deepest, and the bloodiest. It resisted, it crawled and hid in the recesses of the world. But like with Gabriel she twisted and pulled, plucked, and coerced it out. She dug her magical nails into the very earth and tore at it.

With a reluctant rush it swarmed her. Her body arched and a scream ripped from her as the pain of the Veil filled her. The magic that had been forced to create such a brutal divide across the world. Within that deepest magic was pain, loss, and grief. Tears streamed down her face, and she fought to not lose herself. The magic belonged to her, but not this, not this pain.

A woman's wails filled her ears. Behind her closed eyelids Aisling saw hot tears falling into the earth and leaving scars behind. A raven-haired woman knelt, her belly large, and her hands clutching her hair.

Kailyn.

A woman grieving a lost love, desperate to do whatever it took to feel okay again. That anguish filled Aisling now. The pain and fear that had been built into the Veil was burning through her. It didn't care what her intentions were. It wanted to be free. The living, breathing, grief she'd pulled from the Veil made her bones ache.

She felt the other woman's pain as if it was her own and with a cry so primal her throat shredded; she released it.

CHAPTER 36

Brynach

Aisling had risen too high and Brynach screamed for her even though it was clear she no longer heard him. He needed her in his arms. It was the only way he could guarantee she was safe. He looked to Riordan who was pale and shaking. The poor Ravdi was being leeched from and Brynach wasn't sure how much longer he'd stay on his feet. Even Brynach was feeling the effects of the large surges in magic. As connected to Faerie as he was, he felt the ebb and flow as they worked to dismantle the Veil.

Eyes locked on Riordan he was gifted an extra moment to register the attack coming from behind him by the look in the Ravdi's eyes. Riordan's mouth opened, but he didn't wait for what came out. Brynach turned, blade out, and cut down the Fae who'd tried to attack from the rear.

"Break the bond!" he yelled to Riordan before turning back to the fight.

"I won't leave her. I've got this. You take care of that," he yelled and pointed to the charging army.

Breena and Brielle moved to his side. His sister turned to him, smiled with teeth, and then charged. Damn her stubborn, reckless nature. Brynach wanted to run after her, to make sure she was protected, but he couldn't leave Aisling.

He registered the police screaming orders and felt the magic of the witches and Ravdi swirling around him. Whatever Aisling was doing was working. The Veil got thinner. The ever-present connection to the magic of Faerie found him. It rushed around and past him as Faerie was pulled through the gap Aisling was creating.

Riordan's voice was raw as he called out, "Bry! We have to stop her. She's taking too much."

Brynach's head swung to Aisling, and he saw the trickle of blood at the corner of her mouth. No. Goddess. As he moved toward her, a new wave of swords and shouts reached him. Brynach had no choice but to engage with them. He tried, between sword thrusts and blows, to check on Riordan. He saw Liam at his side and had to trust the man to see to him while he fought.

Brielle helped divert some of the foe. "Slowly, make your way to her," she screamed over the battle.

Riordan was shouting for Aisling. The deafening blast of gunfire filled the air. There were bodies at his feet, Fae and human alike. An officer with an arrow in his belly. A Fae with a bullet wound in their forehead. This is what it had come to, so soon.

What had they done?

Brynach let go and allowed the rage that lived right below his surface go. He needed the calm that came with his bloodlust. Emotions had no place here, not with his loved ones in danger. Brynach swung his sword, taking the arm off an attacker and then plunging it behind him toward an armored Fae trying to take on Brielle. He caught him under the armpit and the Fae went down.

"Thank you," Brielle called as she faced down another threat.

He didn't pause to address her, instead he looked back to Aisling and what he saw made his blood run cold. Trent stood before Aisling. He was calling to her, trying in vain to get through to her. Damn it, he was far too mortal to be in the throes of all this fighting. Ollie was trying to pull him back, but he himself was unarmed and unprepared for battle.

Trent's voice was loud as he screamed at his boyfriend, "Get me on your shoulders, now!" And then Aisling's best friend with his perfect balance and lean frame, was standing on the Fae's shoulders eye level with Aisling.

It was a good idea, but Brynach understood what it took to call her back from the edge. Trent wasn't ready for what he was about to face. Aisling would hurt him. He saw the same fear in Riordan's eyes.

She couldn't control herself right now. She looked like she had at the soul prison, wild with magic. Her very skin crawling with it. Whoever that was, it wasn't his Aisling. She'd never forgive herself when she came out of this if she hurt Trent.

"Ollie, she'll kill him! Get away from her," Brynach yelled. He didn't wait to see if the Fae listened to him. A voice cried out and Brynach turned. He reached for a throwing knife and tossed it at a Fae charging his sister. He didn't wait to see where it hit, he knew the blade would find its target.

Then he felt it, magic stroking his skin. Whatever Aisling had taken on was building until she physically couldn't hold it any longer. It leaked off her. Like lightning to a rod, it found Fae, witches, and Ravdi. He watched, powerless, as they were struck with magical blasts.

He saw more than a few cops with their guns pointing toward her. Damn it. Lettie was clawing at the arm of an officer with a gun trained on Aisling. Sean was trying to pull her back. Trent fell to the ground as Ollie was struck with a blast.

Finding Ceiren he screamed, "Stop them!"

His brother moved to the cop closest to him and knocked their gun down. Then he charged the police chief to make sure they understood that threatening Aisling wasn't acceptable.

His Fae senses were overwhelmed. Riordan was crying.

Liam's eyes were wild. "She's killing him!"

To protect Riordan he had to stop Aisling. If he could reach an ankle and tug her down, hold her close, and force her to listen to him. He could survive her wrath and if not, he'd happily die to bring her back. His mind made up he turned toward Aisling, but a voice stopped him.

Breena.

Screaming.

He spun and found her in the crowd. With a curse he surged toward her only to remember Aisling and stop. His sister was engaged in a sword fight with their father and over her shoulder Jashana was fighting with Levinas. Gabriel may be human now, but he was still a threat. He was strong, he was trained, and he was angry. It was a deadly combination. The man had nothing left to lose and too much hate in his heart. Aisling was out of harms way, his sister was not.

As if he felt Brynach's gaze, his father's head swiveled, and those brilliant citrine eyes seared into him. He snarled and started toward Brynach. He had no choice but to brace for the fight that was clearly coming to him. A cry came from behind him and had it been anyone else Brynach would have ignored it, but it was Riordan.

Brynach turned his back on his father and saw Riordan on the ground. Fuck! All his instincts told him that his father was the largest threat, and you never turn your back on a threat, but his entire being was screaming to get to Riordan. He turned to his father in time to see Breena charge in front of him and deflect a sword strike.

"Sneaking up on people's back's now, you fucking coward?" Breena growled.

Damn it, that girl was going to get herself hurt. Jashana was backtracking, bringing Levinas toward Breena and his father to offer backup. He couldn't afford to be frozen right now.

Brynach ran to Riordan and dropped to his knees. The

Ravdi was still breathing, which meant he could wait a little longer.

"Protect him. I'm getting Aisling," Brynach told Liam who nodded with tears in his eyes.

Brynach assessed the situation. Hordes of Fae sifted in, and he had no idea whose side they were on. The human side of the Veil was panicking. He had no time to waste. This had to end.

He searched for backup, but Brielle was engaged in a fight with a tall dark-haired man. The poor bastard she was fighting didn't stand a chance. They had horrible form and the lethal pixie-like Fae had a clear upper hand. Brynach gasped when the fight shifted, and he saw who she was clashing swords with. Ollie was actively trying to kill Brielle. That had to be a mistake. Why in the hell was he fighting and where had he gotten a sword?

Then he registered Trent, screaming and fighting against Sean's grip to try and reach his boyfriend. The cries went unanswered, though the Fae had to hear them. Liam screamed for Brynach, Breena grunted from behind him somewhere, Jashana cursed, and Trent pulled free of his friend.

He was needed elsewhere but he couldn't look away. His head swiveled to Brielle, and Brynach saw how this was going to end. Time froze as Trent reached his boyfriend. There was no stopping the momentum of the killing blow and no stopping Trent's trajectory right in front of it. Brynach lowered his chin and closed his eyes but there was no denying what he'd have seen.

Aisling's friend fell, and his partner screamed. Before Brielle could react, Ceiren was behind the rogue Fae, severing his still screaming head from his body. Brynach knew Trent couldn't have survived Brielle's attack. Still, he felt the twinge of pain when Ceiren knelt next to Trent and shook his head.

His eyes found Breena who was now fighting Levinas. Where was Gabriel? Brynach scanned the battle and found him engaged with Alex. Brynach had a moment to worry over his best friend, but at least his sister wasn't facing him down anymore. Alex could hold his own. Breena was bleeding, her arm hanging at her side, though luckily not her sword arm.

"Brynach! Please!" Liam's voice broke through the din.

Witches and Ravdi behind a wall of police officers in riot gear were moaning and clutching at themselves. He'd have questioned what was wrong but even he could feel it. Raw magic was clawing at everyone near them. The Veil was leaking magic, and it needed a home. Aisling was throwing it out, and it was overloading the magical around her.

Eyes on Aisling, Brynach stepped up to her, gazing into the bright light of her aura. Blood dripped from her mouth onto his cheek. She was killing herself. Then he felt it, the vortex of a magical pull. Panic spiked through him.

She wasn't just pulling from the Veil, it felt like she was trying to pull from him. He reached up for her, leaping and still missed her. Damn it. His head was swimming. He felt dizzy. He scanned for anyone who could help him, anyone he could boost. But around him others were feeling the same effects he was. Breena must have felt it, too. Felt it and faltered for a moment. He watched in horror as Levinas used that moment to lunge toward Brynach's twin. Breena fell backward and Levinas advanced.

Brynach's vision swam, the vice like pressure in his head intensifying. And then it happened. The Veil imploded, sucking inward before bursting outward. Brynach was thrown off his feet. All around him, people were pulling themselves up off their asses. Aisling still hung in the air, and not far away his sister lay on the ground.

"Breena!" Standing, he ran to her, laid out on the ground with Levinas's sword through her stomach. Her arm was pinned beneath their brother, her sword piercing his neck and exiting his skull. Of all the ways to kill a Fae, a sword through the brain always worked. He rolled Levinas away, disregarding him.

"Breena, are you okay?" He knelt and tried to stabilize the blade.

"It hurts," she moaned.

"Shhh. It's okay. I'll remove it. Bite something." He gripped the handle but stilled when she screamed.

"No!" Blood dripped out of her mouth. She wheezed, "Don't."

"You'll heal." He shook his head and gripped the handle once more.

"No, brother," she coughed more blood. "I'm...I don't...I won't." Breena shook her head, hands around the blade.

Brynach cursed. He spotted Jashana nearby and yelled to her. When the warrior approached, he gave her specific instructions. "Get her to the hospital ward of the Unseelie Court. Be careful with her. If she dies, I'll skin you alive myself."

When Jashana sifted he looked for Aisling. She was still hanging limply in the air like a broken rag doll. He could see her chest rising and falling and breathed a sigh of relief. He found Riordan and saw Liam leaning over him with Ceiren standing guard.

Lettie and Sean were crying over a still dead Trent. Ollie was forgotten at Trent's side. Brielle was absolutely horrified as she protected them while they grieved for their friend. When she met Brynach's eyes he nodded, and she gave a small shake of her head. He knew she hadn't meant to hurt Trent. He also knew the Fae well enough to know that wouldn't ease her guilt.

The crowd was collectively freaking out. He saw Dawn and Mrs. Quinn huddled together talking, though Mrs. Quinn kept her eyes on her daughter. The Ravdi in the crowd looked lost and the witches were quiet by their side. The fight still raged on, but they stood still amongst the chaos.

The police chief took out a bullhorn and called for a stop to all fighting. For the most part, it worked. With fights dispersing and Fae sifting out of the area, he could take a moment and focus on Aisling. Brynach longed to have her in his arms, but he wouldn't bring her down while threats remained.

He turned to Brielle, whose strong wings could be used to fly short distances. He nodded up to Aisling and she looked down at her feet. Brynach moved to guard Lettie and Sean while she retrieved Aisling.

"Lettie. I'm so sorry," Brynach offered kneeling down.

Her blue eyes were blown out. "Why did he do it? Ollie was going for Aisling. One minute he was with us and then he was running with a fucking sword," she sobbed and put her hand on Trent's hair. "Trent thought it was just a misunderstanding. He. Oh god," she wailed. Sean was absolutely broken, an arm around Lettie.

"You stupid son of a bitch," the pain evident in Sean's voice.

Brielle touched down and Brynach ran to Aisling. He relieved Brielle of his bride and held her close. With Aisling in his arms, he moved to Liam.

"How is he?" Brynach asked as he knelt and laid Aisling next to Riordan.

"Drained. I thought we had lost him but he's coming around. He shouldn't be able to this fast. He should be comatose right now." Liam looked at Brynach with fear in his eyes. "Something is different."

"Different how?" Brynach asked, his eyes not leaving Riordan and Aisling.

"I can feel it. Faerie. I can...do this." Liam put his hand on the ground dotted with blood and closed his eyes. Where he touched the grass grew tall.

"Did you just use magic?" Brynach wondered.

Liam's eyes were wild. "Yeah. I was full of magic to assist the witches and then the Veil did that exploding out thing and...something changed."

Brynach wasn't following. His fingers were checking

Aisling for injuries. Carefully he wiped the blood from her face with his shirt.

"Brynach, I can hear people talking all the way across the street," Liam's voice was rushed.

"You're Fae," Ceiren said from above them.

"What?" Liam and Brynach said together staring up at the Prince.

Ceiren nodded to where Riordan was laying, eyes open.

"What happened?" Riordan winced as if the very act of talking pained him.

Liam laughed and hugged his brother. "You stupid arse! Don't you ever do that again."

"Ouch! Not so tight. Where's Aisling?" Riordan tried to push himself up. Brynach put an arm under him and helped.

"She's okay. Well, she's breathing. That magical blast hit her hard," Brynach explained as Riordan leaned down to hold Aisling.

"How do we help her?" he asked, eyes on Brynach, pleading with him to have an answer.

Liam, meanwhile, was staring at his brother like he was a miracle and Ceiren like he'd delivered a killing blow.

"Can you sense her through the bond?" Brynach asked.

Riordan was still a moment and then frowned. "Nothing. It feels like it does when we're in Faerie." He searched the area. "But we're not, are we?"

"There is no Faerie anymore, but no, we're on the human side of where it was." Brynach shook his head.

Riordan reached into his pocket and pulled out his phone. Behind him his brother's phone dinged. "Tech works. Why can't I feel her? Or you?" Riordan asked, a hand in Aisling's hair.

"Blondie over here seems to think it's because we're not Ravdi anymore," Liam said standing next to Ceiren.

"What the hell else would we be?" Riordan asked, annoyed. His eyes scanned the area, landing on Sean and Lettie kneeling while EMTs saw to Trent. "Is that?"

Brynach moved to block his view, but it was too late, Riordan had seen.

"Is Trent..." he asked, weakly,

Brynach nodded and placed a hand on the Ravdi's shoulder.

"Let's get Aisling out of here," Ceiren said. "Where to?"

Brynach scanned the fallen. Lettie was being led away by Sean as an EMT put a sheet over Trent and loaded him onto a stretcher. Breena had been removed, but the area his brother had occupied was empty. He didn't see Levinas anywhere. Maybe the Fae were sifting the dead away? The police were pushing the bystanders back.

"The castle. The doctors can help her, and we can check on Breena." Brynach decided. "Can you handle a sift?"

"Whatever it takes to get her help." Riordan nodded.

"Hey, wait!" Liam called out, but Brynach gathered Aisling and Riordan to himself and sifted.

The gates were open and the sentinels were still. Panic lanced through Brynach.

"Kongur?" He tried.

"Do not come in here!" his familiar warned. *"Get far away. Now."*

"What is going on?" Riordan asked, taking to the sift incredibly well. Brynach looked past the gates and that's when the sight and sound of the fighting registered.

"They're attacking the castle." Brynach grabbed Riordan and sifted again.

"What the fuck!" Riordan exclaimed when they popped back into existence outside the condo. "You can do that now?"

"I figured I'd try. So, um, yes." Brynach shrugged. "Can you open the door?"

Riordan dug in his pockets, still pale and shaky but nowhere as weak as he should have been. Could Ceiren be right? The door opened and Aisling stirred. Brynach carried her straight to the bedroom. They both climbed into bed and held her. Riordan spoke softly into her ear while stroking her hair, and Brynach rubbed circles on her back as she woke up.

"Did it work?" she mumbled with her eyes still closed.

"Perhaps too well," Brynach answered.

Aisling shook her head. "What do you mean? I have to get back."

"Like hell you do," Brynach growled, and Riordan pulled her closer to him.

Her boyfriend had tears on his cheeks. "I thought I lost you. It hurt so bad, Ash. I've never experienced something like that before."

She shook in his arms and Brynach moved to her back, holding her and Riordan close. When her cries stopped, she spoke, "I felt her. Kailyn. I lived her pain. It cut through me. I saw the magic that made the Veil, it's how I was able to unweave it. That last bit of the Veil was pure anguish and I had to house it. I thought it would break me. I didn't know if I'd be able to come back."

Brynach's fear was visceral. He'd watched Riordan drain of life. He was forced to watch Aisling bleed and break above him. His sister defended him and what had he done? Frozen up. When push came to shove, he was useless. He hadn't protected them. He hadn't done anything.

"Hey, you're scowling really hard." Riordan's hand found his and unclenched it from Aisling's shirt.

"I failed you," he said. He couldn't meet their eyes. Brynach let them go and left the bed. "I couldn't keep either of you safe. And Breena, she got hurt and I didn't go to help her. I let everyone I love down."

"Bry, no," Aisling began to argue.

"Don't, Aisling. I vowed to protect you. To put you before myself. And Riordan, I may not have said it in so many words, but you are mine to protect, too. And today, I let myself pause. I questioned myself and what to do. In doing so, in my indecision, I hurt you both. It's unacceptable." He tore at his hair and then beat his chest. "I was supposed to be better than that."

Aisling started to stand but it was Riordan who launched himself at the Fae. He tried to grab Brynach's fists and stop him from hurting himself. But he was too lost in his own pain. Riordan's fist connected with his jaw and had him stepping back.

"Fuck that! And I hate that I'm about to pull some "you made me do that" bullshit. But fuck it, you made me do that. What will it take to get through to you, you fucking oaf? We love you. There's nothing to forgive. You didn't fail us. You got us home safe. You protected us. You did your best. You're only one person." Riordan continued to push at Brynach's chest.

His anger, the pure indignation in his voice, warmed Brynach. Aisling moved to hold Riordan tight until he calmed.

"I seem to recall you yelling at me for saying things that hurt you and Riordan," she began.

"Riordan was balls deep in you at the time," Brynach huffed.

Now it was her turn to hit him, and her doing so made him feel a little better. "Don't be an ass. You told me that when I talk about myself like that it hurts you. I'll give you one chance to guess how your words are making us feel right now."

The two of them waited, staring at him until he felt like he had to look away.

"It's not the same."

"Bullshit," Riordan bit out. "That's bullshit and you know it. It's not any different. You love us. We love you. When you do things like this it hurts us. What do we have to do to prove that to you? How have we been failing you?"

"You haven't!" Brynach yelled. "Damn it. You don't understand."

"Do not," Aisling warned. "We understand. You think we

don't see you, but we do. We know, Brynach. We know you think you have to be strong all the time for us. Be the lover, husband, and protector I need. Be the patient partner to Riordan, taking things at his pace while making sure he feels valued. And we thought we were giving you what you needed by caring for us. By giving you a place you felt seen and where you belonged."

Riordan took over for the now crying Aisling, "But we failed you. Because you still don't get it. We haven't convinced you."

"Damn it, no. That's not true," he argued.

"Then what is it?" Aisling asked.

He sat on the bed, head in his hands. "I don't deserve what you've given me. I'm not a good man. I hurt things and when I don't, I want to. You don't understand how often I crave violence. I'll hurt you."

Aisling moved his hands and sat in his lap, "The only time you've hurt me is when I've begged you to. I see your darkness, Brynach. I saw it in the alcove at the Unseelie Court and I let you punish my mouth and soothe yourself. I see your barely contained control and let you unleash it on my body in the most deliciously dark ways. We see you and we love you because of what we see. We trust you and if we're the people you say we are, then we're smart enough to know where that trust belongs."

Brynach wanted to believe them so badly his heart nearly burst from wanting.

"Fucking thick-headed Fae," Riordan cursed and put his hands in Brynach's hair until he was looking at him. Slowly Riordan leaned past a smiling Aisling and kissed Brynach. It was a chaste kiss, but it meant the world to him.

"I'm not the only thick-headed Fae anymore." Brynach shook his head. "You're Fae now, too."

"Excuse me?" Aisling sat back, staring at the two men.

B rynach had a theory about what had happened, but anyone who could confirm it was long since dead. Everyone but one person he trusted to tell him the truth. Brynach watched Riordan and Aisling sleeping, curled up in one another. Slowly, he slid out of the bed. It was time to get answers.

Brynach didn't want to believe the worst of his people. What he was theorizing was downright horrific. Sirens blared outside, police cars raced by, and the sound of glass breaking filled the air. Things were already changing.

It was strange having no Veil to part, no border to cross to enter Faerie. But it was even more unsettling to not know where it was safe to sift to. He had so many questions. Brynach seethed at his mother and brother. No way a ruler in Faerie wasn't aware of exactly what the Veil was.

Gemma would know. He'd made sure his trusted nurse-maid was placed in the Seelie Courts, an unassuming plant. She'd left before the Veil dropped. Brynach had demanded it for her own safety. But he knew where to find her. Brynach sifted to her quaint cabin. Before he even raised a hand to knock the door opened.

"Well met, Prince." She smiled and invited him in.

"How'd you know?" He took the seat she pointed him to.

Gemma settled into a padded chair across from him. "You were always too curious for your own good. I figured you'd be here sooner than later. Congratulations. It looks like you succeeded in uniting the realms."

Brynach shrugged. "Gemma, you have to know that's not all we did."

The Fae nodded, her eyes avoiding his. "No, I imagine not."

"Please, tell me what happened. Why are the Ravdi different? What happened to their bond with the witches?" Brynach needed to know.

"I think you already know," she hedged.

"I want to hear it from you. I don't trust anyone else to tell me the truth." He moved to where she sat and placed himself on his knees before her just like he had as a child. "Please."

With a sigh she nodded. "Keep in mind that this is a myth, something I never believed. Didn't want to believe."

Brynach looked in her eyes and tipped his head to indicate she should continue.

"Kailyn's pain was so raw. That's what happens when men meddle in the lives of women, I suppose. Her father believed he knew what was best for her, and caused her the worst trauma of her life. And with no way to contain that pain she lashed out."

"And created the Veil." Brynach remembered that much.

"She got the same witch who cursed her to construct the Veil. And then she forced countless others to fortify the magic. Many died," her voice trailed off. "Perhaps there were witches then, true witches who lived among the Fae. But the witches we know today are a shadow of those witches."

He feared what would come next. "And what are the witches we know today? The Ravdi?"

The older Fae's eyes met his. "They're Fae. The Veil severed them from their lands and their people. Their magic weakened and over time they changed. They became two halves of a magic meant to be one. They called to one another; the twin souls designed to be whole. Somehow, magic found a way to try and repair itself by uniting the two."

The air was stuck in Brynach's chest. The shock and horror that surged through him threatened to make him physically ill. "Who knew?"

Gemma shook her head. "I don't know, Prince. I have to assume the knowledge was passed to those who hold power, but any oral history of the Veil died long ago with the Fae who lived through it."

His eyes burned and his throat constricted with unshed tears. "They'll never forgive us. They'll burn Faerie to the ground, and we'll deserve it."

Gemma placed a hand on his cheek, and he rested his head on her lap. "You'll find a way to protect them, Brynach."

"I'm one person." He couldn't hide the doubt in his voice.

"Oh, darling, you've always been more than you realized. And now you have Aisling, and dare I say, Riordan, by your side. You have never been alone." Gemma let him stay until he had control of his emotions and then he returned home.

An exhausted Brynach climbed back into bed with his partners and allowed himself one last night of peace before absolutely everything changed. If they thought that bringing down the Veil was the worst thing to happen, they'd been wrong. But at least the two people he loved, who he wanted to spend his life with, were immortal like him. For tonight, he'd cling to that blessing.

Because tomorrow, a war would come.

THE END

If you enjoyed this story, please consider leaving a review on Goodreads, or the bookseller where you purchased *A Prophecy in Ash*. Reviews help authors more than you know.

For updates on the final book in the *In Ash* series, sign up for Julie's newsletter.

She only emails once a month. Plus, it's where you get bonus content and the chance to be an early reader for the final book.

SCAN ME

ACKNOWLEDGEMENTS

For everyone who read, reviewed, and raved about *A Curse in Ash*, I give you my heartfelt love and appreciation. Thank you for the fan art, reader theories, DMs, and the tags on social media. You truly made my debut one I'll never forget. Thank you for welcoming Aisling, Riordan, Brynach and their gang of friends and family into your hearts and shelves. To Melanie and the Unplugged Book Box team for including *A Curse in Ash* in their January box, thank you for trusting in a debut author!

My small but mighty arc team for *A Curse in Ash* – your enthusiasm and willingness to take a shot on me and promote me to your followings is so appreciated.

My eternal gratitude to Lilly (LairofBooksBlog.com), Madison (Princess of Paperback on YouTube), Chelsea (Chelsea Palmer on YouTube), Samantha Leighanne (Leighannes Lit on YouTube), Jessica (Jessica Williamson on YouTube), Leah (Booksnmylouie on Instagram), and Chelsea (Chelseadollingreads on YouTube). You are an absolute dream team. Thank you!

To my team at Atmosphere Press, thank you for guiding me through this series. To my developmental editor Megan Turner for your work on books one and two for ensuring my world and characters shine. To my cover designer Kevin Stone for giving me the most bookstagramable covers! To the rest of the Atmosphere team from internal formatting, to proof and copy editing, and more, thank you for your time and talent.

To my early readers, writing friends, and Sunday sprinting community. Thank you for your support, encouragement, advice, and patience. Building a community with you has been amazing. As always, a huge thank you to Amber McManus

(@amberlashell on Twitter) and Katlyn Duncan (Katlyn Duncan on YouTube) for their advice, guidance, and critique partner talents and time. The appreciation and thanks I have for you are endless.

While I was finishing this book, my parents sold their home of forty-four years. I know how privileged I am to have had a childhood home that constant. Saying goodbye to a lifetime of memories within those walls was more difficult than I expected. But from the process I came to truly understand the strength and beauty of family. It's not a place, it's not walls and floors, it's people. I'm blessed with a fantastic foundation. My family is irreplaceable. I love you.

Thank you to my readers for continuing the journey in *A Prophecy in Ash* and for seeing Aisling, Riordan, and Brynach through pretty tough times. Although, I like to think there were amusing and steamy times as well. A lot is changing for our trio, and I appreciate your support of my career and my characters as they see their journey through. Be sure to use #AProphecyinAsh, or tag @according2jewls wherever you discuss the book.

The world is shifting for Aisling, Riordan, and Brynach and I know how unsettling that can be. I hope you'll join me in book three for the conclusion of their journey.

ABOUT ATMOSPHERE PRESS

Atmosphere Press is an independent, full-service publisher for excellent books in all genres and for all audiences. Learn more about what we do at atmospherepress.com.

We encourage you to check out some of Atmosphere's latest releases, which are available at Amazon.com and via order from your local bookstore:

Dancing with David, a novel by Siegfried Johnson

The Friendship Quilts, a novel by June Calender

My Significant Nobody, a novel by Stevie D. Parker

Nine Days, a novel by Judy Lannon

Shining New Testament: The Cloning of Jay Christ, a novel by Cliff Williamson

Shadows of Robyst, a novel by K. E. Maroudas

Home Within a Landscape, a novel by Alexey L. Kovalev

Motherhood, a novel by Siamak Vakili

Death, The Pharmacist, a novel by D. Ike Horst

Mystery of the Lost Years, a novel by Bobby J. Bixler

Bone Deep Bonds, a novel by B. G. Arnold

Terriers in the Jungle, a novel by Georja Umano

Into the Emerald Dream, a novel by Autumn Allen

His Name Was Ellis, a novel by Joseph Libonati

The Cup, a novel by D. P. Hardwick

The Empathy Academy, a novel by Dustin Grinnell

Tholocco's Wake, a novel by W. W. VanOverbeke

Dying to Live, a novel by Barbara Macpherson Reyelts

Looking for Lawson, a novel by Mark Kirby

ABOUT THE AUTHOR

Julie Zantopoulos grew up in Havertown, Pennsylvania but spent weekends and summers in the Pocono Mountains where she wandered the woods and daydreamed of the world beyond the Veil. When she's not writing she's running her YouTube channel, hosting writing sprints to encourage the online writing community, or reading. If all else fails, you'll find her enjoying "bad" SyFy Channel made for television movies.

Find her online at JulieZee.com, Pages and Pens on YouTube, and @according2jewls on Instagram and Twitter.

9 781639 884971